The Zanzibar Affair

The Zanzibar Affair

A novel out of Africa

Samantha Ford

DIADEM BOOKS

The Zanzibar Affair: A Novel Out of Africa

All Rights Reserved. Copyright © 2011 Samantha Ford

Published by Diadem Books
Distribution coordination by Spiderwize

For information, please contact:

Diadem Books
16 Lethen View
Tullibody
ALLOA
FK10 2GE
Scotland UK

www.diadembooks.com

ISBN: 978-1-908026-32-3

Chapter One

A **LOW SCREAM** coming from somewhere deep inside woke her. Kate sat up and fumbled under the mosquito net to turn on the lamp, knocking over a glass of water in her haste. She stared at the shards of broken glass and the water pooling under the bedside table, and breathed deeply, her heart shuddering uncomfortably in her chest. The memories of that terrible day still haunted her. She had watched people jump to their deaths from hundreds of floors up and wondered how she would have coped with making such a terrifying decision. For months afterwards, the whine of a jet engine had made her look up in fear. An aircraft glimpsed between the great skyscrapers of New York City, an aircraft that seemed as though it could hit the side of a building, brought her out in a cold sweat. The images were impossible to bury. She had not been unhappy to leave Manhattan and return to East Africa.

The room was hot and stuffy; her back and belly slick with the sweat of fear and memory. Kate got out of bed, anxious to leave the room. She turned on a small lamp in the living room. The three-roomed cottage was set back amongst the palm trees in the large walled compound. Normally light and airy, it now huddled in the shadows of the approaching storm. The table with her laptop, completely useless with the erratic power cuts, stood in the corner.

His letter lay open next to it.

She walked out onto the veranda and stared into the night, her mind racing. Thunder rumbled in the distance. Lightning split the sky above, briefly illuminating the dark empty villa at the end of the path. The rain arrived with spiteful intent, drumming on the tin roof of the cottage. Wind tore through the wet palm trees, pulling off branches, the debris flying across the veranda, driven by the storm. A lone plastic chair lifted

1

up, banged against the wall, and, ricocheting back, caught Kate on the shin; she yelped in surprise more than pain. Glancing up, she saw that the normally placid Mombasa sea had become violent and ugly. Crashing onto the beach it pulled and sucked at everything in its path, before hurling it all back again onto the shore.

Driven inside, Kate lit some candles. The electricity would certainly go off with such a powerful storm. She smacked her leg viciously as she felt another mosquito biting her. She picked it off with her nail, the blood-infused body leaving a brief red streak on her skin.

Suddenly the cottage was plunged into darkness. She sat watching the flickering candles and rubbed her bruised shin. Maybe it wasn't too late to go back to the house in Zanzibar? She put that thought aside, knowing that there was no going back. She picked up his letter but didn't need to read it. Like a nursery rhyme learned as a child, she had memorised every word.

Kate stood up and walked to the window, seeing a softer younger image of herself reflected in the glass. Her large amber eyes stared back. That's how I used to look, she thought; the years have passed quickly. How did I end up in this remote place? She knew the answer. She had been here before, but for a different reason.

A crack of thunder overhead unnerved her. Shakily she sat down and reached for the framed photograph of Molly. She stared at her daughter's smiling face, seeing only a whisper of her own features – nothing else, nothing more. She tipped her head back, banking up the tears flooding her eyes, attempting to stem their flow.

She stroked the silver frame with her thumb and sighed. How would her daughter react when she read the letter she had left for her in Zanzibar? The truth of what had happened, so carefully guarded over the years. Kate wondered whether she would ever be forgiven for what she had done. The slender silver bracelet she wore on her left wrist glinted in the flickering candlelight; she glanced down, her fingers moving protectively over it, remembering with perfect clarity when he had given it to her, and where.

Kate shivered and pulled a shawl around her shoulders. Her body ached, and the headache she had tried to ignore was intensifying like the storm outside. Holding the photograph close to her chest, she lay back exhausted and gave in to her memories.

She had loved him in a way she could not have imagined possible. He had evoked a passion in her she hadn't known existed. She had not wanted to sleep at night, only wanting the next day to arrive so she could be with him, knowing that each day would bring him into hers.

Running the lodge in Kenya had been the challenge needed to distance herself from what had happened. Afterwards, New York City had been an irresistible adventure, a fresh start. But what happened there had changed all that.

She remembered when the impossible news had come. The frantic search in Nairobi had ended in a way she couldn't think about, even now. Rousing herself, she returned to the window.

Raindrops formed perfect tears on her reflected face. She traced one with her fingertip. "As you lay there, so far away from Africa, did you think of me at all?" she whispered.

She felt heat surge through her aching body. Pulling off the shawl and her shirt she walked outside to stand naked in the rain. She lifted her long hair from her neck, feeling the wetness running down her back. Another flash of lightning illuminated her thin body; she closed her eyes with relief. The heavy rain gave some respite to the burning, itching bites and cooled her down. Within a minute she began shivering. Feeling dizzy and nauseous, she went back into the bedroom and, stepping gingerly over the broken glass, lay down. The pain tightened like a band of steel around her head.

Malaria.

The area was well known for it and she recognised the symptoms. Throughout the remainder of the night she tossed and turned, her body wet and burning. The fever took hold and the heat raged through her as she tried to sweat it out, the noise of the storm adding to her torment.

In the morning, she woke up disoriented and thirsty. Disentangling herself from the wet sheets she walked through to the kitchen. It was light outside and the storm had passed. She drank long and deeply from a glass of water. I need to be in the sea, she thought. I need to stop this unbearable heat in my body. I need to stop the pain in my head. I don't want to think about anything anymore.

With shaking hands, she reached for a cotton dressing-gown lying on the chair and tied it loosely around her. Carefully she picked up his letter and held it briefly to her lips, before putting it into her pocket and stepping off the veranda. The wooden gates leading to the beach looked far away today, but even in her feverish state she knew that could not be possible. She sat down heavily on the grass lawn as another wave of dizziness engulfed her. Then, with what little strength she could muster, Kate stood up and walked slowly down the path and out on to the deserted beach.

A falcon flew high above the heaving sea, watching Kate moving between the palm trees below. He saw her shadow across the path, then bright and clear as she moved into the sun again. He felt the warm winds blowing gently against his feathered body; his sharp eyes missed nothing as he soared overhead.

Kate looked upwards, flinching at the glare of the morning sun. Blinded, she swayed, unbalanced, and collapsed on the sand.

The falcon saw how the sun threw light into her hair and had turned her skin to a burnished gold. He watched her get up, then stumble and fall again. He flew low in front of her and then banked sharply before veering upwards again, seeking a rising thermal where he could be still and watch her.

Kate felt the soothing coolness of the wet sand beneath her. Sitting upright and with slow movements, she patted the cool sand on the vicious bites on her legs. Then, without thinking, she slowly filled her pockets. The letter curled with the weight of the sand, the dampness already eating away at the words so carefully written. She stood up unsteadily and walked into the sea.

The falcon swooped down again, briefly casting a shadow over her. She looked up and he knew that she had finally seen him. "Let me go," she whispered. "Let me go."

She stood still, feeling the cool water against her ankles. She needed to go deeper, away from the heat and glare of the sun. She moved forward, feeling the swell of the ocean surrounding her.

A sudden wave unbalanced her, her arm moving feebly against the strong current that was pulling her under. Kate struggled for a moment and then gave in, too tired and weak to fight any longer.

He watched her. Somewhere deep inside he felt fear for this woman, now so deep into the sea. He watched as she sank below the surface. Swooping low and fast, he came to where she was.

Chapter Two

T HE SKY OVER LONDON was dark and depressing. Molly closed her umbrella as the taxi hissed to a halt next to her.

"Heathrow, Terminal One please," she instructed the driver. Sitting back, she looked at the rain splashing against the window. Everything seemed too black and white today: the houses, the people, the cars.

I'm going back to Africa, back to Zanzibar, she thought. But this time, it won't be the same. She won't be waiting for me at the ferry, waving and laughing as she catches a glimpse of me.

Molly's tears, like the rain outside, blurred the images speeding past the window. She reached for the chain around her neck and felt the two small keys. They had arrived by courier yesterday, just as their lawyer, David, had promised.

"Kate sent them to me not too long ago," David had said when she telephoned him in Johannesburg with the terrible news. "I didn't think much about it then. I just put them with her personal papers for you. She left instructions, Molly. The keys are for her Zanzibar chest. There's a letter for you inside. That's what she told me to tell you." She sensed his sadness across the miles. David had known her mother for thirty years.

"You will be financially secure, as she wanted you to be," he continued. "Kate had a good life, Molly. She packed more experience into hers than most. She had moments in her life of great happiness. Try and remember that."

When David put the telephone down, he was overwhelmed with the reality of the situation. Now she would find the letter – the one he had tried to persuade Kate not to write. What good could possibly come from telling Molly a truth that would be best left hidden? But Kate had insisted, uncharacteristically disregarding his normally sound advice. Reaching for Kate's file on top of his other paperwork, he sat back and wondered where to begin with the life contained within it; a life that had ended so suddenly. Had Kate had some kind of a premonition? Was that why she had sent the keys to him? Or even worse – had she planned it? He rubbed his hand across his face, suddenly tired, trying to dispel the thought. Just what had happened to Kate in Zanzibar?

The aircraft taxied to a halt at the airport terminal in Dar es Salaam. Molly disembarked and deeply inhaled the warm dusty smell of Africa, instantly evoking memories of her childhood and her mother. She felt already that Africa was emptier without her, flatter somehow.

When the call had come from the British Embassy, asking her to come to Nairobi as soon as possible, she had hesitated. Her first instinct was to go to her mother's house in Zanzibar. She had told the official that she'd go to Nairobi a few days later than requested. One or two days would make no difference now.

A small ferry brought her across to the island. Molly stood still, a wave of loss and panic washing over her. Upon arrival the other passengers disembarked, leaving her alone on the deck. The ferry rocked gently under her feet, soothing her, and the sun felt comforting on her skin. She lifted her chin, inhaling the smells so evocative of Zanzibar. The cloying perfume of the frangipani trees, the spices and dried fish, the pungent odour of garlic mixed with the sea air, all carried on the afternoon breeze. She took a deep breath and stepped off the ferry, heading for the old Stone Town.

Threading her way through the narrow streets, Molly passed tall compressed, white-washed traditional houses, each built around a central open-air inner courtyard, most of them adorned with intricately carved wooden doors, studded with conical brass spikes. Malnourished stray cats warmed themselves in the shafts of sunlight that reached the dusty paths, along hidden alleyways. Scrawny chickens pecked in the dust, squawking indignantly at her as she made her way past. Squeezing past a donkey, she arrived at the house.

Pulling out her set of keys with a feeling of dread, she hesitated and wondered whether she should ring the bell. The house didn't feel like her home any more. Pushing aside the sudden sense of formality that came with the realisation that Kate was not going to be there, she unlocked and opened the heavy doors, entering the open courtyard within. A trickling fountain gave an illusion of coolness in the hot muggy air. Boughs of scarlet, red and pink bougainvillea cascaded down the white walls; the blue of the sky above added to the palette of pure colours within.

Abraham, their house servant, having heard the door open, shuffled across from the kitchen, his hands outstretched in greeting to her.

"Jambo Abraham," she said softly, smiling at the kindness in his old face. "Habari ya siku nyingi... how have you been since I saw you last?"

"Njema Miss Molly, lakini... So sorry to hear this bad news," he murmured, his dark eyes expressing how pleased he was to see her, his smile revealing perfect teeth. He was dressed in a long white Kanzu and a red and gold waistcoat which he reserved for special occasions. He had known she would come.

"Ndio...yes, I know Abraham, it is so sad about Miss Kate."

Taking her hands together in his, he seemed unable to speak. She knew if he could, he would call Kate to the top of the stairs to welcome her daughter home. They both involuntarily glanced up.

Abraham knew Kate's routine as well as he knew his own: breakfast on the roof terrace, the morning shopping in the market, or visiting one of her friends for coffee or lunch. Her afternoons were spent quietly in her rooms, on the second floor, reading or writing. In the early evening, just before the muezzin called the sunset prayers, she would change for dinner. Busy preparing food in the kitchen, he would wait for the sound of her high heels tapping down the stone stairs, a cloud of perfume following in her wake. He shook his head sadly. Remembering the last time he had seen her, over a week now – before she vanished.

Looking back at each other, Abraham squeezed her hands before letting them go. Moving with scarcely a sound he left her, sensing her need to be alone. He padded away on bare feet, disappearing between the courtyard alcoves, their thickness muting sound and adding to the effect of the cool quiet rooms inside.

Molly turned towards the stairs and ascended with a heavy weariness. She continued on up to the roof garden, not stopping at her mother's rooms on the second floor.

The breeze lifted her hair from her neck, cooling her. She placed her hands on the warm stone wall and gazed at the sea. As always, she marvelled at the same view that remained unchanged every time she returned and in fact, had changed little over the centuries. Her mother had loved it too. Flat rooftops made festive with washing lines hung with colourful clothing and materials, bright against the white; the rounded, rocket-shaped minarets unique to this part of the world; and the sea, a sparkling intense blue that almost hurt to look at. She looked out at the same scene that other eyes had watched for centuries. The wooden dhows, with their stiff grey-white sails, drifted past with a lingering elegance unaltered even in the twenty-first century. The island was an addictive place and had been the crossroads for human traffic from all over the world. Traders of spice or slaves, travellers from one land to another: all had left their mark, as her mother had.

Turning away she touched the hammock, bringing countless memories of the evenings she and Kate had shared together up here on the roof, lying back on the stone beds surrounded by cushions, enjoying the night sounds around them. The roof garden had a glorious view over the minarets and rooftops to the sea. They would lean over the low wall and watch families preparing and eating their evening meal, old women sweeping out their back yards, calling out gossip to those who passed, and children playing in the dust. They would listen for the haunting, echoing calls of the muezzin calling the faithful out of their homes to the final *Isha*, the night prayer.

Perhaps, Molly thought anxiously, one of them may have seen or heard something the night before Kate disappeared? Had she been up here on the roof with someone? Did she leave on her own? When exactly had she left? She shook her head with frustration, then taking a final look at the placid sea she turned and made her way back down the stairs.

She paused on the second floor outside of Kate's bedroom; she thought she could smell her mother's perfume. She stopped mid-step and froze. Her heart squeezed in the pain of remembering her mother was gone. She took a breath to steady herself. Molly knew that once she unlocked the chest in the lounge, the chest for which David had sent her the keys, she would find a letter addressed to her. An important letter, David had re-iterated before they had hung up. Kate had told him that if something happened to her, Molly should be sent the keys and must return to Zanzibar to read the letter. With her eyes full of tears she gently pushed open the door to her mother's bedroom.

A breeze had navigated its way through the shuttered windows and riffled through the pages of an open book on the chair by the window. The room was large and airy, and almost overwhelmed by the presence of a four-poster bed, swathed in white mosquito netting. A fresh vase of flowers, one of Abraham's daily routines, was positioned on the bedside table. Lazy motes of dust, passengers on the breeze from the streets outside, filtered through the sunlight. Her attention returned involuntarily to the bedside table and the flowers. Surrounding the vase was the habitual cluster of photograph frames. The largest of them, in a shiny silver frame, was of Kate and Molly on safari in Botswana, the sun bloody and red behind them.

One photograph in particular, scratched around the edges as if having spent some time facing down, was a new addition. Molly picked it up, recognising it instantly. Kate must have changed her mind about something, she thought. Molly had not seen this one for years. Why would it be on display now?

It had been taken in Cape Town. He was sitting on the side of a swimming pool, his arm around her mother, his hand on her shoulder.

Adam.

Kate was leaning into his body, smiling up at him, her hair covering his hand. He too had gone. Africa, it seemed, demanded a high price for happiness. Carefully she put the photograph back where Kate had left it.

On the dressing table lay her mother's make up and perfume. Lifting the bottle she sniffed the familiar smell. Her throat tightened as burning tears filled her eyes. She remembered how she knew when Kate was around by the fragrance left lingering in school corridors, the car and their homes: Molly's beacon when she returned from boarding school, always leading to her mother.

Opening the wardrobe Molly saw the rows of neat coat-hangers, the clothes uniformly beige, white or black, with the odd splash of pink.

Her choice in jewellery was always different. Bones, feathers and beads – no diamonds or pearls. But there were two bracelets she had loved. One was a simple slim hoop of silver which she had worn on her left wrist and never taken off. The other was made of old silver and large opals. Kate had bought it in a shop on Park Avenue whilst living in New York City.

Molly looked down at the silver and opal bracelet on her wrist, remembering when it was given to her the last time they were on safari in Kenya.

"Take it, darling," Kate had said laughing. "It suits you and besides I'm already carrying around too much baggage. If I can lighten the load it all counts in the end." Molly had taken that literally, but now she wondered if there had been some other kind of message in that statement. She thought back. Once, in Cape Town, she had asked her mother if she ever took the silver bracelet off and who had given it to her. Kate had been driving at the time, concentrating on the heavy rush-hour traffic.

"No. I've never taken it off." She had looked at Molly briefly, a soft smile playing on her lips. "Never."

For the rest of the journey Kate had been quiet, preoccupied; but Molly wanted the rest of the story. Who had given it to her? Now she tried to remember the name. Tim? Ted? Tom? She shook her head with frustration. It was all too long ago to remember.

She trailed her fingers through the wardrobe touching the fabric of the clothes. Kate's perfume clung to everything, reaching out with ghostly fingers to touch her face. Why did she take so little with her? What had she been thinking? What had happened here in this house?

She closed the wardrobe door and leaned her back against it, casting around the room for any clues.

On an antique table next to the chair by the window was her mother's CD collection. She had always said she could travel anywhere, as long as she had her music with her. Only classical though, Molly remembered. Music with words had made Kate sad; classical was much safer, easier somehow.

Colourful scarves were draped over an old hat stand, creating a riot of colour in the otherwise cool white room. Abraham had cleaned and dusted the room, and had made up the bed; he would have hung anything up that Kate had left lying around. She would ask him later if he remembered anything unusual here. Anything at all that might have explained her hasty departure.

Descending to the lounge, on the ground floor, Molly lay back on a sofa and looked around the familiar room. Two paintings depicting scenes from a market and a harbour, which Molly recognised as the old town of Lamu in the archipelago of Kenyan islands, dominated one wall of the room. Pale pink cushions added a touch of colour to the cream sofas. Over the fireplace hung a painting by her mother's sister, Lucy. Molly had always loved it. In gentle hues of creams, greys and blues, the painting was of a windswept beach with a rough sea gnawing at the sands. Lucy had been beside herself with grief when she had told her the news.

A Zanzibar chest dominated the centre of the room. Molly felt the panic begin to rise within her. In there were her mother's private papers and diaries – and the letter. A pair of binoculars, some antique compasses and a pile of fashion magazines lay on top; the pages tickled by the air circulating from the ceiling fan above. On the other side of the door which led into the dining room, tall shelves were home to hundreds of books on Africa, the Middle East and Asia. Coffee-table books featuring safari lodges, four of them authored by Kate, were piled on an intricately carved wooden box. Tall turquoise Moroccan lanterns stood either side of the fireplace.

Kate had loved all the good things in life; the famous hotels, luxury trains, designer clothes and spectacular game lodges. But Zanzibar was the island she had finally chosen to live on. A place where she had thought, and hoped, she could be happy. Molly had believed that Kate had been happy here.

But what had happened to make Kate leave the island so suddenly, Molly puzzled? Why had she been found in such a remote place?

Her gaze fell on the bronze statue in the alcove lit by a single light. It was her mother kneeling naked, long hair down her back, given to her by her lover. He had wanted her to be immortalised in bronze.

Adam.

How did he have this hold over her so many years later? "Surely he had nothing to do with her death?" she murmured to herself. She looked around the room uneasily and shivered. He was the only person she could think of who might have provoked Kate into doing something unpredictable, something out of character. He was implicated in all of this, of that she was certain. But how could that be? It was impossible given what had happened to him.

On the wall to the left of the fireplace were six boards covered with photographs of Kate's life and those who had played a part in it. Molly stared at the photographs, her amber eyes moving from board to board, from face to face. Such a life she thought; and all these people making up the sum of her mother's. She looked for one photograph in particular. Yes, there he was. The well-shaped head, the smile, the inevitable cigarette.

Molly rubbed her eyes, knowing what she now had to do. Kneeling in front of the Zanzibar box, she reached for the chain around her neck and the keys. She opened the first lock. As she reached for the second, her courage failed her. She sat back on her heels with tears in her eyes, beginning to panic now that she was close to finding out what Kate had wanted her to know after her death.

"How am I going to do this?" she whispered shakily.

You can do it, Molly, she heard her mother whisper. *Have courage.*

Molly held her breath and turned the second key. Then with both hands, she lifted the heavy lid.

Chapter Three

TOM FLETCHER looked out over the bush, enjoying the silence of it. Impala grazed on the young green shoots, brought out by the rains the night before. It was good to take this weekend break in Botswana, after his business meeting in Johannesburg, far away from the nerve-racking world of international terrorism. The Okavango Delta with its enduring beauty calmed him and helped him to get his thoughts together. He thought about Kate, as he had often done over the past twenty years. Where would she be now? Somewhere in Africa, he thought, smiling; the place she loved the most. And looking out over the whispering yellow grasses he could understand why.

His company had been busier than it had ever been since the horror of the Twin Towers the previous September. Traversing the world, he advised governments and multinational companies on how to deal with potential terrorist attacks and the effects that such attacks could have on their business. It was a highly paid profession, but his life was rarely his own. He travelled extensively, leaving little time for any private life. That hadn't changed.

He leaned back, stretched his long legs and let his mind drift. He thought about his life in the United States working for the CIA as a security expert, which had given him the qualifications he had needed to start his consultancy business. His marriage to Sarah had been fraught with difficulties and betrayal. Her death almost eighteen months ago had brought to a close that unhappy period in his life.

He had met her in California at a dinner party and had been attracted to her immediately. A year later they had married and bought a house in Cold Spring Harbour.

The news of Sarah's pregnancy had been a surprise to both of them. With their busy lives, the subject of children had rarely been mentioned.

But when he saw his daughter for the first time he was smitten with her. They called her Cassandra. From an early age she had fallen in love with horses, a love she had inherited from her mother. It had always made Tom nervous to watch her tiny frame riding on the back of her pony even at the age of five, but she was fearless. He admired that courage and gave in to her persistence, as he always did. Sarah tried to juggle her career in fashion with being a good mother but it proved impossible. There was talk of hiring a nanny. Tom was against it but Sarah was hard-headed. When he returned from his next overseas trip the nanny was already installed and there was nothing he could do about it.

During a conference in Mexico the following year, he was summoned to the telephone. Irritated at the interruption he took the call only because he had been told it was urgent. Minutes later he felt the colour drain from his face. Cassie was dead: a riding accident.

After the funeral, barely able to contain his grief, he had the pony put down and fired the nanny. Sarah had been in New York when the accident happened; it was something he had not been able to forgive her for.

"You should have been here looking after her, Sarah, not leaving that responsibility with the damn nanny!" His rage and anger had known no bounds as he lashed out at her. "That's what mothers do, Sarah, they look after their own children. They don't hand them over to someone else for safekeeping!"

Wanting to spend as little time as possible at home he travelled relentlessly, putting as much space between himself, Sarah, and the little girl's empty bedroom.

His security company expanded as terrorism made itself manifest worldwide. The months of separation, whilst he was away on business, had taken their toll on Sarah and their marriage. She knew that Tom blamed her for their daughter's death, and miserably she had cast around for ways to fill the hours whilst Tom was away. Knowing that her marriage was in trouble and needing to leave her own grief and guilt behind, she slipped easily into a series of affairs.

Tom had had his suspicions. Returning home from Australia a year after Cassie's death, and a disastrous Christmas together, Sarah wasn't at the airport to pick him up – something she always did if she was in town. He had paid off the taxi and walked into the empty house. Sensing that something was amiss, he went immediately to their bedroom and checked her wardrobe. It was empty. After walking through the house, he found no evidence or explanation anywhere of her intention to leave him. He had called her sister in New York City.

"She's not coming back, Tom. It's all over. She wants a divorce."

Tom had closed up the house in Cold Spring Harbour and moved his company to London. He bought an apartment in Holland Park, and threw himself into his work and business, travelling more than he needed to keep him from brooding on what had happened. He had loved Sarah, despite what had happened, and thought they were as happy as could be expected. However he was astute enough to know that being away so often and the death of their child had put a great strain on their marriage. Deeply hurt and disappointed he was loath to get involved with any new relationship.

He was a good-looking man and his personality and quick sense of humour guaranteed him a dinner invitation to many a hostess's dinner table, be it in London, Rome, Kuala Lumpur or Beijing. His physical needs were met by various girlfriends around the globe and this suited him. One or two nights with a female friend and he was gone, until the next time. He started to enjoy life again.

Meeting Kate, eighteen months later, had been the turning point in his carefully constructed life.

Tom was the keynote speaker at a late afternoon seminar at a hotel in London. He was talking about the role of security in the world of tourism. The hall was packed with delegates attending the International Travel show. He was an eloquent speaker and spoke with authority, amusing his large audience, even though the topic was serious. He wore a crisp white shirt, blue tie and an expensively cut navy blue suit; his dark curly hair skimmed the shirt collar, his grey eyes moving over the crowd as he talked.

Afterwards, at the cocktail party, Tom circulated amongst the guests meeting game lodge owners, CEOs of hotel groups, tour operators and major players in the travel and safari business. Exhausted after two hours of talking and mingling, Tom made his way out of the noisy room and headed for the private bar. It was mercifully quiet after the cocktail party. He leaned back into the leather chair and ordered a gin and tonic. The bar was empty.

Then the door opened, letting in some of the conversation and noise from the party across the hall. He looked up. The woman made her way to the bar, ordered a flute of champagne and sank into a chair nearby. She took a delicate sip, put her head back and closed her eyes. He studied her casually, and made some deductions. No wedding ring. Tanned. So lived somewhere sunny; possibly a delegate at the show? Her cream suit complemented her golden skin, the matching cream choker around her neck adding an exotic touch. Her long hair, catching the light from the lamp, reflected the gold in it, making him think of the sun, the sea and long white beaches.

Sensing his scrutiny, she opened her eyes and looked straight at him. Her eyes. He searched for a colour to describe them. Amber, yes that was it, he thought of autumn in England, and the fall in Vermont. She smiled at him.

He smiled back and raised his empty glass. Calling the barman over, he ordered another and paid for the woman's glass of champagne.

Uncrossing her long legs and collecting her handbag, she stood up and walked towards him. Uncharacteristically, he felt his heartbeat increase as she held out her hand to him.

"Hello, I'm Kate."

They met for dinner the following evening and continued the easy pattern of conversation they had enjoyed in the hotel bar as they exchanged edited life histories. He told her about his security company and the places he had travelled to.

"Yes, I was listening to your talk," Kate said grinning. "I've rarely seen so many women in the audience paying such attention. We're normally rather a jaded lot after a long day at the show but you certainly got our attention."

Changing the subject she told him about her life in Swaziland, with her husband Jack, a doctor, and how they had moved there after living in

Nigeria. She regaled him with incredible stories about life in Lagos, which he found almost impossible to believe.

"A place I have yet to go to," he said, "and probably won't after all your hair-raising stories." He enjoying listening to her; he liked her wide happy smile, her infectious laugh, the way she used her hands to illustrate a point.

"You don't wear a wedding ring, Kate?"

"No," she said abruptly. Wisely he changed the subject.

"Where is Swaziland exactly? I've heard of it but haven't had a reason to go there. Not yet anyway…"

"It's a tiny country, a Kingdom, and very dependent on South Africa. It's about two hundred miles from Johannesburg, with lots of green hills, golf courses and good hotels. The Swazi people are charming; very gentle and courteous. It's a lovely place to live, I enjoy it there and I love my job. Swaziland has a fledgling tourism industry, that's why I'm here at the travel show. We need to persuade tourists to extend their safaris in South Africa and include Swaziland. I've a weekly television programme, which I present myself…" Her voice trailed off. "Sorry, talking too much, as usual! It's a pretty little country. You should come and see it for yourself one day."

"I'd like that very much. I'm not sure when though. I have a pretty tight schedule for the next few months. But if an opportunity arises I promise I will come and see you." The idea had appealed to him enormously.

"Do you have brothers and sisters? Where do your parents live now? I would imagine they found it difficult to settle down after all the years of living abroad? Where did they end up?" He took a sip of his wine and grinned at her. "Sorry for all the questions, but you've had an interesting life and I want to know all about it before you fly off back to Africa in five days' time!"

"Yes, they did find it hard in the beginning," she said, flattered by his interest. "My father's life in the Diplomatic Corps took us all over the world. I thought everyone lived like that: two years here, two years there. I've always been very close to him. I have a sister, Lucy. They all live in South Africa now, so not too far away for regular visits. Our childhood was unusual, but in many ways it made us a very close family. We keep in touch on a regular basis. I think out of all the countries we lived in, Kenya was my favourite. It was my first taste of Africa when I was twelve years old, and I've been hooked on it ever since, well, maybe not Nigeria! And you?"

"Just me. Born in the States. No brothers or sisters. My parents are dead, I have some distant aunts and uncles apparently, but I've never met them."

He told her about Sarah and how she wanted a divorce and that they had been living separately for nearly two years now. He didn't mention the accident.

"Keep on moving," Kate said, laughing. "It's the best way to outsmart your past! Now I know you travel a lot, but surely someone as attractive as you, with your sexy American accent, must have piles of girlfriends in London?"

"Yes, I have one or two girlfriends here, nothing serious. It's difficult to have a permanent relationship with my nomadic lifestyle. Not that I am looking for one at the moment. Having said that, if you were single and lived in England, I might become very interested indeed, but as you're not, I'm safe!"

She laughed nervously, and then switched the focus back to him.

"You've no idea how refreshing it is to talk to someone who has at least some idea of where Bahrain or Djibouti is. I love my life in Africa, but sometimes I long to talk about other places in the world. Jack had never been out of England until he went to Africa. Sometimes I find it frustrating; most people are not remotely interested in where you have lived, unless they have lived there as well. I enjoy talking to you Tom." She had an unnerving way of looking at him, making him wonder what she was thinking about.

Emptying the last drops from the bottle of wine they had shared into her glass, he smiled at her across the table then glanced at his watch. "Time for bed I think."

Kate looked up quickly, startled by his suggestion. The nervous look on her face surprised him and then made him laugh, realising that she had misunderstood him.

"Now surely you would expect me to be a little more romantic, more subtle, if I were inviting you into my bed? Your face is a picture and I do believe you're blushing!"

Kate laughed, her face getting hot with embarrassment. "I have an early meeting tomorrow morning, and I still have some work to do before then. So, how about if we meet again for dinner tomorrow?" He paused, "And every night after that?"

She looked at him and smiled at his audacious suggestion. "I do have other commitments, Tom…" Her voice trailed off as he raised his eyebrow at her.

"Cancel them, Kate. Would you do that for me, please?"

Tom waited in the bar at the Ritz hotel. Kate was doing some last minute shopping and they had arranged to meet there. He glanced at his watch despite himself. He found that he was waiting with impatience to catch a glimpse of her as she walked through the door. He forced himself to re-focus on the briefing documents in front of him.

He heard her before he saw her. She was half an hour late and he didn't want to waste one more second of their last two evenings together. "Sorry Tom! I got a bit carried away and didn't notice the time." She swept into the bar, her arms laden with carrier bags. "Such fabulous shops here, we don't have them in Swaziland, needless to say."

She shrugged off her coat as he took her bags and scarf, and ordered a drink for her. "It's obviously raining." He shook her coat. "Should we just eat here tonight?" he asked her.

"Sounds great, and yes it's very wet out there!" Kate said, settling herself in a chair.

After dinner Tom stirred his coffee thoughtfully. "I'll miss you Kate. London will seem empty without you. I don't suppose there's any chance of you staying for a few days longer?"

Kate hesitated and then covered his hand with her own. "Tom, I have to go home. I have a husband and a life there. I have a job and responsibilities. You know I can't stay. I've enjoyed all our evenings together and all the lovely restaurants you've taken me to. Spending time with you has been fun and I've enjoyed every minute of it, but I have to go back." She hesitated. "I'll miss you though…"

He sighed. "I know you have to go and it's wrong of me to try and persuade you to stay. How would you like to spend your last evening having dinner at my apartment tomorrow? I don't know about you but I'd like some home cooking. Let me throw something together for you." He looked at her and realized she wasn't listening to him, she seemed lost in thought. "Hey Kate! You're miles away, come back to me."

Roused from her reverie she looked at him and raised an eyebrow. "You're not going to try and seduce me are you Tom?"

"No," he smiled ruefully at her. "Just dinner." He stood up and looked down at her. "Come, we both have a full day tomorrow, I'll expect you around eight. Here's the address." She glanced down at the card and then up at him.

"I'll look forward to that, thank you Tom. Baked beans on toast have always been a favourite of mine: it's the first thing I have when I get home. Dinner at your place sounds perfect."

He helped her on with her coat and wound her scarf around her neck, the back of his hand briefly brushing her face. He felt her shy away at his touch and smiled to himself.

"I think I might be able to manage something a little more exciting than beans on toast, but I know what you mean about eating out. The novelty does wear off after being on the road for weeks on end."

He flagged down a taxi to take her back to her hotel, and watched the red tail-lights until they disappeared. He hadn't felt this strongly about anyone since Sarah and as much as he tried to suppress his desire for Kate, he knew he wasn't winning. Often, when they were talking, she would lightly touch his hand or his arm, to make some point or other, not realizing how much it affected him. Shaking his head he hailed another taxi and headed in the opposite direction for his apartment. Although getting involved with a married woman had not been on his agenda, he wondered just how happy she actually was with her husband and why she didn't wear her wedding ring. Surely if she was happily married she wouldn't have spent so much time with him?

He looked up at the clock – she was ten minutes late. He hoped she hadn't changed her mind about dinner. Then there she was, ringing the doorbell. Smiling he opened the door, kissed her on both cheeks and helped her off with her coat. He saw her close her eyes briefly, when his hand brushed her neck. She brought her own hand up and stilled his; then, flustered, she quickly shrugged her arms out of her coat.

"Are you cold?" he asked. "Shall I turn the heating up a bit? In America we've always got the heating on full blast but I've become more conservative since moving over here." He touched her cheek lightly. "I guess for you its cold no matter what."

"No, thank you, Tom, I'm absolutely fine," she said, moving quickly away from him. She walked around the apartment, looking at his things whilst he got her a drink.

He had bought champagne to celebrate her last night in England. He knew his apartment was empty, filled only with the bare necessities. To him it often felt like an airport terminal: the place where he waited between flights. Only, it was more comfortable and had better coffee. Despite its shortcomings it was large and airy and had a view onto the private gardens shared by the neighbours on his square.

The lounge was expensively furnished with three large, comfortable sofas. The kitchen was open-plan and doubled as a dining area. Kate had taken all of this in with one glance and had wandered over to the window to look out at the gardens. Beside the window, in the corner of the room, was an antique desk supporting two framed photographs. Kate picked up one of them.

Tom stood still on the other side of the room, holding the two glasses watching her. He knew the next question was inevitable. His first instinct was to distract her attention away from it and where the conversation was going. Instead, he took a sip from one of the glasses and waited. He couldn't keep hiding his past. It was an integral part of him.

"Is this Sarah?" Kate asked, looking over her shoulder at him.

"Yes," he smiled, putting his glass down. He crossed the room and handed her a glass of champagne.

"And the little girl?"

"That's my daughter, Cassandra. Cassie."

"Tom!" Kate exclaimed, looking amused and genuinely surprised. "You haven't said a word all week about her. Where is she?"

He remembered how much he hated that part of any conversation which began about his daughter. It was the having to tell what had happened and then the wait for the inevitably sympathetic response. It was easier not to say anything at all. But he spoke about Cassie so rarely and he missed her.

"She died three years ago. Sarah used to take Cassie riding and she loved it. So, we bought her a pony for her fifth birthday. She'd only had the damn thing a month. It was spooked by the neighbour's dog whilst she was out on a ride across a field alongside our house. The riding instructor was trying to catch the dog to get it out of the field and had let go of the reins. The horse reared and Cassie fell off. It was a simple mistake. I blamed Sarah for not being there but, in fact, I blamed myself for not being there too. I blamed both of us. Even if we had been at home, it wouldn't have made any difference. She's still gone." Tom returned the photograph carefully to the small space on the table that his daughter now filled, and smiled sadly at Kate.

"Oh Tom. I'm so sorry." Kate struggled to find the appropriate words and instead, put her glass down and put her arms around him and said nothing. He pulled back, alarmed by her close proximity and his overwhelming desire for her. He cleared his throat and looked down at her, seeing she was tearful. Embarrassed, he pulled a handkerchief out of his pocket and made to hand it to her. He hesitated briefly and then pulling her into his arms he kissed her gently, feeling her respond.

Reluctantly Kate stepped back from him. "I'm sorry, that wasn't supposed to happen." Flustered, she pushed her hair behind her ear.

Tom saw the look of guilt pass across her face, whilst fighting his temptation to kiss her again. For the first time in years he felt a rush of strong emotion. He could see that she felt, as he had, the first physical jolt of something between them.

"Come on," he said quickly, walking towards the kitchen, "help me make dinner. I need to keep my hands busy with something; you've given me an appetite Kate, one way or another."

Their dinner conversation was as light-hearted and full of banter as it had been all week. Tom was relieved that the kiss hadn't altered anything. After they had cleared the table Tom had made a pot of coffee and brought it to the table. Now he looked at her, his thoughts in turmoil. Kate placed her hand over his.

"In a different world you would have been the perfect man, lover, friend and confidant for me, Tom. But the only world we have is the one we are in right now. Since the moment I saw you, I haven't been able to get you out of my mind. We were never meant to be, Tom. Or perhaps if we were, we've got the timing wrong. I should go now, whilst I still have the courage of my convictions."

"Kate," he said, bringing her hand to his lips. He reached out, touching her face with his fingertips, and cupped her cheek in his hand. He waited. She covered his hand with hers.

"Tom, I hope you'll forgive me but I'm going to go now."

"Stay with me tonight, Kate," he said quietly.

"I wish that I could but it's not fair to any of us. I can't Tom…"

Kate stood and Tom followed suit. She picked up her handbag and walked to the front door. Automatically, Tom helped her on with her coat and handed her back her scarf. He walked with her to the end of the street where they waited for a taxi to pass. He realised, standing there, that they were holding hands. She kissed him on his cheek. Turning his head slightly, he kissed her on the mouth again. She didn't pull away this time.

He saw a taxi coming on the other side of the street and reluctantly let her go, waving to catch the cabbie's attention. It slowed and pulled to a halt opposite them.

"Are you sure you want to go?" he asked her gruffly.

She nodded her head. "Goodbye, Tom," she whispered, the words catching in her throat.

Kate turned away and quickly crossed the road to the taxi. She looked back briefly, waved, and gave him a bright smile before disappearing into the back of the vehicle.

Back in his apartment, Tom stacked the plates in the dishwasher. For the first time since he had moved to London, he felt lonely. Kate had only spent a few hours here with him but the space already felt emptier. He washed and polished their glasses and as he turned to put them away, he noticed her slim briefcase next to the chair.

He didn't hesitate. That one split second decision would bring him, more than twenty three years later, to a remote beach in East Africa in a desperate attempt to find her.

Seven months after meeting Kate in London, Tom was on a business trip to Johannesburg. He had had no contact with her since their last night in London.

After three days of meetings, Tom was looking forward to a few days break before his flight back to London the following Monday. He had hired a car and was planning to drive up to the Kruger Park. He wanted to get out of the city and see the rest of the country he had heard so much about. Sitting in the hotel lobby on Friday evening, with a map spread out in front of him, he was planning his journey. Idly his eyes roamed the rest of the map of Southern Africa, and there it was – Swaziland.

Kate.

He made some rapid calculations in his head. It was a four-hour drive from Johannesburg, and if he left early tomorrow morning he would easily be there before lunch. He hesitated then shrugged his shoulders, suddenly feeling happy. She had practically invited him in London to come and see the country and he wanted to see her again. He would take a chance.

Early the next morning he set off, leaving the bustling city of Johannesburg behind. He was soon out on the open road and heading east to Swaziland. The road was excellent and he enjoyed the miles of emptiness, the small towns he passed through, and the expanses of forest on both sides of the road as he approached Swaziland. With the border formalities completed, he entered the country and headed for the capital, Mbabane. During his journey he had wondered how Kate would react when she saw him. He hoped she would be pleased to see him and maybe he would finally get to meet her husband, if she was still with him.

After she had left London he had resolutely tried to put her out of his mind by focusing on his business. The two women he had dated before meeting Kate had drifted away. Perhaps, he thought, sensing his heart wasn't in the relationships anymore. He had dated an Australian girl for a couple of weeks before losing interest in her as well.

He looked around as he drove carefully along the main road. The country was beautiful with its rolling green hills, and he felt the pressure of the past week seep away. He passed the open markets at the end of the main road where street traders were selling fruit and vegetables, melons, tomatoes, oranges, limes and lemons, making a bright splash of colour on the green landscape. Corn on the cob hissed and spattered as they cooked on open fires burning in empty fuel drums with chicken wire stretched over the top, which stopped the corn from plunging into the fiery depths. Hungry customers waited patiently and Tom's mouth watered as he drove past: they certainly smelled good.

Just outside the centre of Mbabane he found the small hotel recommended by the concierge at his hotel in Johannesburg. Nestling amongst heavy trees, it looked cool and welcoming; he checked in.

Turning on the television to break the silence of the room, and with practised ease, he unpacked his overnight bag. When he had finished, he sought out and found a slim telephone directory. Flicking through it, he was disappointed to find Kate's number wasn't listed.

He walked over to the large glass doors that opened out onto the hotel gardens and the swimming pool. Sprinklers on the grass shot out streams of water in jerky movements, their clicking sound the only challenge to the birdsong erupting around the garden. Wondering how he would set about finding Kate now that he was actually there, and also beginning to question exactly what he intended to get out of the trip, he heard Kate's voice behind him.

Turning sharply, he looked with surprise at her face on the television screen. She was presenting a local news programme, the one she had told him about in London. She looked exactly as he remembered: a little fuller in the face perhaps, but still lovely. He watched the programme until its conclusion and studied the credits. Picking up the telephone directory, he found the number for the television studio. After the call he sat back smiling. Kate was having lunch at a hotel down in the valley, a favourite spot for the locals on a Saturday. One of her work colleagues, hearing he was visiting from London, had been more than helpful. He had left the hotel telephone number in case he missed her. They were expecting her back later in the afternoon.

The hotel receptionist gave him directions and he set off, fully expecting that if she was having lunch there then it was highly likely that she would be with her husband, Jack.

The car park of the hotel was packed and he had to park on the grassy verge outside the entrance gates. Squeezing his way through the busy tables out on the hotel lawn he was lucky to find a couple just leaving. Thankful he sank into a chair, ordered a beer and looked around. The hotel was surrounded by verdant hills; an immaculately manicured golf course was set to the left of lush lawns and to the right a sparkling blue swimming pool. Sitting in the sun admiring the golf course with its majestic backdrop, he wondered how on earth he would find her in amongst so many people.

He reached for his cold beer, his eyes raking the crowds which were now beginning to disperse. Under the shade of a tall palm tree, four tables away, he saw a woman sitting alone. Her hair was swept up on top of her head. She was wearing sunglasses and reading the newspaper. He stood up, and then hesitated.

Unaware of his presence, Kate closed her paper, glanced at her watch and gathered her things together. She stood up. Tom saw immediately that she was pregnant. She dropped her newspaper and Tom, galvanized into action by her clumsiness, walked over and picked it up for her.

"Hello, Kate," he said, smiling as he handed it back to her.

Startled at the sound of his voice, her head snapped up as she looked at him puzzled. Then a wide smile lit up her face.

"Tom! What on earth are you doing here?"

He held out his hands grasping both of hers. She looked marvellous. He smiled at her, hoping his disappointment at seeing her pregnant didn't show in his eyes. This put her in another league altogether – it put her in a place that was now far removed from him. If her marriage had been in trouble then those issues had obviously been resolved.

"I was in Johannesburg on business. I had planned to go on safari but changed my mind and decided to come and see you instead! If you recall, you mentioned that I should come and see Swaziland if I was in the neighbourhood. Remember? I called your television studio and left my name and number in the faint hope that you wouldn't be away for the weekend. They told me this was your favourite haunt on a Saturday. Have you got time for a coffee, or something?"

Once again she glanced down at her watch and hesitated, then smiled up at him, aware that he was still holding her hands in his. Gently disengaging them she sighed and shook her head.

"Your timing is terrible, I'm afraid. I'm heading to the studio now for a meeting. But shall we have dinner tonight perhaps? I'm so sorry, but this is such a surprise! Please say yes about dinner?"

"Dinner sounds great. Will Jack be joining us? I'm looking forward to meeting this husband of yours and the father-to-be. You look wonderful, Kate, absolutely wonderful."

She hesitated, her smile dropping a fraction, and she bit her lip. "Jacks not around at the moment, so I'm afraid you'll have to make do with just me. Sorry." She laughed up at him. "Look, here's my address." She pulled out her business card and wrote down her address. "It's not difficult to find; it's the other side of the golf course in Mbabane. Shall we say seven thirty? Oh, it's so good to see you again, Tom!"

She kissed him on the cheek and walked towards the glass doors of the hotel. Glancing back at him she smiled and raised her hand, before disappearing into the cool shadows of the hotel lobby.

Tom glanced at the card. She had been pleased to see him, he was quite sure about that. But she seemed nervous and distracted. He shrugged his shoulders. It might have been a shock for her to see him there with no warning, or maybe she wasn't having an easy pregnancy. He would find out more over dinner that evening.

He finished his beer and paid the bill, then wandered into the hotel shop. Perhaps he could find a gift for her to celebrate the birth of her forthcoming child. He had to admit that seeing her pregnant had been a surprise, but then why not, he reasoned: it was what most married women wanted.

That evening he pulled up in front of her house, the gravel of the drive crunching beneath the tyres of the car. The house was large and built on one level. A verandah skirting the front and sides, housed large pots of flowers and plants. He was about to get out when the front door opened and Kate stepped out. He jumped out and, opening the passenger door, he helped her in.

"Not quite as nimble as I was in London, Tom. I feel like a hippo these days. I've booked a table at my favourite restaurant. I know you'll like it." She waved at a young African girl standing in the light of a small cottage next to the main house.

"Who's that?" he asked as he backed out of the drive.

"That's Rosemary. She looks after the house and tries to look after me! She'll be such a help when the baby comes, I think she's more excited about it than I am... I'm terrified." She touched his hand briefly. "Turn left here, Tom, the restaurant is about ten minutes away."

Once settled at their table, and impressed with the number of people that she knew in the room, Tom lifted his wine glass.

"Here's to you Kate, I hope the baby will bring you and Jack much happiness," he said, putting as much warmth into his voice as he could muster. She inclined her head and thanked him. "So, where is this husband of yours then?" he asked eventually. "You have got one I presume?" He grinned at her. "Or did you make him up to keep me at arm's length in London?"

"Um, at a conference in Durban I think. Well, that's what he said when he left yesterday morning. I'm not sure really."

My God, he thought, if you were mine I wouldn't let you out of my sight

They both studied the menu and having made his choice Tom sat back and glanced around the restaurant. "Won't all these people wonder what you are doing dining with a complete stranger?" he teased her.

Kate laughed. "Jack and I entertain our friends at home. If I have a tour operator or travel agent interested in promoting Swaziland, I normally bring them to a restaurant, like this one. Sometimes Jack joins me, but more often than not I do it on my own. So don't worry Tom. There won't be any gossip; everyone will assume you are in the travel business. Anyway, it would be highly unlikely that we are having an affair, when I'm so pregnant!"

Kate took a tiny sip of her wine. "Anyway, I don't want to talk about Jack or the baby or anything else. I want to hear all about you. Are you divorced yet? How did it all work out with Sarah?"

Over dinner he filled her in on his past seven months, and told her
that Sarah wanted a reconciliation. She had begged him to take her back,
to give her a second chance at the marriage. Then he abruptly changed
the subject.

"So when is the baby due?" he asked with his soft American drawl.

She looked at him. His grey eyes never left her face. He pushed his
dark hair back and covered her hand with his.

"Kate?"

"Any minute now I would think, the baby has been so active
today…" Her voice trailed away as the conversation was interrupted by
a woman who had stopped at their table.

"Kate! So good to see you. I insist that you introduce me to this
gorgeous man. Who is he?"

Kate laughed. "Tom, this is Felicity. She runs the local newspaper
here, so she always wants to know what's going on. Felicity, this is a
friend of mine from London."

Felicity raised her eyebrow and held out her hand to Tom.
"Delighted to meet you Tom. I do hope you are planning a long stay
here in Swaziland – we could do with some fresh meat."

Puzzled at this remark, Tom shook her hand. "Good to meet you
ma'am."

"Oh, you're American? How exciting!" Felicity gushed, and then
turned back to Kate, "I saw Jack this morning, in a hurry as usual, why
isn't he here tonight?" She didn't wait for an answer. "Anyway I must
dash. Lovely to meet you, Tom. Take care Kate."

Tom looked at Kate uneasily. The colour had drained from her face.
So her husband was actually in town, he thought, and not in Durban at a
conference. He felt awkward and signalled for the bill, giving her time
to compose herself.

"Kate? Perhaps we should call it a night, you look exhausted. Maybe
a quick coffee, at your place?" She had nodded at him and then hastily
rose from the table. Tom felt as though all eyes in the restaurant had
been on their backs as they walked out.

For the first time in each other's company, they were silent on the
drive back to her house. Tom could feel the anger building in him. Jack

had lied to her and now she had been confronted with the truth which, unfortunately, he had been witness to.

Tom walked her to the front door and hesitated. Maybe coffee was not such a good idea. But she opened the door and he followed her inside, reluctant to let her go.

She led him into an open-plan lounge and dining room. It was a big house from inside. In the lounge there were plenty of books and a pile of records and cassettes. There was a bowl of white roses on the coffee table and a Siamese cat who stared at him with a great deal of interest, whilst Kate was in the kitchen. She reappeared after a few minutes with a tray.

Over their coffee he was careful to keep the conversation light. He told her about his recent trip to China, pleased to be able to make her laugh at some of the things he had encountered there. He handed her his cup for a refill and gently asked her about her future career plans, and then changed the subject when he saw her hand shake, splashing the coffee into the saucer. What had happened to the bright and breezy woman he had fallen in love with in London?

She handed him back his cup. Their fingers touched and, flustered, she let go. The cup and saucer fell to the floor, the coffee seeping into the cream carpet.

"I'll get it," Tom said going to the kitchen and finding a damp cloth and soap. He insisted she stay in her chair whilst he scrubbed the stain out. When he returned from the kitchen, she was crying. He knelt down in front of her, putting his hands on her arms.

"I want to help you," he said, his words catching in his throat.

"You can't help me, Tom. Things are not going well at the moment. I hardly see Jack. He doesn't seem interested in me or the baby. I think he might be having an affair. This is a small town and gossip is rife... I try to ignore it but sometimes it's impossible. I'm tired Tom. I'm trying to hold everything together as best I can."

He handed her his handkerchief and watched as she wiped away her tears, her hands shaking.

"I have to give up my job at the studio. Pregnant women are not in demand on television. Not what the viewers want to see." She looked at him miserably. "My marriage was in trouble long before we met, Tom.

But I hoped my job would fill the gaps in it. I've tried so hard to make it work, but it just hasn't happened."

He stroked her arms and, when she had calmed down, Tom suggested that she go to bed. She nodded in tired acquiescence. He stood up, pulling her up with him.

"I don't know what to tell you, Kate. I've been where you are. Sarah had affairs and it destroyed our relationship. It wasn't just Cassie dying; it was Sarah and I turning away from each other. If you love Jack, and you want him to be in your child's life, talk to him. Sarah and I stopped communicating and that's where we unravelled. I was terrified when Sarah got pregnant. I didn't know what it meant for me and for our relationship. And then Cassie was born and I knew exactly where I had to be every day for the rest of my life. I don't know Jack but he might feel differently after the baby is born."

Kate stood in front of him, looking tired and vulnerable. He put his arms around her and gave her a hug, feeling the hardness of her stomach between them.

He stroked her hair. "I wish things could be different Kate, but somehow you have to make this work."

He pulled back from her. "I'm sorry that you're so unhappy, but this will pass, you'll see. The baby will come and make up for a lot of things in your life. Have courage. Keep going Kate."

Kate smiled at him sadly. She took his hand and walked him to the front door. "Good-night, Tom. Thank you. I'm sorry the evening ended in tears. It was so good to see you again. I wish…" she said, raising her hands and them dropping them. "I wish we could have London all over again."

Once she was safely back inside he walked over to the car. Feeling for the keys in his pocket, he felt the small box. Damn! With all the drama of the evening he had forgotten to give Kate the gift he had bought for her. He glanced back at the house and decided to leave things as they were.

He drove back to his hotel, mulling over the evening. He did a quick calculation in his head; she must have been pregnant when he had met her in London, but maybe she had been unaware of it. There's nothing I can do to change her situation, he thought, absolutely nothing. She's married, her marriage is in trouble and she's pregnant. I can't be part of her life. I should leave tomorrow and hope that she works things out for herself. He didn't want to complicate her life any further. Besides, he and Sarah had begun to talk about giving their relationship another shot and, despite everything that had happened, there was a part of him that was still fond of her. He'd gone to Swaziland hoping to find Kate in happier circumstances. He knew that the kindest thing he could do for everybody was to leave Kate, and never be in touch again. Coming here had been an unsettling mistake.

He drove out of the country late the next morning, heading back towards Johannesburg. He thought about her all the way back to the city.

Tom threw his jacket on the hotel bed and sat down. It had been a long day, not helped by the heavy traffic as he came into Johannesburg.

He sat there staring out of the window, drumming his fingers on the side of the chair. He had to talk to her and see if she was all right. He looked at his watch. She would have finished whatever she was scheduled to do at the studio.

Hesitating briefly, he reached for the telephone and called the television station; they hadn't seen her. Concerned, he called her home number. The telephone rang and rang. No reply. As he turned to put the receiver down someone said hello.

"May I speak to Kate, Rosemary?" he asked quickly. "Is she all right?"

"No sir. Miss Kate is in hospital in Johannesburg. The doctor had to come to the house last night, and he drove her there. Miss Kate is very sick." Kate's housekeeper began to cry softly. "Maybe the baby is coming soon." She gave him the name of the hospital.

"Is Kate's husband back, Rosemary? Is he with her at the hospital?"

"No," she whispered unhappily. "He is not with her."

Tom raced down the stairs, taking them two at a time, not bothering to wait for the lift. He commandeered the hotel courtesy car, and gave the driver the address of the hospital. He cursed as they crawled through the heavy traffic. A little before seven the car pulled up outside the hospital.

Her room was in darkness save for a lamp on the locker next to her bed. Quietly he approached the bed. How small she looks, he thought, how vulnerable. He watched her as she slept. He took her hand and turned it over in his. If only I could read palms, he thought, maybe I would be able to work out what will happen to this woman. His eyes travelled back to her face. She was awake, watching him, her eyes brimming with tears.

"Don't cry Kate, don't cry."

He fumbled in his pocket and brought out the small box. Not letting go of her hand he flipped the lid off with his thumb and held up a slender silver bracelet. Carefully he placed it on her left wrist and covered it with his hand.

"I'll always be with you, Kate, wherever you go. Be brave and strong, but most of all be happy. I have to go now." He felt his throat tighten with emotion. "I have to let you go Kate, I'm sorry."

"Don't let go of my hand, Tom. Don't let go of my hand," she whispered.

He brought his thoughts back to the present as he watched the impala feeding. Twenty years since he had seen her, and yet she still had this strong hold over him. He closed his eyes and saw her, recalling the scent of her on the warm wind blowing across the Delta. He imagined her golden hair tangled between his fingers and felt his chest tighten with the longing for her.

Chapter Four

KATE AWOKE from a drug-induced sleep to find her doctor standing next to her bed. He smiled down at her.

"Kate, we need to do a Caesarean today as I don't want to wait any longer. I've scheduled you in at half past one. Try not to worry; you're strong enough for this."

She watched the doctor's back as he left the room.

"I'm not ready," she said, but the doctor was out of earshot. "I need more time," she said to herself. She put her hand on her belly and thought about Tom. How he had been concerned enough to come to the clinic. She pushed away the angry thoughts about her husband, Jack. The hospital staff had tried to contact him but with no success. She had telephoned her parents, and had had a long conversation with her father. She had felt comforted by his words of reassurance; although she could tell he was angry that Jack was not with her.

Tom. Was she mistaken, she wondered, or had he been close to tears when he had said goodbye? She looked at the bracelet on her wrist and felt oddly comforted.

At a quarter past one, they came to collect her. They wheeled her through the long corridors to the operating theatre. Kate was frightened and wished with all her heart that Jack was there or that Tom had stayed longer. She had always had a fear of hospitals and hated the smell of them and now when she needed Jack most he was nowhere to be found. She was on her own. Once in the operating theatre, she looked around at all the nurses and doctors busy around her, anonymous figures behind their masks in their scrubs. Her anxiety increased. Her head snapped around to her left as she felt the sting of the needle in her arm and after that, nothing.

When she came around from the anaesthetic she found herself back in her room but it was empty. She looked down at both sides of the bed, expecting to see her baby but it was only her in the room. Panicking, she pressed the buzzer.

A nurse bustled in with an expression of expectancy and kindness when she saw Kate's obvious distress. She told Kate that her baby was in intensive care and that she'd had a girl.

Kate fell back on the pillows, overcome with relief. "May I see her?"

"Not right now, Kate, the baby is very weak and so are you. I want you to rest until tomorrow and then we'll see how things are."

Kate stared at the ceiling, her belly hot with pain. When she awoke some hours later, the doctor was leaning over her, his face full of concern.

"What's the matter?" Kate asked automatically, trying to sit upright. He put both hands on her shoulders and gently pushed her back against the pillows. He sighed heavily. Kate's stomach contracted in fear.

"Your baby is sick, Kate, and very weak. The chances of her survival are very small. You may see her, but you won't be able to touch her or pick her up. She only weighs three pounds and she's fighting for her life." He waited a moment as though letting it sink in. When Kate didn't say anything, he continued, "Have you decided on a name for her yet?" Kate's breath caught in her throat.

"I want to call her... Molly," she said, her voice shaking. "I want to see her as soon as possible. May I see her now?"

"Of course, I'll send a nurse with a wheelchair. She'll take you to see your daughter."

The nurse pushed her wheelchair into a closed-off room. The light from the window opposite didn't quite reach across the small space. The room consisted of six glass incubators, in three of which Kate could see tiny little figures. One of these is mine, Kate thought nervously. Helping her out of the wheelchair, the nurse led Kate to one in the far corner of the room.

"This is Molly, Kate," she said quietly, "I'll leave you to get to know her."

Kate looked down at the tiny baby. There seemed to be wires and needles inserted everywhere. She put her hand on top of the incubator and watched the tiny chest caving in and out, her daughter fighting for each breath. Kate's own breath caught raggedly in her throat. She hadn't expected her to look so fragile, so small. Her daughter's eyes looked up at her; they were dark and large in her tiny face. Shocked, Kate stepped back, trying to take it all in. The nurse, seeing her distress, hurried over with the wheelchair and Kate stumbled back into it. She squeezed her shoulder.

"Yes, she is tiny, but babies are much tougher than they look. I've seen smaller babies than this who have grown up strong and who are going to school now. Come, let me take you back to your room. You can come back whenever you feel you want to." Deftly, she turned the wheelchair around. What she hadn't told Kate was that the baby was very sick and had little body weight with which to fight. It would be touch and go. There was no point in worrying the distraught mother even further.

Kate went to see Molly each day for hours on end, until the nurses finally persuaded her to go back to her bed and rest. Jack had finally been contacted, four days after his daughter's birth. When he arrived at the hospital, Kate was furious. She refused to go with him to see Molly. When he returned to her room looking as shocked as she had felt the first time she had seen Molly, she watched him coldly.

"God, Kate, she is so tiny. You must prepare yourself. She might not make it."

"Molly will make it, Jack. I've been watching her the last four days and she's getting stronger. Not that you would know, or be able to tell. Did you have to drag yourself out of someone's bed to make it here? I know you weren't at a conference. No-one knew of any conferences going on in Durban. I'm not even sure you *were* in Durban. So, just get out, Jack."

He didn't move. He sat watching her, her face and body full of hurt and fury. He rubbed a hand over his face, feeling the stubble on his cheeks. God, I should have been more discreet, he thought miserably. She's always been astute, always had good instincts. She's not easy to live with, but betrayal is something she will never tolerate. This is going to take some putting back together, especially now there's the baby. He knew with absolute clarity that if the baby died, Kate would leave him.

He figured she would probably leave him anyway but not whilst the baby was sick.

His shoulders slackened as the full weight of the situation hit him. He sat back abruptly in the hard chair, thinking quickly. Perhaps Kate's parents could come and stay with them in Swaziland for a few weeks. He opened his mouth to ask Kate what she thought but hesitated. He knew there would be some ugly scenes when she got home – with or without the baby. Having her parents, and in particular her father, there might diffuse the situation. He would call them tonight and, if they agreed to come, he would book their tickets straight away. Once everything had been organised, he would tell Kate what he had arranged. He stood up and bent to kiss her goodbye, but she turned her back on him.

After he left, she lay back, exhausted and frustrated. He hadn't said a thing, she thought. He didn't even deny it. Any of it. I need to divorce him, she said to herself. But even as she thought it, her previous resolve to do so dissipated. I don't have the energy, she thought. Maybe if this had come out before Molly had been born, but now… The baby is all I must focus on. Jack never needed me but Molly does. I have to stay strong for her sake.

When Kate was discharged from the hospital she went to stay in a hotel ten minutes from the clinic. The doctors had become more hopeful and although Molly was still in ICU, she had been taken out of the incubator. Kate could touch her now and she would visit every day to watch her, stroking her tiny fingers as they curled around one of hers, praying for a miracle, willing her to live.

"Hold on tightly to me, Molly, and I'll pull you through this," she said quietly. "I want to see you grow up. I want to hear you laugh. I want to see what your handwriting will look like and what sort of sense of humour you'll have. Don't take that away from me, darling. Give me something to hold on to as well."

On one of many similar afternoons, Kate began to cry. She was living in a hospital with her husband nowhere near her and she now had a new-born baby that may or may not live through another day. A single tear splashed onto the baby's face. Molly's body twitched gently and her little face registered surprise. Despite herself, Kate laughed. Wiping away her tears, she began to feel more hopeful.

Six weeks later, Molly was released from the clinic. She was still fragile and tiny, but could now be fed normally and not through a tube. Jack arrived to take them home. Gingerly, Kate lifted her daughter from the cot, feeling the lightness of her. She knew she would not have the backup of the doctors and nurses from now on; it was a terrifying thought. Holding her daughter as tightly as she dared, she fought back her feelings of panic. Breathing deeply, she carried Molly out of the clinic towards the car – and to Jack.

Jack had organized for Kate's parents to come stay. Their presence did make things easier between them although Kate was obsessed with the baby and fiercely over-protective. She spent the nights sleeping in Molly's room, watching over her, giving her the medication that would keep her tiny heart going, checking her pulse, making sure she was still breathing.

"Come on, Kate," Jack would say in frustration, "Give yourself a break. Let me help you with Molly. I'm a doctor, I can help."

But Kate refused every offer, even though she was exhausted. Her mother took charge of the house and with Rosemary, the housekeeper, tried to make things easier for Kate. She too offered to look after the baby, but Kate refused to let her.

One day, Kate's father had come into the nursery to check on them both. Seeing Kate asleep and the baby awake, he had picked up Molly, careful not to disturb Kate. He took the baby out into the garden with him, talking to her as he walked with her nestled in the crook of his arm.

Kate woke up slowly. She glanced at her watch and was surprised to see it was late afternoon already. Molly usually woke her up at this time for her feed. Kate looked down into the empty cot and felt a rush of panic. She ran out of the nursery and into the lounge, catching a glimpse of her father in the garden through the French doors. She ran out onto the patio and caught herself before crying out to him. Her father said something to Molly and Kate saw that she was smiling. Tears welled up in Kate's eyes. In a moment of clarity, she knew that everything was going to be all right. For the first time since Molly was born, she knew without doubt that she was going to live. Quietly, she returned inside the house and left them in the garden together. She felt relieved to have her father take over for a while. She knew now that at some point she would need to sit down with him and talk to him about her future and the future of his granddaughter.

Later that evening after Kate had put Molly to bed, she sat thinking about Jack. She wished she could have loved him more. Unexpectedly her mind travelled back to what was then Rhodesia and how they had met there.

Chapter Five

KATE WAS SETTLED IN a small cottage in the outskirts of Salisbury. She had spent two years previously in London working for the BBC. After a while, the cold and grey of London became too much for her. She wanted to return to Africa.

Rhodesia had often been in the news at that time for one reason or another. Ten years before, on the 11 November 1965, Rhodesia's Prime Minister, Ian Smith, had signed a Unilateral Declaration of Independence from the United Kingdom. Kate had often wondered whether he had picked that particular date because it had signalled the end of the Great War and the beginning of his with the rest of the world.

After two years as a journalist, the prospect of living in a country where history was in the making appealed to her. She resigned her job, telling her boss that if he wanted a correspondent in Southern Africa, she was his girl, packed up her things and booked passage on a Union Castle ship, sailing from Southampton to Cape Town.

Standing at the rail of the ship in the early hours on the morning of her arrival, she watched a flat-topped mountain loom up almost as though out of the sea. As the ship neared land, the bowl of the city revealed itself: Cape Town. She was at the furthest tip of Africa.

With reluctance, swiftly followed by a wave of excitement, she caught the overnight train heading north to Rhodesia. As she watched Cape Town retreat around her, she wondered if she would ever be back.

Within months of arriving in Salisbury, she was in demand as a scriptwriter for the top broadcasters on radio and television. Jack Hope was one of the freelance broadcasters and came in twice a week. After having qualified in England as a GP, he too had been drawn to

41

Rhodesia, like so many others, for the pure adventure. He worked in the main hospital in the city and saw, first hand, the terrible injuries wrought by the bush war. The first time she met him at the Salisbury radio station, she had stayed to watch him record his piece from the script she had prepared for him. Mid-way through the recording, he looked up and smiled at her, before carrying on. She hadn't hesitated when he asked her out for dinner a few days later. She knew his reputation with women but one by one, he soon dropped his posse of girlfriends and the two of them became inseparable.

Despite the guerrilla war and the worldwide hostility against Rhodesia, the social scene amongst the white community was vibrant. There were cocktail, dinner and drinks parties almost every night of the week. The weekends were a marathon of barbecues, lunches at the Club, tennis, riding and horse racing.

Sometimes, Kate and Jack would take time out from the whirlwind of parties to spend a quiet weekend with Jack's friends, Mark and Jane Wilding and their three young boys, who lived on a farm just outside of the city. One weekend, six months into her and Jack's relationship, Jane called and invited them to stay.

"I could do with some female company, Kate. Sometimes all this talk of war and farmers being killed really gets to me. Bring me some glossy magazines if you can find any. I've been feeling really spooked lately and I need something to take my mind off things. You will come, won't you?"

Ten years of the bush war was taking its toll. Pro Ian Smith supporters fought doggedly on fighting a war they were beginning to despair of ever winning. Peace talks with the leaders of the black majority and international negotiators were fraught with difficulties, both sides determined to fight to the bitter end. The situation in the country was volatile and dangerous. Young able-bodied white men were called up to fight for their country, farmers were exempt; their duty was to protect the women and the farms around them as part of the Police Reserve.

Civilians were required to travel in a military convoy to minimise the opportunity of being attacked by insurgents. Peeling away from the convoy, Kate and Jack drove down the long bumpy dirt track to the farm. Kate rode shotgun, with Jack's rifle poking out of her window, nervously scanning the bush. Jack always laughed at her but never had the heart to tell her that if there was an attack, they wouldn't survive it... The terrorists normally attacked in groups and two people in the middle of nowhere would not stand a chance. Families often travelled in two vehicles, the parents splitting the children between them, to ensure that if there was an attack part of the family might survive. The gun reassured them both to a degree.

The farmhouse was large and sprawling and, as their family had grown, Mark had added on more rooms, as had the two previous generations. The spacious stone-floor lounge was cool and dark; a welcome respite from the brutal summer heat. Shelves filled with books, magazines and photographs lined one wall whilst the others were hung with fierce-looking shooting trophies, covered with dust. The furniture was shabby but comfortable, passed down from generation to generation; the chair covers so faded it was difficult to work out their original patterns and colours.

Kate loved pulling out old books filled with newspaper cuttings or forgotten bookmarks. An old bible fascinated her the most. Each child's birth had been carefully recorded in the front, as well as each death. It chronicled five generations of Mark's family. The tooled leather cover was oily with old hand and finger prints and the pages within were fragile like cobwebs. The magazines and comic books sometimes dated back twenty years and copies of the *Farmers Weekly* kept her amused for hours with quaint adverts and illustrations of the latest fashions: the dresses with wide collars and the women wearing white gloves. It was a charming journey back in time.

Jane kept a diary and Kate was impressed with her friend's diligence: every single night Jane wrote up the day.

"Why such a huge diary, Jane?" Kate had asked her one evening, during their last visit. They had been sitting outside on the verandah, and Jane had looked up and grinned at her.

"A diary has always been kept on the ranch. I've got all the originals. They're not very exciting though, just daily happenings on the farm, such as the milk yield, how many calves born, how many chickens, the maize harvest, a list of supplies and so on. All mundane stuff, really. Of course there are little personal anecdotes, babies born, weddings, old folk dying, illness and accidents. I'm trying to spice up my contribution; it's always been the women in the family that have had this task. I'm trying to modernize things a bit, so I write about the world today, the war of course, what's happening here in the country. I need to produce a girl baby soon." She patted her swollen stomach. "I can't see those sons of mine labouring long and hard over this every night!"

Kate had watched her fondly. "Don't you ever long for a bit more glamour in your life, Jane? A trip to Harrods? Tea at the Savoy? A trip on the Orient Express?"

Jane had sighed and put down her pen, shooing away one of their four big Dobermans who seemed determined to sit on one of the chairs. "Off you go Max, you're supposed to be guarding the farm, not lying around here." She turned back to Kate. "Glamour in my life? No. I know it's hard for you to understand. You see my parents and grandparents were also farmers and my brothers run their farm now, just as Mark is doing here. We farm folk are inclined to marry each other, we understand each other and it's the only life we have ever known. I'm not remotely interested in a more glamorous life. These Rhodesian farmers carefully select who they will marry. They might lust after the glamorous types they see in town, or at the club, but they never marry them. Affairs yes, but marriage no. They know instinctively that a marriage will never survive with someone who hankers after something different. When you marry one of these guys, you're not just marrying the man; you're marrying the entire family, the land and their history."

Kate remembered how she had felt a stab of envy; envy for someone so content with her life and her place within it. However she hadn't envied their lifestyle, living day to day on a knife edge.

On their second afternoon, Kate had been buried in the bookshelves when Mark came into the room. She had smiled at him wistfully. "How lucky you are, to have such a history all in one place. It must be wonderful to feel so rooted, to know exactly where you are in life and know that the landscape will always remain the same for you, even with all these troubles going on."

"It's all I've ever known, Kate," he had answered, swirling the ice around in his glass. "I couldn't imagine being anywhere else. I could walk around this farm blindfolded and know exactly where everything is. There are three generations of us buried here. I will be buried here, as will my sons, and their sons. It's the continuity that makes this place so special; as if we are still all together here and always will be. Wedded to the land, so to speak. It's in our blood. I won't give up my land; it belongs to me and future generations. If I have to, I'll die fighting for the right to keep it."

They dined outside beneath the enormous trees at the back of the house that night, once the boys had gone to bed. Years before, Mark had laid a large square of concrete beneath the heavy boughs and it was there they entertained their friends and farmer neighbours. The view stretched out indefinitely over hundreds of acres of land.

The conversation inevitably turned to the war. They ran through those whom they knew had been killed or ambushed, which farms had been burned to the ground and where. The windows of the house were all open and occasional squawks and squeaks from the two-way radio in Mark's study would ebb out and for a few seconds they all held their breaths, listening. Many of the farmers in the area around Marandellas, a town about sixty miles from the capital, had been attacked and killed by bands of marauding terrorists. The white farmers in every area kept in touch with each other by radio, checking at the end of the day that everyone was safe and locked in. They would repeat the process again each morning, making sure everyone had made it safely through the night.

Propped up next to Mark's and Jack's chairs were their fully loaded guns. Before bed, Mark, Jack and the four dogs went out to check the perimeter fences of the ranch, securing the sandbags, ensuring that the heavy padlocks and chains were in place, and that the powerful security lights were working.

Later, Kate and Jack lay in bed, listening to every sound in the night, trying not to imagine what could happen. Any loud noise had them sitting bolt upright in their bed, Jack reaching for his gun, Kate's heart beating rapidly in terror.

The next morning they took their leave, Mark having already left to take the boys to school, a half an hour trip he undertook twice a day, determined that his sons should live as normal a life as possible under the circumstances.

Kate hugged Jane tightly. "You have more courage than I have Jane, living out here with all the problems. You should think about coming into town for a few days, give yourself a break. We could have lunch and do a bit of shopping."

"Not possible, I'm afraid. We need to guard our farm. But you must come again soon. I so miss having some female company. Goodbye Jack." Her eyes narrowed as she scanned the perimeter fences, then she looked down at her watch. "Better get going otherwise you'll miss the convoy; if you're late they'll go without you!"

The war raged on, and as with most wars, people got on with their lives, almost accepting the daily bad news of casualties on both sides. Kate and Jack and everyone else ensconced themselves in the parties and being together; it felt safer that way.

"Jack, let's give Jane and Mark a ring, see how things are out on the farm. Maybe we should go and visit them, cheer them up a bit. It's weeks since we saw them. The news has been so bad lately and that latest farm attack was not that far away from them."

On the Thursday night before they were due to go Jack cancelled at the last minute. He tried to persuade her to go alone, telling her she would be safe enough in the convoy and that Mark could come into town to collect her. But Kate said she'd rather not go alone. She tried to call Jane but the farm lines were down and she couldn't get connected.

"This blasted war," she said to Jack, "it's impossible to ever get through to anybody!"

The twenty African terrorists quietly surrounded Mark and Jane's farm just before sunset. Dressed in combat fatigues they watched the family of five as they had dinner outside in the garden. As night fell in shadows across the house, they crept through the electric fence, which they had soundlessly disabled. The leader of the group silently signalled to his men. They rose up as one. The four big Dobermans scrambled to their feet and started to bark, startling the family. As Mark reached for his gun the terrorists opened fire.

Kate and Jack heard the news on the radio the next evening. The family was slaughtered where they sat and the dogs too. After ransacking the house, the terrorists had set fire to it and then melted away into the night. Kate and Jack, and what seemed like the entire Salisbury community, attended the funerals the following week. There were those there who knew Mark and Jane as well as Jack and Kate had known them; others who had met them briefly at some of the parties. There were even those who hadn't known them at all but who felt, as an act of solidarity, that they should attend and pay their respects.

The hot African sun seared through the stained glass windows in the great cathedral, spilling a kaleidoscope of vivid colours over the hundreds of sombrely dressed mourners attending. Five coffins lay in front of the altar. Kate was relieved, in many ways that they had all died together, but she felt grief-stricken that they were all gone. Mark and his family were no longer and their beautiful home was gone. She knew that this small family, with their roots so deeply embedded in a country they had loved so much, would in time be forgotten.

Close family and friends followed the cortège out to the farm for the last time; a long stream of shiny cars and military vehicles in convoy. The sun beat down on all of them, black-clad and overheating, as the last five of the Wilding family were laid to rest with their ancestors.

Afterwards, Kate wandered through the burnt out remains of the house. There was little left to see. She found an edge of the leather cover of the family bible but the pages recording the lives of the generations past were gone. She felt overwhelmed by sadness. She nudged a pile of charred remains with her foot and watched it disintegrate. She looked down to get a closer look, a sob catching in her throat. The diary. Words that would not be whispered through the generations to come. She sank to her knees and wept with the hopelessness of it all.

The whole incident had shocked Kate more than she would admit. What if she had decided to go and visit them that weekend? There would have been another coffin – hers.

Shaken, she hurriedly left behind what remained of the house and the choking smell of the smouldering ashes. It was a smell that she would come to know again, across the other side of the world, in a terrorist attack which would stun the world with its breathtaking audacity.

During the wake that evening, in a hotel in Salisbury, Kate and Jack discussed the future of the country and the part, if any, they would play in it. Neither of them felt optimistic. Losing their friends as they had, and the reality of life outside the expatriate bubble they lived in, stared them straight in the face. Jack felt that it was time to move on. The war was out of control and the terrorists had the upper hand. They were all at risk. It was only a matter of time before the black majority won the war. It was *their* country after all. The British had taken it away from them and then a small white minority had attempted to colonise it for themselves. They'd been lucky enough to have it for as long as they had.

On the drive home and without very much ceremony, Jack asked Kate to marry him. Shaken by recent events and longing for something normal, something happy to look forward to, she accepted. They were both too shell-shocked to feel anything other than safe in, and reassured by, their decision to marry and leave the country to its inevitable fate.

Chapter Six

JACK FOUND A POSITION at a hospital in Johannesburg and a month later they left Rhodesia. Their wedding was planned for later in the year but they hadn't yet decided on a date. Kate was keen to meet his family and she wanted him to meet hers. However, Jack was too new and busy in the hospital to make the trip to England, or to make time to visit her parents who now lived in Durban. He promised he would do this when she returned.

With no job of her own and encouraged by Jack, she decided to go alone to England to meet his parents and spend some time with her sister Lucy, who had left South Africa a year ago to spend a year working in an art gallery in London. With nothing keeping her in Johannesburg, she booked her flight.

Kate's meeting with Jack's parents had been a disaster. When the train had pulled into the station in Winchester she had spotted them straight away, based on Jack's description. More than a little nervous Kate had politely answered their questions about her journey, her parents and family and how she had met Jack.

Over dinner that evening, aware that she was under close scrutiny, she had looked at her surroundings and the beautiful country house that Jack had been brought up in. Somewhat different to the wooden house on stilts that I had lived in, in Malaya, when I was a child, she had thought wryly.

Sitting opposite Jack's parents, Kate realised they had very little in common and they had even less interest in her. She wondered what had compelled her to do this on her own and why Jack had let her. They

49

made no effort to get to know her and asked barely one question between them throughout the meal. Kate filled the long silences with stories about her and Jack in Rhodesia, and about her childhood in Malaya and how, at school there, they would all run wild in the jungle and hunt for pigmies.

Oh God, she thought to herself, they probably think I hunted pigmies down with a bow and arrow, or a blow pipe. She had felt her spirits plummet and counted the hours before she could excuse herself, blaming jet lag, and go to bed.

Jack's parents didn't like her. No wonder he took off for Rhodesia, she thought. Cold, aloof and arrogant, they had obviously come to the conclusion that she was not good enough for their only son.

Apprehensively she thought about her future with these two in it. Perhaps she and Jack would not be so well suited after all. Kate was well aware of how influential relatives could be and the pressure they could put on a marriage. She already knew that Jack's parents visited him when they could and he made a point of returning to England every two years. They had just left the country when she had met Jack and he would have come with her for his normal visit, had it not been for the new job at the hospital. Jack's parents would play a big part in their lives once they were married. She knew they didn't approve of her, because she was too different. Doubts about getting married to Jack began to pool and fester in her mind.

That night, the whole ghastly evening over with, she lay in bed and wondered what she should do next. How could she get out of staying even one more day with his parents?

The train rushed through the English countryside en route to London. Kate looked out of the window, deep in thought.

An awkward silence had fallen over the breakfast table that morning and, after what seemed like an interminably long time, she had fled to her room and sat on her unmade bed. Visions of the years to come, with visits from his hostile parents had made her shudder. Maybe she had agreed to marry Jack for the wrong reasons. Maybe the events at the farm had unbalanced her for a while; perhaps she had been too hasty with her decision. All she had thought about then was leaving the country and starting a new life away from the bush war. Maybe this was all going to be a mistake. Quickly she had made a decision and returned to the icy atmosphere of the dining room. She had a week to kill and, with her decision made, she would be able to spend more time with Lucy. She had to get away and think things through.

The taxi had arrived and she had taken her leave of them. His mother had stood there at the front door with her arms crossed looking triumphant. Their eyes had locked and then Kate had tossed her head and walked away from them.

The train's arrival at Kings Cross roused her from her reverie. She collected her luggage and went in search of a taxi.

Now the two sisters grinned at each other across the dining room table, delighted to be together again.

"So, how did the meeting with Jack's parents go? Did you manage to endear yourself to them, as anticipated?"

"Oh, I don't know!" Kate said, almost wailing and putting her face in her hands. "To tell you the truth, Luce, I'm getting cold feet about the whole thing. Jack's parents were incredibly difficult. I didn't get on with them at all. They didn't like me and I didn't particularly like them. Jack telephoned his mother and gave her the date of our wedding, without even letting me know first! It made me think that what his mother thought was more important than what I thought. It made me angry, as if he had already taken over my life. I've always been a free spirit, as you well know, and I like to have a say in where my life is going and with whom. I'm not particularly keen on living in Johannesburg either."

Lucy listened to her carefully as she spoke.

"He's a wonderful man and in a way I do love him, but I can't help feeling that there's something missing. It's not an easy decision to make. I've given up my job, my cottage – everything – to be with him so that we can get married. Now, I have to reinvent my life. The trouble is I'm not sure where I'd be going next if I wasn't getting married to Jack. Besides…" Kate paused and looked away, "If I was absolutely certain I was doing the right thing, I wouldn't be here with you now, would I? I'd be with his parents, trying my hardest to make things work and planning our wedding with them. But I'm not."

"How on earth did you manage to get away so quickly Kate? What was it, one or two nights? What excuse did you give for cutting the visit short?"

She giggled. "I told them I wanted to visit our Grandmother in Scotland for a few days."

"Kate! She's been dead for over twenty years."

"I couldn't come up with any other reason to leave so suddenly. I think they were relieved when I announced my imminent departure. I don't think they approved of me at all."

Lucy threw her head back and laughed. "Well, I have to say that you're not the run of the mill English rose. I mean, look at you, bare legs with that beaded thing around your ankle, ivory bangles and all that blonde hair, they must have found you terrifying. They would probably prefer one of those Sloane Rangers, all terribly correct with a posh accent and someone who can make a perfect soufflé. That's definitely not you, Kate."

She leaned towards her sister, suddenly serious. "Kate, if you have any doubts at all about this marriage, don't go ahead with it; so far it hasn't exactly been an auspicious start, has it?"

Kate shrugged her shoulders. "No, you're quite right." She slowly pulled the engagement ring off her finger and placed it carefully on the table between them. "I'll post this back to him tomorrow and tell him I don't want to go ahead with the wedding. I've thought long and hard about it, on the journey down here and it just doesn't feel right any more, not now that we have left the war zone of Rhodesia."

Quickly she changed the subject, relieved that she had made her decision. "Now, what have you been up to? How's life in the world of art? Have you met anyone you need to tell me about?"

"Nope. I have dated a few guys but to be perfectly honest I didn't seem to have much in common with any of them. I feel as though I've been brought up on another planet. I went to a dinner party last week and met a whole bunch of people who had lived in Africa at some point in their lives; it was so refreshing, and I realised that I wanted to go home, so that's what I've decided to do. I've loved spending time in all the galleries here in London but I need to go back to where I belong. It's been fun but it's not enough for me."

Kate jumped up from her seat and hugged her sister fiercely. "That's fabulous news Lucy, at least we'll be living on the same continent. I know you wanted the London experience but I hated you being so far away." She yawned expansively. "The past few days have exhausted me, I need to sleep."

Lucy cleared away the debris of their dinner thinking about their conversation. Kate had told her about meeting Jack in Rhodesia and the reason why they had both decided to leave, not a moment too soon by all accounts – it sounded like a dangerous place to live, but then Kate had always loved a bit of adventure, even when she was a little girl. Calling off the wedding was one thing, now her sister would have to start life all over again. She turned off the kitchen light and headed for bed. If there was one thing her sister was good at, it was catapulting herself into a new life.

Chapter Seven

WHEN KATE'S FLIGHT touched down in Johannesburg, Jack was waiting for her. She had sent him a brief note and the engagement ring, saying that she would not be going through with the wedding but that she would be returning to collect her things. The last thing she expected was to see him in the arrivals hall at the airport. He must have used his considerable charm to have found out which flight she was on, she thought apprehensively.

Jack collected her luggage and put it in the car. They drove through the busy streets of Johannesburg, neither saying a word. It was only when they pulled up in front of their house that Jack finally turned to look at her.

"I heard that the visit to my parents didn't go too well, Kate. I'm sorry about that. My mother is an extremely difficult woman. Even I don't get on with her. I want to marry you and I want you to reconsider your decision. I've been offered a three-year contract in Lagos, in Nigeria. I thought that it might be fun. It could be a brand new start for both of us. Will you give it some more thought? Stay with me for a few days, let's talk things through and see if we can put ourselves back together?"

That evening, out on the patio under familiar star-filled skies, Kate sat and thought about the proposal. If she married Jack she would be in Africa and in a part she had never visited. That would be a big adventure in itself. Despite what she had said to Lucy, she and Jack had been good together in Rhodesia. Perhaps she had been too hasty with her decision.

She turned to see where he was. She could see him in the lounge, reading. She felt a stab of guilt that she had treated him so badly – that she had dismissed him and their future together so quickly and based entirely on her meeting his parents. Feeling her gaze on him, he looked up. She was reminded of the first day they had seen one another and she smiled, as she had done then. He stood up slowly and came to join her outside.

"All right, Jack. I'll stay with you here for a while; let's see if we can work something out."

He kneeled in front of her and pulled her to him, holding her tightly. "Thank you, Kate. I want to marry you more than anything in the world. I can make you happy, just give me a chance."

She held him close and prayed that she would make the right decision.

If Kate had had any inkling of what it would be like to live in Lagos, she would never have considered it as the place for their new start. There were no travel brochures to be found on Nigeria or Lagos and after some weeks there, she understood why.

On the flight over Jack had warned her about their new life there. "Nigeria, like most other independent African countries, despises the white regimes in both South Africa and Rhodesia. It's against their law to enter the country if you have lived, or even visited, either of those countries. It carries a jail sentence and deportation. That's why we had to get brand new passports in London with no incriminating stamps. As far as everyone is concerned, and I mean everyone, we have been living in London. You must not mention Rhodesia or South Africa to anyone, Kate; it would be dangerous for us. When you send letters to your family in South Africa they'll need to go in another envelope and sent via London; the company will post them on to Durban."

Kate thought about Jack's explicit instructions. Now the new adventure seemed tainted with danger and she wished he had told her all this before they had left Johannesburg. Anyway, it was too late now, they were about to land. Looking out of the window as they started their descent, all she saw was a seething mass of humanity below. Shacks and tin roofs spread endlessly across the city, squashed between multi-storey buildings. The roads and motorways were jammed with cars, all shimmering in the dusty heat.

The heavy aircraft door opened and the humidity snaked its way through to the passengers. To Kate, it felt like a hot steaming blanket had been thrown over her head. They fought their way through the noisy crowds, towards immigration. The Immigration Officers sat on high stools with even higher desks, so that they were both forced to look up at the Nigerian who was closely examining their passports.

Kate wiped her clammy hands on her sleeves. With a great flourish he stamped Kate's, pushing it back to her with a flick of his wrist. The passport tipped off the end of the desk and fell to the floor. Kate and Jack looked at each other. Jack shook his head slightly, knowing Kate was about to re-act to this blatant rudeness. She bit down on her lip and bent to retrieve it.

The short drive to the house was a nightmare. Kate had never seen a place as noisy and as filthy. Huge piles of smouldering rubbish lay uncollected on the sides of the road; unfinished flyovers ended in the middle of the air. The traffic moved at a snail's pace clogging every inch of road as they crawled through the heat and noise of hundreds of honking cars.

Their new house was nice enough. It was fully furnished and came with a cook, a cleaner, a gardener and four guards.

Why so much security, she thought, nervously?

There was also a car with a driver, Joseph. They unpacked their suitcases in their bedroom and went downstairs. It was getting dark outside. Jack's colleague at the surgery had stocked up the larder and the bar for them, ready for their arrival. They sat down in the lounge with a glass of wine and surveyed their new home. The cook, Ezekiel, busied himself in the kitchen preparing dinner for them. Suddenly, and without warning, everything was plunged into darkness. There was a curse from the kitchen before the door swung open and Ezekiel came bustling through with two candles and a broad smile on his face.

"What's happening, Ezekiel?" Kate asked.

"Ah, these electricity people, this happening all the time. They are called NEPA, the Nigerian Electrical Power Association, but we call them Never Expect Power Again." Laughing, he went back into the kitchen to fire up the gas stove. Kate looked at Jack pensively.

"Let's hope he's kidding, Jack. It's eight o'clock, and still as hot as hell. We need that air conditioning if we plan on getting any sleep at all."

Just then, there was a great thudding and rumbling all around them. Kate's expression turned into one of alarm.

"It's all right, Kate, just the generators. Our neighbours are obviously very well prepared and we might have to look into getting one ourselves, if the power really is that erratic."

It turned out it was. They learned that the power would go off for five days at a time, causing all the food in the fridge and freezer to rot. There would be no hot water and no air-conditioning. After two weeks, Kate demanded that Jack install a generator sooner rather than later. Whilst she waited for this to arrive from England and trying to fill her time whilst Jack was working long hours at the surgery, Kate set about making some friends. She decided to start with her neighbours. In particular, the American couple next door who had a massive generator pounding away night and day, no matter whether there was electricity or not. It was their iced up windows that drew her to them first.

Kirsty and Jim welcomed her into their cool home; Jim mixed her an ice-cold martini and invited her and Jack over for dinner that evening.

They feasted on shrimp and steak, whilst the windows dripped with condensation as the cool windows fought against the hot night air outside. Kirsty and Jim had lived in Lagos for ten years and knew the ropes.

"I don't see any of this food in that dreadful place they call the supermarket," Kate said to Kirsty.

"That's because all our food is flown in from the States, honey. Americans here are well looked after by their government. I wouldn't shop here if they paid me. With the power cuts that meat could have been thawed and frozen Lord knows how many times, it's not worth taking the risk." Kate and Jack were horrified at the thought.

The rest of the evening was filled with tales about life in Lagos and Kate laughed nervously with the rest of them, not quite sure whether to believe all the stories.

The power went off again the next day. In desperation, Kate decided to take their meat and store it in the fridge at the surgery. Jack was surprised and hesitant at first but tried to accommodate her. He cleared aside the drugs that had to be kept at a certain temperature to make room for their week's meat supply. A few days later and fed up that their generator had not yet arrived, Kate came bounding into Jack's office to raid his fridge. Finding that he was in the middle of a consultancy, she apologised and quietly continued into his dispensary.

"How about these for dinner tonight, Jack?" she whispered to him, over the head of his patient, holding up a bag of lamb chops. His patient looked up in horror. Jack got the message and promised to chase up the generator.

Six weeks later a large truck trundled up the driveway and there it was: the generator. Once installed, life improved for them almost instantly. They entertained more and, as the expatriate community was fairly small, before long they were very much a part of it. Kate was very happy with Jack and they got along well together. Life, despite the difficulties of living there, was good.

However, Jack struggled daily at his surgery. With the erratic water and electricity supplies it was difficult for him to maintain the high standards he was used to. He found the challenges and the work exhausting, but once at home Kate was always able to bring a smile to his face, when she told him about her day.

She had a great capacity for adapting to whatever life threw at her, treating it all as a big adventure. He guessed that that had come from all the years she had trailed from country to country with her parents, living in some kind of magical travel bubble. Coming from a stable background in England it concerned him slightly that she didn't have any particular country that she belonged to. But in time he was quite convinced that she would put some roots down with him and when the babies came, if they did, she would soon settle down.

Ezekiel, who had looked after the company house for ten years, had told them that the telephone in the house had not worked for five years and so they depended on their driver, Joseph, to deliver invitations for dinner. Even if only driving ten kilometres he could be gone for seven hours, stuck in the traffic. For Jack's birthday, six months after they had arrived in Lagos, Kate arranged a dinner party. The invitations had been delivered weeks before. With growing consternation she and Jack sat waiting for their guests to arrive. An hour passed, and then a second, with no sign of them. At ten o' clock, they decided to call the whole thing off and go out for dinner instead.

Joseph battled through the thick traffic heading into the centre of town. Traffic on the opposite side of the road was worse. Kate sighed with frustration and turned to look out of the window. Suddenly she sat up straight and grabbed his arm.

"Jack! Jack! There are our dinner guests. They're stuck in the traffic!"

Jack turned around and sure enough, there were their guests, sitting sedately in their car, amidst the heat and the suffocating choking fumes of cars and lorries. Kate and Jack waved frantically. Their guests looked across the traffic chaos and recognizing them, raised their wine glasses in a toast and waited with good natured resignation, looking steadfastly ahead.

Kate giggled. "So that's how they handle the frustration of a traffic jam! Joseph, turn the car around, if you can, let's get back to our dinner party – it looks as though our friends will arrive after all."

One Sunday Jack decided to take Kate to a different beach from the one they normally went to. The traffic was not as bad at the weekends and he was getting bored with going to the same place every Sunday. Kate packed a picnic and put it in the cooler box, along with a chilled bottle of wine, and they set off.

"I heard about this beach from a patient of mine. Apparently it's not quite as crowded as the one we always go to." Now he looked around with satisfaction. Not many people at all. "I'll set up the picnic table and chairs and you can have a swim. There'll be a cold glass of wine waiting for you." He set to work.

"This was a great idea Jack," she said, settling back in her beach chair contentedly. From where they sat they could see before them a wide expanse of beach and the blue sea sparkled beneath the sunlight. From the road, a black van drove over the pavement and pulled up on the grass verge. The van was followed by four cars, out of which jumped three TV crews. They quickly went about setting up their cameras. From out of the back of the van, eight men, chained together, were pulled to the ground by four policemen.

"Oh, they must be making a documentary or something," said Kate sitting up straight and watching the proceedings with interest.

The prisoners were released from their chains and tied to the stakes. From a second van, which neither Kate nor Jack had noticed before, were carried out eight wooden coffins. With very little warning and in a sudden blast of gunfire, the policemen shot the prisoners.

Kate and Jack hadn't moved. They sat still with their mouths open in shock, the cucumber sandwiches in their hands, forgotten.

"Jesus Christ!" Jack said, standing up quickly and knocking the picnic table over in his haste. "This is no damn film! That was real. Look at the blood."

He pulled her out of her chair and held her, whilst they watched in horror as the dead prisoners were untied and thrown in the coffins. Within minutes the coffins had been returned to the van, the policemen drove off in a now empty vehicle and the TV crews packed up and left.

They drove back to their house in silence, shocked by what they had seen. Kirsty and Jim came over for a drink and Kate and Jack told them what they had witnessed.

Kirsty laughed. "Oh that! That's a public execution. They have them often on that beach. The expatriates who live nearby turn up their music so they don't hear the gunfire and have a stiff drink for their nerves. Anyway," she lifted her martini glass, "Cheers everyone."

"Doesn't it shock you?" Kate asked, her voice sounding strained even to herself. "This country shocks *me*," she said, suddenly angry. "Everything about it shocks me. The filth, the heat, the lack of food in the shops, the bloody traffic and the traffic jams, the dead bodies left on the side of the road. God, even I'm using them as landmarks!" Laughing hysterically, she continued. "I was driving into town last week and saw two dead bullocks on the road, all bloated and horrible. Ah, I thought to myself, turn left at the next road. I mean, don't you think the driver of the truck carrying the livestock would have noticed if two thundering great bullocks had fallen off? And you know that bloated corpse of a man on the road to Appapa? Well, he's been there for over a week now. I know when the turning is coming up and I use him as a beacon!"

Laughing and crying at the same time, Kate tried to get control of herself. Jack passed her two valium and a large glass of wine.

"Come on, Kate. I know it's a nightmare but there's nothing we can do about it. I still have a year to go on my contract."

Kate looked at her American friends. "How can you stand it? How can you live here?"

Jim glanced across at her, shrugging his shoulders. "It's the money, honey. It's the money. This is not called a hardship posting for nothing!"

Lying in bed that night Jack could feel how tense she was. He held her close and stroked her hair, knowing that she had been shocked by the incident on the beach, just as he had been.

"I'm proud of you Kate. It's not easy living here. I don't think anyone ever really gets used to the traffic and the chaos of day-to-day living. We only have one more year left on the contract and then it will be all over. I'm making good money here, more than I could make anywhere else, and I wouldn't have been able to do this on my own, not without you."

"I don't know if I can take another year, Jack. I don't know if I ever want to live in Africa again. I can't get a job here because I'm white. I can't tell anyone where we lived before or what we went through. It's as though I didn't exist before this. It just doesn't feel right. The white community here lives in some kind of whimsical world, all for the sake of making big money. This isn't real life and the money is just not worth it. Thousands of Nigerians live in terrible squalor, the authorities don't bother to pick up a dead body on the road and we sit around having gin and tonics laughing hysterically at life here. I've had enough Jack; I want to leave as soon as possible."

He fumbled for the light switch and looked at her helplessly. "If you really feel that strongly about life here then I won't force you to stay. I have to finish my contract Kate. You could go and stay with your parents until it's finished, if that would make you happier? Think about it anyway. I want you here with me but I don't want you to be unhappy." He glanced at the clock and rubbed his eyes tiredly. "I'd better get some sleep, I have an early start tomorrow. I could do without attending that conference in Port Harcourt."

He would be away for three days. She hated being on her own and always worried for Jack's safe return.

For three days she waited anxiously and was relieved when it was Thursday and time for Joseph to collect him from the airport. Late that evening, Joseph returned without him. He had not been on the flight.

"Not unusual Madam," Joseph said, seeing how worried she was. "I will wait at the airport every day until Doctor Hope returns."

She sent Joseph back to the airport each day for three days, cursing the fact that the telephone didn't work. There was nothing else for it but to sit and wait for his return. Finally, Joseph returned with Jack, who was glassy-eyed with exhaustion. His clothes were wrinkled and stained with sweat. She ran out to him as he came up the steps to their front door.

"Where have you been, Jack? What happened? Did you miss the flight? I've been sick with worry! I tried not to think the worst but I didn't know what to think!" She burst into tears and he held her tightly.

"You'll never believe it…" he said, walking her into the house and going straight to the drinks cabinet. He poured himself an enormous gin and tonic, which he downed in one long series of thirsty gulps. He poured himself a second and topped up Kate's glass before sitting down with her.

"For God's sake, Jack, tell me what happened!" Kate said impatiently.

"I left here and went to the airport on Monday morning, as you know. I had my return ticket to Port Harcourt. I boarded the flight. The plane took off and after a couple of hours I realised that we should have reached Port Harcourt by that time. Everyone else on the flight had started to realise this too. We asked the air hostess to tell us what was going on and she said that the plane was going to Kaduna. The pilot, for reasons known only to himself, had decided that he didn't fancy flying to Port Hacourt after all, that he preferred to go to Kaduna. Maybe he wanted to visit a relative or something. No idea. No explanation either. Anyway, that's where I ended up – unbelievable! When I eventually got a flight from Kaduna to Port Harcourt the next day, I had missed half of the conference. Then – and it gets worse – when I went to get on the return flight back to Lagos, it was overbooked." He took a deep drink from his glass and shuddered at the memory.

"They took us out to the aircraft and made us all run around the plane. The fastest passengers were the first on and they got the seats. I wasn't sure what the hell was going on, so I was one of the last ones trying to get on-board. Needless to say, I didn't get a seat!"

Kate was laughing so hard her stomach ached. All her worry from the last three days dissolved as the tears streamed down her cheeks. After a while, Jack started to laugh too. Now that he was home, he saw the funny side.

They looked at each other, laughing helplessly. She put her arms around him, happy to have him back. "I'll stay with you Jack and see our last year out on the contract. I can't leave you here on your own, it wouldn't be fair. For better or worse, isn't that what we said? It can't get worse than this!"

Jack's three year contract was finally up. Kate held her breath as their flight took off for England. They knew that they wouldn't relax until they were at least two hours away from Lagos. After that, if there was a technical problem, they would be diverted to Nairobi. Kate didn't want any eventualities to take them back to Lagos. She reached for Jack's hand.

"That pretty much does it for me and Africa. I don't think I ever want to live on that continent again!"

Jack smiled at her. It had been tough, but she had stuck it out.

He wondered when he should tell her. He had accepted a position in Swaziland. Based on what she had just said, he wasn't sure if there was ever going to be a good time. He hoped that she might change her mind. He had done some research before accepting the position. Swaziland had a fledgling tourism business and, coupled with this, there was opportunities for someone like Kate in the media business. Unlike Nigeria, where she couldn't work, she would be able to use her journalism experience doing something he knew she loved. If he could sell her this idea, it might well take the sting out of the fact that he had accepted the offer of the job without consulting her.

Whilst Kate dozed, he worked out his strategy for telling her.

"Kate?" He shook her arm gently.

She smiled at him sleepily. Pushing herself up in her seat she squinted at her watch. Only two hours before they landed and already she was dreading the next part. With no job in the pipeline for Jack, they would be staying with his parents until he found something. She prayed that it would be weeks rather than months. She hadn't seen them since her disastrous introduction to them over three years ago.

They hadn't come to the wedding. Kate had felt her new mother-in-law's sour disapproval across the miles. Now they would have to stay with them for the foreseeable future. The thought made her feel ill.

"I know how much you hated Nigeria," Jack said, "and I understand why. It was a difficult contract but we did it and survived. I also know how much you're dreading staying with my parents – almost as much as I am. I think I could easily get a job in the UK, but I know you don't particularly want that either."

He went on to tell her about the job offer in Swaziland and the opportunities for her. The fact that she could carve out a career of her own this time. The country had a good infrastructure, there was no need for a generator, there were no traffic jams and it was only four hours from Johannesburg. Their lifestyle could be good there.

Kate listened to him intently. Despite herself she began to imagine the possibilities. She felt a little piqued that he had kept all this to himself but she quickly saw that it would mean a minimum amount of time spent with his parents and that she wouldn't have to live in the UK. The thought of being able to work again was the deciding factor for her. She saw that Jack was watching her and waiting to see her response.

She shrugged her shoulders and smiled. "Why not? It might be fun."

Jack breathed a sigh of relief. "The job comes with a house, so that's a weight off of our minds. You can have a cat and if we get really bored, we can go away for the weekends in South Africa, go on a safari somewhere."

Kate's mind raced for the last hour and a half of the flight. She barely noticed the plane landing. She felt a curl of excitement at the prospect of living in a new country and the chance to get back into the media industry.

Chapter Eight

BRINGING HERSELF BACK to the present, Kate glanced at her
watch. Jack still wasn't back. She checked that Molly was asleep
and then went outside to look for her father. She knew he would still be
up. The night was cool and clear; thousands of stars littered the sky
above. She found him on the patio and smiled at him fondly. It had
been good of her parents to stay on longer than they had intended to:
three months now.

They wandered around the garden, discussing the best place to start a
rose garden. Of Peter's two daughters, Kate was the most headstrong.
Lucy, by comparison, was quite different; she was the dreamy child.
From a very young age it was apparent that she was a gifted artist. Lucy
could always be found sketching, drawing and painting; smudges of
paint on her face and on her clothes. Kate was the curious one, always
asking questions about the world and her place in it. Lucy could always
be found around the house, whereas Kate was always climbing a tree or
out with her friends playing. She was wilder and more confident than
her older sister.

Lucy had never married; she had decided against the ties that bind,
preferring to float through life untethered. She now lived on her own by
the sea in a place called Wilderness in South Africa and was a
moderately successful artist. Kate had married Jack four years ago but
Peter knew that she was unhappy. Lucy had been the one that wanted
the babies. Now Kate had Molly and Lucy was childless.

With only two years between them the sisters were very close and
kept in touch regularly. Peter had retired from the Diplomatic Corps
after forty years of service, and was quite content to spend time in his
garden or with his daughters. Despite Jack being the one to invite them,

and Peter having some idea as to why Jack had wanted them in the house, he was quite besotted with his granddaughter. She had the same big amber eyes as Kate and he spent all day with her until Kate wrestled her away from him, to feed and bath her.

"Daddy?" Kate asked.

Peter smiled at her, knowing with that tone in her voice that she was going to ask one of her tricky questions. "How do you work out who are the most important people in your life? How do you know which ones to trust, which ones to love?"

He wondered why she asked him this. Why she always seemed to need some kind of guarantee for happiness. He knew from experience that there was no such thing in life. Finally, he answered her question with as much wisdom as he could muster.

"Firstly, Kate, it's not such a good idea to look too far down the road. You can't plan these things in advance. Experience usually reveals the answers to those kinds of questions. I think the real question you are trying to ask me is who do *you* love and have you loved the right person? Could you have loved someone else more? Take a piece of paper and write down the names of all the people you love. Imagine that they are all dead. How much would you miss each of them? Then list them accordingly. I think that might give you the answer you are looking for."

Kate linked her arm through his and together they walked back to the house. She stretched, looked up at the stars and kissed him goodnight. She checked on Molly before going to bed. She saw that Jack had come home whilst she had been outside in the garden with her father. Kate sighed as she slid into bed next to him. She was careful not to wake him.

Molly was making excellent progress, becoming stronger with each passing day. Having her parents living with them had taken the sting out of the situation between her and Jack and she had returned to sharing his bed. They now rubbed along together, presenting a façade to everyone around them. Her life slowly started to find balance and they got along as well as they always had. Their relationship had always thrived in stressful situations. Plus, Jack was making the time to be at home and occasionally came back early to spend time with Molly. Finally she drifted off to sleep.

She awoke with a start in the early hours of the morning. Her mother stood next to her bed, shaking her gently.

"Come Kate, something is wrong with your father."

Kate jumped out of bed and rushed into her parents' room. Her mother walked slowly behind her as if sleep-walking. Her father was lying in bed, his eyes closed, a slight smile on his lips. She lifted his hand but he didn't stir. She looked at her mother, a question in her eyes, then turned back to her father.

"Daddy? Wake up. Please wake up," she asked gently. But he didn't move. He just seemed to smile at her. She realised that his hand was cool in hers, not warm like it usually felt.

Kate stepped back from the bed aghast. She turned to her mother again.

"He's gone, Kate," her mother whispered. "He's gone. Go and get Jack."

An ambulance came for him an hour later. Kate was in her bedroom. From there, she listened to the soft murmur of voices as Jack took control of the situation. She heard the sound of her father's body being pulled from his bed and placed on a stretcher, then the sound of the engine of the ambulance starting. She watched from the bedroom window as the ambulance drove past, its lights flashing. It turned right out of their driveway and disappeared, taking her father away from her forever.

The next morning, Kate sat on a grassy bank in their garden and tried to remember her childhood with her father. She was flooded with memories of the different countries and houses they had lived in. He had loved his life with the Diplomatic Corps and when he retired his thoughts had turned to returning to England. They had talked about it often but his heart wasn't really in it. Too many years abroad had shown him an entirely different life. It would have been too difficult to adapt to a life he had left as a young man. Her mother longed to go back, but years of following her husband had become a habit. Where he went, she followed.

Kate knew he would leave a big empty space in her life. She already felt it. The only thing that made his death seem real to her was the sound she kept hearing in her head of his body being pulled from the bed and the soft thud of his arm when it had fallen from her grasp. She was too shocked to cry.

She lay back against the grass and stared up at the sky above her. She watched as a falcon circled slowly above her. It was close enough for her to see the brown and cream feathers beneath its wings. It was the only movement in the sky, and the garden was still and breathless around her. She felt the sun, already hot, against her skin. The moment felt timeless and surreal. Kate watched as the bird flew higher until it was just a speck and seemed to disappear. Slowly she stood up, glancing at her watch. Lucy would be here soon. They would have to start the painful process of arranging their father's funeral.

After the funeral her mother made plans to return to England, not wanting to be in Africa anymore. She was taking her husband's ashes with her to scatter them in England, the land of his birth. Kate doubted that he would have attached much importance to that. Lucy and Kate had tried to persuade her to scatter his ashes here in Africa, a place that he had loved. But she was adamant.

"I spent years following him around the world and now, for once in his life, he's coming with me." A ghost of a smile had played around her lips.

Now Kate sat with her mother at the dining room table, Lucy had left early that morning. Molly was in her high chair banging her breakfast bowl enthusiastically with a rubber spoon, oblivious to the sad atmosphere.

"You know that you'll always have a home with us here. Please don't feel that you have to start making big plans for your future now," Kate said as she rubbed her mother's arm gently.

"Kate, I have spent most of my life trailing around after your father. It's time for me to go home. I have loved my time abroad but I've always missed the changing seasons of England. I'll be quite happy there. Your father left me well provided for. Rosemary is very capable of running the house and taking care of Molly; you don't need me here anymore. You must try and make your marriage work. Jack isn't such a bad person, he will settle down in time. Having children is the best cure for that. I'll come back and visit you, I promise."

The house felt unbearably empty without her parents. Every day Molly crawled from room to room. Kate was sure that she was looking for them. After a few weeks, she stopped looking, as if she had accepted that they had gone. But Kate struggled. She found it hard to believe that her father was dead and that he wasn't with her mother in some other country. She felt a strong urge to leave the house and run away from the memories held there.

She held Molly in her arms and walked through the empty rooms wondering what time Jack would come home. How would it be now, living in the big house, just the three of them? Her parents had been the buffer between any arguments about Jack's frequent late nights and weekends away. Now she would have to confront him and see where their marriage was actually heading. She knew that Jack loved the company of women, and he was an outrageous flirt. She remembered the big party at the British Embassy in Lagos to which they had been invited some months after they had arrived there. Jack had disappeared for nearly two hours that night. She had searched the grounds of the house for him, asking if anyone had seen him. But no-one had.

Finally she had found him coming down the elegant stairway which led to the rooms above the ballroom. He had told her that someone had had a bad turn and that he had been asked to help. She had accepted that story at face value until she had overhead a discussion in the Ladies' room a little later.

"I see Rebecca has already laid claim to the handsome new doctor! She didn't waste much time getting him up the stairs on the usual pretext, did she?"

Kate had carried on washing her hands pretending she hadn't heard the conversation. He had had lots of girlfriends when she had met him in Rhodesia and on a couple of occasions, when they were going out together, she hadn't been sure if he had been completely faithful to her. She knew without a doubt that he was not being faithful to her now.

Over dinner one evening Kate mentioned to Jack that a business was up for sale in Tinder Bay, a small sleepy town halfway down the Garden

Route in South Africa. She told him a little about it. His reaction seemed to explode out of him.

"What on earth are you thinking, Kate? A boatyard? Neither of us knows anything about building bloody yachts!"

"We don't need to know anything, Jack. There are forty craftsmen that will do that for us; all we have to do is run the place. It's something completely different. You're bored with medicine, bored with being a doctor, so why not try this for a couple of years? We can build the business up and then sell it."

Jack looked at her as though she was mad. He knew Tinder Bay was a lovely part of the world and it was true, he was bored with his practice in Swaziland. In his mind he began to see himself out on one of the big yachts, and imagined himself at the yacht club. Kate had planted the seed well.

They had driven to Tinder Bay the following month to take a look. The size of the boatyard took her breath away. It was a cavernous place, holding yachts in various stages of construction. The huge ramp leading out from the building led down into the cool waters of the lagoon. She could imagine launching the finished yachts, all white and gleaming and smelling of fresh paint. They had looked at property to buy, finally settling on an unusual house high on the hill with views across the lagoon.

The negotiations for the boat yard were finalized and within weeks it was theirs. Confidently they returned to Swaziland to pack up their home there. Kate had found a new position for Rosemary – the couple who had taken over their house was more than happy to keep her on. Satisfied that everything had worked out well, they looked forward to a new life on the coast.

Kate sat in the back of the car holding Molly. It had been a long drive. "Tinder Bay is up ahead, Kate. We made good time." Jack slowed the car down and glanced at Kate in the driving mirror. She sat up straight and looked around. Tinder Bay lay spread before them.

"Oh, it's lovely, Jack. If we can't be happy here, we won't be happy anywhere!"

She didn't see the frown on his face. He had enjoyed his freedom in Swaziland. Kate had been so preoccupied with the baby that she hadn't noticed his discreet affair. It wasn't as though he didn't love his little daughter, he did; but he resented the time and attention Molly got from her Mother and felt there was very little left over for him. He was going to miss his mistress and her undivided attention when they were together. It had certainly taken away some of the boredom of living in a small town.

Unfortunately for Jack, Kate was well aware her husband was having an affair. His lover had torpedoed her marriage but Kate was determined to hang onto him. They had been through too much together to let it all go. She had thought very carefully about a divorce but had decided to give it another try. Her first move had been to get him away from Swaziland.

Molly needed a father. To go it alone would be too hard and would mean a full-time job for her, which in turn meant she wouldn't be able to spend the time with the baby. Buying the business had been a good idea. It would take Jack far away from his mistress. Now they were here, ready to settle down and make a new life.

Within twelve months the business was in ruins. Jack quickly got bored with spending hours and hours in the boatyard, for it wasn't as glamorous as he imagined it would be. Kate valiantly tried to keep things going but even she had to admit defeat. The men that worked there were uncooperative and surly. Jack's short temper did nothing to foster any good relationships. One by one the men resigned. Customers who had ordered yachts found that production had almost ground to a halt, and threatened to sue for breach of contract.

Cracks once more appeared in the marriage. The strain of Jack's affair before Molly was born, the months afterwards when she had been totally devoted to looking after her, the death of her father and now the failure of the business, had all taken their toll on an already fragile relationship.

Jack came into the kitchen and sat down heavily on the window seat. Kate stopped unpacking her groceries and turned around. She looked at him steadily, her instincts already telling her what he was about to say.

Even so she felt her stomach clench with anxiety. She picked Molly up and held her close, then waited for him to speak.

"Kate, I'm sorry, this isn't working for me. I hate the bloody boatyard and I hate this small-minded town. We need money. We've put everything we have into this disaster of yours. I'm going back to Swaziland – back to the practice. I hate to do this to you, but I suggest you wind the whole thing down and admit defeat."

He leaned across the kitchen table and ran his fingers through her hair. "I'm so sorry, Kate, really I am. For everything."

She listened to the sound of his car as he drove away from the house. The clock ticked loudly and steadily in the room. Not really surprised with this turn of events she wandered through into the bedroom. His clothes, shoes and suitcase were gone. He must have packed everything up when she was out shopping with the baby.

Jack had left her. She started to reason with herself. Of course he would have taken his things if he was going back to Swaziland? But there was something final about the look of the empty cupboards; he had left not a trace of himself. Why hadn't he packed after he told her he was going back?

So sorry, Kate, really I am, he had said. Sorry about what? Sorry the business didn't work out or sorry I'm leaving you, literally, holding the baby? Why hadn't he asked her when she would be following him back? Because, she reasoned, he was going back to his mistress...

Two weeks after Jack had gone, things went from bad to worse. The workmen were paid off, and all production on the yachts stopped.

Straddling Molly on her hip she opened the door from the office which led into the production area. All was quiet. There were no longer the indications of high activity: the whining saws and the smell of sawdust and fresh paint. She wandered amongst the hulks of the half-finished boats and looked down at the sawdust on the floor.

It was all over.

The bank had called her the previous afternoon. They would be taking the house to offset the massive overdraft she and Jack had been unable to service. The liquidators would be arriving at the end of the week to wind things down. David Warner, her lawyer, was flying in that afternoon, from Johannesburg, to help her with the legal side of closing down the business. He would also deal with all the creditors. She was glad he was coming. At least he was a familiar face and a friend.

"So, Kate," he said, sipping his coffee after dinner. "You tell me that Jack has gone back to Swaziland. Where does that leave you? Will you go back and join him there?"

She put her cup down carefully and looked at him. "I'm not really sure, David. I don't want to go back. I've never thought it was a good idea to go back anywhere. I thought I might go south and try Cape Town. There might be more opportunities for me there. I would imagine that Jack will eventually want a divorce. If it should come to that, then I'll give it to him. It's been a bit of an up and down affair, this marriage. My whole focus now must be on making a secure future for Molly. Most of our money and savings have gone down with the boatyard. I still have my inheritance from my father, it's not huge but it will be enough to get me started in Cape Town. I'll have to start making my own money pretty quickly." Kate paused. "Thank you for coming to my rescue, David, I really appreciate all your help, it means so much to me. You do realise that you might have to wait awhile before I can pay your fees though?"

David chuckled softly. "Don't worry about my fees. Let me clean this mess up first, and then we'll work something out. I should be able to wrap things up by Thursday and then I must get back to Johannesburg. I don't want you to worry about any of this, just leave it to me."

The Friday morning after David had left, Kate sat on the jetty at the boatyard, dangling her feet in the sea. Molly sat on her lap. Looking up she saw helicopters in the distance. Here they come, she thought. Here come the vultures. Angry customers, hearing of the liquidation, were determined to rescue their half-finished yachts. In the other direction she saw a line of transportation vehicles waiting patiently in the loading bay.

Kate watched the hulls of yachts being loaded onto flatbed trucks; they rumbled past her on the jetty. Kate didn't move. Soon afterwards there was only the sound of the rotor blades retreating as they all left.

She listened to the silence, watching her toes through the clear water of the lagoon. What a disaster the whole thing had been. Now everything was gone. The house, the business, and Jack. Molly squirmed in her lap, restless after watching all the activity around them. She still had Molly, Kate thought, and her cat. They would move to Cape Town and start something new.

Swinging her legs back up on the jetty and carefully standing up with Molly, she locked the big doors of the yard for the last time.

"Come on, Molly, let's go home whilst we've still got one. It's all over here."

Molly gurgled and pointed over Kate's shoulder, laughing. Kate marvelled at how she could be so happy without any awareness of what was going on around her. Looking up Kate saw a falcon perched on the highest apex of the roof of the warehouse behind them. With a jolt of surprise she tightened her grip on Molly. Shading her eyes from the sun, she watched the bird lift off from the roof and fly away over the lagoon. A familiar feeling came to her. She frowned, turned, and walked away. She had still not made the list that her father had suggested. I'll do it tonight, she promised herself, when Molly is asleep.

She sat looking at the blank piece of paper. Molly lay peacefully next to her, filling the space that Jack had left behind. What had her father said to her? *List all the people you have loved, and then imagine they are all dead. Who would you miss the most?*

She smiled. The first name would be easy: Molly. She ran her finger softly down her daughter's cheek, feeling the warmth and silkiness of it. After Molly was her immediate family: her parents and her sister, Lucy.

She hesitated. Where was Jack going to be in the scheme of things? She left him out for the moment. She tapped the pen against her teeth and slowly wrote a name down.

Tom.

She looked at his name and glanced at the bracelet on her wrist. Guiltily she squeezed the piece of paper into a ball and tossed it into the wastepaper basket. Turning off the light, she snuggled down into the bed. Holding her daughter closely she tried, unsuccessfully, to block out the disturbing memories of Tom Fletcher and his grey eyes steadily watching her across the table.

The next morning Molly lay contentedly next to her mother in the big bed. "Well, darling, we're on our own now, all packed and ready to go, just you, me and dear old Mr Cat. Tomorrow I hand over the house and then we're off to Cape Town. This place was a disaster all round." Molly smiled, too young to understand what was happening. Happily, she chewed on a piece of her mother's long hair.

The next day they set off on the six-hour drive to Cape Town. As they came over Sir Lowry's Pass, Kate could see the city of Cape Town in the distance and the curve of False Bay below. Table Mountain loomed in the background with white clouds tumbling over the top and down the sides. She stopped the car in a layby, unbuckled Molly from her seat, and they got out to look at the view. It was spectacular. The huge expanse of sea glittered in the afternoon sun. Hundreds of houses shimmered in the heat. A large white sandy bay curved in a half-moon crescent. Kate sighed, rubbing her chin against Molly's silky head.

"We can make something out of this, darling. There's a whole big new world waiting for us down there. Come on, let's go and get it!"

They got back in the car and began the steep descent down the mountain pass towards the City of Cape Town.

Chapter Nine

THEY STAYED IN A SMALL HOTEL until Kate found a house to rent in the leafy suburb of Constantia, in the southern suburbs of the city. When their furniture arrived from Tinder Bay, she set about making a comfortable home for them both.

I *can* make a life for us, Kate thought. All the opportunities are here. Within a month she decided to start her own company and get in on the ground level of the fledgling tourism industry. She did her research and realized there was a gap in the market place for what she wanted to do. She set up her business in the spare room of the old house. She wanted to produce glossy books featuring the best game lodges throughout the country. The second stage would be to include East Africa in another series of books.

Despite having lived much of her life seeing very little of Jack, life was lonely without him. When she was settled, she spoke with him briefly. He told her that he was staying in Swaziland, for the time being, and had no plans to join them in Cape Town. She didn't ask where he was living or with whom.

Two months later he called her. "There's no easy way to say this, Kate. I'd like a divorce. I've met someone..." Kate bit her lip anxiously. She had known this was coming but she hadn't anticipated it being this soon.

"Is it someone I know? Actually, don't answer that. It doesn't matter," she paused for a moment. "All right Jack, if that's what you really want, if she will make you happy, then go ahead. I'll ask David Warner to handle my side. Let's just get it over with. Fortunately for you, you don't need to give me grounds for a divorce, it's quite simple really; just a breakdown of the marriage is all that is required legally."

"There's something else, Kate. She's Canadian. There are some great opportunities over there for doctors. I've been offered some very attractive jobs." It was his turn to pause. "I've accepted one in Toronto. I'll always look after Molly, you know that. Maybe when she's older she can come and spend some time there with us. Let's see how it all goes. I'm sure you'll meet someone else, and I really want that for you. You were never easy to live with, but life certainly wasn't dull with you around." He smiled ruefully into the phone; there were many things he would miss about her.

After hanging up she sat back. Their marriage had been on a rocky path since Lagos. Kate had known the relationship was in trouble, and had known it would reach an end at some point. She felt a little sad, but she wasn't unhappy. In fact, she felt surprised. Not that it was officially over but that their relationship had lasted as long as it had. She also felt disappointed that he was so disinterested in being a part of Molly's life. He would never be her father now. It would have been nice if Molly could have seen him now and again, but his proposed new life would not allow for that. It would probably be years before he saw his daughter again. Kate certainly wasn't going to let her go to Canada until she was old enough to travel alone. For now the most important thing to Kate was that Molly was happy. There were good schools in Cape Town, which would give Molly the kind of education Kate wanted her to have and their lifestyle was predominantly outdoors and safe; it was a wonderful environment, and a healthy one, to bring up a young child. Molly's relationship with her father was something they would have to navigate in the future.

Thoughtfully she picked up the telephone and called David. "Jack wants a divorce, David, and it looks as though he will be going to live in Canada somewhere. He's anxious to get things wrapped up before he leaves at the end of the year. I won't be contesting it, so it's all quite simple really."

The divorce came through six months later. The evening she received the papers Kate sat outside in the garden and tried to work out how she felt now that the divorce was final. She would miss the financial security of the marriage, but had to admit to herself that being single was less stressful. When Jack had had his affairs, she had felt nothing but disappointment in him. She wondered what she had lacked that had made him stray as much as he had. She wasn't sure exactly when it had started but she wondered now whether it had ever stopped. All she knew for sure was that he had become less discreet when they moved to Swaziland. They had got along well and had had a similar desire for adventure. Thinking back, she realised a turning point had been when she was pregnant with Molly. It was as though a switch had been flicked. Jack just lost interest. She tried to think if that was it, or whether it was something in her and that perhaps she had pulled back from him.

She went to pour herself a glass of lemonade. Her feet felt cool on the stone floor of their house. She took the glass outside and sat beneath the vines outside the back door. The sun had set and the sky was a burnished orange. She took a sip from her glass and ran her fingers over the bracelet on her wrist. She was free now, but was Tom?

She hadn't expected to see Jack again but before he and his new wife left for Canada, he came alone to say goodbye to them. They had lunch together in the garden. Kate watched him closely, wondering how his life would turn out now. She tried to figure out whether he looked happier. Tired, she thought. He looks tired. Maybe Africa had brought out the worst in him; too much freedom had made him take risks that he wouldn't normally have taken.

Molly studied her father with big round eyes. He was almost a stranger to her now. She hid behind Kate's skirt when he went to kiss her goodbye. For the last time he held Kate in his arms, and buried his face in her hair.

"Be happy, Kate. Take care of our little girl. Don't let her forget me, will you? I hope you'll be happy." She looked up surprised to see the tears in his eyes, and in turn, felt her own eyes filling.

"Goodbye, Jack."

She opened the door for him to leave, and then firmly closed it behind him. She knew that she would probably never see him again. Needing something to hold onto she lifted her daughter into her arms and held her tightly, until Molly squealed in protest.

She came to the decision that she would need to have help with Molly. Initially, there would be a fair amount of travel, visiting the game lodges she wanted in her book. That would mean being away from home. She placed an advert in the local paper, specifying her requirements. For a week she interviewed candidates; all unsuitable.

She ran the advert for a second week and on the first afternoon she began running a second series of interviews. Kate was running late. When her first applicant turned up, she had to ask her to give her fifteen minutes to finish a document she was working on. She showed her into the sitting room to wait. When she was finished, she went through and found Molly sitting on the woman's lap, being read a story. It was a positive start. Hannah Wood had been an English teacher and had recently retired. She had taught at one of the best schools in the country and her references were impeccable. She had brought up two daughters of her own and when they left, to go to university in Scotland, she found her life empty and quiet. Kate hired her on the spot and Hannah was given her own small cottage in the grounds.

Kate's mother had passed away a year after her husband. She hadn't adapted to life in England and had found it difficult living on her own. She had died in her sleep and all alone. Unintentionally, Hannah became a mother figure to both of them. She ran the house with superb efficiency, shopping and cooking for them, leaving Kate with the time she needed to concentrate on her burgeoning business.

Before long Kate had a good circle of friends and neighbours. She travelled around the country gathering content and photographs for her book. She tried not to be away for longer than four days at a time. The schedule was exhausting, with many flights backwards and forwards over the vast country and long hours on the road driving to remote lodges. Sometimes, Hannah would come into the house in the morning and find Kate slumped over her desk, or curled up on the sofa, fast asleep.

The game lodge owners liked the idea of her book, with her fresh approach and vision. South Africa was a difficult place to attract tourists given its history, but Kate knew that one day the tourists would come in their droves, once the country had resolved its political problems. Even now there was a steady stream of visitors to the country.

Her proposed book was generating considerable interest within the travel industry. She moved her company from the house and took a suite of offices in town. Her business was starting to grow and she realised that she needed an assistant to run the office if she was going to be away. Emily had been highly recommended to her and they hit it off immediately. The tall attractive French woman was highly efficient and had immediately starting to implement systems which would soon have the business running smoothly, and efficiently.

Christmas came and went and the months flew past. The launch of the book was a huge success and Kate travelled all over the country promoting it. Sales were higher than she could have imagined and the money started to roll in. She bought a dark blue Mercedes, which she had coveted for months. Every weekend she and Molly spent hours looking at houses for sale, eventually finding the perfect place: big, bright and beautiful with views across the ocean. It took her breath away and was exactly what she wanted. "Do you like this house Molly? Shall we buy it?"

"I love it Mommy, look it has a baby pool!"

Kate hugged her, laughing. "It's an outside Jacuzzi darling, but you can still swim in it. I love this place and just look at the view! We did it Molly, we made it on our own!"

Chapter Ten

KATE WALKED ALONG the beach, unaware of everything around her, including the man who was watching from the bar of the hotel. It was impossible to walk on the hot burning sand and the water of the sea was achingly icy cold. She went for the happy medium, which was to walk on the cool wet sand at the water's edge. A large straw hat protected her face from the heat of the midday sun. She had an hour before she had to collect Molly from playschool and she had taken the opportunity to take a walk on the beach, giving herself a much needed break. Reaching the end of the bay, she turned and looked up at the immaculately white hotel. It looked cool and inviting and she was thirsty. She hopped her way over the scorching sand and was grateful for the cool of the hotel lawn. She hoped no-one would notice as she washed the sand from her feet in the water from a sprinkler.

Tom Fletcher sat in the hotel bar, nursing a cold beer; he looked out over the palm trees and watched the people on the beach. There were not many out, as it was too hot for most people. Camps Bay looked beautiful, as always. It was an arced curve of white sand, surrounded by palm trees. The blue-black mountains of the Twelve Apostles made a dramatic backdrop and the heat shimmered off their façade.

He knew he had to call Sarah in London. He hesitated. They had had another furious row before he left for Cape Town. Living together again had been more difficult than he had ever imagined. In his experience, most Americans loved London; the history and the magnificent buildings. Sarah could find nothing right with the city. She hated the weather, hated the crowds and sometimes, he thought she hated him too. The endless complaining and fights were taking their toll on him. He had decided on the way back to the hotel that he would add an extra week to his business trip, just to put off going home.

Tom's attention was drawn to a woman in a straw hat walking on the beach. Suddenly she turned and started to head in the direction of the hotel. He watched, amused, as she nimbly negotiated the burning sand, crossed the road and surreptitiously washed her feet in the water from the sprinkler system.

He had thought of Kate often over the past four years. He wondered where she was. Her child would be nearly five now. Would she still be with Jack? Or had she divorced him by now? Perhaps she had married again and was living in another country, somewhere in Europe perhaps? Her French was fluent, he knew, and she had talked about living there. "But only if I ever get tired of Africa," she had said, grinning at him across the dinner table in London.

Tom sighed heavily and turned back to his drink, feeling unaccountably depressed and lonely. He finished his beer and walked towards the lift. It was time to call Sarah.

The phone call had not been a success. Sarah had, predictably, been furious that he would not be returning to London for another week. He had heard her out, holding the phone away from his ear and then, with a curt goodbye, he had hung up.

He looked around his room, then did what he always did after a fight with Sarah – he buried himself in his work. He unzipped his laptop and, pushing aside the books on the table, he waited to get started on his report. Idly, he picked up one of the books and flicked through it. Impressed, he turned to the dustcover to see who had produced it.

There she was. Her photograph. Kate Hope.

The book had been written by Kate and had been printed and published in Cape Town. Her biography said that that was where she lived. He checked the publication date. It was that year. He felt a punch of excitement. The hotel he was staying in was featured in the book; they must have her contact details.

Quickly he picked up the phone again and asked to speak to the manager.

"She often pops in to the hotel," the manager told him. "She likes to walk on the beach here." A fact that Tom dearly wished he had remembered when she finally went missing in East Africa. "She was here a couple of hours ago actually, you just missed her. What a wonderful woman, we love what she's done for us in the book." He gave Tom the number of her office.

Now he paced the floor of his hotel room. He had to speak to her; he wanted to see her again, despite all his promises to himself that he wouldn't.

He dialled the number the manager had given him.

Emily picked up the call and asked him to hold on a few moments. She went through to Kate's office. "There's an American on the line, Tom Fletcher, he says it's a private call. Will you take it?"

Kate looked up surprised, then smiled with pleasure. "Yes, absolutely, put him through Emily." Discreetly Emily closed Kate's door and put the call through.

"Tom!" He smiled down the phone; he could tell she was pleased to hear from him.

"I'm here in Cape Town on business. I saw your book in my room here at the hotel. I have to see you, Kate, unless that rogue of a husband of yours is still around, but even if he is I still want to see you."

She laughed happily. "No, we're divorced now. I would love to see you, Tom; how long will you be in town for?"

"A week. God, it's so good to hear your voice again. I can't tell you how much I have missed it, and missed you. When can we meet?"

"I have a business dinner this evening, but we could meet for a quick drink before that?" She gave him directions to her favourite bar at the Waterfront, arranging to meet him there at six. "I missed you too, Tom..."she said quietly. "See you later."

He watched her walking towards him, her hair glinting in the late afternoon sun. He stood up immediately and went towards her, crushing her in his arms and holding her tightly. "Kate, Kate," he murmured into her hair. He pulled back and held her at arms- length. "Now I know what has been missing in my life all these years – you!"

She laughed up at him, kissing him lightly on the mouth; then, taking his hand, she led him to a quiet table in the corner. They sat and looked at each other unaware of the waiter hovering, ready to take their order. The waiter cleared his throat and Kate dragged her eyes away from

Tom's. "A glass of wine for me please. Tom?" He nodded, not taking his eyes of her. "Make that two then, thank you."

He took both her hands in his feeling happier than he had for years. He was still in love with her, of that he had no doubt.

"So, you're divorced. I'm going straight for the jugular here – is there anyone else in your life? Please say no?"

"There is someone in my life, Tom, someone I love more than life itself." She watched the happiness and hope fade from his face, and went on hurriedly. "Her name is Molly and she's my daughter."

He grinned at her. "Sounds like I may have some tough competition then. A girl, and I bet she looks just like you."

The waiter appeared with their drinks. Impatiently Tom waited for him to leave. "I want to hear all about everything, Kate. I know we only have an hour right now, but tomorrow is another day and I want to spend all of it with you, and the rest of the week. That secretary sounds super-efficient, I'm sure she could run the show perfectly well without you there. I'm not going to let you escape this time, I can promise you that."

"Still making demands, just like in London…" she squeezed his hand delighted to see him again, "but this time Tom I'm free, no husband to hold me back. Where shall we meet? Where are you staying?"

"At The Bay."

She interrupted him. "I was there early this afternoon walking on the beach! I stopped at the hotel for a drink. Why don't we meet there then? I'll pick you up around two, give you a quick guided tour of this wonderful city, and then we can go back to the hotel and take it from there."

"I'll count the hours Kate, and I'm pleased that you're wearing the bracelet I gave you."

Kate looked down at her wrist. "I'll never take it off, Tom, never, and I'll never forget you sitting there holding my hand and the despair when you said goodbye. I really didn't think I would ever see you again and here you are – it's wonderful!"

On the dot of two Kate pulled up outside the hotel, Tom was waiting patiently. He whistled with appreciation when he saw the car. "Nice ride, Kate. That book of yours must be selling well." He levered his tall frame into the passenger seat and buckled up. He glanced behind him. "Where's Molly then?"

Kate chuckled. "I wanted you all to myself today. Hannah, our nanny, has Molly for the rest of the day."

He looked at her and took her hand. She pulled it away quickly as she negotiated the way out of the hotel drive, then took his hand in hers.

"It's so good to have you with me again, Tom. The last time we met, in Swaziland, everything was so difficult. My marriage to Jack was pretty much over, although I did stay with him for two more difficult years, then he went off to Canada with his new wife."

For the next two hours they drove around Cape Town and Kate pointed out places of interest. "I love walking on the beach so here is my favourite one in the Cape. Noordhoek."

He eased himself out of the car and stretched. "Come on then, let's kick off our shoes and take a hike. It looks terrific down there."

They walked along the beach holding hands and catching up on the past four years.

"So, you're still living with Sarah then. I guess you didn't divorce in the end?"

He stopped walking and pulled her towards him. She tasted the salt on his lips as he kissed her gently, then he ran his fingers through her hair and held her.

"I would have divorced her after I met you in London, if you had been free, which, of course, you weren't. I fell in love with you Kate. Sarah and I have tried to get the marriage back together but it hasn't been easy. She has a lot of problems and I feel responsible for some of them. But she is difficult to live with. I still travel a lot and that helps the situation. I have left her a couple of times, but then she threatens to kill herself if I don't come back – that's a heavy gun to hold to my head. Come sit down here a minute."

She sat down frowning at his problems with Sarah. He sat behind her, encircling her with his arms, his chin resting on her head, as they looked out at the surf crashing onto the sand.

"I know what I want now Kate, and I will pay whatever price there is to pay. I want you. I want you in my life. I want to be happy and I know I can make you happy. Me living in London and you living here won't make it easy, but in time we can work something out. I can't think of any reason why I can't run my business from here."

Kate turned in his arms and looked up at him. He traced her face with his fingers, his gentle eyes full of love for her.

"Let's go back to the hotel and have a glass of ice cold wine. It will take over an hour to get back, what with all the rush hour traffic. The drive will give me time to work out what I'm going to do with you! Come on Tom, the day is too beautiful for such serious talk."

He brushed the sand off her legs and his trousers and took her hand, kissing her sandy fingers. "Ah, but I am serious, more serious than I have ever been in my life. I'm not letting you go this time Kate."

The sun sizzled and hissed its way into the sea; they watched the fiery sky as they sipped their wine. A cool breeze lifted the heat from their bodies as they sat watching the end of a perfect day.

"Will you stay with me tonight, Kate? We've already wasted so much time. I want to lie with you in my arms and make love to you, and then I'll probably want to marry you, if you'll have me."

She smiled at him happily. He was a good man, decent and compassionate; it wouldn't be difficult to fall head over heels in love with him and stay with him. She sighed. "I should go now, Tom, it's been an emotional day, a wonderful day. I'll be counting the hours until we can be together again. I can't disappear from Molly's life for two days. I'll organise things with Hannah and then see you around five tomorrow, then we can have two whole days and nights together."

He watched her drive away feeling ridiculously happy. He would take his chances with Sarah's threats of suicide because nothing was going to stop him having Kate in his life now – nothing.

He turned back to the hotel and made his way to his room. Whistling through his teeth he opened the door to his suite. Dropping his clothes on the floor he headed for the shower.

Wrapping a towel around his waist he wandered through to the sitting room and stopped dead in his tracks. "Sarah!" he said incredulously. "What on earth are you doing here?"

"I know you're not pleased to see me, you never are. But I have something to tell you. Come and sit down."

Puzzled, he sat down. Surely she would not come all this way to ask for a divorce? But maybe she had met someone else. He leaned forward. "Tell me then."

To his horror she burst into tears. He reached for the box of tissues on the side table and passed it to her. "Come on, Sarah, things can't be that bad surely?"

"I was going to tell you on the phone, but when you said you were staying on here for another week I just lost it. I was so angry with you and angry with the world as well. There is no easy way to tell you this, but I thought it should be done face to face, and I can't wait a whole week and live with the terror of it. I've got cancer, Tom. It doesn't matter what type or where it is, but I've got it. I have to start the treatment in two weeks' time and I'm terrified, absolutely terrified. Promise me that you will stay with me, don't leave me to grapple with this on my own?"

Sarah burst into tears again. Tom went and sat beside her. He put his arms around her, his own thoughts reeling. "Will you take me on safari again, Tom? Can we go tomorrow? It's not much to ask, is it?"

He watched her as she slept. She certainly didn't look good, that was true. He was still reeling from the shock of seeing her here and trying to grapple with her bad news. How could he leave her to fight this battle on her own?

With a heavy heart he phoned down to reception and asked them to book a four-day safari, and two seats on the morning flight to Johannesburg, then two more on the short flight to the game reserve.

He sat in the dark with his head in his hands. Yes, Sarah had very likely been given a death sentence, but so had he.

Kate pulled up outside the hotel just after five the following afternoon. Quickly she ran a brush through her hair, checked her face in the car mirror then climbed out of the car. She would leave her overnight bag in the boot for the time being.

She waited at reception whilst a group of six people were checked in. Finally she had the attention of the receptionist. She smiled brightly and asked for Mr Tom Fletcher. She rolled his name around on her tongue whilst the receptionist checked the computer; it had a good solid ring to it.

The receptionist looked up puzzled. "I'm sorry, but Mr and Mrs Fletcher checked out this morning. They have gone on safari, a last minute change of plan I think."

Kate drove slowly home, her mind working furiously. So he had been here with his wife all the time then. What on earth had he been thinking when he said he wanted to spend the night with her? What was he going to do with his wife – pack her off somewhere? And now, without even a goodbye or a telephone call, he had flown off on safari.

Chapter Eleven

Molly

KATE, MY MOTHER, wasn't like my friends' mothers. They were all very nice, very comfortable, reassuring in their constancy. Kate was different. I was never sure what she would do next. All I did know was that whatever it was, it would be fun and exciting. She had a lot of energy. If she had a good idea, everyone around her would be drawn into it, catching her enthusiasm. It was contagious. Looking back now, forty years later, I am surprised at how much I remember as a child of five.

Whatever she did, she always made sure I was included. When her first book came out, I was four years old. We sat together in the garden. I was on her lap. We flipped through the pages of her book. She tried to tell me funny stories about the animals in the pictures and pointed out things that she thought would interest me. I liked the pictures the most.

Sometimes, if it was school holidays and I wasn't staying with my Aunt Lucy, Kate would take me on safari with her. During the game drives, we would sit right at the back of the vehicle to make sure we had the best view. Kate – I started to call her that when I was twelve years old and it used to amuse her no end – would put her arm around me and point out all the animals and birds. She often spotted them before the ranger or tracker. I guess that was because she spent so much time out in the bush.

I don't remember my father very well. He went to live in Canada when I was very small. Every year though, on my birthday, he would send me a card. He had two more children and I thought that they must

89

have taken up his time over the years because the card sending became sporadic and finally stopped altogether. Then he was killed in a skiing accident.

Kate was always busy doing something and she was often away. However, at the end of each day when she was home, she would pack all her files away so that we could spend time together before I went to bed. She would cook dinner and ask me about school and my friends. If she found out I was working on a project or presentation for school, she would pull out the scissors and glue and a stack of magazines and travel brochures and we would cut and paste for hours on end. When she was at home the best part of my day was when she would sit on my bed, put her arms around me, and read me a story.

I don't remember her going out much when she wasn't travelling, unless it was a cocktail party or something important. On those nights, Hannah, my nanny, would come up from her cottage and look after me, or I would go to stay with her.

Even though she had such a busy life, Kate always managed to get to school for concerts, or parents' evenings. Most times she was a bit late, but she always came.

I loved Adam. He was funny and generous and always happy. He arrived in our lives like a thunderbolt. He made her as happy as he was. Our lives shifted slightly and it wasn't just because I went to boarding school. Instead of just the two of us, we became three. But he was good about it. Sometimes, I would want my mother to myself and Adam would somehow know. He would disappear for hours on end and he had his own apartment in the city. He never stayed with Kate when I was home from school, although I'm pretty sure he stayed in our house during the week, when I was away boarding at the school. They were together until I grew up, so he was very much part of my life.

They travelled often. Kate would send me wonderful postcards. I have them here in front of me. She must have chosen every single one of them with care. The backs of them are crammed with descriptions and anecdotes. The weeks passed quickly until there she was again, laughing and waving to me from the school car park, both of us crying as I tumbled into her arms.

Thinking back now, Adam seemed almost too good to be true. I never heard them argue or raise their voices at one another. They looked so right together, but deep down inside I always felt, perhaps with some sort of premonition, that something would go wrong to spoil everything. When that did finally happen I lost my mother. Both our lives changed forever. When I finally read that letter, the one her lawyer told me was waiting for me there on the island of Zanzibar, and was to be read in the event of her death, I started to understand some of the things that had always puzzled me. I finally had the answer to why my mother and her sister appeared to have drifted so far apart.

But I will never understand how she and Lucy got away with what they did.

I still have that letter. It would mean absolutely nothing to anyone now. Most of the people who were involved have gone. It's for another reason that I hold onto it, because it carries her voice to me. It's a voice that I miss every single day. There was another letter, Tom found it. All that remained of it was a tight ball of paper, like a tissue you find in a pocket after a wash. Over time, I managed to piece almost everything together and I now understand why Kate did what she did.

I still have questions though and for these I don't think I'll ever have answers. Why did I have to meet Tom under such cruel circumstances? Why did Kate not stay with him? Her life would have been less tragic had she chosen that path. Why did they cross paths over the years but never see each other? How did such a passion between two people – Kate and Adam – go so badly wrong? And perhaps, above anything else, how did we all get it so very wrong with Adam?

But that is Kate's story. Just as he had destroyed her, so she destroyed everything he had ever given to her. Letters, cards and notes. Words of love that she couldn't bear to read again. Amongst her things I found the only journal that she had ever kept that connected her to him, her own recollections of how she first met Adam and the catastrophic impact he had on her when it was all over. It must have been written thirteen years after she had first met him, and I would have been eighteen years old. I would imagine that after she had written it she probably never read it again, but she did keep it.

I hadn't planned another trip to New York City, but when the news came through I knew that I had to go to her. She wrote about Adam around that time and I think it was because she couldn't accept what had happened to him. I remember watching her write, that hot airless night and, hours later, when she had finished, she put her face in her hands and cried as though her heart might break.

This is what she wrote:

New York City – 2000

I had heard about him, of course, but had yet to meet him. By all accounts he was attractive, articulate, amusing and one of the best safari operators in the business. He was extremely popular and well-liked by everyone – especially women. I had met many attractive men in my life, but there was more to him, something deeper. I saw past the blue eyes, the blond hair and the laugh. I was drawn to him immediately like a moth to a candle.

I had been checking a recently opened boutique hotel for inclusion in my book. Having done so, I decided to have a glass of wine, before heading home. I sat beneath the shade of a tree in the rose filled garden, sipping my drink. The hotel was nestled at the foot of Table Mountain and it made for quite a view. I sensed, rather than saw, him approach. Flopping down in a chair opposite mine, he pulled out a packet of cigarettes, lit one, and blew a perfect circle of smoke up into the air. He looked at me and smiled slowly. He smoked as I watched him. Neither of us said a word. The garden now seemed still and silent almost as though even the birds were holding their breath.

Tall and slim, he had elegance in his frame and his gestures. From where we sat, the sun glinted through his hair, which was the colour of butterscotch. His eyes were very blue. Looking up, I could see their similarity to the skies that hovered over us. I studied a face that instantly communicated that I was sitting opposite someone who lived for the moment and didn't take life too seriously.

The word 'beautiful' makes me think of him. If a man can be beautiful then he certainly was. In time, he made me feel beautiful too. What greater gift could he have given to me? When he leant forward, to stub out his cigarette, his white shirt parted and I glimpsed a strong tanned body. I saw a slim silver chain with a small cross on it. My heartbeat seemed to speed up. I swallowed hard and held out my hand to introduce myself.

"I'm Kate." I said.

"Yes, I know," he said, smiling again, "and I'm more than delighted to meet you underneath this tree."

He had a well-modulated English accent and, as he talked, his eyes travelled over my face as though he wanted to remember this defining moment. I found out later that he'd been born in England but educated in Europe where he had learned to speak Italian, French, German and Spanish. In the years that were to come, I never ceased to be impressed with his ability to switch from one language to another. I became impressed with everything that he did. He was the most extraordinary man I had ever met or would meet again.

On that beautiful evening in Cape Town we sat and talked about the safari business. He knew far more about it than I did and I listened attentively, or tried to. He didn't take his eyes off me for a minute and I could feel my carefully constructed world slowly unravelling like a ball of wool. The powerful attraction between us was obvious, and I knew without any doubt that my life had taken an irretrievable turn.

When I reluctantly stood up to take my leave, Adam stood up too. He came around to my side of the table and gently ran his finger down my cheek.

"Beautiful," he said. "So very beautiful. I think I could fall in love with you, Kate Hope. It would be quite easy."

The touch of his finger made my stomach lurch. I wanted to run my fingers through his hair, feel the texture of it, and taste his lips. I inhaled the faint scent of him and deep inside of me I felt something shift, something old and ancient and as pure and enduring as the love and passion I would have for this man.

I drove back to the city hearing his voice, hearing him laugh. I was already lost to myself without even realizing it.

Adam called the next day. He invited me for lunch. Although the sound of his voice enticed me more than I wished it would, I knew that I had to be absolutely sure that this is what I wanted – instinct was already telling me that it would be a heady ride. I made some excuse not to see him. He called every day, and every day I had a reason why I couldn't meet him.

As I came to learn in time, Adam never took no for an answer. A few weeks later, on a Friday, as I was leaving my office, I found him waiting at the bottom of the stairs. He watched me descend and when I reached him, he held out his hand for mine. Pulling me towards him he said quietly:

"I've been waiting years, maybe all my life for you, Kate. Why are you avoiding me?"

He was irresistible. I tried to fight my feelings for him on a daily basis. I think it amused him to watch me try, knowing with certainty that I would fail.

We had lunch, then dinner. He didn't push me. He waited for me to feel comfortable, to trust him. We talked about everything and yet there never seemed to be enough time. He was intoxicating company and I felt as if I had known him my entire life. I couldn't get him out of my head for longer than a few seconds; he consumed my every thought.

A messenger arrived after lunch one Monday and delivered an envelope. Opening it I found a first class ticket to London, leaving on Saturday night. Smiling at his impudence, but very much liking his style, I decided to go. Thus began my life with Adam.

The gods must have been laughing but I didn't hear them, my head was full of Adam.

He was waiting for me in the lounge at the airport, smiling his slow smile. He knew I would come, of course.

He had booked a suite at the Mandarin Hotel in Knightsbridge. He had thought of everything and, in time, I would become accustomed to that. He was born to travel and his knowledge of the world was encyclopaedic. He shuffled and exchanged tickets as if he were playing a game of cards. He knew all the terminology and the configuration of every aircraft. He always made sure we got the best seats. All I ever had to do was grab my handbag and follow him. On long flights, he taught me to do crosswords and word games, until I was as good at it as he was. He had endless energy, in and out of bed, and he never ran out of things to say. With him as the pivot in my world, it became the most beautiful place to be in and every day felt pure and new and full of endless possibilities.

Love made everything bigger, brighter somehow; people seemed nicer, views more perfect, food and wine more piquant. The world was a wonderful place, as long as Adam was in it with me. He was the most stimulating man I had ever met and his zest for life was contagious. He made me wild, reckless and brave; with him I could, and would, do anything

Those first days with Adam in London are imprinted on my memory. He made everything special, from a cup of coffee in a humble café, to dinner at The Ivy. We spent more time in the bedroom than we did anywhere else, always hungry for each other. I would lie still watching him, my eyes travelling over his face and naked body. I would touch his hair and face and wonder how I could be so very happy, so lucky, to have him in my life. It was in London where he found a matching silver cross, which he bought and placed around my neck. I never took it off and wore it for years, until I couldn't bear it any longer.

All my memories of Adam are crystal clear and if I close my eyes, I feel as though I could touch him. Even now I dream about him... and my dreams are so vivid that when I awake and turn over, I still expect to find him there. But of course that is impossible now.

After London we were inseparable. Both of our businesses started to grow. The following year we decided to take bigger premises and house both companies under one roof. That way, we could be together all day as well. We chose the largest office and shared it. I would often look up and find him watching me, smiling happily.

I knew he loved me. He told me so, many times a day. If I was away from him for too long, he would come to look for me. He liked to surprise me. One wet and windy Friday afternoon, he looked up from his desk and stared out of the window. Turning to look at me, he said, "The thought of sitting in Cape Town for the weekend has no appeal whatsoever. How would you like to go to Paris for a few days?"

We left that evening. He was unpredictable and exciting and fiercely protective of me. Despite all the promises to myself not to fall in love with him, I did. I fell hard and I fell fast. Working in the same office meant that we soon learned each other's talents and it wasn't long before we merged our separate businesses. It turned out to be a winning mix. Security and love made me brave and creative. Before long we became well known for our unusual safaris and journeys. This meant more travel for us and we didn't hesitate to go. Leaving the shackles of the office behind we jetted off into the endless sky, happy to be together in a world of our own making.

Adam had been married, but that too had ended in divorce and he was in no hurry to marry again. I didn't trust marriage after Jack. It seemed to me that marriage made a relationship dull and predictable, exhausting and depleting it of fire and passion. I didn't want to spoil one second of my time with Adam. I had the very best of him and he had the very best of me. It was more than enough.

For ten unforgettable years it was everything.

The years passed swiftly but I was unaware of time. We worked hard and we played hard, but we were spectacularly successful. Together we travelled the world gathering in the business.

On business trips years afterwards, when it was all over, wherever I was in the world, Hong Kong or New York, Kenya or Canada, I would search the crowds on busy streets, looking for him, or someone who looked like him. I didn't find either. By that time, he had gone far away and left a cavernous hole in my life. It was one which I tried to fill with all manner of things: I tried other men, moving to New York City, long holidays in far off places and new business ventures. None of them came close. Those long sparkling days of love were replaced with endless others, filled with shadows and memories, and I felt a weariness inside of me, a weariness that often threatened to overwhelm me. The sound of his voice echoing through my thoughts, his whispered words of love, would bring me to my knees with grief.

No matter how far away I went, Adam was always with me, like a demented spirit who wouldn't let go. I tried everything I could but was never able to find that joy in my heart that he had evoked, when the world was such a beautiful place to live in and he was completely and utterly mine.

Chapter Twelve

"**WELL, THAT'S ANOTHER SHOW** wrapped up," Adam said, closing the last box of brochures, sweat glistening on his chest. "How the hell did you manage to play hockey in a climate like this, Kate?"

Kate clung onto his hand as they crossed a busy road in Singapore a few minutes later. He pulled up on a traffic island and whilst waiting for a gap in the traffic, he pulled her towards him. "Do you know I would love to see where you went to school? Shall we take a few days to go have a look?"

She kissed him, oblivious to the traffic hurtling past them. She wanted to show him where she had grown up, wanted to show him her old school up in the cool green highlands of Malaysia. "Can we?" Kate asked. "Is there time?"

"We can do whatever we want to do, Kate. Luca is capable of running the office with Emily, and with Molly in boarding school, no-one will even miss us. We can call Molly later and tell her you're going back to your old school. She'll love that."

Kate thought quickly. It would be a pity to miss the opportunity of seeing where she had lived as a child. Adam was right. Molly was a weekly boarder now. She had friends she could stay with over the weekend or if she wanted to go home, Hannah was there. Luca could easily look after the office for them for a couple more days. Seeing that she had consented, he grabbed her hand and navigated them through the traffic.

"We'll leave in the morning," he said, deftly avoiding a trishaw. "It's only a short flight to Malaysia from Singapore." She could tell that he was looking forward to the trip.

The heavy doors of the plane swung open. As they stepped out, almost immediately, Kate could smell a familiar sweet creamy scent of Frangipani flowers and warm spices that transcended thirty years. The heat was tremendous despite being eleven at night. The next morning, they hired a car and driver and began the long and winding journey to the Cameron Highlands. Kate didn't remember the road snaking as much as it did. After several hours, they still hadn't passed anywhere that looked familiar to her. They stopped several times to ask passing locals if they knew of the old colonial school but they were met with blank faces. No-one remembered it.

She knew that the locals may have chosen to forget the British Army's posting in this part of the world but she was surprised that no-one recalled the school. Thousands of children had lived and been educated there and she was sure that the local population would recall the number of British brats running around their jungle.

She was about to give up hope when the car banked sharply on a turn in the road. Kate glimpsed a green rounded corrugated tin roof. Instantly, she recognised it as the old school church. Yelling to the driver to stop, she jumped out of the car and ran towards it. It was *exactly* as she remembered it!

"I remember sitting in this church, boiling away in the heat and hoping the padre would get to the end of the service before we all keeled over and fainted," Kate said, happily throwing her arms around Adam. From the church, it was easy to find the school.

Bizarrely, the jungle looked bigger to her now; the trees so much taller. Following a narrow path, they walked up an incline and came out on a clearing. Down to the right was the old playing field. They were quiet and empty. Closing her eyes, she tried to recall the yells of the children as they tore across the fields on their way to play in the jungle, or the shrill whistle of the games mistress during a hockey game.

Walking on, they came to a barrier, which had always been there. Kate caught glimpses of the roof of the old staff room and a corner of the dining room. A guard was blocking their path and he refused to let them in. The school was now a military barracks and out of bounds to civilians. Both Adam and Kate did their best to argue their case. Despite never taking no for an answer, Adam always knew when a game was lost.

Gently taking Kate's hand, Adam led her back along the path they had just walked and returned them to the car. "Come on, my love, let's find a hotel and a bottle of champagne. I don't suppose you can remember any hotels around here?" he asked hopefully.

They checked into an old hotel and then wandered around looking at the memorabilia now used to decorate the lounge. Adam could tell that Kate was disappointed but he soon had her laughing again.

Later that night, whilst Adam slept, Kate spent hours staring out at the jungle, thinking of her father and trying to remember things. But too many years had passed and she regretted her decision to come back. Some things were best left in the past, she thought. But Adam wanted to see her old house tomorrow, so she would have to go along with that.

The next day, they started their descent back to Kuala Lumpur. Kate's next plan was to try to find the house where she had lived.

Her heart sank as she reached her old home. Her father's garden was overgrown with weeds and the house stood empty. The windows and doors were long gone. An old shutter, eaten away by termites, clung precariously to its rusting bolt. Trees had taken root inside the house and bushes covered with dust cowered in the corners. A broken table with three legs missing leaned against a wall. An air of finality had settled on the place, sucking any memories into damp wet corners. Kate walked around the back where the kitchen had been. Stretched from one end of the back garden to the other was a rusting piece of wire. Her father had bought her a monkey when she was nine years old and had put up the wire so that it could run up and down the garden on a chain, but could not escape. Forlornly, she ran her fingers across it now. It was the only thing left that she recognised in its original form. Coming back had definitely not been a good idea. Taking her hand again, Adam once more led her back to the car.

"Come on," he said, kissing her forehead, "It's time to get back to real life."

They flew back to Singapore the next day, flying low over the cruise ships anchored in the harbour.

After checking into Raffles Hotel, they showered and headed for the famous Raffles Bar. Kate's journey back to her past had evoked many memories. It was definitely time for one of those famous Singapore

Slings. And then she would take him to bed, Kate decided. Taking her hand Adam settled her into a corner, making sure that there was room for him to come and sit next to her. He walked up to the bar and ordered the cocktails.

Tom sat in the hotel foyer waiting for Sarah to come back from the Spa. He thought about the trip so far. His company had added two new accounts to their portfolio. He still enjoyed watching the business grow but was increasingly concerned about the growing threat of terrorism and the 'chatter', which he was privy to. Because the trip necessitated going to Australia, Thailand, the Philippines and Malaysia, and would take a month, he had reluctantly given in to Sarah's insistence that she join him in Singapore at the end of it. The intense treatment for her cancer seemed to have worked and six years on there had been no sign of its evil return.

He saw Sarah walking towards him. She looked hot and cross. "I hate this heat and humidity, Tom. For God's sake, let's go have a drink somewhere cool!"

They walked through to the bar, which was mercifully cold. He ordered their drinks, nodding at the man who had just ordered his. Returning to their table, he listened to Sarah talk about her day; the shopping, the botanical gardens, the butterfly farm, and how clean the city was. Tom half-listened.

The couple sitting at the corner table were obviously very much in love, he thought enviously. They were oblivious to everyone. After some time, the man stood up and walked to the men's room. The woman he was with had her back to Tom and when her partner returned, he blocked his view of her completely.

Sarah was watching Tom carefully. He had stuck by her during her illness and for that she was grateful. He had become a stranger to her over the past years but she had ceased to care. She knew that he didn't love her anymore and she suspected that, like her, he had had the odd fling, but that didn't bother her either. He gave her a generous allowance each month and, if he wasn't away on another business trip, they would occasionally go out for dinner together. But on those occasions, as now, there would be long silences between their stilted conversation, which made the time together feel arduous.

They were both still careful to avoid any mention of their daughter. Drinking gave her some comfort, as did shopping for clothes and shoes. She enjoyed her time staying in hotels on the infrequent occasions she was able to wear Tom down enough to let her come on a business trip with him. He looks so unhappy, she thought. But then, so am I. What a waste of two lives. Frustrated with his silence, she picked up her drink and finished it. "Get me a drink, Tom."

Tom went to the bar and ordered Sarah another glass of wine. He felt inexplicably sad. I should never have taken her back, in the first place, he reflected, but then there was the cancer scare and he had not deserted her. But he had paid the ultimate price and lost the woman he had loved, and still loved. He glanced back at his wife's angry face and with a sinking heart he knew that the evening would end with yet another interminable row. When he returned to the table, he noticed that the couple in the corner had gone.

Chapter Thirteen

KATE LOVED THE BUSINESS but sometimes it was draining and she longed for her own kitchen and bed. The scramble at the airports and the long flights were exhausting. The social side of the business was also beginning to pall. Entertaining international tour operators for dinners and lunches, attending functions, seminars and cocktail parties – and they were expected to be seen at all of them – left them with very little time for a family life or making friends who were not involved in the travel business. Their next big trip was to the States and Canada. She shuddered, remembering their last trip there. Twenty-four flights in thirty days. It had been a nightmare with all the different time zones.

After that particular trip, instead of flying back to Cape Town, they had arrived in Johannesburg from New York and gone straight to their favourite game lodge to recover from all the travelling. Kate had been unusually quiet during dinner that evening. Adam had watched her, trying to work out what was bothering her. He waited for her to tell him.

Later, they sat around the campfire relishing the peace and quiet after the madness and noise of New York City. Kate turned to Adam and reached for his hand.

"Adam, we are so lucky to have all this; some people only go to one game lodge in their entire lives, we have been to hundreds, and there is still a magic in being out here. I love it and I love you for making it happen for me." She lifted her glass and toasted him. She continued, "But sometimes, when I wake up in the morning, I have no idea which country I'm in, let alone which hotel. All these lodges are starting to look the same to me. I love the bush and the game but occasionally I feel that if I have to do one more game drive I'm going to scream."

Adam laughed and poked the fire with a stick, sending up a shower of sparks. She was right; he had been wondering himself how much longer they would be able to keep up with the relentless travelling. He felt worn out himself at the moment.

He stroked her arm absently as he gazed into the fire, thinking about what she had said before replying. "We've been doing it for nearly seven years, Kate, and perhaps it's time for a change. I'm happy to let Luca take over some aspects of the business, but not all of it. I'll go mad if I have to spend every day in the office. That will take a lot of pressure off both of us. Maybe after a month or so, we'll feel differently."

"Absolutely, I'm happy with that, as long as you don't go away too often!"

They left the lodge two days later, Kate feeling relaxed now that they had agreed to ease up on their schedule.

Adam watched her out of the corner of his eye as he negotiated the vehicle down the narrow bush track. If it will make her happier to spend more time with Molly, then so be it. He pulled her across to him and put his arm around her.

"I love you, Kate. You know that, don't you?"

"Yes, I know."

"So, are you going to tell me why you always scan the horizon for something?"

She smiled at him. "It's just something I do. But, when I'm with you, it's not really necessary because everything is perfect and I'm safe. You'll think I'm mad if I tell you."

"You can tell me anything, Kate, you know that."

"Well," she looked at him. Perhaps he *would* understand. "When my father died, I was devastated. I remember sitting out in the garden the day afterwards and, high above me, I saw this falcon. I needed – wanted – something to hang on to and I know it sounds ridiculous, but in my mind, a falcon has become the spirit of my father. Strangely enough, over the years, whenever something has gone wrong in my life, I do always see a brown falcon!" She glanced sideways to see if he might be laughing at her ridiculous theory, but he wasn't. "So, that's what I do. Although, I really wish he would pay me a visit when I'm really, really happy. If it is my father, he'd like to have seen that."

Puzzled and amused with her answer, he drove on through the bush.

Chapter Fourteen

LUCY stood on her wooden deck, shading her eyes from the sun. In the distance, she could see Adam and Kate walking along the beach back towards her house, holding hands. She watched twelve-year-old Molly running in and out of the water. She would bend down occasionally and pick up shells and run to show them to Kate and Adam. Lucy smiled. Finally, it seemed that Kate had found the right man – a man who obviously loved her as deeply as she loved him. But, more importantly, Molly had taken to him too. She had never seen the child so happy.

Lucy distinctly remembered Kate's telephone call to her some seven years ago.

"Luce, it's me," Kate had said breathlessly, laughing. "I've met someone. His name is Adam Hamilton. I don't know where to start! I'm still reeling from meeting him two weeks ago."

"Whoa! Slow down Kate," Lucy had said, laughing in turn. "Tell me everything." She had listened carefully whilst Kate told her about Adam and how they had met.

"I want you to meet him, Luce, not right now, of course, but soon. I know you'll like him. Everyone likes him! God, I'm so happy. I spend the entire day thinking about him and counting the hours until I can see him again. I feel like a teenager! Something happened. I can't explain what. I've never felt like this in my life before. Every man I have ever met pales into insignificance compared to Adam. I'm crazy about him…"

After the call, Lucy went and sat outside on the deck. She was delighted to hear Kate sounding so excited and happy. Adam sounded nice enough and her sister had obviously fallen head over heels in love with him. She had wondered then how Molly would feel when she met him.

But, that was seven years ago and everything had seemingly worked out well; much better than expected, in fact. When Lucy had finally met Adam, she had been very impressed with him and had understood why Kate was so besotted with him. He was striking to look at, utterly charming, and he had a great sense of humour. She had understood the attraction straight away.

Over the years, she had stopped worrying about Kate and Adam. They were perfect together and had even amalgamated their businesses successfully.

Lucy always looked forward to getting postcards from them when they travelled all over the world. They seemed to have everything: love, money and a very glamorous life-style. Sometimes, she envied them but knew she could never handle their brutal business schedule. Although, Kate had told her in confidence that they often took some extra days either side of their trips just to have some time alone. They would jet off to the Caribbean, if they were in that part of the world, or take a long weekend in a chateau in France. They had also spent many weekends with her here in the Wilderness. She loved their company. Adam let Kate grow and he boosted her confidence. There were never any awkward silences or bad atmospheres filled with heavy resentment. They were exactly what they were: perfect and happy together.

When they returned from their beach-combing, Adam sat down to help Molly with a school project. Lucy and Kate walked back down to the beach and sat on a sand dune watching the curling waves crash onto the beach. There was a rotund full moon that had begun to rise. Lucy looked at her sister.

"It's almost too perfect, isn't it? What are the plans now, Kate? Things are going well for you and Adam and Molly is blossoming. Have you thought about marriage?"

Kate laughed. "No. Marriage would spoil all of this. We don't need it. Somehow, we don't need that kind of old fashioned commitment. I love him and he loves me. That's enough for both of us. I don't want anything more than I have now."

Lucy nodded and then turned suddenly, a big smile on her face. "Did you ever hear anything from that man in London – the American? What was his name again?"

Kate lifted her head and stared into the dark. "Tom. His name was Tom. No, I don't expect to see or talk to him again. He turned out to be such a disappointment." She smiled brightly at her sister. "But that was so long ago and is now all in the past. He probably stayed with his wife and they returned to America. I have no idea."

Lucy picked up a small stick and doodled in the sand. "But you did like him, didn't you?" she said softly. "I mean, at one point, you did think about leaving Jack and going back to London to be with Tom... I guess falling pregnant was the deciding factor for staying with Jack. Do you have any regrets at all?"

"Lucy, stop digging around in the sand and also in my past!" Kate laughed. "I don't have any regrets about anything anymore. Look at my life now. I have a beautiful home, a new car every year, my lovely daughter, a hugely successful business, pots of money, world travel and the love of my life – Adam. What more could a girl wish for?"

"But don't you get tired of living out of a suitcase, Kate? I know it all sounds very exciting but you must get fed up with it sometimes. I certainly would."

"Now and again I do. It's hard work keeping up with Adam dragging a suitcase from airport to airport, staying in a different hotel every night, entertaining people you know you will never see again," her voice trailed off. "It's exhausting actually. There are also all the shows that we know we have to be seen at. I won't be able to keep this up forever. I know that. But Adam and I have talked about it and we've decided to ask Luca to take over the visits to the lodges that we normally do every year and also some of the international marketing trips. He would be very good at it."

"It must be hard though, Kate," Lucy continued, "trying to sell South Africa at the moment. I mean, the international community feel very strongly about apartheid, although there are big changes coming, but not soon enough for the ANC. With all the violence going on in the country, it's surprising that anyone comes here at all. If things get any worse, won't the tourists just stop coming?"

"Possibly. I'm well aware of all the problems. Adam has put every penny he has into the business, and I've put in a considerable amount myself. But, things will come right Luce, we just have to hang in there until there is some resolution with the government. Did I tell you that we've taken on more staff? I know it sounds crazy with all the uncertainty but there are young Africans out there bristling with degrees and they are so keen to get into the tourism business. I've taken on two and they are brilliant! It's the way forward, Lucy, we have to embrace change because it *will* come. We have to offer job opportunities to the previously disadvantaged. I know it's the right thing to do. So, I've put John into the marketing department and I'll train him myself. Amos wants to get into logistics and the itinerary side of things. He was talking about incorporating some tours into the townships – the Americans will love that, once things have settled in the country. We might still get the odd bump in the road but this country's tourism will boom. Just wait and see."

Lucy was quiet for a few minutes. The silence suspended easily between them. "Let's hope you're right, Kate. Where are you off to next?"

"The States and Canada." She grinned at her sister. "After that, it will all be up to Luca. We'll still do the odd trip. I don't want to give it up altogether. But, we'll be able to pick and choose where we want to go and what we want to do. I'm looking forward to it."

Lucy stood up and stretched. She brushed the sand off her trousers and extended her hand to Kate, pulling her up. She had met Luca once and although he had been pleasant she had disliked him, even though she knew he was Adam's closest friend. There was a hardness and ruthlessness to him and she didn't trust him at all.

"I think it's a good idea to bring Luca in to do some of the travelling," she said hesitantly. "You don't want to look back in years to come and wish you had spent more time with Molly. She needs you, Kate. She's growing up fast. Try and spend some more time with her."

Chapter Fifteen

LUCA SAT AT KATE'S DESK. He enjoyed running the company when they were away – there was always something going on. Their clients were well heeled and came from all over the world, paying top dollars for a safari experience with them. They needed a lot of looking after, especially the Americans, who were always a little nervous of Africa and what happened in it.

He checked the huge calendar on the wall. The year's activities for Kate and Adam were all there. He saw that another trip to the States and Canada was coming up, in three weeks' time.

He looked at the photograph of Molly in the silver frame on Kate's desk. She was a pretty little girl with a lovely personality. He made a mental note to ask her if she wanted to go riding with him at the weekend. He enjoyed her young company and had been happy to teach her to ride. In his austere bachelor world it made a pleasant change to his normally dull weekends.

He glanced up at the clock and quickly finished his coffee. It was time to pick Kate and Adam up from the airport.

"So, how was the trip to the Far East?" he asked, smiling at them both. Adam and Luca had been friends for twenty years.

"Hello Luca," Kate said, grinning at him. "Going back in time is not a good idea, but business was good, except in Malaysia, that needs more time, and when this country sorts out its politics I think we will get some good business from the Far East."

Luca smiled back at her. He had been attracted to Kate from the moment that Adam had introduced her to him. You're a lucky bastard, he often thought.

Now they were back in the office sitting around the board room table. Adam lit a cigarette. Kate frowned slightly. "Adam, I thought we were going to make the offices smoke free?"

"We are, darling, just as soon as I finish this one." She rolled her eyes at him.

Kate looked at the clock in the office. "Let's go around the corner to Max's and have dinner. I'm in the mood for pasta, after all the noodles and things. Also we have a proposition for you, Luca…"

She was intrigued with Luca's past. She knew that he was French, that much was obvious. He was as tall as Adam with dark curly hair and deep brown eyes. She had never seen him in anything else other than long khaki trousers, safari boots, shirts in various shades of blue and a safari jacket with many pockets. He was never uptight or angry, he just seemed to float through life, finding it all rather amusing. Rumours abounded that he had been in the Foreign Legion, had been a mercenary in the Congo, and had been a Selous Scout in Rhodesia. He had certainly travelled in some of the hot spots of the world and he always carried a small pistol. When she had asked him about the pistol he had just mussed her hair and laughed.

Kate and Adam always used Luca to dry run some of their safaris. He had a pilot's licence, so would charter an aircraft and fly the routes across Africa, checking out the logistics for them. He was always alone, never seen with a woman. If he entertained them at all, it would be at his apartment in town, to which neither of them had ever been invited.

Having finished dinner, the three of them sat back enjoying their coffee. "So what's the proposition then, tell me?"

Luca listened carefully, noticing how tired they both looked. When Adam had finished speaking, he quickly came to his decision. "Sure, what's not to like about it? It will be good to get out of the city and into the bush. I'll need some kind of contract from you both." He turned to Adam. "Do I get to take Kate with me, by any chance?"

"In your dreams, Luca. She stays with me, always has and always will."

"Right, thought I'd ask anyway. Just kidding, Adam. Now tell me how it all works and what you expect from me?"

"Well," Kate said mischievously, "you need to try and visit about four or five lodges a day and then check into one around four in the afternoon, ready for the famous game drive, which I normally find far too long. I mean, to leave at four thirty and get back to the lodge at nine is a bit much. The first couple of hours are fine, then a stop for sundowners, which is always very pleasant. All the guests certainly enjoy that part; then they normally need the loo. The women are always nervous though, I mean they tell you how dangerous the animals are and then they expect you to bare your bum in the bush. All very well if you are wearing a skirt, but difficult indeed, if you are wearing tight trousers!

"The drive back, in the dark can be a bit tedious. Limbs so cold you can't feel them anymore, bugs ricocheting off your eyeballs. At that point I am always pleased to see the lights of the lodge in the distance." She sipped her coffee and grinned at Adam.

"Anyway, after the game drive and the mad dash for the toilets, it's time for the evening's entertainment. You get about ten minutes to shower and change, then it's back up to the main camp for dinner. Now, anyone who has watched the film 'Out of Africa' before they go on safari, has a fixed image in their mind as to how it should all work out. Robert Redford waiting at the campfire, looking fabulous, peeling an orange. Meryl Streep stepping out in the long skirt, sexy boots and shawl, lions roaring away in the background, a bit of Mozart perhaps.

"The rangers, having been up since four thirty for the morning game drive are dead on their feet. It's in their best interests to get you into your room and tucked up for the night, so they can crash into their beds and sleep. In order to do this, during dinner, they put a lot of emphasis on the fact that there are man-eating lions roaming around outside the rooms, leopards looking for lunch, hyenas waiting to haul you off and eat you; there is bad stuff out there, so don't you dare come out of your room once we have seen you to your door."

Adam chuckled; she certainly knew how it all worked.

"The rangers can't leave the camp until everyone is locked down. No room service either. After all, why would you order an expensive bottle of champagne and ask for it to be delivered to your room, when you know the barman may well be eaten en route, if all is to be believed?"

Kate took a deep breath. "I am not sure how long it takes before a ranger succumbs to sleep deprivation, but one thing I do know is that they get huge tips, especially from Americans: guests leave the rangers their telescopes, cameras and sometimes their wives. Don't laugh Adam, you know it's true.

"Woman in particular, who have subscribed to the great African adventure, have fixed ideas of how their safari should be: they saw that movie too. A little bit of Mozart, safari clothing, hair sparkling in the light of the campfire, drop dead gorgeous game rangers, hyenas cackling in the bush somewhere. The reality is quite different. Having got back from your bladder-bursting game drive and $10,000.00 worth of cosmetic dentistry destroyed by bugs, and with your hair looking like rope, you have precisely ten minutes to appear around the campfire looking like a goddess.

"The bath in your room is so modern, so African in design, so bloody deep, that it takes an hour to fill and fifteen minutes to get the energy to crawl out from its cavernous depths. The lighting in the rooms, designed by some appallingly camp guy who has been let loose in there, challenges even those with eyes like a hawk. It's supposed to be seductive and soft, sure, but it is so bad that you can't even find one eye to apply make-up to. Stumbling around in your tent, hurricane lamps waving in the breeze puts even the most docile female in a foul temper. She wants to look fabulous – this is her dream of Africa. There are lovely game rangers out there and she wants to impress."

"She's kidding, right?" said Luca, looking at Adam. He laughed and shook his head.

Kate continued. "Over dinner and a couple of glasses of wine, the thought of an early morning game drive seems like a really good idea, until the ranger mentions what time they would have to get up – five o' clock. But, too late, it's all been agreed. Having been regaled with stories of man-eating animals lurking around your tent, listening to the strange sounds of the night and not getting much sleep, a new day has begun. The rangers seriously expect you to get out of bed at five a.m. and within ten minutes, be up at the mess tent all bright and breezy. Well, I can tell you that's not possible for a start. Only puppies look good first thing in the morning, not women who have survived on three hours sleep." She was in full swing now and enjoying making them both laugh.

"I often wonder, on those evening game drives, why ordinary civilised people from first world countries, always want to see a kill. Where is the pleasure in watching the guts being ripped out of the unfortunate animal? Intestines spilling out into the dirt, blood all over the place; also lions have a gut wrenching stench about them. These seemingly normal and civilised people would not sit around, with a drink in their hand, watching the aftermath of a road accident, would they?"

She sighed dramatically. "I would love to have my own game lodge and get everything just right."

Adam shook his head at her. "Be careful what you wish for darling…"

"So, Luca. Are you still up for the job?" Kate asked innocently.

Luca wiped the tears of laughter from his eyes and nodded at her. "Can't wait, Kate."

Luca drove back to his apartment in town. It was perfect, he thought to himself – the opportunity he had been looking for had fallen right into his lap. He could benefit very nicely from the job that Kate and Adam had offered him, and widen his own business interests considerably. If they wanted him to do some international trips, that was even better. Once everything was in place he would look at East Africa and work out the logistics of the market there.

They wanted him to start after their trip to the States and Canada. He would let his contacts know that his private business was about to expand considerably.

Chapter Sixteen

ADAM AND KATE settled into their hotel in Toronto. Deciding to have a drink before dinner, they headed for the bar. It was absolutely packed with men in dark suits. Perched on their seats, Kate and Adam chatted away to each other, hardly noticing how quiet the crowd in the room was. When they eventually did, Kate glanced around and saw that everyone was looking glum and that not much conversation was being exchanged. When she looked more closely, she saw that everyone looked thoroughly miserable.

"Maybe it's the thought of another ferocious winter that makes them look so unhappy?" Kate whispered to Adam. "I'll be back in a minute. Maybe you can strike up a conversation with someone and see what's up?" She slid off the bar stool and headed for the bathroom. As she washed her hands she thought briefly about Molly's father, Jack, and how he had died here in Canada. She had never seen him again.

Adam watched her returning to the bar within minutes. She was laughing so much she couldn't string a sentence together. She kept starting to tell him but then she would laugh so much she couldn't get the words out.

"Come on Kate! Share the joke," Adam said starting to laugh with her. With an enormous effort, Kate dabbed at her eyes and managed to get control of herself.

"On my way to the bathroom, I saw an events board on display outside the bar." She started to laugh again but checked herself. "There's an undertaker's conference taking place here in the hotel tomorrow. I think this gloomy bunch in here are the delegates!"

"Well in that case I don't want to hang around here for the next hour. Let's go back to the room and celebrate life instead."

Later, Kate lay on Adam's chest listening to his heart beating steadily. She looked up at him suddenly.

"Adam, are you frightened of dying? When Molly was very young I used to think about it and it made me keep going when things were a bit tough. Then, when Jack was killed in the skiing accident, I worried that if I died too that Molly would have no-one. It's a horrible thought. Adam, I can't imagine a world without us in it together."

She lay her head back down, running her hand over his familiar body, a body she knew as well as her own.

"I don't want to talk about death and dying, Kate. It's about the only thing that spooks me. I just can't imagine it, and I don't want to either. We'll always be together, just like this; just you and me." He tightened his hold on her. "I'll always be with you and should something terrible like that happen, you'll only have to hold still and you'll sense me; feel me with you. Promise me that you'll do that if I die?" She shivered and nodded her head, trying to push away the thought of a world without him.

"As for you Kate," he carried on, "You'll go on forever, capturing and captivating everyone and everything in your path. You'll probably forget all about me and fall in and out of love a dozen times more. Come on, enough of this talk! Let's get dressed and go down for dinner. It's that bloody undertakers conference that's brought all this on. I swear that if they are in the hotel dining room tonight, I'm not going to eat here."

During dinner, he seemed more quiet than usual, and she cursed herself for bringing up the subject of death and dying. Sometimes, she wondered if she was not more realistic about life than he was. Life was a huge adventure to him, full of fun with interesting places to visit. He was rarely serious and it was one of the things she loved most about him.

She looked up and found he was watching her steadily, looking very serious indeed.

"Marry me, Kate. We belong together," he said. It was more of a statement than a question. "Molly needs a father figure in her life and I know she's fond of me, after all these years. I could adopt her and we could all live happily ever after. What do you think?"

"I think it's a fabulous idea, Adam. Truly, wonderful," Kate paused. "We've both tried it before though and it didn't work, did it? There's something about marriage that kills all the passion and all the fun. I love what we have at the moment – you, me and Molly. I don't want to lose that. I never want this relationship to become dull and ordinary like all the others. We have such an exciting life. It's perfect and wonderful and unlike the life of anyone else that I know. I love it. I am terrified that it would all go wrong if we got married. I'd love to marry you if you can guarantee that that won't happen and that things won't change."

"Nothing in this world is ever guaranteed, Kate. I can guarantee that I love you and that my love for you will never change. The thing is, I knew you'd say this. I knew the answer to my question was going to be no, but I thought I'd ask anyway. I don't want to make our relationship ordinary by getting married. Definitely not. But I've been wondering how to ensure that you are going to spend the rest of your life with me." Saying this, he put his hand in his pocket and pulled out a small black box.

"I've been carrying this around with me for the past three years. I want you to wear it for me, nothing more, nothing less. Just a private commitment to each other that no-one ever needs to know about, unless you want to tell them. Go on, open it up."

Speechless, Kate opened the lid and lifted out a ring. She knew he would have searched long and hard to find something so perfect. It was a perfectly rectangular stone surrounded by intricately plaited white gold set on a wide band.

"It's so beautiful," Kate whispered, looking up at him. "It's so unusual. Where did you find it?"

"In a tiny shop down an alleyway, in Zanzibar. Remember when we were there with Molly?"

"Yes, of course. I remember how smug you looked when you came back from one of your jaunts around Stone Town. Adam, I love it!"

"The stone reminded me of the colour of your eyes, the way they light up when you have one of your 'Guess what?' moments. I know you don't like conventional jewellery but this just jumped out at me. Here, let me put it on your finger."

"Which one?" she said innocently.

"The finger where your wedding ring should go, but, as you turned me down, this will have to do in its place. I'm glad you like it though. It's a long way back if I had to change it." He slipped the ring on her finger. "It looks nice with your silver bracelet. Come on, let's go and have a glass of champagne and I can pretend that you said yes to my proposal."

She stood up and hugged him tightly. "I love you, Adam. You've no idea how much. I love my ring and all the reasons why you gave it to me. Thank you."

Feeling a little emotional himself, he led her through to the bar. They both knew that something special had just happened and that married or not, they had just made a deep and serious commitment to each other.

The only two people she would tell would be Molly and Lucy. She would call them just as soon as she could.

Chapter Seventeen

ADAM WAS WAITING for her in the arrivals hall at Johannesburg International Airport. He watched her push her way through and run straight into his arms. "Oh, it's so good to be back! I missed you so much. How was Milan?" She chattered all the way to the car.

When the invitation had come through to visit two new lodges in Botswana, Kate had decided to make the trip on her own. Adam had been in Milan at a travel show, showing Luca the ropes.

"We have an invitation to visit some game lodges in Botswana, Adam," Kate had told him when he called her, "but they want us there this week! I thought I might go solo on this one. What do you think?"

"Well, of course I would prefer to come with you but, if they insist, you'll have to go on your own. Just behave yourself! I don't want you falling for one of those good-looking rangers."

"Why would I go looking for a game ranger when I have you, the love of my life?" She smiled down the telephone.

"I never want to lose you, Kate. I know what it's like, sitting around a campfire, the sky full of glittering stars. It's romantic and anything can happen." Years later he would recall his words to her with bitterness.

"Why don't you fly back from Milan to Johannesburg and then when I'm finished in Botswana we can have a few days in the bush? Yes?" Adam agreed. "Good! I'll see you then. Have a good flight back to me," Kate said, hanging up the phone.

Now, over dinner, Kate told him about the lodges in Botswana.

He listened and watched her. She had blossomed in the nine years they had been together. She was no longer the shy woman he had met in the hotel garden. She could hold her own in any situation. He was proud of her, but even so, he couldn't help remembering her when she was vulnerable. She had clung to him, needed him, and she had brought out the best in him, he knew that. He loved her now, more than ever. Did that make him the vulnerable one? He shook his head, irritated with his thoughts. He was just tired from the long flight, that was all.

When she had finished telling him about her trip, she sat back in her chair and smiled at him. "So, how did I do on my first solo trip for the company?"

"You did a terrific job. I'm very proud of you. Milan was not the same without you. It was no fun at all. But, Luca was great and he enjoyed it. Come on, we've got an early start tomorrow. Let's get out of this city and into the bush. The noise in Milan was ear-splitting. I need some peace and quiet."

The next morning, as he loaded their bags into the back of the hired car, he told her he'd booked two nights for them at her favourite lodge. "I'm glad we're taking this break, Kate. You can try out the spa when we get there this afternoon – go have a manicure or something – and we can just relax. What do you think?"

She put her hand on the back of his neck and ruffled his hair; she noticed how tired he looked. "I can think of something far more exciting than a manicure and, after that, we can order a bottle of wine and sit out on the deck and watch the animals come to drink at the waterhole. It's my favourite time in camp when everyone is out on a game drive and we have the place to ourselves. Forget the spa, I'd much rather spend a few hours in bed with you…"

Kate wound down the window as they left Johannesburg far behind them and drove into the game reserve. She breathed in the dry dusty smell of wood, trees and animals. The vehicle brushed against a wild sage bush and the pungent smell drifted through the vehicle. Adam drove slowly, careful to avoid any animal that might bolt across their path.

They arrived in the early afternoon and spent the afternoon making love. After taking an outdoor shower together they sat out on their private deck. A hurricane lamp hissed on the table between them, although it was not quite dark yet. A bottle of wine cooled in a silver ice bucket. Suddenly, Kate sat bolt upright. "Adam," she whispered urgently. "Look, elephant!" He had already seen them and was waiting for her to do the same. "I must have been looking straight at them but didn't *see* them. How can they just arrive like that, without making a sound?" she said, shaking her head in wonder.

Quietly, he poured her a glass of wine. Contentedly, they sat and watched the elephant until they were swallowed up in the shadow of darkness. In the far distance came the distinctive roar of a lion. Kate shivered and reached for Adam's hand.

The next evening, Adam opted to stay in camp. Once again they had spent the afternoon in bed and he needed to catch up and write his notes on the trip to Milan. "Are you sure you won't change your mind about the game drive?" she said hopefully, picking up her hat and her jacket.

"No, you've worn me out. Anyway, I'll probably see more animals around the camp than on a game drive. They're not that dumb, you know. It's quieter here and they know they won't have to dodge safari vehicles. I'll see you later." He handed her the camera and kissed her on the mouth, pushing her out of the tented suite.

Kate walked up to the main camp for tea and cake. The guests were all there with their binoculars, cameras, hats and jackets. Once the sun went down it could get cold quickly.

Kate sighed, worried, as she watched the Vervet monkeys being shooed away by the staff. They had come close to camp, hoping to snatch a couple of the cakes on the tea table. She knew how naughty they could be. The guests were given strict instructions to zip up their tents when they left them, as the monkeys were curious creatures. They liked to go foraging for food when everyone went out. In this camp, there were biscuits in a jar in each of the tents and the monkeys were sharp and adept enough to help themselves. And not just to the biscuits, they liked to ferret in guests' luggage and admire themselves in the shiny taps and mirrors.

Kate watched the safari vehicles pull up and, along with the other guests, she gathered up her things. Adam really didn't look well.

Chapter Eighteen

KATE PUT THE TELEPHONE DOWN and hugged herself happily. Lucy had met a Frenchman. Jean-Philippe had been on holiday in South Africa and had wandered into the art gallery, in Wilderness, exhibiting Lucy's paintings. He had purchased one and asked if he could meet the artist. The gallery owner called Lucy to ask. She was flattered as it was one of her most expensive pieces and the money would be enough to keep her going for months. Besides, no collector had ever asked to meet her before. She agreed immediately.

They met for lunch the next day. Jean-Philippe had been collecting art for years. He hung the majority of his collection on the walls of the farmhouse he owned just outside of Cannes. The remainder of his collection, which he circulated regularly, was stored in a warehouse near the harbour. He lived alone in France, with two Labradors. His marriage had ended in divorce and there were no children. He told her that he had a small law practice in Cannes, which he had inherited from his father. Lucy liked him almost immediately. Jean-Philippe extended his stay and they saw each other every day for two weeks. When he couldn't justify being away any longer, he invited Lucy to come and stay with him in Cannes. Lucy had never been to France but it was one place she had often thought of visiting.

Kate encouraged her to go. She was delighted to hear Lucy sounding so happy.

"He really is the nicest man I have ever met, Kate. I really didn't think that I would ever fall in love, but I have," she gushed, laughing nervously. "I'd like to be with him all the time, just like you with Adam. Now I understand this thing called love!"

Lucy had originally planned to spend two weeks there. Two months later, she called Kate out of the blue. "This is going to come as a bit of a shock to you! I do love France. The people are so friendly and polite. Jean-Philippe has asked me to marry him and I've accepted. It was totally unexpected. He took me out to dinner and just asked!"

Kate could hear the joy in her sister's voice.

"That's the most wonderful news, Lucy! I knew something had to be going on with not hearing from you for ages. Congratulations to you both. How fantastic. Does that mean you'll be moving to France?"

"Kate, you should see the house. It's beautiful. It's an old farmhouse with huge grounds. I can garden to my heart's content! I've already started. And the light, Kate, the light here is so magnificent. I can see why the great masters came here to paint. It's golden and pure and it reflects off the stone in this way..." she laughed. "It's hard to describe! All I know is that when I'm not in the garden, all I want to do is paint. I'll be back for a few weeks to pack up my things but then I'll be coming back here. You and Molly must come and stay, and Adam of course! Please come. I want you to meet Jean-Philippe. He's already said that you're welcome anytime you like. You will come for the wedding, won't you?"

As she had said, Lucy returned to South Africa, packed up her house and paintings and moved to France. Kate hadn't been able to go to the wedding but Molly went and was Lucy's bridesmaid.

"She looked so beautiful and happy and he is *such* a nice person," Molly told Kate when she collected her at the airport. As they stood waiting for Molly's luggage to come through, Molly told Kate more. "The farmhouse is très French with those pale blue shutters and it's such a cliché! He has a view from the upstairs windows out over fields of lavender. Really! Lucy sits out there with a big straw hat on her head, surrounded by a purple haze and bumble bees, as she paints. She's so happy, Kate. She wants you and Adam to come and see her soon."

Kate smiled, "How funny, that's exactly how I imagined her: sitting in a field, painting. Jean-Philippe sounds as though he is the best thing that could ever have happened to her. She's been gone for six months now and I already miss her terribly. I will go and visit her as soon as I can. At least you'll have a lovely place to go to for your holidays. It sounds so perfect." She hugged her daughter. "I wish I could have made it to the wedding, but with Adam away, and Luca, it just wasn't possible. I am so proud of you flying all the way to France on your own, not many thirteen year olds get that opportunity. I remember not being able to imagine you being old enough to fly on your own!"

"I know! I did feel ridiculously grown up. I didn't much like the long journey though. I don't know how you do it so often. All those people pushing and shoving and the long queues for everything. I don't think I am going to go into the travel business when I grow up." Molly's luggage arrived and they wheeled the suitcase across the car park.

"Oh, dear! I was hoping you would follow in my footsteps and take over from me. Then Adam and I could go and lie around on a beach somewhere and let you do all the hard work instead. Come on, I don't know about you but I'm starving! We're going to that little fish restaurant at the Waterfront. I've asked Hannah to join us. I think she misses us terribly. She moved into that little flat overlooking the sea whilst you were away and she's found a job giving extra English lessons to children at the school near her, but I know how much she misses you." Kate slid behind the wheel of her Mercedes and looked contentedly at her daughter: the last three years had given them all the time they needed to be together. Luca had taken over most of the travelling now, although she and Adam still managed to steal away for long weekends up the coast or in the bush. Now and then Adam would get bored with the office and opt to attend one of the travel shows, or check out a new lodge, but nothing that would keep them apart for more than a week. Everything had worked out perfectly and she had never been happier.

Chapter Nineteen

KATE LET HERSELF INTO THE OFFICE. It was a Sunday but there were a few things she still had to finish before Adam got back from a business trip tomorrow. A new lodge had opened in Botswana and she had suggested that before he took off for London he should take the short flight from Johannesburg to Maun and check it out. Luca could easily have done it but as Adam would be flying out of Johannesburg anyway, it was more cost effective if he did it. He had been looking preoccupied and worried lately and she had felt that a break in the bush would be good for him. She frowned to herself as she watched the rain slash across the windows, feeling uneasy but not sure why.

She sat down at her desk and looked out of the window. Heavy black clouds hung over the city and she could hear thunder in the distance. One of Cape Town's famous storms was coming. She opened the report from the auditors.

The company was in real trouble. The continuing violence in South Africa had ended its reputation as one of the top new destinations to visit. Two bombs had gone off in town. There had been one at a restaurant and another at a small hotel on the beach. Dozens of people had died. International travellers were not prepared to take the risk and the cancellations kept coming in. Their overheads were high and the fleet of vehicles, the Range Rovers and Mercedes, all stood empty in the driveway of the offices. The thirty-five people who worked for them would have to be cut to fifteen.

Kate scanned the figures anxiously. They would not be able to crawl their way out of this financial disaster; she could see that for herself. She knew there was only one solution. She would have to sell her house to pay off the money owed to all their suppliers. Kate loved her house and she was filled with sadness at the thought of having to sell it.

The phone rang, making her jump. She knew it was Adam.

"What are you doing sitting in the office today? You should be here with me in London. It's beautiful here and I have no-one to spend the day with!"

Kate smiled down the phone at him. "Well, someone had to be here to answer your call! It's horrible here. Dark and gloomy, like my mood," she said ominously. "I've just finished reading the report from the auditors and it doesn't make for pleasant reading. Please tell me you've managed to pick up some new business? God knows, we're going to need every scrap we can get! How was the lodge in Botswana, did you manage to relax a bit?"

"It was fine, just fine. Not many tourists around though, so the camp wasn't full. Come on, Kate, cheer up. I'll be back on Friday. We can go through everything together then."

"Friday! I thought you were coming back tomorrow?" Kate said, surprised.

"I've decided to make a quick trip to New York. I'm pretty sure I can push for business there. Besides, there's not all that much to do in the office at the moment, is there? I can make good use of the time and it's cheaper to fly to New York from London than from Cape Town or Johannesburg."

"I'll pick you up from the airport on Friday," Kate said, trying to keep the disappointment out of her voice. "We're going to need to sit down and make some pretty hard decisions, Adam."

"Fine. See you then, Kate." The phone went dead in her hand. Puzzled, she stared at it for several minutes, before carefully putting it down. He had told her precious little about the new lodge – maybe he hadn't liked it. She dialled her sister's number in France, needing to talk to someone.

They quickly caught up on each other's news. "We had a lovely French Christmas, Kate. What a change from Christmas in Africa. No turkey and stuffing in the sweltering heat, we had lobster and oysters. The weather was mild enough for us to sit outside. The cruise was fabulous, such a civilised way of travelling. I don't think I will ever go near an airport again. Anyway, enough of me, how was your Christmas and how are you all?"

"Christmas was Christmas – terribly hot. But that was months ago. We should have been really busy here, but business is so bad at the moment. You probably heard about the bombs going off in South Africa. It is so bad for tourism. Adam is in London at the moment, then he's going on to New York, trying to drum up more business, but it's difficult. We'll have to do some drastic cost cutting here, if we're going to survive."

"Surely Adam should be with you there and not running around London and New York costing the company more money? Is everything all right between the two of you?" She knew her sister better than anyone else and she knew that something wasn't quite right; she could hear it in her voice. "Come on, out with it. Tell me what's going on," she heard Kate sigh.

"I don't really know what's going on. We seem to have paddled into very troubled waters with the company. I think I'm going to have to sell my house, which will break my heart, but I can't see any other way around it. We desperately need some cash flow. I don't think Adam realises the trouble we're in. He was never that good with figures and he seems to think that everything will turn out all right. But, Luce, I don't think that's going to happen. He's always been like that. When there's trouble, he sticks his head in the sand and hopes everything will go away."

Lucy listened quietly. She felt sure there was more to her sister's concern than money. "You're still not telling me everything, Kate. What else is bothering you?"

"I can't put my finger on anything but I have this feeling that Adam is keeping something back from me. He was kind of preoccupied before his trip to London, which I put down to the state of the business, but I think it's more than that. I've known him for ten years now and he seems to be almost secretive these days. Maybe I'm just over- reacting what with everything else going on. I don't know – something's not right. I'm not travelling with him as often as I used to, but he still goes off. I mean there is absolutely no point in him going to New York, the Americans will not come here whilst all this violence is going on. He doesn't seem to be worried about the business, or rather, the lack of it," Kate paused for a minute.

"A couple of times I've come back to the office and he's been on the phone. Normally, he'd just wave his cigarette at me, but twice he's lowered his voice and then hastily hung up," she carried on quickly. "I'm trying not to think about the classic answer to this. I don't believe Adam would ever betray me, we've been so happy together. Anyway, he couldn't have met anyone else because he's always with me. Well, except when he's travelling. But we call each other every single day, when he's away, so it can't be that. Can it?"

Lucy frowned, not sure of what she should say. She felt pretty certain something was going on. She was extremely fond of Adam – he had turned her sister's life around when she had needed it most. She felt grateful to him for that and for that she decided to give him the benefit of the doubt.

"Kate, I'm quite sure there is nothing to worry about. You're probably just hyper-sensitive at the moment. Please think carefully before you say or do anything. Look, this call must be costing you a small fortune. I don't suppose there is any chance of you coming over for a week or two, what with things as they are at the moment?"

Kate hesitated and Lucy knew her answer was no. "Goodbye Kate, take good care of yourself and come and see me when you can. Love to Molly," and then as an afterthought, "and to Adam."

Kate put the phone down and leaned back in her chair, tapping a pencil nervously on her desk as she tried to work things out. If Adam's company went down, then hers would too. It was as simple as that. When she had agreed to combine the two companies, she had not even thought about things going wrong. The bank would come after her home and everything else she possessed, just as the bank had taken her house in Tinder Bay thirteen years ago. Reluctantly, she opened the property section of the Sunday newspaper and tentatively looked for an estate agency. There was no point in waiting to discuss it with Adam: something had to be done now, and the only asset they had was her house. Adam didn't own any property and had ploughed what money he had had into the business. She looked at the clock on the office wall and hastily tidied her desk. It was

Molly's seventeenth birthday, and she had promised to take her out for lunch. Seventeen; she could hardly believe it.

They drove back from the airport. Kate listened whilst Adam told her all about his trip, the people he had met and the new business he hoped for.

He reeled off the names of companies there, companies that she knew herself from their last trip there two years ago. "Well, I'm sure it was all worthwhile, Adam, but unless this country gets its problems sorted out, things are just going to go from bad to worse." He nodded in agreement, suddenly quiet. They didn't talk for the rest of the car ride to the office and the silence hung heavily between them.

Back at the office, they pored over the figures together. Kate had made a short list of the creditors who had to be paid immediately. "I've put the house on the market, Adam. I've already had one offer that I'm considering." He saw the tears in her eyes and leaned across the table to brush them away as they slid down her cheek. He got up and put his arms around her, holding her close to him.

"I'll get you another house, Kate. Don't look so distressed. All this will blow over. You've made a good plan here and it should save the company. Let's go and have dinner and work out our next move." He smiled brightly at her. A little too brightly, she thought.

Kate accepted the offer on her house and began to look for a place to rent. The contract went through quickly and within a month she had handed her house keys to the new owner and settled into her rented apartment.

With the crisis of the company over and the creditors paid off, she felt the pressure begin to ease. It had been a tough six months. David Warner, her attorney, who had handled the contract with the house, called her from Johannesburg.

"Kate, you must go for half of the company now, you've earned it. Without your money, from the sale of the house, the company would have collapsed. At the moment, Adam owns half of your company but you have no shares in his. I strongly advise that you rectify this position. It would not be unreasonable to ask for fifty per cent of his company. I can handle it for you. If something goes wrong, or if your relationship with Adam should falter, he will take everything and you will be left with nothing. I saw that happen to you with the boatyard and I won't let it happen to you again."

Kate saw the sense of what he was telling her. She had let Adam buy shares in her company two years after they had met.

"All right, David. You're absolutely right. I'll speak with Adam this evening. Don't sound so worried, we'll get through this. Adam has never let me down before and I'm sure he won't do so now. We love each other. We trust each other. I wouldn't have done this for anyone else but I'd do anything for him and someone had to bail out the business or we'd both have been sunk."

Over dinner, Kate brought up the subject of the shares. At first Adam resisted. Kate repeated what David had said to her.

"It's not what I want. I trust you with everything but from a legal perspective he has got a point. I have to think about Molly," Kate finished quietly, hoping he would understand.

"I don't know why you feel so strongly about having half of my company, Kate. How can you say that you trust me but then ask for half of the business? What difference will it make anyway? I promised you that I would pay back all the money you have put into the company, surely that's enough?" he demanded angrily. It was the first time in their relationship that Kate had heard him raise his voice to her. It was the first time in ten years. He crushed his cigarette out in the ashtray and sat back exasperated. After a few moments, he leaned forward and looked into her eyes; his anger seemingly had passed as rapidly as it came. He smiled at her suddenly but his eyes were sad, something else she had never seen before.

"It's all right, Kate. Go ahead and do the paperwork with David. I'll sign it off. By the way, I'm planning another trip, New York again. I didn't have time to see as many agents as I wanted to on this trip. I want to make sure that when the time comes and they start to come to South Africa, that we get the lion's share of the business. Get Emily to put it up on the board, will you? It's probably better and less expensive if you stay here and run the company, especially as very soon you'll own half of it!" He reached over and took hold of her hand. "Come on, it's been a long day. I need some sleep."

"Hold on, Adam," she said, dismayed at his suggestion. "You can't keep flying off to places whenever you feel like it any more. We need to plan the trips carefully and evaluate their importance."

"Oh, come on!" Adam interrupted sharply. "You know as well as I do that the American market is extremely important to us. What happened to the impulsive and positive Kate? You're beginning to sound like the accountant!"

This stung her as he knew it would. She replied coolly. "Impulse and adventure come with a price tag, Adam, and we can't afford either at the moment. I'll do as you suggest and stay here. Whilst you're gone I'll call David and have him restructure the company."

Kate watched him carefully. It had been easy, too easy really, but she had what she wanted and if he wanted to go to New York again then she wouldn't be able to stop him; she would have to go along with it. She had big plans for the company and it would probably be easier if she implemented the new systems whilst he was away.

Long after he was asleep, she lay in his arms, wide-eyed. Something fundamentally had shifted between them. She could feel it. Was it things going wrong with the business or was something wrong with them? She thought back carefully over the past few months, looking for anything that might explain the way she was feeling now. Something was not right.

It would be many years before she found out the truth and the lengths that Adam had gone to, to keep it away from her for as long as he did. Luca had been involved, but she had been completely unaware of that as well.

Chapter Twenty

E MILY STOOD AT THE WINDOW of Kate and Adam's office, gazing out to sea. Kate finished her telephone conversation and looked up at her, smiling brightly.

"Okay Emily, let's go through all the expenses from Adam's latest trip to New York and see what it cost the company. Let's see if he managed to keep within his budget this time."

They worked on the figures for an hour. As Emily stood to return to her desk in the office opposite theirs, Kate stopped her.

"Hang on, Emily. Where's the bill from the hotel in New York? Whilst you're looking for that, could you please bring me the company telephone bill? It seems a bit high and I want to re-check it."

Ten minutes later, Emily returned with only the telephone bill. "I can't seem to find the hotel bill, Kate. I'll ask Adam for it when he gets back from his meeting with the bank."

Kate scanned the telephone bill. It *was* very high. Her eyes travelled down through the dialled calls. She began to notice that one number was repeated frequently. It was a New York number. At that moment, Adam strode back into the office and came to stand in front of her desk. He grinned at her. "Let's go back to your place and spend the afternoon in bed," he said, rubbing his hands in anticipation.

Kate looked up anxiously, not having heard him. "This number in New York, Adam, do you recognise it? None of the staff can make long distance calls, so it can only be either you or me. I don't know it. Do you?"

Adam came over and put his arms around her, resting his chin on her head. He glanced down at the bill. "Yes, I recognise it. That's the Tourism board in New York City. I needed a lot of information from

130

them before I left on the trip. Now that South Africa has a new government and apartheid is finally over, there are tons of new agents and tour operators popping up; they know all of them so it's important to keep up to date."

Emily came into the office, knocking lightly on the door. Adam stepped away from behind Kate's chair. "Hello, Adam. Sorry to bother you. I was wondering if you have your hotel bill? I need to file it with your other expenses from the trip."

Kate watched his face closely, but saw nothing.

"I'll find it for you Emily. If it's not here in the office, I'll bring it in tomorrow, that's if I can find it. See you back at your place, Kate. Don't keep me waiting too long." He gave her his slow seductive smile and left the office.

Kate turned off her computer anxious to join Adam. The business from his three trips to New York was certainly coming in, she had to admit that. The telephone bill was high, but now she understood why. Happily she drove back to her apartment – Adam had promised to make love to her for the entire afternoon and speak only Italian; she shivered with anticipation. No point in bothering about a couple of bills.

Luca tapped on her office door and raised an eyebrow when he saw Adam's normally untidy desk was clear. "Where is he? Out of town again?" He kissed Kate on both cheeks and sat down in front of her, noticing how tense she looked.

"Yes, New York seems to be his favourite destination lately. I'm planning on joining him next time he goes. I'll need to do something when Molly leaves for London, it will take a lot of getting used to, not having her around. I'm dreading it really."

"Yes, I can understand that. We'll all miss her. So when will Adam be back?"

"Next week. Then he's promised to stay in Cape Town until we go to the travel show in London, in November. Sorry Luca, I'm so busy at the moment, trying to check the end of month figures. Emily will make you a cup of coffee if you like, but I must get on." He held his hands up in front of him.

"No thanks. I'm on my way. Let's all have dinner when Adam gets back, it's been a while?" She nodded at him and blew him a kiss.

Luca left the office and walked towards his car, thinking about his meeting with Adam after his last trip to New York. Adam had insisted that they should meet somewhere private. Reluctantly Luca, seeing how agitated his friend was, had suggested his apartment. Adam had asked for his help.

"Give me twenty four hours to think about this, Adam. I can help you but there is no way that you can ever tell Kate that I have; it would be far too dangerous. You might not like what I'm going to suggest, but it's the only way I can give you what you need. I don't want to know any of the details. None of them. I'm a loner as you well know, but if I decide to go ahead with you there will be no turning back – ever. You need to be quite clear about that Adam."

Adam had nodded. "I'll do whatever it takes, Luca. I'll do anything. Just tell me what I need to do…"

Adam had agreed to Luca's plan. There was a lot of risk involved but Luca seemed to have a good system in place, a system that had worked well for years. It was worth the risk when there were absolutely no other alternatives.

Now Luca turned the keys in the ignition and backed out of the parking bay. They would have to make absolutely sure that Kate didn't join Adam on any trip to New York.

Emily popped her head around the door. "Molly's on the phone, but she said not to disturb you if you were busy, she just wanted to let you know that she is staying over with a friend tonight. Any message for her?"

Kate shook her head as her fingers flew over the calculator on the desk. "I'll see her tomorrow then, oh and Emily, would you mind staying behind for half an hour, I need you to check a couple of things for me?"

Kate's stomach tightened as she rechecked the telephone bill. Why would Adam still be calling the tourism office in New York so often? Surely there couldn't be that many new agents springing up wanting to sell South African holidays and safaris? And why could he never produce his hotel bill? She had asked him why the hotel bill never appeared on the company credit card statement, and he had told her that because things were tight with cash flow he had put it on his personal card and would claim it back when business improved. She frowned, trying to ignore her instincts which were telling her something was definitely not right. She sat still, needing to know the truth but not wanting the answer. She felt her scalp prickle with anxiety; she pushed her chair away from her desk and slowly stood up.

She went into Emily's office and asked her to call the hotel in New York and ask for a copy of Adam's last three hotel bills. Returning to her desk, she picked up the phone, checked the time difference and dialled the number for the tourism office in New York.

The phone rang a few times and activated an answering machine for a woman called Elizabeth Green. As she was hanging up, Emily came into her office and told her that the hotel had no record of Adam staying there on his last trip or any previous trips.

Emily watched, her face frozen, as Kate wrestled with the truth in front of her. Kate felt the bile rise in her throat as she stared at the telephone bill. So he had betrayed her then. Ten years of her life with him evaporated in that moment. She looked up at Emily, with a sadness in her eyes that was heart piercing in its hopelessness.

"What happens now?" Kate asked her. "How can I fix this?" Her head was starting to pound.

Emily shook her head slowly, as shocked as Kate. She had moved with Kate into her and Adam's premises and seen how their business merged and grew together. She had offered gentle words of encouragement and support to the staff that were let go when business began to dry up, and now there was this.

They were such a golden couple, she thought to herself, always together, always laughing, obviously very much in love with each other. She had often had to curb her envy for their relationship but right now, she was glad she was not in Kate's shoes. Molly was leaving for England soon and it was a long way from Cape Town. Emily knew that would be devastating for Kate too. What would happen to the company?

Who would get what, would it survive a split? Emily felt her own stomach clench with worry. How would Kate cope with this?

Emily walked around to Kate's side of the desk and put her hand on Kate's shoulder. She squeezed it gently. "We'll get through this, Kate. It's not going to be an easy ride, but I'll help you as much as I can. You need to work out how you are going to confront him with this information you now have." She paused suddenly uncertain, "You *are* going to confront him aren't you?"

"Yes, of course I am. I still want to believe him." Her conviction sounded hollow, even to her own ears, "Maybe there's an easy explanation for this, Emily. It's the last thing I thought he would do to me, especially after all we've been through," her voice faltered. She looked out of the window, absently fondling the bracelet on her wrist, and began to feel her life splinter and fall apart in front of her.

Adam lay in bed holding her. It was dark outside but too early to go to sleep. He thought about the company and the mess they had only just managed to crawl out from under.

Kate had set up all sorts of systems, ones he had never bothered to implement. She had taken on two accountants to keep an eye on the budgets and the cash flow. He knew she had made a big sacrifice by selling her home. He had been with her when she handed over the keys and walked away from it. He had driven her back to her new apartment and watched as she fought back her tears. He had promised her that he would recoup the money so that she could buy again, but, as he had discussed with Luca, that was going to take time.

He sighed quietly and felt her move next to him. The trips overseas took a lot of their cash flow but unless they did the marketing there would be no business. Kate was not as eager to travel anymore: she wanted to spend time with Molly.

Kate was also savvier technologically. She felt that a lot of the business could be done by video conferencing and e-mail. He knew she was right in many ways but he preferred to be out of the office these days. It bored him to go there every day. It always had. Until Kate came along. Now, she was spending all her time at her desk poring over budgets and figures, or in meetings with the accountants and auditors. All the fun had gone out of the place and he didn't enjoy it any more.

Kate was keeping a tight rein on him and the money, and it filled him with dread that she might stumble on the truth. It irritated him when she asked to see all the expenses he incurred on his trips, although he was astute enough to know that this was the only way for them to keep their business under control. He turned over on to his back and stroked her hair. He ran his hand over her smooth skin.

He hated himself for having to keep up his end of the bargain.

"Turn around, Elizabeth. God, it's good to be away from Africa for a while."

Adam strolled into the bar at the Four Seasons hotel in Manhattan. He saw her waiting for him and tensed. "Hello, Elizabeth. How was your day?"

"It was good, how was yours? Did you manage to get through to your office?"

"Yes," he replied curtly. "But Kate was out for the day. I'm not quite sure where she is but I guess she's with Molly. I spoke to Emily and, I have to say, she was pretty short with me." He ordered a Martini and whilst he waited for it to arrive, he thought about Kate and the impossible situation he now found himself in. Elizabeth chattered away but he wasn't listening.

"So what are you going to do about Kate, Adam? When are you going to tell her about us? Are you listening to me?" she snapped, and repeated her questions.

Adam thought quickly. "It's not as easy as you think, Elizabeth. We're business partners and this means more than the end of a love affair." His Martini arrived and he took a sip.

"Well, you had better do something and sooner rather than later because I've booked a flight to Cape Town. Remember you said I should see it one day? Well, on impulse, I bought a ticket. I'm coming for three weeks over Christmas. I'll be staying with you. That gives you ten weeks to finish the thing. I expect you to do it."

Adam drained his glass. Christ, he hadn't planned on this. He also had no intention of ending his affair with Kate. He loved her. He would have to think of a very good reason for Elizabeth not to come. She was a tough cookie. Having been born and bred in New York into a very wealthy family, she was used to having her own way. It wouldn't be easy. He called the waiter over and ordered another drink. Things were becoming complicated.

He noticed that Elizabeth was tapping a manicured nail against her glass and that she was waiting for him to respond to her news. Her jaw was clenched and her eyes had narrowed.

He had met her whilst she was on safari in Botswana. He had been checking up on the newly opened lodge there, before his trip to London. He had noticed Elizabeth watching him as he chatted to the lodge owner during the day, and she had made sure she sat strategically positioned to survey the bar, and his entrance into it, that evening. He had felt her eyes on him throughout dinner.

He was a good story teller and had kept all of the guests amused throughout the meal. Adam knew he epitomised everything anybody had ever read about game rangers and the kinds of men who live in Africa. After dinner when everyone reconvened by the fireside, he had not been surprised to find Elizabeth had carefully manoeuvred herself next to him.

They talked about New York and she told him about the specialist practice she had just started with a fellow physician. He listened carefully to what she was saying. This was her first trip to Africa and she had fallen in love with it.

As the night lengthened, one by one the guests retired to their rooms, until it was just the two of them left. The rangers had excused themselves; they knew Adam was perfectly capable of getting back to his luxury tent without fear of the animals and he had promised to see Elizabeth safely to hers. He walked her back and she invited him in for a nightcap. He hesitated, but then accepted.

They sat outside on the deck with drinks in their hands. He listened carefully to her proposition and felt appalled by it. Later, as he dressed, he couldn't help but supress a terse laugh. Elizabeth demanded to know what was so funny.

He put his jacket on and told her it was something he remembered he'd said to someone once about the seductiveness of an African night in the bush and game rangers. She didn't see the humour and from the expression on her face, he was glad to leave her tent.

Back in his own, he cursed himself for what he had done, for what he had had to do. But, that was Elizabeth's deal. He sat outside smoking until the sky lightened and the dawn chorus of birds began.

The next morning, Adam left the camp without saying goodbye to Elizabeth. He found her business card in his shirt pocket on the flight to Johannesburg. He would have to come up with something to say to Kate and why, after his London trip, he would be going straight to New York.

He looked out over the landscape below. He remembered the look on Kate's face when he had hurriedly cut off that telephone call at the end of January, when she had walked back into the office unexpectedly. It was a call that had made him question the future, and his place in it.

"Well Adam, have you got anything to say about my proposed visit?" Elizabeth was still staring at him. She looked ready to start a scene. She was ten years older than him and looked it. She had sharp features and short black hair. She was as high maintenance to be with as it took to keep her looking as good as she did. He glanced away, despising her and what she was making him do. He knew he would have to make some very tough decisions.

"I'll see how the land lies when I get back to Cape Town but I wish you'd discussed your plans before you booked your flight. I don't like this sort of pressure being put on me, Elizabeth. I have enough on my mind, as you well know. I don't need this as well." He stood up abruptly. "I have to leave now for the airport." Angrily he left the bar, leaving Elizabeth with her half-finished drink and his untouched. She shrugged her thin shoulders at his retreating back. He wouldn't leave her, she knew that. He needed her far more than she needed him. She knew exactly how to bring him to heel. She smiled quietly to herself and finished her drink.

Kate sat in the office waiting for Adam, her mind distracted. Not having Molly at home would be a terrible wrench for her. It would have been easier somehow with Adam beside her. She knew that she was losing them both and she felt profound sadness and grief. She wrestled with how to confront Adam with the facts as she knew them. Although devastated by what she had found out, she had soon become increasingly angry. Today she felt quiet and calm. It was a quiet fury that sat icily in the pit of her stomach.

She heard the car pull up outside. She always collected Adam after a trip, always anxious to fly into his arms and hold him, but this time she had sent Bradley, one of their drivers, to pick him up. She heard his footsteps as he walked the corridor to their office. She stood up and walked towards the door to meet him. Adam walked in, surprised to see her standing there.

"Kate, what are you doing here all alone? And why didn't come to the airport? I looked for your beautiful face amongst the crowd and then I spotted Bradley. I've missed you!" Smiling he pulled her into his arms. Holding her closely, he breathed in the familiar scent of her and felt the softness of her hair. He noticed that she was rigid in his arms. He pulled back from her and saw that her eyes were glittering with anger and tears.

"Who is Elizabeth Green, Adam?"

He stepped back as though she had hit him. She had caught him unprepared and he could tell by her face that she knew.

"Elizabeth? What on earth are you talking about, Kate? Who's Elizabeth?" he said defensively, trying to buy himself some time.

"Don't you even try to lie to me, Adam! I know you don't stay in a hotel when you're in New York. You stay with her and..." her voice faltered and broke as her rage grew. "I called the number that you told me was the Tourism Board in New York and Adam, she answered the phone! She told me that she was with you yesterday and that you had just left for Cape Town. Why, Adam? Why?" Kate shouted, pushing him hard with both hands.

"You've got it all wrong, Kate. All right, yes, I do know an Elizabeth Green in New York. She runs a big travel agency. We could get a lot of business from her. I have to take her out for dinner. You know how it all works!"

"Yes," Kate spat out the word, "I'm beginning to see how it all works. Quite clearly. Which agency does she run, Adam? Perhaps I'll recognise it?" she retorted icily. She crossed her arms against her chest to stop her hands from shaking. He searched desperately for a name, hesitating a moment too long.

"She's a doctor, isn't she, Adam? Dr Elizabeth Green. I had her checked out. So, you're still lying to me. I'm waiting for the part where you explain everything to me and show me how I've got everything wrong. I want you to take your stuff out of my apartment immediately. Do whatever you want to do but this whole thing between us is over. I can handle most things in life but betrayal – and yours above anyone else's – is not one of them. I will never trust you again."

Kate snatched up her handbag and walked to the door. She stopped briefly, turned and looked at him, and fought back her tears.

"Adam...why?" her voice wobbled. "How could you do this?" Without waiting for a reply she walked away from him, her legs shaking.

Adam sat down at his desk like a lead weight. Jesus, what a mess, he thought. Now what? He heard Kate's car tyres skidding out of the driveway and knew it was all over. Kate was normally so easy-going and he had never seen her so angry. He knew she would never forgive him. He could barely forgive himself.

From where he sat, he watched the rain sweeping across the harbour. He knew his life would not be the same without Kate in it.

His hand shook as he lit a cigarette. He inhaled the smoke deep into his lungs and shuddered. Yes, it was all over. She had caught him out. She now owned half of his company and, if this was the end of everything, then that was another nightmare to add to the whole thing.

He knew she would take everything she could. Not out of greed but out of pure fury. Inhaling again, he blamed himself. He had started out on this road of hope and it was far too late to tell her the truth. He had had his chance to tell her but he hadn't. He would now have to keep going and let her believe what she thought was the truth – and that would destroy them both. His sudden hatred for Elizabeth galvanised him. He reached for the phone, intending to phone her and call the whole thing off. He would live with the consequences, come what may. But, he couldn't do it. He had to see her again.

He closed his eyes and bit his lip. This was the closest he had been to tears for years. A life without Kate and Molly in it was unimaginable, unthinkable.

He slammed the phone down, ripped it out of its socket threw it across the room. He began to pace the office, his mind racing.

Then he made one of the most difficult decisions of his life.

It wouldn't take much more to make Kate hate him but that's what he had to do. It was the only way he could protect her now.

It was a huge gamble, but he didn't have any other choice.

"I'd like to go on a cruise," Sarah said, sounding bored. She looked up from a pile of travel brochures spread out on the table in front of her. "I hate London at this time of the year." She looked across at Tom, seeking a reaction.

"This one sounds really fabulous," she said, holding a brochure up, "It goes all around Europe and then heads for Africa. The first stop there is Cape Town, then Mombasa, Zanzibar, Singapore and Sydney where the cruise ends. We could spend some time there and then fly back to London."

Tom sighed and put down the notepad he was writing on. "Sarah," he said, barely containing his exasperation, "I can't just take off like that. It sounds like a six week cruise. I can't be away from the business for that amount of time."

Sarah frowned and threw the brochure at him in frustration. It fell on the sitting room floor between them. "Tom, you travel all the time. Don't you think it would be nice if we could do it together when it's not tied to your business? I'm sick of this weather. Every day it's grey and depressing. Besides," she tried another tack, "it's our twenty-fourth wedding anniversary next month. We should do something to celebrate the fact that we've been together that long. If you can't take that much time off then maybe we can get off in Mombasa or Singapore and fly back?"

Tom turned his head and looked out of the rain-splattered window. The clouds outside looked bruised. A cruise with Sarah was the last thing he needed. He saw the wind pick up. It was grey and depressing, he had to admit.

Africa. Without having to try very hard, his thoughts went back to the last time he had seen Kate in Cape Town. Even to this day, he felt appalled at the way he had left her without so much as a goodbye, or even an explanation. He had wrestled with his conscience for days afterwards, desperate to talk to her, to explain things. Back in London, after his safari with Sarah, he had made several calls to Kate, but she had refused to take any of them. A leaf smacked against the glass of the window and clung to the glass, startling him.

Tom turned back from the window and looked wearily at his wife. Time had not been kind to her. Her hair was thinner now and shot with grey. She had gained weight and her face was puffy and lined with years of heavy drinking.

"Well, what do you think?" Sarah demanded, seeing she had his attention back. "The cruise leaves in eight weeks' time. That gives you plenty of time to sort your business out, doesn't it? We'll only be gone for three or four weeks, depending on where you want to get off."

Resigned, he nodded his head. "Fine, Sarah. Go ahead and book the cruise but make sure we only go as far as Mombasa. I can't be away any longer than that." What he didn't say was that any longer than that in her company would be too much for him to handle. He was grateful that his business demanded that he travelled as much as he did. It was the only way he had stayed married to her. He stood and went to the kitchen, pouring them both a glass of wine.

Sarah watched him suspiciously and took a long sip from her wine glass. That damn woman, she thought. She wondered if he had had an affair with Kate. Her affairs had given him ample opportunity and reason to do the same thing.

She had found out about Kate during one of their blistering rows. Sarah had been drunk and had taunted him, trying to get some sort of reaction from him. Instead of the usual disinterest, he had finally admitted to her that whilst she had been busy with her affairs, he had met someone. Surprised to have finally had a reaction out of him, she punished herself by asking who this other woman was. "Kate," he had said simply. In that one word, Sarah knew that Kate had meant far more to her husband than he was letting on. Despite her prodding and prying, he didn't say any more about her. Sarah felt so threatened by the unspoken depth of feeling she sensed that she never mentioned it again.

Maybe Kate had been married when they met. Whatever the reason, she knew that when he went quiet in that way, that he was thinking about her. Sarah hated her for that; he was her husband but that damn woman had somehow managed to capture his heart, and wouldn't let go.

Chapter Twenty-One

S IX WEEKS HAD PASSED since her bitter confrontation with Adam. Each day, Kate had gone into the office they shared together. She had nowhere else to go. She listened to him on the telephone, laughing and joking and watched him, aghast. How could it have come to this? It was as if ten years had never happened, as if they had never existed together.

Four weeks ago she had come into the office and found that it had been divided by a dry wall. It had been completed overnight. There were two doors to their previously large spacious office and now they both had a private entrance. Adam had blocked her off, cut her out of his view. Luca had come to the office once or twice but had found the atmosphere so tense and volatile that he now chose to meet Adam in the bar around the corner. Day after day Kate had sat in stony silence trying to work out a plan for the future. The wall was the last straw.

The lawyers and accountants had come up with various suggestions for splitting up the company, all rejected by Kate.

Earlier that year they had booked to go to the London travel show. The situation had been impossible to get out of or change in any way. Kate now sat next to Adam on the flight there. Neither spoke to each other. This is probably the last time I will fly with him, she thought miserably. Desperately, she turned to him.

"Adam, we've slowly managed to build up a good company again. What will happen to all the people we employ if we tear it all apart? Is there any way we could try and put this back together? Despite everything, I still love you. You've hurt me badly, more than I can tell you, but I can't imagine my life without you in it. Please think about it. Please don't leave me…please."

Adam kept his eyes trained on the back of the seat in front of him. He turned his gaze to look at her. Her large amber eyes were filled with tears. "Kate, get yourself a life. I have a new lover. I don't want you anymore. I don't need you in the business. Luca has turned out to be an excellent partner. I just don't need you anymore. I don't love you anymore. It's over. Finished." He looked away quickly so that she wouldn't see the pain in his own eyes, or witness the terrible pain in hers, as he delivered the final blow.

Kate fell back as though she had been hit. All the air was knocked out of her and she couldn't breathe. Tears began to stream down her face and she knew that if she didn't move that she would start to sob for air and would draw attention to herself. She couldn't bear to look any more foolish in front of him. She rushed blindly to the toilet. When she came out, he had moved to a different seat.

She would never forget the agony of that show in London. Kate had pretended to their colleagues in the travel business that everything was fine. She couldn't help remembering all the previous shows when they had waited for the end of the last appointment before making excuses not to attend the endless dinners and cocktail parties. They had just wanted to get away and be with each other.

This time, she manned the stand with him, her face frozen in misery. Adam laughed and smiled as normal beside her, but not with her. Not being able to stand his indifference to her any longer, she chose to walk around the show instead. She passed three days wandering blindly around the vast halls, frequently being stopped by someone who recognised her but on the whole, being left entirely alone.

On his way back to the office after a lunch meeting, Tom saw the advertising for the annual travel show. His afternoon was free and on impulse, he decided he would go to see if Kate was there. He took the opportunity that presented itself.

Navigating his way through the crowds, he came to the African section of the hall. He wandered looking for her, but after an hour he gave up and left, sorely disappointed. He hadn't really known what he would do had he seen her. He had had no intention of talking with her, feeling sure that she would cut him dead. He just wanted to see her, needed to see her. He had made a promise to himself that he wouldn't approach her. Too much time had passed and he didn't want to complicate his, or her, life. If she had wanted to see him over the years, she would have found him. She knew the name of his company and that he was based in London. He chastised himself and wondered for the hundredth time why he was still thinking about her. She obviously had no interest in him after what had happened in Cape Town, and he couldn't blame her for that. With a heavy heart, he walked back through the crowds. Tomorrow he and Sarah would set sail on their cruise. Miserably he plucked a brochure advertising cruises from one of the stands. When he got outside he threw it in a rubbish bin.

The days at that show were very hard. Kate would have done anything to get Adam back had he shown one shred of interest in her. Her fury and anger had been replaced by hurt and neediness. She couldn't believe he felt nothing for her and every day she hoped there would be some crack in his icy cool that would let her in again. She hoped in vain.

At the end of each day, they would get into a taxi together and return to the hotel, the air heavy and silent between them. He would head for the bar and leave her standing in the foyer. Every night it hurt as much as the first night he had done it. She would numbly stumble to her room and cry.

In the weeks beforehand and in those endless days in London, she had thought long and hard about their relationship. He had cheated on her but, she reasoned, she could forgive him that. She could forgive him anything, just to have him back in her life. The days were long and empty without him and the nights even longer. She imagined him going to all the parties without her, doing all the things he had never wanted to do when she was with him. After the third day and in total despair, she changed her flight and went back to Cape Town.

Finally accepting that he was never going to come back to her and after he had made it clear that he wanted to buy her out of the company,

Kate had no choice but to go ahead with it. His lawyer put together a package, convinced she would accept it and go quietly. However, she was incensed with the offer. What irked her most was the fact that he would get the company, retain all the business and carry on with his life, unaltered and with his new woman.

In the meeting, where she had been presented with the package, she and Adam sat surrounded by his lawyer and their accountants. The papers were spread out in front of her, ready for her signature. Kate looked steadily across at Adam, who was studying his nails, avoiding looking at her. She felt the anger rise inside of her. She pushed her chair back with such force that it tipped over, and she stood up unsteadily. Even Adam was jolted from his studiousness to look at her.

"No, absolutely not! I will not sign it. I need more time to think about this and I want my lawyer here before I sign anything," she said angrily, her voice shaking with the effort. She needed David Warner to help her undo what he had set in place for her when he had insisted she took fifty per cent of the company.

The following day David arrived on the afternoon flight. He tried to hide his shock at seeing Kate so thin and pale.

"Come on, Kate," he said, "let's go through our plan and afterwards I'll take you out for dinner. You need some food, some ammunition, for the fight ahead. I'm meeting Adam tomorrow with the amended deal and the way I would like to see it structured."

Kate felt herself let go. With David there, everything would be all right. But she knew that it wouldn't be. That nothing would ever be all right again.

Stuck in the annual December traffic jam surrounded by the hordes of tourists who fought to get themselves to the beaches, Kate thought ahead to the meeting that was going to take place that morning. It was scorching hot. She put the roof of the car down trying to find a breeze in the still air. After not moving more than an inch or two, Kate edged forward until she could turn right up a side street and take what she hoped would be a faster route to David's hotel. At the top of that street she made to turn left and hit a second traffic jam. "Dammit," she exclaimed, glancing quickly at her watch. Then, with a sudden dawning of horror, she realised she was caught right beneath the balcony of

Adam's apartment. Glancing up with morbid curiosity, she saw him with a woman. They were sitting apart from one another but looked close enough from where she sat. She was filled with fury. Was he living with her now? Was that Elizabeth? Glancing around in sudden fear of being seen – in particular by them – she pushed the button to get the roof of her car back up.

Later that morning, she and David drove to the office in her car. David went into the office with the offer Kate would accept to buy her out of the company. She sat in the hot car, drumming her fingers on the steering wheel. She felt her fury tight across her chest.

David returned to the car twenty minutes later with Adam's offer.

Kate scanned it quickly. "Double it, David. Double the price of buying me out and take it back to him."

Three times Kate sent David back. On the fourth occasion, even she felt impressed with the final figure Adam was prepared to pay to eliminate her from his life. With a shaking hand she signed the document, the words blurring in front of her.

She returned to the office a few days later, for the last time, packed up her things and said her goodbyes. As she was about to leave the accountant came out of his office to stop her.

"I'm sorry, Kate. I need your company credit cards."

Her breath caught in her throat. It was all becoming real now. This was it. She was out of the company.

"You won't be able to use any of the company accounts any more either, I'm sorry; it's a direct order from Adam."

With as much dignity as she could muster, she handed over the credit cards and walked to her car.

All gone, she thought. All those years of my life. She felt as though the slightest knock could unhinge her. She had lost her home, the man she loved, her business, and soon, her daughter.

Had Kate looked up, she would have seen that up above in the endless blue expanse of the sky, a falcon circling slowly overhead.

Molly knocked softly on her mother's bedroom door. She had come home last night and found Kate crying on the sofa. Kate had always seemed so strong and brave, even over the past few months when everything was going so badly wrong. To have found her like that had been a shock. Molly had sat beside her and stroked Kate's hand, unsure of what to say.

Molly knocked again and quietly pushed the door open. Sunshine filled the room and she blinked at the empty bed. Kate was curled up in the corner of the room on her sofa, crying as though her heart would break.

"Can you get up, mummy? Can I get you into bed?" Molly said, starting to cry.

"No… I can't," Kate whispered distraughtly.

Molly covered her with a duvet and went to call their family doctor. Her voice shook as she explained the situation.

Hours later, Kate was in a bed in the hospital, heavily sedated. Molly filled Dr Williams in on all that had taken place over the past few months. He shook his head as he watched Kate sleep. Adam had sworn him to secrecy on his last appointment but he still felt that it was the wrong decision especially as he could now see, with his own eyes, the effect Adam's decision was having on Kate. He turned to Molly who was watching him anxiously.

"Molly, your mother is having a nervous breakdown. The human mind and body can only take so much." Dr Williams paused and looked at Molly. He could see that she looked scared. He had been Molly's doctor her whole life and had seen her through measles, re-occurring tonsillitis and a host of other childhood ailments. He put his arm around her and squeezed her shoulders reassuringly. "You're off to London in a few weeks, aren't you?"

Molly nodded miserably, more frightened now than she had ever been in her life. Seeing her mother so broken and unhappy was a shock to her.

"Don't worry, I'll have her back on her feet by then. I promise." He looked at Kate again, trying to hide the worried look on his face. "Come on, Molly, let's leave her to sleep. That's the best thing she can do right now. You can come back tomorrow to see her." They left the room and he watched Molly walk away down the corridor. He went back into Kate's room. He knew he had to tell her but he simply didn't know how to do it. He knew she was in her early forties and had taken a battering emotionally. He sat down and took her hand in his and tried to figure out the best way to tell her that she was pregnant. He decided to wait until Molly had left for England before he told her.

Kate slept almost all of the time she was in hospital. When she wasn't asleep, she stared out of the window, her mind completely still. On the fourth day, she woke up feeling stronger and decided to check herself out. Molly was leaving in two weeks' time and she had to help her get ready. She wanted to spend the last precious days with her daughter, wanting her to have a memory of her as she had been, and not this person she had become.

The two weeks passed in a blur for them both. On the evening Molly was leaving, Kate drove her to the airport with a heavy heart; her little girl was leaving home. Kate bit hard on her lip to stop herself crying. Molly sat quietly next to her, worrying how Kate would cope on her own.

Once Molly was checked in, they both walked slowly towards the departure gates. Kate hugged her daughter fiercely, both of them crying. "Go well, darling. Be brave, be happy. I'm here if you need anything."

"Will you be all right?" Molly asked anxiously.

"Of course I will be. I'm going to take on new projects, keep myself busy and be thinking of you when I'm not. Now, off you go, they're calling your flight." With a wobbly smile, Molly hugged Kate tightly and hurried away.

Kate drove away from the airport, managing to keep her tears at bay. She drove to her favourite lookout spot overlooking the ocean, and parked her car. She got out and sat on the bonnet, wrapping her arms tightly around her body. She had often seen airplanes from this spot when she had sat up there before. She knew from Adam that the pilot took this route as it offered tourists a final scenic sweep of the city.

She heard the great jet engines in the distance and glanced at her watch. That would be Molly's London flight. The airplane lights came into view appearing out of the black night. She watched as it gained height, banked in an arc and began its journey north to England. She felt her throat tighten and her eyes burned with the promise of hot uncontrollable tears.

"Goodbye, Molly," she called into the night air, half lifting her arm in a wave before pressing her hand to her mouth, the tears already coursing down her cheeks and over her fingers. My life will be so much emptier without you in it, my darling girl, she said to herself. She watched the pulsing tail and wing lights fading into the night, and then there was silence.

She got back into the car, put her head on the steering wheel and wept.

Kate woke early the next morning. Her eyes were puffy and gritty from crying. She lay on her back and stared at the ceiling. Her life felt bottomless. Molly had gone. Adam had gone. The business had gone. She had absolutely nothing.

Wearily she got out of bed and pulled on her clothes from the day before. She wandered through her apartment, finding it bigger and emptier. She sat on Molly's bed and looked around. A hockey stick stood forlornly in the corner with her roller skates. The wardrobe door stood open with just a few clothes left hanging in it, the empty coat hangers now abandoned.

No-one can prepare you for this, she thought.

She made herself a cup of coffee and went to sit on the balcony in the sunshine. With no office to go to anymore and with no job, she wondered how she would fill the hours in the day until something came along. She knew something would eventually, and that gave her hope. She had put feelers out for consultancy positions over the past weeks but, so far, nothing had materialised. She wondered whether the news of her nervous breakdown had trickled through the industry. She knew the news about her and Adam would surely have.

She stared out to sea, unable to make any decisions about anything.

When the sun became too hot to sit out in, Kate went indoors. She looked at herself in the mirror and didn't like what she saw. She needed to get out. She pulled on a baseball cap, put on a pair of her largest sunglasses, clipped on her earrings, and went to sit in her car. She didn't know what to do or where to go. She started the car and headed out of her driveway. I'll just drive for a while, she told herself. After twenty minutes, she found herself at the Waterfront, the huge shopping and hotel complex in the old Cape Town harbour. Autopilot, she thought to herself. How many weekends had she and Molly spent here? How many evenings with Adam?

She tried to not look for him amongst the shopping throngs but she did.

Tom wandered through the Waterfront, trying to decide on a restaurant. The ship was leaving Cape Town early that evening. Sarah had decided to take one of the tours offered around the city. Tom had preferred to walk around the busy harbour. He found a seafood restaurant that looked promising. It was busy and full. The sun was hot so he volunteered to eat inside where it was cooler. Almost everyone else was out on the terrace. Once seated, he asked the waiter what he recommended and made a decision based on that. He waited for his bottle of water to arrive.

It really was busy. He had learned over the years that one of the most enjoyable pastimes on his travels was to watch the people around him. In restaurants and airports, especially; places where he normally found himself alone. After his lunch, he was leafing through a book he had bought earlier when he heard a chair fall. He glanced up startled, and saw that a woman was hurriedly trying to place it upright. She looked as though she was on her way out. As she righted it, the handbag beneath her arm slipped and fell to the floor. He bent down and retrieved the bag for her, handing it to her as she passed. She mumbled her thanks and hurried past.

When he had paid the bill, he made to leave but his eye caught sight of something on the floor. He bent down and picked up a simple clip-on earring. The crowds in the restaurant had thinned and there were no fellow diners around. He wondered whether it had fallen out of the woman's handbag. He untangled a strand of blonde hair from the earring and slipped it into his pocket.

Cape Town lay bathed in a soft pink glow, the evening lights beginning to sparkle like jewels, in a sumptuous jewellery box, the famous mountain now slightly diminished by the majesty of the ship's graceful carriage and its own cascading lights.

As the ship pulled slowly away from the quay, Tom gazed at the mountain, watching the tiny cable car skimming down its great side. He looked down and watched the crowd below. He looked out at the harbour and watched the progress of a tall slim woman, as she walked along the quayside. Her walk was slow and steady as she made her way to the small outside bar where she sat down and ordered something from the waiter.

A breeze blew her long hair away from her face. He thought his heart would stop beating. His fingers tightened on the ship's rail. He only just stopped himself calling out her name. His heart hammered in his chest as he watched. She turned her head, as if sensing him, and looked up; seeing only hundreds of passengers. She didn't see him there, staring intently at her.

"Is that you, Kate?" he said incredulously, cursing himself for leaving the binoculars in the cabin.

He heard the change of rhythm in the great engines, rumbling and vibrating as the ship prepared to head out to sea. He watched her, willing her to look up again and see him standing there.

She sat quite still, a glass of wine on the table in front of her, a cigarette held motionless between her fingers. She watched the ship and the passengers crowding around the rails.

Kate reached for her wine. "Oh God, I wish I was on that ship," she whispered. "I need to get away, go somewhere completely different and get out of this town with all its memories."

She turned and watched as the big mountain turned slate grey then disappeared into the darkness of the night, the massive outline hidden by the black sky. Her tears slithered down to her mouth and into the wine. She knew she had to find her way back to reality before she became a spectator of her own life. She had to accept all that had happened. It would be a long journey and she would be alone, without Adam or Molly. She watched the fading lights of the ship until they tipped over the horizon.

"I think back on those times with you," she whispered softly. "You consumed my every moment, Adam. Now there is only the empty nothingness of the long evenings ahead and the numbing reality, with everything sucked and drained out of the day. And another week is gone. You're never coming back to me, are you? At night I lie consumed, staring into the night, I torture myself with images of you lying in someone else's arms, all of me forgotten." She sipped her wine and looked into the dark night, alone with her memories.

Tom stood at the stern of the ship. The ship ploughed through the inky waters, kicking up silver spray as the mighty engines relentlessly pulled him further away from her. Wearily he looked up at the blanket of stars overhead. Had the woman sitting alone at the table been Kate? He wasn't sure, she had been too far away to see clearly, and he hadn't seen her for twelve years.

He turned and made his way back to their cabin, dreading the evening ahead and all the evenings that would follow with Sarah.

Chapter Twenty-Two

KATE WANDERED through the quaint cobbled streets of Antibes, enjoying the bustle of the small seaside town. Lucy had dropped her off and promised to pick her up before it got too hot.

"There are some gorgeous little shops in Antibes," Lucy had told her. "You need to go up all the side streets to find them. There are loads of tourists around at the moment but they are more inclined to promenade along the rue de la Republique where all the cafes are. If it gets too hot go to Place Nationale; there's a little hotel there that's always cool and shady. That's where I'll pick you up. Oh, and watch out for dog poo – it's everywhere! It's one of the few downsides of living in this neck of the woods. That and noisy mopeds."

Kate had been walking through the town all morning. She had fallen in love with the market and bought lots of fresh food for lunch. Lucy had been right about the shops. She glanced at her watch and decided to stop for a coffee. She found the hotel Lucy had mentioned and sank gratefully into a chair, her bags piled up on either side of her. Small shops lined the quadrant and in its centre were a couple of outdoor restaurants. The leafy trees surrounding the square offered much-needed shade from the sun. In the distance she could see the old Antibes fort and the tri-coloured French flag giving a half-hearted flutter every now and then when a breeze lifted it. She ordered her coffee and watched the people wandering past. She had always loved her and Adam's trips to France. She loved the French people and their way of life, so very different from hers. She felt the baby move inside her and shifted in her chair. The news of the pregnancy had been a shock. For many months it was hard to tell that she was pregnant with her being so thin. She had wrestled with her emotions and then come up with a plan. She had called Lucy.

They discussed the future at great length. Kate was not in any position to bring up another child and Lucy had been unsuccessful at falling pregnant. Jean-Philippe, Lucy and Kate, swapped phone calls for a week before they finally agreed. Adam's child would be brought up by them. Three months before the baby was due, Kate flew to France.

Kate looked at the bags full of baby clothes that she had bought that morning. It felt strange. It was not something she had anticipated would happen again. It was agreed that the baby would remain a secret between all of them. Not even Molly would be told the truth. Kate wondered how it would feel to hand over her child and her heart ached at the thought. But she had thought long and hard about it over the past few months, and it was the only solution. She had a consultancy project coming up in Kenya and she didn't want anyone to know about Adam's child, least of all Adam.

She felt the tears welling up again. Oh God Adam, we have a child.

Chapter Twenty-Three

K ATE COLLECTED HER FILES and put them in her briefcase. She had enjoyed working with the management of Pelican Place, in Kenya, for the past two weeks. The five-year marketing plan had been well-received and if they followed her plan, they would soon be up and running.

That evening the owner of the lodge, Robert Smart, had joined her for dinner. He had offered her a two-year contract to manage and run Pelican Place. He had checked out her CV and was suitably impressed with the feedback he had received.

Back in her room that night she had run through the contract. She would have free rein over refurbishing it to a standard she thought would be suitable. She tapped her pen on the table next to the bed, already imagining how great she could make this lodge look. After all, she recalled dryly, she had been to hundreds of them over the past ten years; she knew what did and didn't work. It would mean she could get away from Cape Town and not run the risk of seeing Adam again. The lease on her flat there was almost up and she could just put her things in storage until she decided where her future might lie.

She signed the contract with a flourish. It was just what she needed – a new start in a new country. But first she had to return to Cape Town and pack up what was left of her life there.

Luca pulled up outside Kate's apartment. He had come to say goodbye to her. He had often seen Kate around after it had all ended. Either driving along in her car, or sitting alone at her favourite restaurant at the Waterfront. He had not wanted to be in the middle of the whole sorry situation. It saddened him to see her looking so unhappy but he had seen the end coming months ago. On the outside she seemed fine, but he had heard about her breakdown and how she ended up in hospital.

Helpless to do anything, Luca watched her from a distance. He saw her at cocktail parties and launches; he watched her watching the crowds, always looking for Adam. Catching sight of him, she would flee from the room. Once Luca had tried to catch up with her, but seeing her with her head down on the steering wheel of her car, he decided not to intrude.

Now Kate sat on the end of her bed, looking at the two boxes of clothes, four boxes of books and her suitcase; that was all she had left. Everything else she had sold.

"Is this all you are taking?' said Luca, leaning against the wardrobe.

"Yes, I don't want anything more. I want a new life, a new beginning, and all my stuff has too many memories. The contents of the apartment have been sold. I'm going to put some things in storage and then I'm moving on, Luca, getting as far away as I possibly can. I'm not even going to tell you where I'm going, but I am, I'm going. It feels liberating to sell everything off, like a snake shedding its skin.

"I don't want to be here anymore. I'm tired of always looking for a glimpse of him and if I do see him driving past, or in a bar, or at a restaurant, I fall apart. It hurts too much, Luca. I won't have to go to any more damn cocktail parties and endure the pitying looks, or tolerate the stilted conversation, when everyone is trying not to say his name in front of me. I will never come back to Cape Town. I thought I would be stronger, and more able to deal with things. But when I see him around town, everything comes tumbling back again. I don't want to live like this anymore, Luca. It's too difficult. He's unlikely to leave town and so it has to be me."

Luca watched her carefully, thinking of all the good times they had shared together, how bitterly it had all ended and the part he knew he had played in it.

"I'm thinking of leaving South Africa myself, Kate. I thought I might take a look at Uganda. There are some interesting business opportunities there and I want to check things out. They're always looking for bush pilots. I might even set up my own show. So, if you ever find yourself in that neck of the woods, keep a lookout for me." He grinned at her.

Luca pulled her to her feet and into his arms. "Be happy with your new life and let go of Adam. You'll never get him back; he's gone from you, Kate. One day you'll understand…"

He felt her tremble. She looked up at him and tears shimmered in her eyes. "You're right and I will let go of him, but it was good wasn't it? We all had a lot of fun together. I honestly thought it would go on forever. But you go off to Uganda and have a big adventure. I'll miss you. I know you hate e-mail and it will be difficult to communicate, but let's try and keep in touch?"

She turned back to her packing. "What does Adam think of you going off to Uganda?" she said over her shoulder, then shook her head. "Sorry, it's none of my business, and I know you won't tell me, with your misguided loyalties. Forget I even asked."

He looked into her amber eyes and dipping his head he kissed her roughly and left the room. She called after him.

"Hey, Luca! How far can falcons fly?" He turned back and raised his eyebrow.

"As far as they want, Kate." Smiling, he got into his car and with a wave he drove away from her.

Kate watched the airport buildings speeding past her window. She felt the powerful surge of the mighty engines as they pulled the aircraft up into the black night. She took a last look at Cape Town glittering below her, knowing she would never return. The aircraft banked slowly and she whispered goodbye to the country that had given her the greatest happiness and the greatest pain she had ever known.

I've blocked and buried how we ended in this beautiful city, this beautiful country, she said to herself. My new life is waiting for me; as far away from you as I can possibly get. I have cut the ties, Adam, and now I'm leaving you far behind. I will always love you. You gave me all those years of happiness. We were so good together, but now – it's time to say goodbye.

The tears came before she could stop them. She pressed her forehead against the window and let them come. "Goodbye, Adam," she whispered, "Goodbye."

Adam watched the night sky from the lookout point. He heard the roar of the jet. He knew that Kate was on that flight. He covered his face with his hands, unable to look up; she was leaving. His shoulders heaved with emotion. He had achieved what he had set out to do, but it didn't make things any easier. It was finally over – he had driven her away.

He drove to Luca's apartment where they had arranged to meet. Luca wanted to discuss the second part of their plan, and with Kate now safely out of the picture they could move ahead with it.

Chapter Twenty-Four

KATE PUT DOWN THE PAPERS she was working on and turned off the computer. It was time for her to check Pelican Place whilst the guests were out on a game drive, and ensure that everything was perfect for when they returned.

She inspected each room, making sure there was a chilled bottle of white wine, fresh towels, that the bathrooms were clean and that the beds were turned down. She had changed the décor entirely. The rooms were high maintenance: when the wind blew across the plains there would be dust everywhere, but it was well worth the finished look, which was luxurious, inviting, and very romantic. The ceiling fans she had installed in each room kept them fresh and cool, even during the searing heat of the day. The bathrooms were spacious and had double basins and a claw footed bath. There were outside showers, which were very popular with the guests, even when it rained. She had replaced the single beds with big double ones and ensured there were large soft bath towels and snug luxurious bathrobes. All were crisply white. Kate had the toiletries flown in from England, which was an expensive exercise but it added to the sense of opulence.

Outside, on the deck of each suite, were long comfortable day beds, covered in white towelling. Between them was an antique chest, binoculars and books on wildlife game and birds. Each deck had a telescope on a tripod and a small infinity pool.

After her afternoon round, she felt satisfied that everything looked perfect. She walked back to the main area of the camp. It was spread over two decks; the ground one for the lounge and bar and the upper one for the dining room which had elevated views of the lake.

She nodded to the barman, who was busy preparing the bar for the evening. He put out glasses and ice buckets, which gleamed in the soft light. Kate walked to the upper deck above, where individual tables had been laid. Silver cutlery and candlesticks had been positioned on stiff white tablecloths. She paused and held a crystal glass to the light, making sure it was spotless. Her choice of flowers that evening was yellow roses. They nestled in shallow bowls. The flowers were flown in from Naivasha every day, from a huge farm that grew them there. The guests would also find a vase full of yellow roses in their rooms that night. It was hard work to keep up the standard but her staff liked and respected her, as she did them, and they worked as hard as Kate did to keep everything looking as beautiful as it did.

Kate returned to the lower deck. The lounge looked inviting tonight, as it did every night. This was always the first space the guests would see when they came up from their tented suites for drinks and dinner. There was no artificial light at all and the entire space was candlelit. The effect was magical. Comfortable cream sofas and armchairs were grouped around a huge stone fireplace, where a fire had already been lit. There were bowls of yellow roses on every table and classical music played quietly in the background, adding the finishing touch.

Kate stood back and took a last look around. Her lodge looked fabulous. Having been to so many others over the years, she knew exactly what worked and what didn't. Pelican Place had appeared in numerous international glossy magazines over the past two years and all her bookings came from that exposure. She was booked up a year in advance and her lodge was considered one of the best not only in Kenya, but in Africa.

She heard the rumble of the safari vehicle returning to camp. Checking her watch, she was pleased to see that the game drive had been precisely three hours.

Kate hurried to the kitchen. They had a full camp tonight and the guests were always hungry after the drive.

Satisfied with the kitchen's progress and preparations, she returned to her own room. Furnished in exactly the same way as the other suites, it could be used, if absolutely necessary, by staying guests. This rarely happened though, unless reservations had overbooked the lodge. It was

Kate's private area and she liked to keep it that way. She never joined her guests in the evening, leaving that to the deputy manager and the game rangers.

Feeling content, Kate poured herself a glass of wine and stepped out onto her deck. It was a beautiful night, still and calm. The stars were fantastic, as they always were in the bush, with no artificial lights to detract from their brilliance.

She wanted to speak to Robert, the owner, about purchasing two Cessna aircraft. Having their own aircraft and pilots would bring the cost of flying the supplies into the camp down. They would also be able to use it to fly their guests in and out, instead of chartering from the company in Nairobi.

She thought back to the previous week after a day's shopping in Nairobi. The chartered plane had been two hours late and it was late afternoon when they eventually took off for the flight back to the lodge. She was the only passenger and was bringing supplies to the camp. They reached the airstrip, an hour from Pelican Place, as the sun was setting. The pilot offloaded the supplies and was anxious to get back to Nairobi before dark.

Kate was left alone on the airstrip. She scanned the horizon anxiously, waiting for the lodge vehicle to collect her. She sat on a crate of champagne as she watched and listened to the wildebeest grunting at each other as they grazed. There were thousands of them waiting to begin the great migration across the Serengeti. The night air was cooling fast. She heard the lions, a little too close for comfort, but she knew they would not be interested in her, not with all the wildebeest around. With an uncomfortable feeling that the vehicle would not be coming, she knew she needed to make a plan.

Looking around, she saw parked on the other end of the airstrip an old two-seater aircraft, which had obviously not been used in years. She looked through the supplies around her. Grabbing some candles, a bottle of champagne and a packet of biscuits, she headed towards the aircraft, picking up a rock on the way. As she had anticipated, the doors were locked. Climbing up on the wing with the rock, she broke the pilot's window, put her hand inside and unlocked the door. She climbed in and tried to get settled. It was going to be an uncomfortable night but at least she would be safe.

Sitting back in the seat and watching as night fell and the stars began to appear across the sky, she opened the bottle of champagne and nibbled on the biscuits. The lodge knew that there would be no flights after dark. As they had arrived so late, she had missed the pick-up. They would presume she would be coming in on the first flight the next morning. Darkness fell quickly. She was conscious of being surrounded by animals. She could hear them and smell them.

Resigned, she settled back. She wasn't nervous but she would be happy to see the sun come up in the morning.

Kate didn't sleep much and when the sun finally came up, she crawled out of the plane, stretching her aching body. In the distance, she saw a swirl of dust and prayed that it would be the vehicle from the lodge.

Paul, her deputy manager, pulled up in a cloud of dust.

"They radioed this morning to let us know you came in last night," he told her. "The pilot arrived back too late and the radio tower had been closed so they didn't radio to tell us. Kate, where did you sleep?"

Kate indicated the old plane. "Thank God that was here, Paul. If it hadn't it would have been a very dangerous night. Thank goodness I'm not a paying guest! If I was an American guest, I would sue the lodge. We really can't have this happen again."

Now she leaned back in her chair and looked up at the stars. A lion roared in the distance calling his pride together for the night's hunting. She shivered, trying to stave off the memories of Adam. She thought instead about Lucy. Her son would be three tomorrow. Lucy had called him Edward and had been with her when he was born at their home. Kate had held him briefly and then handed him to her sister. Two days later she left France and returned to Africa. It was hard to watch Jean-Philippe and Lucy with him and know she mustn't hold him. It was agreed that only Lucy would refer to him as her son. It had not been an easy thing to do but that was the deal.

She spoke to Lucy often and always asked after Edward. In time it became easier but she had not seen either Lucy or Edward for three years and she had not asked for any photographs. A lion roared again, closer this time. Her contract at the lodge was due to end, although Robert was keen for her to stay on for a further two years.

Adam. She had tried everything to get him out of her mind but he still strayed back in. Despite her success, she was lonely. There had been no-one else and for this she was grateful. The thrill of being so much in love was something she desperately missed but once had been enough. She had decided never to let herself be so vulnerable again. Sometimes she thought that loneliness was worse than death. The world seemed dull and empty without Adam in it. She took another sip of her wine, the memories jostling for position. She tried not to think of how it had all ended. She tried to remember only the good times, but it didn't always work that way. Being swamped and overwhelmed with grief for so long wasn't something she ever wanted to go through again.

It would have been far less painful if he had died, she thought. That would have been easier to accept. It would have been better than this.

Close by a hyena giggled, a sound she had always disliked. She squinted into the dark, trying to see what else was out there. The elephants were down in the dry river bed to her left, and a large herd of impala grazed some metres away. There was a full moon that night. Without warning, a large male rhinoceros emerged from behind a bush. Kate caught her breath. They moved so silently when they wanted to. The moonlight turned its normally dull grey body to silver. He was magnificent. She watched him graze and thought about the offer she had been made. It would take her far away from here. It was an attractive four-year contract with a prestigious British company; they wanted to grow their company and include photographic safaris. It appealed to her.

There were no wild animals in New York City, only predatory females like Doctor Elizabeth Green. Foremost in her mind was that it would take her even further away from Adam. With a final look at the rhino, she picked up her glass and went back inside. She had made up her mind.

Chapter Twenty-Five

Molly

THE ATMOSPHERE AT HOME, before I left, had been awful – terrible, in fact. Kate walked around like a ghost, or she sat and stared out of the window, completely lost to me. I knew she was not really watching anything in particular. Just thinking about him.

So my greatest fear had come about, it was all over between them. She looked so sad on her own; she hadn't told me much about what really happened, just that it was all over and she had sold her shares in the company. Sometimes I thought she was unaware that I was in the same room, so deep was her grief for Adam.

She had always been so strong and in control of everything. Nothing had ever seemed to pull her down, but he had. I went with her to the hospital and sat by her bed for hours; she looked suddenly fragile. I thought about all the happy years we had shared, and Adam was included in that. But now I hated him with such fury, for what he had done to her.

When she came out of the hospital we had our last Christmas together. She really made an effort to make it happy. I desperately needed to know that she was going to be all right on her own. She told me she had various ideas about starting another business and, depending on how Cape Town felt without me in it, she might even consider moving to another country, maybe Kenya. Although she wasn't the same as before, I saw her starting to fight back from the circumstances she now found herself in.

The day we had both dreaded came all too soon. She took me to the airport and we stood there awkwardly, neither one of us wanting to say much. In a way it was a relief when my flight was called. We hugged each other fiercely and then I let her go, before she could see that my heart was breaking too. It was one of the most difficult things I have ever had to do.

I got on with my life in London. I had decided against going to University – I wanted to study interior design. Through her many contacts Kate had arranged for me to study at one of the great interior design companies in Chelsea Harbour. I rented a tiny flat and got on with my life, but we called each other every week. It was strange not to be in Africa, a place I had known all my life and I missed it. Getting used to low grey skies was something I have not achieved, even now.

A few months after I left Cape Town, my mother went to stay with her sister in France. Lucy was finally pregnant and she wanted to spend some time with her, and be with her for the birth of the baby. I suggested going over to see them both in the summer, but apparently it was a difficult pregnancy and no visitors were allowed. I did manage to spend a few days with Lucy, Jean-Philippe and little Edward the following Christmas. He didn't look very much like either of them, but then it's sometimes difficult to tell with small babies, but they were both over the moon with their new son.

Kate found a project in Kenya which led to her being offered a great contract to actually run the lodge; it was called Pelican Place.

I could hardly pick up a magazine without seeing the lodge featured. I have been out there a few times to stay with her and it really is stunning. I was so proud of her and what she has achieved in spite of her personal pain. As far as I knew she had kept well clear of any involvement with another man. I could understand that. But it was sad nevertheless, she was such a loving person with so much love to give and no-one to give it to.

I shall cherish the memories of us sitting out on her deck, at the lodge, listening to all the nocturnal noises around us. We sat for hours and hours talking about our life together; she rarely mentioned my father, but she did tell me she had forgiven him for walking out on her, and how sorry she had been when he had been killed. They had had a few happy years together and those were the memories she wanted to remember.

Then she told me about Tom, how they had met in London, and then again some years later in Cape Town, and how attracted she had been to him. I'm not sure if she was married when she first met him, and somehow I didn't feel I should ask. Tom was an American and he lived in London. Then she had laughed and said that that was so many years ago she could hardly remember what he looked like. But I'm not sure that that was entirely true – she just didn't want to forget Adam and pushed any other man, and memory, away.

I noticed over time that she didn't mention Adam's name as often as she had done and I thought she was gradually coming to terms with everything. We were still as close as we had always been and she seemed glad I had met James. It was nothing serious at first, but now we were thinking of moving in together and I wondered how she would feel about that. Would it make her feel excluded perhaps? Envious, maybe, because of what she had lost and what I had found? But she had told me how happy she was for me, and yes, why not live together. That's what I loved about her – she never reacted like a typical mother might. So, with her blessing, James and I moved in together and he has given me the stability I so desperately needed.

Kate invited both of us out to Kenya. She had wanted James to have some sort of idea of our life in Africa, he had never been there before. It was a wonderful and memorable trip. They got on well together even though I think James found her a bit daunting at first. She was now fiercely independent again and back in control of her life; well, at least I thought she was. Every evening she would commandeer one of the safari vehicles and with our own private ranger we would set off into the bush for a game drive. I'll never forget the three of us sitting high up on the roof of the parked vehicle at sunset, a cold glass of wine in our hands, watching a huge herd of impala following a pride of lions.

"Isn't it supposed to be the other way around with the impala being followed by the lions?" James had asked puzzled.

"The impala are safer following the pride, than being in front – less chance of getting eaten that way!" Kate had laughed and raised her glass in front of her. I wasn't sure if that was a toast to the intelligence of the impala, a toast to the beautiful sunset or a toast to Adam, or a sort of salute to the fact that she had got her life back together again and could manage quite well without him. Anyway, it was an unforgettable two-week safari and I was very proud of my mother and it wasn't long before James fell under her spell.

My life with Kate has been a huge adventure, a bit like her own childhood I would imagine, but unlike her I yearned for some roots.

Gradually, over the years, I found my mother again. The laughter and fun came back into her life. She could have become bitter about things, but she didn't. Then she moved to New York City. That was something I hadn't anticipated, but she embraced it, taking everything in her stride. She loved it there and so did I. I would fly out and see her and she would meet me at the airport, laughing and waving as usual, and I allowed myself to hope once more.

Then came September 11th. Like the rest of the world I watched it all on television, unable to believe what I was seeing. I knew my mother was somewhere there, right in the middle of it. It was days before I could speak to her; the telephones and computers in the city were all down.

She survived that terrible day, but she told me she still has nightmares about it, so I'm careful never to mention what happened that day and she never talks about it. Eventually she returned to East Africa and went to live in Zanzibar. That's where everything went wrong again. I knew without any doubt at all that Adam had had something to do with what happened there – and why she had disappeared without trace.

Chapter Twenty-Six

LUCY HEARD THE TAXI pull up outside and rushed out of the front door to greet Kate. Three years was the longest they had ever been apart. They hugged each other tightly.

"Come inside, Kate, I'll sort out the taxi. Edward is hiding behind the sofa, go and introduce yourself."

Kate felt gratitude wash through her. Lucy would have guessed that meeting Edward for the first time since he was born would be emotional for her, and she was giving Kate some time alone with him.

Kate sat down on the sofa, knowing that curiosity would get the better of him eventually. "Hello Edward, come and meet your aunt," she said softly.

Shyly, he looked out from behind the back of the sofa. Kate's breath caught in her throat. He had Adam's eyes. He was almost identical with the shape of his face, his blue eyes and blond hair. She held her hand out to him and saw that it was shaking. "You are so beautiful, Edward. So beautifully perfect. Will you shake my hand and say hello?" She smiled at him.

Lucy bustled in, looking nervous.

"He only speaks French, Kate. He understands English but doesn't know how to say very much. He will, when he starts school." Lucy scooped him up and hugged him, whispering to him in French as she brushed the hair back from his face. "You could try Swahili though…" She looked anxiously at her sister, torn between her love for her and the son she was holding in her arms.

"He's lovely, Lucy. You must be so proud of him. He's even beginning to look like you," she said generously. They sat outside that evening and caught up on each other's news. Kate tried hard not to stare at her son and she avoided picking him up. She was wary of how emotional she was feeling, looking at Adam's son, their son.

They spent a week together. After a couple of days, she knew she had made the right decision. The child had brought them both so much happiness. They gave Edward security and unhampered love, which he needed and deserved.

The day before she left, Lucy and Kate went for a walk through the countryside together, leaving Edward with Jean-Philippe.

"Molly and James were here a month or so ago," Lucy said to Kate as they walked across a large field opposite the house, heading towards a small copse of trees in the distance. "James seems like a good sort and he very obviously adores her, as she does him."

"Yes, I like him. I think he is perfect for her. She's so like me in many ways. The older she gets, the more I see of myself in her. James will make a fine doctor when he graduates. Molly showed me the photographs of their apartment before they moved into it together. I thought it was awful but she has turned it into a masterpiece. I saw it before I left London to come here. She's going to make a wonderful interior designer."

They walked through the soft surroundings of the fields that were gentle and melodic in the afternoon sunshine. Kate could hear the breeze in the trees ahead and felt the sunshine on her face. She closed her eyes and instantly imagined herself back in Africa.

Lucy studied her sister, noting the dark circles underneath her eyes. She looked tired and weary.

"I'm so sorry it didn't work out with Adam. I'm sorry that it all came at such a price to you, Kate. Have you met anyone else – when you were in Kenya?"

Kate opened her eyes, shook her head and smoothly changed the subject. They turned back in the direction of the house. "I'm really looking forward to living in New York City, Luce. The company and the safari project sound as though they will keep me busy. There's a lot to do for them and I can't wait to get started."

They talked on about Kate's hopes for New York and the job and Lucy talked to her about Edward starting school and her hopes for him.

After dinner that night, Kate stood up, yawning. "The taxi will be here early tomorrow morning. Please don't bother getting up. It's an inhuman hour. I'll give Molly your love; I'm staying in London for two days before I leave for New York. Goodnight Lucy, good-night Jean-Philippe. Thank you both."

She turned to go upstairs then paused and looked back at her sister. "Would it be all right if I kissed Edward goodbye? I won't wake him, I promise."

"Yes, of course it's all right. Spend whatever time you need with him. He sleeps like a little log so he won't wake up."

Jean-Philippe reached over and took his wife's hand in his and gently wiped the tears from her eyes. He knew how hard it was for Lucy to see her beloved sister so broken and alone.

Chapter Twenty-Seven

TOM SAT NEXT TO HIS WIFE'S BED. She was very ill now. He was tired and exhausted both physically and mentally. When the cancer returned with a vengeance Sarah had begged him to take her back to America, to die in her own country.

They had returned to Cold Spring Harbour and opened up the house again. He was still involved with his security business, but he had handed the day-to-day running of it over to his senior partner. The time now was spent looking after his wife, as best he could.

Two days ago he had taken her into the hospice, where she now lay dying. He sat next to her bed, giving her as much comfort as he could. He didn't know if she was even aware that he was there. She called him softly. He moved closer to her, trying to hear what she was saying.

"I'm sorry, Tom, I've made your life so unhappy," she whispered. "Forgive me for what I did. I missed Cassie too, you know. Terribly."

He held a glass of water to her dry cracked lips, encouraging her to sip. Now she lay back again reaching for his hand. "I know it won't be long now, before I can be with Cassie. But I want you to find happiness too. I want you to go and find her. Go and find Kate. I don't want to think of you on your own now," she whispered, "Will you do that Tom?"

Sighing softly, she left him, her hand going limp in his.

He waited for the tears to come, but they didn't. He sat there with her, shocked by her final words. He had only mentioned Kate's name once to her, during a terrible row. Had she known, then, that he had stopped loving her after their daughter's death? That he had fallen in love with someone else? Through the ensuing years he had tried to be civil with his wife even though they shared separate bedrooms and had

172

done for years. Yes, he had slept with a few other women, but none of them had meant anything to him. The marriage had been a sham and they both knew that.

What a waste of two lives, he thought, as he gently covered his wife's face with a sheet and pressed the buzzer next to the bed. Yes, he was sad that her life had ended in such pain, but he grudgingly had to admit that it had taken a lot of courage for her to ask for his forgiveness and encourage him to make a new life for himself.

Tom waited in the chapel. He felt, rather than heard, the gathering of their friends and her distant family behind him. He looked with sadness at the coffin as it passed him. He knew that Sarah had been no happier than he had been, and apart from his little daughter, he had few lasting memories to live on.

Later that night he watched television, trying to distract his thoughts. Flicking through the channels, Tom saw that 'Out of Africa' was showing: that seemed good enough. The magnificent music swelled and filled his living room. The vast plains of East Africa filled the screen and opened up in front of him, the old train in the distance, chugging its way from Mombasa to Nairobi, smoke from the engine billowing into the sunset. He put his head back and closed his eyes, feeling drained.

When he woke up the film had finished. He got to his feet abruptly. With all his international connections it would be easy enough to find Kate, but he wasn't sure if that would be the right thing to do. Understandably she would be angry and disappointed with him. He had walked out on her in Cape Town.

Tom had sold the house in Cold Stream Harbour; the buyer had wanted all the furniture and fittings so it was a clean move for him. He hadn't wanted to keep any of it anyway. Once he had disposed of all Sarah's belongings, he packed a couple of boxes of his own things and had them sent on ahead of him. He closed and locked the door, walking away from his few memories, and headed out to the airport and his flight for London. He still had his apartment in Holland Park and that was where he was going.

Chapter Twenty-Eight

KATE HAD BEEN LIVING in New York City for six months. A limousine had collected her at the airport and driven her into Manhattan to the hotel on Fifth Avenue that would be home until she found a place to live. Kate had smiled at the familiar skyline.

She loved the buzz of the city; it never seemed to go quiet. There was a reassuringly loud aspect to the city with taxis honking their horns and police sirens howling through the streets. Looking out of any window at almost any time of day or night, she would always see people hurrying along the sidewalks. There was never any doubt in her mind as to where she was living. It was irascibly New York. She could define her route to work just by the smells and sounds along the way. There were drills and jackhammers that pounded on pot-holed roads and sidewalks accompanied by the stench of hot tar. There were the floral scents of fabric softener as she passed the Laundromats. The smell of food was all pervasive: from the stalls selling coffee, hot dogs, fruit smoothies, bagels or carmelised nuts to the pizza parlours and Chinese take-aways. She would feel ice-cold blasts of air conditioning as she passed the great grand stores on Fifth Avenue and know she was almost at their office building.

The store was on Madison Avenue and Kate's office was on the fifth floor of the beautiful building. It was a little chunk of England in Manhattan, she thought on her first day there. Wooden floors were partially covered by expensive rugs and there were leather wing-back chairs, oak tables and huge glass-fronted display cabinets. The fifth floor was divided into three sections: an art gallery, a book department and a safari desk. On her first day there, Kate was slightly concerned that she seemed to be the only person on the fifth floor, and glanced nervously at the art and books, hoping that someone would be handling that.

On her third day, she realised she was meant to be managing the entire floor, including art and books. Although Kate was highly skilled in her own field, she had never been involved in the world of retail. She watched elegantly clad shoppers wandering around the art gallery and book department. They always stopped at the safari desk to ask questions about Africa and what it was like there. She quickly realised that the art and the books provided an excellent opportunity for her to engage future business. Kate's enthusiasm for safaris and Africa and her impressive knowledge of the lodges and landscapes there, soon had the business rolling in.

Kate settled into the rhythm of life in the city and enjoyed the challenge of Manhattan and its inhabitants. She struggled at first to understand New Yorkers. They spoke fast and said things that made sense to them but none at all to Kate.

Her greatest challenge was managing the art gallery. The pieces were spread throughout the store and were frequently moved around to aid display.

On one of her first mornings, the phone rang. A customer who had been in the store a few weeks previously was interested in purchasing a painting by the artist Cox. Kate's heart had sunk.

"I'll call you right back," she had said, "Once I've located them and found the price." She had sat back in her chair dumbfounded. "Isn't Cox some sort of apple or potato?" she muttered to herself. The customer had told her the paintings were of grouse and that they were hanging on the third floor. Kate didn't know a grouse from a pheasant and when she went to the third floor there were no paintings of birds of any kind.

Kate ran up and down the stairs, searching every canvas for a signature with which to identify the artist. She finally found a painting of two birds flying out from amongst some dark reeds. She found the signature buried amongst them in the water. She was impressed to find out what grouse looked like. She returned upstairs and called the customer back.

"I found it. It costs $1000," she said triumphantly. She was about to ask him how he would like to pay for the piece when he demanded to know what kinds of grouse they were.

"Are they Ptarmigan or Snow Grouse? Are they Willow or Ruffed Grouse? Are they Capercaillie, Gunnison Sage or Dusky Grouse?" he asked impatiently.

Kate smiled at the memory; it had been a baptism by fire all right. A few weeks later, a taxidermist had dropped into the office to ask if he could display a piece of his work in the store. Kate had been busy with two clients who wanted to go to Botswana on safari.

"Yes, why not, send it and I'll see what I can do," she had said flippantly, turning back to her clients.

A week later, the security guard, Jon, called her and told her there was a large crate out on the sidewalk addressed to her. They had to open it because the crate was too big to get through the door.

"That's fine," she said. "Bring the contents up to me, would you?"

Half an hour later, Jon called again. Kate detected a slight note of panic in his voice. "Ma'am, you had better get down here because it's stuck in the door."

Puzzled, Kate ran downstairs. Wedged in the door was a fully grown male lion. She stifled her laughter with great difficulty. "Pull it out and try the other end," she offered. "That might work better."

The lion was navigated out with some difficulty and as Jon and two other members of staff caught their breath, they placed it on the sidewalk. People stopped and stared and shortly, a small crowd formed outside the shop. Kate looked around inside, desperate to find a solution to the problem. Her other colleagues inside the store were laughing hysterically.

Kate found a large piece of cloth and valiantly attempted to cover the lion with it. A brisk wind kept whipping the sheet up, revealing claws and teeth. Out of the corner of her eye, she saw a TV camera being set up. This will be really bad publicity, she thought frantically. "Throw the damn thing down the stairs into the basement!" Kate yelled. She had been laughing so much that she could hardly see. There was a round of applause from the crowd before it dispersed.

The lion was removed from the street but went no further than the basement. It was too large to get into the elevator or up the stairs. All the staff entered the building through the basement and the lion became the staff mascot. It was hugged and patted every morning and soon after was used as a coat stand.

A few weeks into her job the accountant came down to show her how to ring up the sales. "Don't look so worried, Kate, it's a piece of cake when you know how. What I want you to do is put it in tutorial mode and practice for a couple of hours. Just pick any credit card out of the system and use the number, but remember it must be in tutorial mode." He left her to it.

Kate randomly picked out a credit card number and started to practice. She rang up a huge safari for $120,000.00, a dozen rare books, some pieces of artwork, and a few expensive fishing rods for good measure. Satisfied she ran it all through on the card and went back to her safari desk, not giving it another thought.

A week later the accountant rushed up to her, his face ashen. "Kate, we have a customer on the line, demanding to know why the store has run up nearly $280,000.00 worth of goods on his card!"

Kate looked up startled. "I'm sure I put it in tutorial mode, honestly. Oh dear, I expect he is a bit cross, sorry." Laughing uncontrollably, Kate fled from the store and into the first bar she could find. Ordering a large martini she tried to pull herself together, but every time she thought about the outraged customer she would start laughing again. It felt good, so very good, to be laughing again. She wiped her eyes and reached for her glass.

The next morning, the cash point had been replaced with a large potted plant. Kate shrugged. That's a relief, she thought, I came here to sell safaris, not books, art, fishing rods or stuffed lions.

The safari business was going well and the company was building an excellent reputation as an operator. Kate's talent for designing safaris that perfectly suited their up-market clients was the company's signature strength.

The London travel show was something Kate dreaded but she knew that the company would not accept her refusal to go. She was expected to attend and learn about any new game lodges that had come into the marketplace. The flight from New York began its final descent into London Heathrow. Kate looked down at the green fields of England and sighed. She had left New York reluctantly. She knew that Adam would be in London. He attended the show every year without fail. How was she going to avoid seeing him? She fastened her seat belt; she would spend one day, and one day only, at the travel exhibition.

Kate walked through the doors of the enormous exhibition centre and took a deep breath. It was hot and crowded already. Despite herself, she was looking forward to seeing her friends and colleagues from South and East Africa. With slight trepidation, she walked towards the African hall.

She knew he would be there. A part of her wanted to see him as much as a part of her didn't. She saw his company – what used to be *their* company – listed above the stand. She breathed a sigh of relief; there was no sign of Adam. After an hour or so, Kate went in to the ladies room. As she came out of the cubicle, she saw a woman combing her hair and touching up her make-up in the mirror. As Kate washed her hands, she smiled at her. The woman turned and Kate caught sight of her name badge. Jessica Theron. She was with Adam's company.

Kate felt an old rage build up inside of her. Maybe this woman had replaced her. Her smile disappeared. She wanted to slap the woman's face. All the memories came swirling back and she felt the familiar weight of loss and despair.

Kate walked along the edge of the stands, trying to extricate herself from the hall. Then she saw him. Adam. He was walking towards her and he was smiling. Kate's heart fluttered. She felt her smile freeze as he walked quickly past her. His smile hadn't been for her after all.

Kate fled from the exhibition hall, and hailed a taxi. Returning to the hotel where she had stayed on her trip to London twenty years previously, she walked into the familiar surroundings of the bar. It was glass-fronted and looked out onto Hyde Park. Sipping a drink, she looked out at the grey, cold afternoon. She remembered meeting Tom there all those years ago. What would he have made of my life, she wondered? He was so grounded, so sure of where he was going in life. She wondered where Tom was living. Then she squashed any thoughts of him to the back of her mind. He had not been honest with her when they had met again in Cape Town. Quite obviously he was after some kind of affair whilst he had his wife stashed away in the hotel room. She had spent days trying to work out what had happened, why Tom had been so eager to have her back in his life on a permanent basis; he had told her he loved her, wanted to marry her. To this day she was puzzled as to what had made him run out on her. It wasn't the sort of thing she thought he would ever do, he was too decent and honest; but then, maybe she had been wrong. She had certainly been wrong about Adam after all.

She looked at the bracelet on her wrist; she had not taken if off since the day Tom had given it to her.

After the first year, Kate found contentment in her life. She had a wonderful apartment on 5th Avenue and she enjoyed her social life, the events at the store, the cocktail parties and the new friends she was making. Spring and then summer came to New York.

Molly came to visit twice a year and spent most of August with Kate. It was early September and Kate had seen Molly off, back to London on a Friday. She walked through the streets of Manhattan feeling sad. She remembered Molly's smiling face in the back of the taxi as she waved goodbye. It never got any easier saying goodbye to her. She spent the weekend walking the city and enjoying the last of the summer heat.

On Tuesday, Kate woke to a glorious day. The sky was blue and clear with bright sunshine. It was the best kind of New York day. She showered and dressed then checked her briefcase. She had an appointment downtown with the company advertising agency. Humming happily she flagged a taxi down and got in. Now she checked her watch. The traffic was hardly moving. Impatiently she told the driver she would get out and walk the last few blocks.

She looked up at the sound of an aircraft; shading her eyes she watched it. She had never seen an aircraft flying this low over the city.

It has to be some kind of publicity stunt, she thought, maybe a film shoot, there were enough of those going on in the city. With a growing feeling of unease, Kate stopped walking, aware of other pedestrians doing the same, and watched the plane. Seconds later it plunged into the North Tower. Bewildered she looked around; everyone had stopped in their tracks, staring mesmerized at the burning tower. Everyone started talking at once. What's going on? What's happening? With frightened and incredulous eyes everyone tried to make some sense out of what was going on. The minutes ticked by. Then the screaming started. In the distance another aircraft was approaching, Kate held her breath, fear and terror beginning to pervade her body. With a roar it plunged into the second tower.

People started to run in every direction, screaming and crying, unable to understand what was going on.

Taking her shoes off, she started to run as well. Unsure of what to do or where to go, she ran blindly on, her mind frozen with fear. Is New York under attack, she thought frantically? Her teeth were on edge with all the people screaming and shouting. Is America under attack? People were frantically punching numbers into their mobile phones, attempting to make contact with family and friends. She stopped running and looked back.

Crowds of people stood around dumbstruck and frightened. Everyone was horrified, holding on to each other in small groups. They too were all trying to understand what was happening. Kate could see that parts of both towers were on fire. With the smoke that was billowing out from the buildings, she could hardly see what was happening up there. Breathlessly she turned to a man standing next to her; he was talking rapidly into his phone. "What's happening?"

He told her that a passenger airplane had been flown into each tower and that the news was saying the planes had been hijacked by terrorists. He told her that two other planes had been hijacked and that one had just crashed into the Pentagon.

Kate looked at him wide-eyed. "We're under attack. America is under attack," he said, putting his head in his hands, as he sobbed. "This could be happening nationwide. We have no idea what's really going on." Kate put her hand on his shoulder. She looked up again at the World Trade Centre towers and watched the drama unfold. Police and fire brigade sirens were screaming all around her as the vehicles drew up at great speed. Fire-fighters and policemen were running all over the place. Kate's heart was in her mouth. She wondered desperately where all the people were who were up in the towers, if some had managed to get out in time.

Kate watched as pieces of paper dropped down from the mighty towering infernos. With sickening realisation, she brought her hands up to her face.

"Oh God, it can't be," she whispered, horrified.

They were not pieces of paper. They were people jumping.

Not long afterwards, there was a series of explosions and the south tower started to collapse in on itself. Everyone screamed and started to run uptown as fast as they could. Kate was pushed and shoved as the crowd surged around her. There was a roar and the most frightening sound Kate had ever heard behind her. Galvanised by terror, Kate ran blindly as a billowing fog of dust and smoke surrounded her. She couldn't breathe. There was no air. She coughed and covered her mouth and face with her shirt as best she could. Her eyes streamed. She couldn't see anything. Occasionally, she could feel someone nearby and would turn her head to see someone else running for their life beside her.

She tripped and fell a number of times but didn't stop. She wondered if she was about to die. When she was twenty blocks away, she turned around and stopped, gasping for breath, her heart hammering in her chest. She couldn't run any more. Big pieces of dust and debris floated to the ground; they were brown and scorched around the edges. Out of the dust that covered everything, white ghostly figures trudged and ran. Kate noticed that shoes, bags and items of clothes were scattered everywhere. Choking, Kate carried on. I have to get back to my apartment, she thought desperately. There was a smell of aviation fuel that was so strong it felt as though it was searing her lungs. Around her, she heard the screaming sirens of more emergency vehicles heading downtown. Miraculously a taxi appeared and she tumbled into it. As they neared her apartment, she changed her mind. She needed people around her. What if there is more to come, she thought? If I'm going to die then I don't want to be alone when it happens. The delicatessen and shops in her neighbourhood had pulled down their steel shutters. The shopkeepers wanted to get off the island as fast as possible. Kate wondered if she too should get off. I have nowhere to go, she thought.

Kate walked into a bar on the corner of her street. It was twenty past ten and the place was full. In the corner was an enormous television screen. All eyes were on the screen where the carnage of what was happening was being shown live. The Americans around her were frozen in disbelief. They stood and watched, unmoving. Some cried. Others had their hands to their mouths. Stupefied, they watched as the drama played out, minute after agonising minute. As she watched, the second tower started to collapse. Everyone around her started to scream and cry.

Kate thought about Lucy in France and Molly in London. They would be watching this in horror. She knew it would look very bad, as if the island of Manhattan was on fire, massive black clouds of burning aviation fuel blanketing out the sun and almost eclipsing the island. They would have watched the planes plunging into the towers and watched the mind-defying images of people jumping alone, or in pairs holding hands, in their last terrified moments of life.

Kate had watched it all. It would be a recurrent nightmare for years to come.

I have to call them, she thought, but she couldn't move. She was rooted to the spot, petrified.

Outside the light darkened and the streets fell into shadow as though there had been an eclipse of the sun. It felt apocalyptic.

Kate lost track of time and at some point reluctantly left the bar and returned to her apartment. The wind had changed direction. Dark pieces of debris drifted past her and she could still smell aviation fuel as well as burning and the smell of burnt hair and human flesh. She remembered the day she and Jack had gone to Jane and Mark's after they had been killed and their house was burnt down. It was a smell she had never forgotten but had never wanted to smell again. Staggering up the stairs to her apartment, she grappled to stop her hands shaking to open the door, then ran to the bathroom and vomited.

She tried to call Lucy and Molly but the telephone lines were down.

Like the other residents of New York who had not made it off the island in time, Kate did not sleep that night. She sat watching the TV in numb shock. It was her only line of communication. Hugging her knees to her chest, she desperately wished she was back in Africa, the place that most of the world thought was savage. In her mind's eye she kept replaying the terrible images she had witnessed and watched as they were repeated again and again on the TV. It still didn't feel real.

"Please, God," she prayed. "Please, God, let the angels have caught them before they hit the ground." The tears came again as she reached for the small teddy bear that Molly had given her; hugging it close, she stared sightlessly out of the window. "Oh God Adam, do you know where I am at the moment? I wish you were holding me now, I'm so frightened."

The following morning, not wanting to be alone, she made her way to the store on Madison Avenue. A shadow passed overhead and involuntarily she ducked her head then looking up fearfully. A lone fighter jet dipped and turned forlornly in the empty sky. The roar of its passage caught up with it, reverberating through the city. It headed up the Hudson River and there was absolute silence afterwards. All flights had been grounded and the skies were now a no-fly zone. The city was locked down with the living and the dead. It was empty. It felt as though there was no-one in it.

She walked along the great big avenues and didn't see one car of any kind. It was as though she was one of very few left. The few people she did see were walking along as dazed as she felt. What if the office was shut and no-one was there either? The silence of the city was suddenly shattered by the piercing siren of an emergency vehicle, screaming towards what would become known as Ground Zero. Kate jumped, hearing it.

Tears welled up in her eyes. All the shops she passed were closed. All the American flags that she saw were at half-mast. Passing Saint Patrick's Cathedral, Kate saw it was full of people, numb in their grief. They were lighting candles for the missing and the dead. Kate walked in and knelt in the aisle. There was hardly any space for her. She closed her eyes and prayed with everyone else around her and found some comfort there surrounded by people.

Leaving the cathedral, she stood at the top of the stone steps and watched a fleet of forty or more military vehicles, bristling with gun-toting, grim faced soldiers, make their way along the avenue; she felt as though she was in a war movie. Kate walked on towards the store, hearing her own footsteps echoing on the sidewalk. It was a totally unheard of phenomenon in this normally incredibly noisy city.

Day after day, Kate sat at her desk, constantly trying the telephone, her e-mail and her mobile phone, desperate to talk to her sister and to Molly. Cut off and isolated with no way of communicating with the outside world, she paced the floor of her office or stared out of the windows at the silent streets below.

There were many bomb scares in the city at that time. There were stories of dirty bombs and Anthrax attacks. In the weeks that followed, as she walked the streets of Manhattan, it seemed there were hundreds of funerals. Sometimes, the only thing to be buried would be a finger. Hundreds and hundreds of photographs of the missing were displayed on the buildings, at the railway, police and fire stations. Family and friends searched frantically for lost loved ones and, as the days passed, hopes of finding anyone alive diminished.

Kate found herself retracing her steps to Ground Zero. Looking at the photographs as she passed, she thought how young they looked. She could smell the smoke from the burning buildings and her footsteps faltered. Rounding the corner, her courage nearly failed her. Somehow sounds seemed muffled and she shivered, sensing the spirits of the hundreds who had perished. Before her was a gaping, smouldering hole in the ground and blackened twisted metal struts thrusting into the air, like accusatory fingers. People around her stared as well, crying and praying.

Kate turned back towards her apartment. New York was supposed to have been a huge adventure. It was meant to be great fun and a new beginning for her. Throwing back her head she looked up at the great yellow sun and the blue sky and she knew something had ended here.

She desperately wanted to be away from the carnage and the terrible sadness corroding the city.

If I go back to the bush and go on safari, she thought, I will see the animals and the trees, the birds and the flowers. They will not have changed at all. Despite all that has happened here, despite how the world will now surely change, the great plains of the Serengeti will be untouched by this. This glittering elegant city, the place I thought would change my life, well it's done that. It's changed the way I think and the way I feel about life. I still have a chance to change my life. I still have choices unlike those terrified people who had only two. To jump, or be burned alive.

Exhausted, she hailed one of very few cabs and sat back, looking at how almost every store window she passed had been hung with a deep purple cloth with black bands across it, underscoring the scale of the whole thing.

After a couple of weeks, Kate carefully placed the magazines and newspapers, which had covered the September 11th attacks in the bottom of one of her boxes. She still had two years to go on her contract. Going back to Kenya was not an option in her current circumstances. She would have to sit it out.

When she finally made her home in Zanzibar and unpacked her boxes she was still unable to look at the images captured on camera in the magazines and newspapers.

Chapter Twenty-Nine

MOLLY ARRIVED to spend Christmas with Kate. It was a year after September 11th and the city had recovered enough to celebrate the festive season. The store would be busy but Molly offered to help. They would have some fun together.

The rich and famous would be coming through the doors, as they always did at that time of the year. Molly enjoyed seeing the film stars whom she recognised from various television series and films.

Kate closed down her computer and pulled on her thick coat and gloves, then headed out. The city looked beautiful, all dressed up for Christmas. I love this city, she thought. It's expensive but I'm enjoying it. Life is good again. She had decided to do some Christmas shopping and then to stop for a Martini at her favourite cocktail bar on 60th Street, before heading for the restaurant where she had arranged to have dinner with Molly.

Molly was standing in for her at the store. It was a late night shopping evening and she would be there for another two hours. Kate's thoughts were on what she would buy her daughter for Christmas as she hurried along the busy sidewalk. She had seen the perfect gift for her; a silver bracelet from Tiffany's.

Tom stopped at a cocktail bar on 60th Street. It was discreet and old school New York with leather Chesterfield sofas and chairs. Looking around, he soon figured out that it catered to the tastes of the staff and visitors to the UN building that was a few blocks away. The bar had a quiet dignified air to it which led him to think of the days when lighting a cigar in an establishment like this would have been the thing to do. Instead, he ordered a beer.

Six months after Sarah died, he had met Nicky. At fifty three he had almost given up any ideas of another relationship. Browsing through the travel section of a bookshop in London he had noticed the attractive dark haired woman working her way down the book shelves until she was standing next to him. Triumphantly she pulled a book out and smiled at him.

"Found it! It's such a satisfying feeling, isn't it? I thought it might be out of stock..." she had flicked through the pages. "I can't wait to get stuck into it."

Curiously he had asked her about the title and soon enough they were chatting about books, recommending titles and authors to each other.

"My name's Nicky, by the way; it's nice to meet someone who enjoys the same taste in books. I never seem to have the time to travel, but I've promised myself a trip to Japan this year. Have you ever been there?"

Impulsively he had suggested they have a coffee together and he would tell her about Japan, what to see and where to go. She had been delighted.

Nicky was in her early forties and rented a small Mews house in Chelsea. Being a successful lawyer had left little time for marriage and children.

"I specialise in divorce cases," she had told him. "When you see once happy couples bickering and fighting over who is going to get what, it sort of puts you off getting married."

He had watched her as she chatted away. She was very attractive with her heart-shaped face and shoulder length auburn hair. She had large brown intelligent eyes and laughed easily and often.

They had spent a pleasant afternoon together and he had asked if he might take her out to dinner during the week. She had agreed with alacrity.

They had dated frequently over the following months and when she came back from Japan, three months later, their relationship had developed further. Occasionally she would spend the night at his apartment and they spent every weekend together.

Although his marriage to Sarah had been fraught with difficulties he had found living alone was difficult, the weekends in particular. When the lease on Nicky's apartment expired he had asked her to move in with him. For the first time in years he was happy and hoped that, given time, he might fall in love with her.

Now he glanced up at the clock behind the bar, it was time to go. He had an hour to spare before he would meet Nicky back at the hotel. He had a new life now. Kate was in the past where she belonged – he wouldn't let thoughts of her spoil his newly found happiness with Nicky.

Kate walked along 60th Street. She had Molly's present, beautifully wrapped, and there was just enough time for a Martini, before joining Molly for dinner.

As she approached the cocktail bar, she remembered she hadn't collected her prescription. Entering a pharmacy, she saw there were four people ahead of her in the queue and she hesitated. Should she leave it until tomorrow? No, she would wait her turn. She wouldn't have time tomorrow.

Tom finished his drink and walked out onto the snowy sidewalk. He looked up and down the street and reached for the gift list inside his jacket pocket. He turned right, heading uptown.

Kate hurried into the bar a few minutes later. There was one seat vacant. She put her parcels down, pushed aside the empty beer glass and ordered her drink.

Tom slowed, weighed down by crispy beautifully wrapped bags and navigated the pedestrians, equally laden, trying to walk past. Regarding his list, he decided to go into the elegant English-looking store on Madison Avenue. He knew they had a superb book department and he wanted to get something special for Nicky for Christmas.

Entering the lift, he alighted on the 5th floor and browsed amongst the books. A young girl was ringing up the sales on the till. She was tall and slim and had long curly hair and large brown eyes. They chatted briefly about the snow outside and hearing her accent he asked where she came from. She told him she was from London, but had been born in South Africa and that she was here visiting her mother; she wrapped the book he had bought and handed it to him.

He told her he had spent some years going back and forth to Johannesburg on business. As they talked, he had the vague sense of having met her before. She looked familiar but he knew this was impossible. Molly handed Tom his gift-wrapped purchase and excused herself, turning to the next customer patiently waiting her turn.

He left the store and started to head for the hotel, thinking over the conversation. There was something about her that nagged him, something about the colour and shape of her eyes. On impulse he turned sharply, retracing his footsteps back to the store on Madison. As he approached, he saw that it was closing. He waited a few moments to see if she would come out. Then feeling rather foolish, and realising he would not know what to say to her, he turned and walked back to the hotel.

Kate met her daughter at the restaurant. Over dinner, Molly talked about some of the customers who had come into the store. She had seen one person she thought might be famous and told her about a man she had chatted to who had visited South Africa, amongst other places in Africa, quite frequently.

Kate didn't pay much attention to the conversation. She had met so many people who had lived in Africa or had been on safari there, what was one more? Suddenly she lifted her head and looked carefully around the crowded restaurant, frowning.

"Sorry darling, I wasn't listening, I had a strange feeling that I was being followed or someone was watching me." She shook herself quickly. "Anyway, tell me again about the man from Africa, or wherever he came from. Did he buy anything?"

The next day, Kate was going through the transactions of the previous day. She was running through the credit card slips. She sat down quickly. Tom Fletcher. There it was. His signature, clear and strong.

He was here in New York.

All the hairs on the back of her neck stood up. She thought back quickly, trying to remember where he had said he lived in the States before he moved to London. Had it been New York City or New York State? She racked her brain but couldn't come up with an answer. She wondered how she would have felt about seeing him. It would have been a big surprise if she had been in the store when he had come in. She looked at the slip again and slowly put it back in the drawer.

She shook her head. He probably wouldn't have recognised her, not after all that time. But he had finally met Molly. She wondered what he had thought of her daughter. She thought back to the previous evening. Had Molly been wearing her hair up or down? Frowning, she tried to recall. It had been down. It would have hidden the unusual birth mark on the back of her neck.

Nervously she fiddled with the silver bracelet on her wrist. He had walked out on her, and besides, there could be dozens of Tom Fletchers on the planet.

She walked back to her desk pushing all thoughts of her past out of her mind

Chapter Thirty

K**ATE LOOKED OUT OF THE WINDOW.** It was another impossibly beautiful spring day. She longed to be sitting in Central Park and not there in the store. She had a year left of her contract. The phone rang, making her jump.

"Kate? It's Emily."

"Hello Emily! How lovely to hear from you," Kate smiled into the telephone, genuinely pleased to hear Emily's voice. "How's Cape Town today?" There was a short silence from the other end. She felt her stomach squeeze with anxiety.

"Kate, I have some bad news for you. I thought I should tell you before you hear it second-hand from someone else." Kate heard her swallow nervously and her heart began to beat more quickly. Adam. It had to be something to do with Adam.

"It's Adam," Emily said slowly. "He died yesterday, somewhere in England, I think. No-one knows for sure. There are a lot of rumours going around, as you can imagine. The details are a bit sketchy. I'm so sorry to be the bearer of bad news, Kate, but someone had to tell you and I thought it should be me."

"Thank you, Emily," Kate said in barely a whisper. "I'll have to call you back, I can't…"

Kate softly replaced the receiver and gazed out of the window, now seeing nothing at all. He was gone. There was a time when she thought that his dying would have made things more bearable but now that she knew, she found it didn't. She waited to feel some sort of reaction but felt only disbelief at the news. One thing she did know now was that he would not be able to hurt her again. She would have to break the news to Molly.

191

Carefully, she walked over to the window and looked down at the traffic below. Leaning her forehead against the cool glass, she felt her body shudder. An overwhelming sense of loss engulfed her. She sank to her knees, the full impact of the news hitting her hard. Surely, I would have known if he had died? I would have sensed it? Felt it? She tried to get her rising emotions under control but unable to hold it back, she gave into her grief and wept for the man she had loved and had now finally lost forever.

New York had been a fantastic challenge, but what next? She had watched the safari industry change over the past years. The internet had made an incredible difference to how people had begun to travel. Research and bookings were being done online. The bespoke safari planner was becoming redundant. Younger people with greater IT skills than she had were swarming forward into the tourism market place.

She drummed her fingers lightly against the cab window. Did she really want to stay in the business? Travelling had become nearly impossible after 9/11. There was no pleasure in it anymore. Taking off shoes and belts, being hand searched; she hated it all.

Molly had called her from London to say that she would fly to New York and spend some time with her over Christmas. "I know it's been difficult for you with the news of Adam's death and that's why you feel so restless. I want to help you make some sort of decision about your future."

She heard her mother sigh heavily, before saying brightly, "You're right, I do need to talk about what to do next; it will be so good to see you Molly, and it's good of you to make the time when I know you should be spending Christmas with James. I'll send a car for you. What would you like this time, the stretch limo? Or something less ostentatious?"

Molly laughed. "This might be my last visit, so I'll take the stretch!"

As Kate walked home, she looked up at the sky. No falcons around here, she thought, far too noisy.

Standing across the road, he watched her. She was still beautiful. Running a hand through his blond hair, he lit a cigarette and melted back into the crowded sidewalk.

Kate left New York for Kenya at the end of December the following year. Her contract was up.

Chapter Thirty-One

TOM SAT BACK in his chair and looked out at the communal gardens of his apartment in Holland Park. He sipped his hot coffee carefully. He had sold his business the previous year and now had enough money to live on very comfortably for the rest of his life. His two-year affair with Nicky had ended amicably a year ago and they had gone their separate ways.

That afternoon he had gone to see a wildlife exhibition being held in a gallery off of Bruton Street. The photographer had lived in Africa for most of his life and his work was outstanding. He had spent an enjoyable afternoon looking at the portraits of wild animals and endless landscapes. Thoughtfully he had returned home.

Idly he had turned on his computer. No harm in seeing if Kate had published any more books, he thought to himself. No, she hadn't. The exhibition had unsettled him. He looked out at the garden; the rain hissed and spat against his window. He needed to get away.

An hour later he had booked and confirmed a safari to the Okavango Delta in Botswana. It would dove-tail nicely with his two-day business trip to Johannesburg in two weeks' time.

He stood up, quickly glancing at his watch. There was a cocktail party at the American Embassy in Grosvenor Square to which he had been invited to attend. In his line of business, over the years, he had become a well-respected figure with British and American Embassies all around the world, exchanging and receiving useful information. The British and American Governments had become close after the destruction of the World Trade Centre. This evening's gathering was to meet High Commissioners, and Consuls from a variety of countries

194

including East and Southern Africa. He would have to leave now in order to get through the tight security at the Embassy, and not be late.

Tom circulated the cocktail party, chatting with fellow Americans, friends and colleagues and catching up on past and current events in the unpredictable world of terrorism. He had been introduced to Mike McNeil who had just finished his three-year service with the British Consulate in Cape Town, and had now been posted to the High Commission in Nairobi. Mike was in his mid-fifties, round and portly from years of social events and too many dinner parties; he constantly mopped his face with a large red handkerchief. A confirmed bachelor, he was invited to just about every social gathering wherever he was posted.

They chatted easily together about the increasing presence of Al Qaeda supporters near Lamu and Zanzibar. Mike McNeil was an old hand in the world of diplomacy; it had been his career for over thirty years and he knew Africa well. He had been closely involved with the American Embassy after the series of bombings in Nairobi and Dar es Salaam in 1998.

As the evening drew to a close Tom asked Mike if he was free for dinner. For two bachelors, with a lot in common, it seemed a fitting end to an interesting evening.

When Tom returned from Johannesburg and his weekend in the Okavango Delta, he immediately got in touch with Mike McNeil, who still had two weeks before he was due to take up his new position with the High Commission in Nairobi. Tom asked for his assistance to try and track down Kate and find out where she was living now. They arranged to meet up at the weekend and Mike had promised he would find out as much as he could.

Meanwhile Tom had been using his impressive list of contacts. She had definitely lived in Cape Town, but he already knew that. Then she had left the country and gone to live in New York City, but after that the trail had gone cold. My email must have gone around the world six times or more, Tom thought. Colleagues and old friends had passed it along and there had been some helpful replies. Kate had apparently spent time in East Africa, managing a game lodge, but whether it was

Tanzania or Kenya his contact could not say. Everyone was vague as to her whereabouts.

London. She had walked through the door, with her beguiling smile and changed his life. He had liked her attitude to life, one big adventure after another; but that had been then. How would she be now, and how had things turned out for her? Realistically he knew she could not possibly look the same, just as he did not. Knowing that she had been in the travel and safari business, she must have travelled all over the world promoting her company and a thought continued to intrigue him.

He had been a prolific traveller himself and the chances of them passing each other on escalators, in lifts, or at airports, was not that impossible to imagine.

He had watched out for her. But had she looked for him, would she remember him at all?

I'll find her again. I don't care how long it takes, but I will find her wherever she is. With that thought Tom turned off the lights and headed for bed.

Mike dabbed at his forehead with his red handkerchief. "Superb lunch, old boy," he said to Tom. "I think I'll have a small brandy and then tell you what I have managed to find out about this woman you're trying to find. But first I have to ask you what your interest is in her, just normal procedure, you understand."

Tom looked at him, amused by the very English accent. He was impatient to find out what news Mike had for him. "I met her here in London many years ago. There's nothing sinister going on. I just want to find out what happened to her and where she ended up. That's it."

Mike watched him shrewdly. Tom Fletcher was a likeable chap and had told him a lot about his business, but very little about his private life. He knew he had been married and that was about it. He had him down for a confirmed bachelor now, like himself, but his interest in this woman Kate made him wonder if there was not a bit more to it.

He cleared his throat. "It wasn't easy to trace her. She has moved around quite a bit. The only place she stayed put for any considerable amount of time was Cape Town, but even then she travelled a great deal

– all over the world in fact. She lived there for around fourteen years with her daughter."

Tom nodded. Mike continued. "She was definitely heavily involved with her partner, Adam Hamilton in Cape Town; whether they married or not no-one knows, but it seems unlikely as we had that checked out and nothing came up. But they were partners in an extremely successful company, but then it looks as though the partnership came to an end. The shares went back to Adam Hamilton and Kate Hope left the country shortly afterwards."

"Is that it Mike? What happened to her after that?"

He shrugged his shoulders. "I would imagine that if she sold her interest in the company back to this Hamilton character it was probably the end of the affair as well. She had probably wanted to put as much distance between them as possible. Anyway we did a bit more digging and it seems she spent two years in Kenya; we have been able to track that. But exactly where she was, I have no idea. The next sighting of her was when she entered the United States. She lived and worked there for four years before returning to Kenya and presumably that's where she is now. I can most certainly find out for you when I get there next week. Give me a month or two and I'll see what I can find out for you. Having been with the Embassy in South Africa for the past three years it shouldn't be too difficult to run a check on this Adam Hamilton chap either."

Mike stood up and held his hand out. "Good to see you again Tom, excellent lunch and now I must get back to the office. Maybe I'll see you in Nairobi one day?"

Chapter Thirty-Two

WELL, IT'S NOT CALLED the Lunatic Express for nothing, Kate thought, standing on the platform in Nairobi's train station, waiting for a train that was supposed to depart at seven p.m. She looked at her watch, it was now ten p.m. Her fellow passengers were lying around on the dirty platform. They were mostly hearty Germans on their way to Mombasa or young students on their gap year. Their rucksacks were being used as pillows; they looked resigned to the way of travel in Africa.

At eleven p.m., the train heaved itself into the station. Hissing and screeching, it ground to a halt. The passengers leapt to their feet in a frantic race to find seats and sleeping compartments, despite the stationmaster's pleas to wait until the train could be cleaned. Arriving passengers looked surly and disgruntled at the late arrival. They squeezed past the enthusiastic crowd, causing more chaos. Kate's cabin was tiny but she edged herself inside, trying to ignore the rubbish on the floor and the dirty hand basin. She stashed her two bags away, sat down, and contemplated her surroundings. She had been on the train many times before but it had never been this late and never this dirty. To add to the misery, there was no electricity and no water and it was a twelve-hour trip.

Resigned, she lit a cigarette and opened her bottle of water. There was still a lot of activity on the platform. Porters were throwing bags upwards through the carriage doors. Traders were bustling from window to window selling bottled water and snacks. Passengers were shuffling up and down the corridors, looking for their seats and cabins. Finally, close to midnight, the train shuddered out of the station accompanied by a great deal of enthusiastic whistling from the guard.

Kate thought about the project ahead. She was to oversee the re-decoration of a large villa south of Mombasa, on the east coast of Kenya. She opened her map, flicked on her torch, and studied the Kenyan coastline. She had never heard of the place where the villa was situated but it was there somewhere. After closer inspection, she still couldn't find it. Resigned she sat back and looked out at the blackening night and the dwindling lights of Nairobi instead.

After leaving New York, she had gone to London and stayed with Molly and James for a few days and then she had spent four days with Lucy in France. Edward was six years old and was a carbon copy of his father. It had been a poignant few days but she had handled it as best she could, almost convincing herself she was indeed his Aunt. But above all else she was grateful she had given Lucy and Jean-Philippe the chance to be the good parents they had turned out to be and her child was safe and protected in their world. Looking at her own world now she realized how catastrophic it would have been to try and bring the child up herself.

Kate returned to London and then flew out to Kenya and stayed with her old friend Trish O'Conner.

She had met Trish when she was running Pelican Place. Trish was a bush pilot and flew guests into the lodge. Often she would stay overnight and then fly on to another lodge the next day to ferry guests back and forth between lodges. Instead of putting her in the basic pilots' accommodation, that every lodge had, Kate had insisted, if they had a spare room, she stayed in the lodge itself. Or, if they were full, Trish would stay in Kate's private accommodation. The two women had got on well together and had remained good friends.

She had called Trish from London to let her know she was coming back and looking for a job. Trish had immediately invited her to stay at her house in Langata, a suburb outside of Nairobi.

A chance remark at one of Trish's dinner parties had set her on this path. They had been talking about a huge villa on the coast and how the owner, who lived in London and rarely used it, was thinking of selling it or renting it out. Kate had listened closely as they talked, her mind already racing with possibilities.

She knew from her experience that not everyone liked to stay in large hotels full of other intrepid tourists. If the villa was as large as it sounded, and she thought that it may well be, she calculated that there could be a good opportunity to convert it into a boutique hotel catering to the more discerning guests.

Trish lost no time in contacting John, the owner, and selling Kate's idea to him.

"John will be in Nairobi next week Kate, he seemed quite interested in your idea. I did a great job selling you as the perfect person for the project. John has piles and piles of money. He was born here but went to live in Brussels – that's where he made all his money – he was a trader or something. But he still has close ties here and comes back as often as he can. The villa down on the coast has been in his family for about eighty years, it was their holiday home. Anyway he wants to meet you. I've invited him for dinner on Wednesday!"

Kate had been excited about the prospective meeting with John. She desperately needed to get her teeth into something. His villa had been on the market for two years and no-one had approached him with a suitable offer. The dinner party had been a success. After a few days of deliberation, he agreed to convert it into a small hotel and then hoped to have a better chance of selling it as a business venture, rather than a private home. The sound of the dinner gong from the dining carriage of the train reminded her that she was hungry.

Back in her cabin after dinner, Kate readied herself for bed. It made her laugh that the train driver had the annoying habit of picking up speed and thereafter tapping the brakes every few minutes, sending anyone not holding on to a surface, to lurch either backwards or forwards. During dinner, an attendant had converted the long carriage seat into a bunk bed. She collapsed on to it and wedged herself in with rather sad-looking pillows. She braced herself for the long night ahead. She closed her eyes and saw his face again, his slow smile seeping into his blue eyes. She smiled as she remembered being on the train with him and how the bucking, rocking carriage had added a different dimension to their love-making that night. She drifted off to sleep, holding his memory close.

The old train hurtled through the night and into the dawn. Kate watched the sun come up changing the sky from a soft pink to brilliant blue. After twelve hours on the go, it thundered into Mombasa station and braked with a toppling lurch.

Porters swarmed the platform touting for business and before long Kate was loaded into a taxi and on her way.

The heat and humidity on the coast drained the energy from her body. Her thighs stuck uncomfortably to the cheap plastic seat of the wretchedly hot car. The centre of town in Mombasa shimmered in the stifling heat. The taxi took her to the industrial harbour and the waiting ferry.

The cacophony of noise, the humidity and the smell were overwhelming. Lorries and cars jostled for position in the burning sun, after which the passengers boarded. The ferry chugged and belched across a narrow estuary, landing with a crunch on the other side. Navigating a slippery ramp, the taxi rocked and bucketed its way around potholes. Traders lined both sides of the road and kept a wary eye on the traffic; one miscalculation by a driver and their stalls would be flattened.

After a while, the number of traders thinned and the road improved slightly. Now also dodging goats and cattle, the car drove towards Diani. Kate saw the signposts pointing left, surrounded by others, advertising beach hotels, car and bike hire and beach safaris. They drove through Ukundu and a seething mass of traders, chickens and goats. It had obviously rained heavily recently and the market wallowed in mud. Children played alongside their mothers who manned the small stalls. Flies rose up like clouds on piles of rubbish. Tucked down dark alleyways, she glimpsed shacks built out of pieces of packing cases and corrugated iron with rags covering the windows.

The car picked up speed once out of the village and she saw the sea on her left. The waving palm trees, the white tip of the surf, and here and there small plots of land under cultivation. They passed village after village, some comprising of just a few huts.

The frangipani trees, with their heavy sweet scent, were everywhere bringing a touch of beauty to the smallest and poorest village.

She caught glimpses of some of the insides of the shacks, wet muddy floors, more chickens, washing hanging on the bushes to dry, woman bent double over small tin bowls, washing and wringing out clothing.

Some just sat on stools watching the world go by, and the men in small groups just talked and watched. She wondered what they did all day.

The villagers openly stared at the car with the white female passenger. Kate remembered with a start that it was an incredibly Muslim area and she felt very conspicuous in her short tee-shirt. Without warning, the car plunged right down a small dirt track flanked by thick bush.

Kate began to feel uneasy. She hadn't anticipated the house being in such a remote spot. Her heart beat uncomfortably in her chest. She wondered how foolish she was being moving here on her own for however long it was going to take her to draw up the plans for the boutique hotel. This had been an impulsive idea, which she had not discussed with anyone other than the owner of the villa and her friend Trish.

The driver looked back at her, waiting for directions.

She had no idea where the house was. She only knew the name of it.

"Keep going, please," Kate said as calmly as she could.

Sweating profusely in the heat and the humidity and with a knot of fear and panic, Kate felt great relief when she saw a large painted stone with the name of the villa on it. Hooting at the gate, they waited for the askari, the security guard, to come. He unlocked the big gates and the car nosed its way in.

Driving slowly through the trees, they came to a low white building and with a shudder the car came to a halt in front of it. Kate unglued her body from the seat. Her clothes stuck to her body.

The cottage was basic. There were two rooms. One contained a writing table, a chair and two threadbare sofas. In the second room, there was a large double bed draped in a large mosquito net with holes big enough to put a fist through. Kate shuddered at the prospect of sleeping under it; her legs were already stinging and burning from bites. Mosquitoes were rife in that area. The kitchen was devoid of cutlery and crockery and there wasn't a pot or a pan in sight.

Kate contemplated her options. The thought of retracing the two-hour drive made her feel faint. Thanking the driver and paying him the agreed fare, she turned to look at the house servant, Titus. He beamed at her expectantly, hopefully.

Let's make the best of this, she thought, until I can come up with a better solution. She cursed herself for not asking more details about the cottage, which sat at the back of the villa itself. It was basic beyond belief.

Tired, hot and cross with herself, Kate wandered down through the extensive grounds of the large estate, passing the empty villa on her right and a huge swimming pool. She walked down some steps and onto a sandy path, lined on both sides by towering palm trees.

Approaching a large wooden gate nearing the end of the footpath, she could hear the sea. Flinging it open, she stepped out onto soft powdery sand. She let her breath out in an amazed sigh. The turquoise sea and dazzling white sand was like something out of a holiday brochure and there was not a soul in sight.

A cool breeze fanned her sticky skin. Kicking off her shoes and hoisting up her skirt, she ran into the water up to her thighs, and looked back at the beach. Large holiday homes, shuttered and empty, sat back in the shade of more palm trees. They had been invisible through the thick bush that they had driven through. The sun burned overhead and her skin tingled from the heat of it.

It was isolated in the extreme, she thought. It would be a huge challenge and her faltering courage rallied itself. Already she could see in her mind's eye how the small hotel could look and how she could design it to fit in with the environment here. Walking slowly back through the estate towards her little cottage, she saw five strong African men walking in single file. They were carrying pots, pans, patio chairs, crockery, cutlery and bed linen from the villa. The last man had tucked a vase of brilliant red hibiscus flowers in the crook of his arm.

Kate felt her spirits lift. She asked Titus to go to the local *duka* to shop for the essentials she would need. Plugging in her laptop, she inserted a CD of Mozart's. The first notes of the Clarinet concerto seeped through the muggy air and soothed her frazzled nerves.

Later that night, sitting out on the verandah with a warm glass of white wine, Kate felt herself relax. When she inhaled she could smell the saltiness of the sea in the air. A sharp sting on her arm alerted her to the advance of the mosquitoes. With a sigh, she stood up and went inside. Using her hair clips to close the biggest holes in the mosquito net, she switched off the light next to the bed.

In the early hours of the morning, the drumming of rain on the tin roof woke her; momentarily, she had no idea where she was. Switching the light on to no effect, she realised that the power had gone off. She lay quietly listening to the rain. It was so heavy that it drowned out all other sound. Pulling a pillow over her head, she fell back to sleep.

The next morning the power was back on, she made some coffee and wandered out onto the veranda. Lush green lawns ran through the property and down to the gates, leading to the beach. Hibiscus and frangipani provided vivid splashes of colour. Purple and white bougainvillea trailed over the high white walls, surrounding the gardens and villa. She picked up her sketch pad and for the next two hours, worked on her plan. A long green snake leapt out of a tree, landed on the veranda near her left foot and wriggled happily away into the grass. Kate froze with terror and shuddered. She hoped snakes would not be a problem on the estate. Guests were always amused by monkeys, of which there were plenty in the large grounds, but not by snakes.

She went back to her sketches and plans.

Kate collected her bag from the carousel and headed for the taxi rank. The train had been fun going to Mombasa, but flying to Nairobi for her meeting with John had been the quicker and more reliable option.

Her taxi wove its way through the heavy traffic in town, dodging the rickety trucks that belched out black smoke. Soon afterwards, the car headed into the wealthy suburb of Langata.

She looked out at the big houses they passed. They belonged to a different era with their colonial veneers, immaculate gardens and security guard huts. The car pulled up at Trish's house.

Trish, hearing the taxi, came out to greet her, her short blonde curls bouncing around her make-up-free face. Born and bred in Kenya she had the wholesome look of someone who spends all their time outside.

Now they were sitting on the cool veranda having coffee. "So Kate, how is the project going? I want to see your designs and hear your ideas! It's in the middle of nowhere, isn't it? I've flown around that neck of the woods many times and I think that stretch where you are has always been deserted. It's a beach-lover's paradise. Except for the mosquitoes."

"It is a challenge Trish, and it's going to be expensive. I hope John isn't overwhelmed by the figures I've compiled. I did tell him that you have to come up with something different to catch the attention of the international market. I think I can do that. Pelican Place was a success and I'm going to apply the same philosophy to the beach place."

"I stayed there last week. It still looks pretty good but they need to change the camp manager. He doesn't have your exacting standards. But the game is still good and my clients enjoyed it. I think it's because I know what it was like before, but if you don't know any better, it's still pretty wonderful. What's your time frame? When can I bring the first guests?" Trish asked, raising her eyebrow.

"Well," Kate said, smiling. "Once everything is approved by John! The local elders in the village and the council down there are content that we will be bringing employment into their area. Molly is going to oversee the interior design, which will be lovely for me. I do miss having people around. I reckon that it'll take about a year. But come on, Trish, enough about the beach house! I need a break. Tell me all the local gossip. There's always plenty!"

Trish topped up their cups. "Yes. Always! I'm not sure where to start. Remember Jonathan?" Kate nodded, settling herself back into her chair with a sigh. This was exactly what she needed – some girl talk and gossip.

"Well, he's just dumped his third wife for a younger model."

"Same old thing!" Kate and Trisha said at the same time, rolling their eyes and laughing.

"Do you remember bald Andy? He's just fathered another set of twins, but unfortunately, not with his wife. I think she's quite relieved about that though... and there's a new chap at the British High Commission who we're all dying to meet. Mike someone or other. He was with the Embassy in South Africa for a few years before coming here."

"What about Deedee? Is she still a wreck?" Kate asked interrupting her.

"Yes, she's become a rather over-enthusiastic supporter of the white stuff, spends most of her day on a different planet."

Kate leaned back in her chair. "So are there any good-looking available men around these days?"

"Well, you know as well as I do that most of the men around are available, married or not! But, actually," she said, sitting up straight and grinning from ear to ear, "I did meet an interesting guy at the Muthaiga Club. Paul someone or other. He's a pilot. Really good looking and very sexy. Of course, flying is my favourite subject so we had a lot to talk about! He's not had his licence for that long but he seems to know what he's talking about and knows his way around the cockpit. I think he might be English but as I did most of the talking there were some subjects we never got around to."

Kate laughed. "So nothing much has changed then? Everyone's still doing the sexual merry-go-round. My remote beach house has something going for it after all. At least there's no gossip. Well, not yet anyway. I'm sure, once we fill up with guests, there will be plenty!"

Trish looked across at her friend. Kate was a bit of a mystery. Although they were good friends, Trish knew little about Kate's personal life. She had broached the subject of men in Kate's life but Kate had laughed and brushed the question aside.

"Would you mind if I go to freshen up?" Kate asked Trish, standing up. "If we've got company tonight, I'd quite like to make myself look half-way presentable. Is that good looking pilot, Paul, coming around?"

"No. I would definitely have invited him if I had seen him again, which I haven't unfortunately."

Sitting in the garden whilst Kate went to shower and change, Trish thought that Kate had always seemed like the loneliest person in the world. She was generous and kind, and always good company, but there was a remoteness to her as well. She always seemed to be keeping her distance. Trish smiled. Not dissimilar from that good looking pilot called Paul.

John looked up from the budgets he had been studying. "It's an ambitious plan, Kate, but I like it. You have a lot of vision. Trish took me to see Pelican Place, just to get a feel of how you work. I was impressed and I can see that you want to use some of that magic for the beach hotel. To tell you the truth, the budget is more than I anticipated it would be."

Kate held her breath. John continued, "But I think it will work, so go ahead. You must be aware though, I will be selling it at some point, once you have used some of your skills to make it internationally famous!"

She beamed at him, relief flooding through her. They discussed the plans and designs for the following two hours and then John took her to the airport for the flight back to Mombasa.

"When we're ready to open, Kate, I want you to think about running the place for me. I'll give you a three-year contract with all the usual benefits, a medical plan, pension scheme etc. I think you'll be impressed with the package I'm offering." He handed her an envelope "Give me your answer as soon as possible. I would feel more secure if you stayed on. After all, you'll soon know the place inside out when it's finished and the staff will be used to you. I don't want to bring a complete stranger in to manage it. It will be a unique place and will take someone with a certain character to be able to live and work there. Would I be right in thinking that you have those qualities?"

On the flight, she studied the sheet of typed paper with John's proposal. It was impressive. She would earn an excellent salary and would live in the cottage in the grounds, which John had promised to upgrade. She looked out at the clouds; it was almost too good to be true. A secure future and three years of hard work was something she needed.

New York had been an expensive exercise. Renting the apartment on 5th Avenue had cost a fortune. She had looked at so many apartments and been appalled at how small they were. She wasn't prepared to pull a bed out of the wall in a one-roomed place. But it had been costly to live the kind of life she had been used to. She was determined not to touch the money she had left in trust for Molly.

The aircraft began its descent. She looked out over hot, bustling Mombasa, as it came into focus. Soon she saw the shacks and shanty towns, the fruit and vegetable markets and the teeming mass of humanity. There were Indians, Africans and Europeans all living in harmony down there. The crumbling grand façades of old colonial buildings, with their rusting ironwork balconies, added to the cosmopolitan feel of the ancient port town. She fastened her seat belt in preparation for the landing and pushed the contract back into the envelope. Yes, she thought, I'll sign the contract.

Chapter Thirty-Three

KATE CLOSED HER MOBILE PHONE, overwhelmed with the news that had come through. She looked down through the trees on the estate and contemplated what she would do next.

John had told her he had sold the villa.

Now there would be no hotel, no project and no contract to keep her occupied for three years. She sat on the veranda and tried not to panic. He had told her she could stay on the estate for two months, but after that she would have to move out. The new owner would be arriving and he had no interest whatsoever in building a hotel.

She knew she now had no home, no job and nowhere to go. Shakily she lit a cigarette and looked at her options. She didn't have any. With the recent political turmoil in Kenya, investors were skittish. Tourism had dropped considerably and the lodges were taking a knock with their bookings. It was the worst time to try and find another job and she needed one.

Numbly she walked down to the beach and sat on the sand at the edge of the water. Her armpits prickled with anxiety. She walked back to the cottage, passing the empty villa and all the dreams she had had for it.

Titus watched her, as he had every day since she arrived. She did not ask much of him. He would go to the village and buy her food, sweep out the cottage and prepare a simple meal for her in the evening. Sometimes the food was left on the plate when he came in the next day. She didn't seem to eat much and he wondered why this white woman would choose to come to this isolated place on her own. He, at least, had his family in the village, but she had no-one to talk to. He knew about the plans for the hotel, and that kept her busy during the day. But the evenings must be very long for her. Now she looked very unhappy and deep in thought. Maybe she had received bad news.

He picked up the scissors and went into the garden to collect some flowers for her; perhaps they would make her smile again. He looked up as a shadow fell briefly over him. He smiled. The falcon seemed to have taken up residence in the grounds. He had seen it often over the past few weeks.

Kate watched the candle flicker in the cool night air. Tomorrow she would have to break the news to the village chiefs. It would be the end of their dreams for a better future too. She hoped that the new owner would keep Titus and the gardeners on. Her thoughts turned to her own future.

Zanzibar was a place she had often thought about and she had been there many times. It had a lot of character and history and she had met interesting people who lived there. That was worth thinking about. It wouldn't solve the problem of a job and making some money to live on, but she felt that once she got there maybe something would come up. It would do as a temporary place to stay until she found something more permanent.

Kate wandered through the narrow streets of Stone Town on her way home breathing in the scent of cloves, vanilla and frangipani which seemed to permeate the air around her. After all the years of uprooting herself from country to country, she had finally decided that Zanzibar would be the place to live, and a good place to try to put down some roots.

She had found a house to rent on the edge of the old quarter. Abraham had worked for the previous family who lived there for five years, and was dismayed when they left. Kate had taken an instant liking to the gentle old man and asked him to stay on with her.

Sending for her boxes in Cape Town, Kate had stayed in an old hotel for a month, until she could move into the house. The island was a hybrid of old and new with a smart beach-front hotel, which attracted a very glamorous international crowd, who had to share the streets with donkeys, and down hidden alleyways were derelict colonial buildings gathering dust and history. The name of the island still conjured up images of its romantic and exotic past, drawing people from all over the world. Kate soon met local writers, artists, poets and people with questionable, but interesting, pasts.

When her boxes arrived, Kate unpacked each one almost ritualistically. They had been in storage for seven years now and she had forgotten what was in them. Taking her time, she pulled out each item. With each one came a flood of memories.

The bronze statues from Paris, her boards of photographs, her library amassed over the years. Opening her suitcases from New York, Kate smiled ruefully. No need for the business suits, designer shoes and handbags or the thick coats and jackets she had worn there.

At the bottom of one of the boxes, she found her scrapbooks. Pouring herself a glass of lemonade, she climbed the stair to the roof garden and sank back into the cushions on the day bed. She opened the first one.

How young I was, she thought, and how attractive Adam had been. Flicking through the pages, she re-lived those good years in South Africa. How successful she and Adam had been. There were newspaper clippings, slightly yellowed, which recounted some of the more spectacular things they had achieved. Here was Adam shaking hands with Nelson Mandela. There was the old DC4 aircraft they had chartered to fly across Africa. So many memories. Abruptly she closed the scrap book. Adam was dead and she had her own life to get on with now. There was no point in hankering after a past she could never have again.

Looking out across the rooftops, she watched a young man swinging in his hammock, a middle aged woman silhouetted by wooden shutters, always writing long into the night, the fat white cat sitting on the wall, waiting patiently for his owner to return.

She padded on bare feet downstairs to carry on the unpacking. Kate unpacked the shoe boxes full of loose photographs, all neatly filed in envelopes. She flicked through them. There must be hundreds here, she thought. All stills from my life and the people who have played a part in it. There was Molly, growing up through the years. She had a few framed photographs in bubble wrap which she carried to her bedroom and positioned next to the bed.

That night, the last person she saw before she fell asleep was Adam. Smiling his insouciant smile; his eyes looking into hers. She dreamed of him that night. He was running towards her on a beach but he was so far away she could hardly see his face. She tried to run towards him but her feet wouldn't move and he receded as though he were running away from her. Stretching out her arms, she tried to go faster; she called him but he had gone.

Kate woke calling his name. Turning sharply, she half expected to see him lying beside her in the bed. She reached out and turned his photograph over so that she wouldn't have to look at him anymore. She didn't want to dream about him. It still surprised her when she realised he was dead. She found it so hard to believe. She wondered if she would ever see where he had been buried and if she saw his grave would it make it more real for her. But she had no idea where that might be.

In the months that followed, Kate walked the island, getting to know it. She liked the way it felt. Molly and James came out for Christmas and the three of them had flown to Lamu in Tanzania before going on safari. She watched her daughter and James, who were so happy together and she felt a degree of envy. She had had an urge to have it all again, but put that down to unpacking the boxes and seeing all her things around her, reminding her of the life she had once known.

Kate entertained once or twice a month and sometimes Trish would come and spend the weekend. Life was going well for Kate; she had finally found the peace and happiness she had craved for so long.

Kate was returning from the market on her way home. She had a basket full of fresh tomatoes and mint, and in the warmth of the sunshine their scent emanated around her. She passed the internet cafe she regularly visited. She paused and wondered if she should see whether the internet was up that day. She didn't anticipate there being much mail to look at but it had been a week and she thought she ought to. She kept her feelers out in case the opportunity to run another project might come up.

Kate scrolled through her email, deleting the ones she didn't recognise. There was one that she hesitated over, from Emily, and below it one from Trish. She skipped to Trish's email. She read it quickly. Trish had heard that a couple were going to Europe for a month and they wanted to know if Kate would be interested in looking after their game lodge whilst they were away. There would be no guests and only a skeleton staff.

A short-term temporary contract suited Kate those days. She Googled the lodge and its location. It was way up on the Northern Frontier. Her heart sank. It looked very isolated with nothing for miles around. She thought quickly. She could do with the extra cash injection. She sent an email back to Trish telling her she was very interested and would almost certainly take up the offer. She asked her what she should do next. Almost finished, she happily returned to the email from Emily and opened it.

Hello Kate,

I hope this email will find you – wherever you are. No-one seems to know exactly where that is or where you are living these days. I don't know how to tell you this. Even to me it sounds too incredible to be true. It will come as a great shock, so I hope you are sitting down and have some company around you.

Adam has been seen in Nairobi. There doesn't seem to be any mistake that it is him. You probably know that he left South Africa. Things were not going well with the business, from what I can gather. No-one was quite sure where he went. Some said Paris, others Italy, maybe England. I remember calling you in New York, two years ago, and telling you that he had died in England and that was based on fact. I saw the death notice myself in the newspaper. Now I don't know what to think, Kate. Perhaps he fabricated his own death to avoid whatever problems he was having, I'm not even sure if they were business or personal. You can imagine the speculation here. He was always clever and knew how to tell a story or two, as I am sure you will remember. He was recognised at the Norfolk Hotel in Nairobi by an old colleague of yours. She contacted me in Cape Town when she returned. She was convinced that it was Adam. This was a few months ago. I didn't want to tell you then because it might have been a terrible mistake and I thought that perhaps the man she had seen was not Adam at all, just someone who looked very much like him.

But, having said that, I always remember you telling me that over the years you have never seen anyone that looked remotely like him, so there could be a lot of truth in this.

I have tried to do some follow-up on the sighting myself but the trail has gone cold since then. I'm not sure what your reaction is going to be to this news, although I can probably guess. I know that you were devastated when he died – if he did, that is. Don't go looking for him, Kate, it will only bring you more pain and you have had too much of that. Anyway, as I said, it could be a huge mistake and I would have upset you for nothing. But again, I didn't want you to hear it from anybody else first. I'll keep my ear to the ground and if there is any more news I will let you know immediately.

Love, Emily

Kate sat back in her chair, not quite believing what she had read. Adam might be alive? Her hands shook as she picked up her bag and left the café. This had to be some terrible mistake. Someone had got something horribly wrong. He could not be alive. That was just not possible.

She thought back to that telephone call from Emily in New York City. Kate's initial reaction to the news of his death had been disbelief. She had been convinced she would have known, she would have felt it, if he had died.

Back at the house, she slowly climbed the stairs to her bedroom. Pulling open a drawer at her dressing table, she retrieved the photograph of her and Adam taken in Cape Town.

She sat down on her chaise longue, tracing his face with her finger, and tried to make some sense of the news. Her gut twisted with the familiar anxiety. What if he came to Zanzibar? A place they had both visited. The place where he had bought her the Zanzibar box, and the ring. It was a small island. If he came here she would hear about it, she would see him. Is he looking for me? She thought. Does he want me back? I have to find him, she decided desperately. I have to be absolutely sure there is no mistake.

Running downstairs to where she kept her photograph boxes, she gathered up a few of the photographs she had of him. They were not recent but they were good enough for what she had to do. She ran back upstairs and packed a small bag. She told Abraham she would be away for a few days, then left the house and headed for the ferry which would take her to Dar es Salaam and from there a flight to Nairobi.

Kate checked into the Norfolk Hotel. She would have stayed with Trish but she wanted to keep her search private. She had never told her about Adam and didn't want to have to start now. For the next few days she worked her way around the city, looking for Adam. She scoured the pubs, clubs, bars and all of the hotels. She made calls to game lodges but there was no record of him staying. Emily had written that it had been some months ago. Kate didn't know how many that meant. Maybe he had only been passing through Nairobi, en route to somewhere else. Maybe she was wasting her time. But she had to know for sure; she had to find out.

She pinned printed copies of his photograph on notice boards outside the local shopping centre where she knew most expatriates went. She showed the photograph around at the Muthaiga Club, the Karen Club and at popular restaurants. Underneath each photograph she had put his name, asking if anyone had seen him. She had included her phone number. She drove out to Wilson airport, the portal for all flights heading out to the game lodges. Desperately she showed his photograph to the busy bush pilots collecting their passengers to go on safari, and to the pilots bringing passengers back. But none of them knew him, or had seen him; they barely had time to even glance at the photograph.

The following afternoon, she sat in her room waiting for the phone to ring. It lay silently beside her. She studied the photograph of Adam she had used. Of course, he would look different now. The picture was over ten years old but she didn't have anything recent.

Her mobile rang. Kate snatched it up and held her breath.

"Kate? It's Trish. I've just come back from the shop in Karen and saw a photograph pinned on the notice board. I recognised your number below it. And I've heard that people have seen you all over town sticking up these photographs and asking questions. Why are you looking for this guy? Who is Adam Hamilton? Where are you at the moment?"

Kate sat up quickly. "He's an old friend, Trish. I heard he was in Nairobi. I'd just like to meet up with him again, that's all. I'm staying at the Norfolk," she said lamely.

"Well, look, it's an odd way to try and find a friend, Kate. You can't go running around Nairobi asking if anyone has seen him. You need to get a grip on yourself. You should have stayed with me and maybe I could have helped you. It's a small place and people talk." Kate felt foolish. She *had* been running around town like a lunatic and hadn't thought for one moment what it must have looked like to anyone else.

Trish was still talking and Kate tuned back into her voice. "Listen, remember I told you about that good looking guy I met at the club, a year or so ago? The pilot called Paul? He looked a lot like this friend you're trying to find. At least I think so. A bit older, but I think it was him, Kate. Different name but very similar in looks."

"Have you seen him since, Trish?" Kate asked quickly. "Did you bump into him again anywhere? I really need to know."

Trish heard the urgency in Kate's voice and frowned. "I know better than to try and ask you what this is all about. I know you won't tell me. Yes, I did see him again, a couple of times actually. He was flying guests around, the same as me, but we didn't have time to really talk, just waved at each other."

Kate cursed. None of the pilots she had briefly shown the photo to had recognised Adam. How stupid she had been. If she had stayed with Trish and shown her the photograph she would have had her answer straight away. She just hadn't been thinking straight.

"There are so many pilots coming and going Kate, they move around a lot, all over East Africa. Unless any of them are in your social circle and live in Nairobi the chances are we wouldn't know each other. What on earth is going on, Kate?"

"I've got to go, Trish. What was his surname, this Paul that you met?"

"Morgan. His name was Paul Morgan. Kate..."

"I'll give you a ring tomorrow, Trish. Bye!"

Kate closed her phone, feeling more unnerved than ever. Her heart seemed to be clattering in her chest and she felt light headed. Trish is right, she thought, I need to get a grip on myself. Paul Morgan. She knew from experience how powerful the internet could be. Adam, if it was Adam, was clever. It would not have been difficult for him to take on a new identity, become a pilot and settle somewhere else in Africa. East Africa had a constant flow of game rangers and pilots who moved around. They would spend a few months in one place, before moving on to another. They were forgettable, dispensable. Private pilots were always in high demand, she knew that from Trish. There were dozens of them around and they didn't necessarily all know one another.

Having exhausted all possibilities in Nairobi, and with no further phone calls, Kate decided to take a break and spend a few days in the bush at her old camp Pelican Place. Perhaps she would be able to think things through more clearly there, more calmly. She called the lodge and made a reservation for three days. She left at dawn the next morning.

It was a short flight out to the Mara. Whilst she waited patiently for the lodge vehicle to collect her, she sat beneath the shade of the old aircraft she had once spent the night in. It was worse for wear these days with the paint peeling off the body; the wheels were deflated and it was badly rusted. Kate heard another airplane approaching the runway. Ah, more guests, she thought. That's why the vehicle's late to collect me. They're going to collect us all together.

Idly, she watched the Cessna land and disgorge its four passengers. They stretched and walked around the aircraft, as they waited for the pilot to unload their luggage. The camp's land cruiser drew up alongside the plane. Kate waved at the driver and he waved back before helping the passengers into the vehicle and loading their bags. Kate stood up and was about to walk over to the vehicle when she saw the pilot turn and climb back up into the airplane. He started the engines quickly. He had been some distance away but she had seen that he was tall, tanned and had blond hair. She caught her breath. Was it him? Was it Adam?

Kate began to run towards the plane as the pilot turned and taxied to the end of the airstrip, preparing for take-off. She watched as the plane advanced towards her slowly. Her heart started to pound.

She was standing at the edge of the runway when the plane was at its closest to her. The pilot turned his head in her direction looking surprised to see someone standing alone on the air strip. He looked at her.

It was Adam.

Kate ran towards him but the plane had passed her and the noise of the engines increased as it picked up speed.

"Wait for me, Adam! Wait!" she shouted as she ran after the plane.

The engines were now at high pitch and the red dust in its wake swirled behind it. With a roar it lifted off.

"Wait for me, Adam! Wait for me!" Kate screamed into the dust.

The Cessna rose slowly into the air. Out of breath and struggling to breathe with the dust, Kate slowed to a halt, shading her eyes, watching the aircraft in the distance. Then it turned in a slow arc and re-approached the runway.

Kate's heart lurched in hope. She saw him smile down at her and then he waved once, before gaining height again and flying off.

Kate sank slowly to her knees in the red dust, tears running down her cheeks, dust crunched in her mouth. She wiped the tears away and watched the plane soaring higher until it was just a speck in the sky. Then the silence of the bush returned and everything was still.

Kate turned back towards her luggage and the vehicle waiting to take her to the camp. She saw the guests staring at her astonished. She didn't care. I should have taken down the registration of the aircraft, she said shakily to herself. But it had all happened so quickly that she hadn't been prepared in the slightest. On the drive to the lodge, the only thought that repeated in her head was: he's alive – Adam's alive.

Sitting in one of the suites in the dusk that evening, she thought about the aircraft and the pilot. Had it really been him? Could I have made a mistake? Sadly, she knew she hadn't and that it had been Adam. She was quite sure he had seen her too. Why else would he have banked and flown so close to her? Why else would he have smiled? Exhausted by her emotions she lay back on the bed and fell into a troubled sleep.

She sat up suddenly. It was pitch black and Kate could hear that the camp generator was off. That meant it was after midnight. She wondered if she had heard an animal shuffling outside her tent and whether it was that which had woken her. She listened carefully but it was silent and profoundly still. She resettled herself against her pillows and closed her eyes. She tried to remember what she had been dreaming about. There had been something that had jumped out at her. She realised that whatever it was had woken her up. She had to remember what it was.

Luca! Kate opened her eyes with that one name searingly clear in her head. Luca. He would be the one person that Adam would contact. He would know. Luca had told her he was leaving South Africa and wanted to start his own business somewhere in Uganda. She clearly remembered him saying that when he came to say goodbye to her in Cape Town.

Kate dressed hurriedly and walked through the wakening camp towards the manager's office. She tried the door handle and was grateful that her habit had not been altered by the new manager, it was unlocked. She searched the shelves and then resorted to opening drawers at the desk, looking for a telephone directory. She pulled it out roughly. All the safari companies operating in East Africa would be listed. Uganda, that's where he would be, with Luca. If Luca had started his own flying safari business and Adam was a pilot, then it all made perfect sense. Luca was the key to it all.

Her heart sank as she leafed through the pages. There were at least three dozen of them. Where would she start looking for Luca, she thought quickly? If I pick one or two companies and call them, one of them is bound to know Luca.

She picked up the phone, her heart beating furiously. A telephone operator picked up immediately and she gave him the number she had randomly selected. She was asked to wait and the lined crackled and spat as she did so.

"I'm sorry, the line to Uganda is down at the moment and unlikely to be working for the rest of the day. There is an engineer working on the problem. Would you like to try again tomorrow?"

Chapter Thirty-Four

"**Y**OU'RE LIVING** on borrowed time, Kate. If I was your bank manager I would say that you are in deep overdraft. You should be taking better care of yourself," Dr Burton said sternly, watching her closely.

Kate had met Charles Burton at one of Trish's dinner parties, and she had seen him several times when she came into town from the lodge, either at one of the clubs or restaurants.

"Where do you live now?" he asked as he made notes in her file. "I haven't seen you around for a few years, although Trish kept me up to date on your travels. Bad business in New York. I expect you're glad to be back here."

Kate turned her head, looked at him and smiled. She's not young anymore, he thought, but she has the most beautiful eyes and smile. He had examined her but there was nothing physically wrong with her. She was highly stressed and far too thin.

"I don't really live anywhere permanently but I am making a concerted effort to settle in Zanzibar."

"You must do something about your life, Kate, this moving around is beginning to take its toll on you. You've lost far too much weight since I last saw you and you seem to be under a lot of emotional strain. You need to take some time off. Can you try to get away somewhere for a few weeks? You need to find someone to look after you. Where's your daughter these days? Why don't you go and stay with her for a while?"

He watched as her eyes filled with tears. "Molly has her own life to live and I don't want her to see me like this. But there's a game lodge up near the Matthews Range, way up on the Northern Frontier. Trish told me about it. The owners need someone to look after it for a month or so, whilst they are in Europe. It could be a good place to be right now."

He watched her carefully, noticing how her hands shook slightly, how she constantly fiddled with the bracelet on her thin wrist. She was very agitated about something. "I can prescribe some tranquillisers for you, Kate. That might help with whatever is bothering you so much at the moment."

Kate shook her head again. "No, no pills. Thank you. I'll be all right. I just need a bit of time to sort some things out."

"Would you like to tell me about it, Kate?" he asked her gently.

She hesitated briefly and then in an outpouring of relief, she told him what had happened since receiving Emily's email. When she was finished, Charles came around to where she sat. Sitting opposite her, he took her hand in his.

"Look at me, Kate. No-one ever died of a broken heart but you need to take better care of yours. I know you don't like taking pills but you are going to have to take something to slow your heart down a bit. These pills will calm you down and give your heart a bit of a break. Let me help."

As he wrote out a prescription for her, he continued. "Surely you must have met some decent men in all these exotic places you've been living? It seems to me that you've been running hard and fast for far too long. Slow down a bit, Kate. You never know, there may be someone out there trying to catch up with you!"

She gave him a wry smile. "Well, there was someone I met years ago in London but I was married and so was he. It was a bit of a non-starter, really. I think of him now and again and wonder how he is and where he is. He was very decent... well, he appeared to be." She smiled ruefully. "I promise to take better care of myself, although I'm not sure what for."

"Do it for yourself, Kate, and for Molly. Think about taking that job looking after the lodge that you mentioned, up in the Northern Frontier. It might be a good place for you to be. You can't go on running all over town looking for this man who has risen from the dead. If you are right and it is him, then quite clearly he doesn't want anyone to recognise him. Let it go, Kate."

He watched her leave. He wasn't entirely sure that the game lodge was such a good idea. He didn't think that she should return to Zanzibar as she would be alone, but he did think she should be surrounded by people and the lodge would provide that. His only concern was that it would be so remote that it would give her too much time to think about things. She seemed fragile and her mind, as well as her heart, was all over the place.

Chapter Thirty-Five

A MARVELLOUS THING, the internet, Adam thought. The internet and gossip. Just a few well-placed pieces of information and a couple of whispers in the right ears and he had managed to create his own demise. The expatriate community in Africa rarely checked the facts of such a story. Within days the news had swept through the continent. He was dead. No-one asked for proof. Why would they? He had changed his name, got a new passport, and headed back to Africa.

Luca had met him off the flight in Uganda, where he had been living for the past eight years, and where he had set up his flying safari business. He, of course, had heard of Adam's death; after all, he had been the one to suggest the idea and had arranged for the new passport.

In the following months, he taught Adam to fly and he shared his home in Uganda with him. Adam was different to how he remembered him. He was thinner, harder and more brittle than he had been when they had met briefly in England. He also drank a lot more than he ever had before. Sometimes, despite being very careful to hide it, Adam's hands would shake so much in the mornings that he would have trouble holding his cup of tea or coffee. This concerned Luca, and he watched him carefully, but Adam was a damn good pilot and seemed sober when he flew.

After Adam had obtained his pilot's licence Luca explained the next part of the plan. He had bought and registered a small aircraft in Kenya and kept it in a hangar at the airstrip in Nanyuki.

"There shouldn't be any need to go into Nairobi on a regular basis, Adam. All you need to do is fly guests from lodge to lodge. I've registered a company there and I've let the lodges and charter companies know that we're ready for business. We already have bookings for next month. It's highly unlikely that anyone will recognise you. Nanyuki is a sleepy little town and I've rented a small cottage for you on the outskirts. It's a bit basic but it's comfortable. It's obviously important that you don't get too close to anyone there. Just keep your head down and don't socialise. I have a contact in Nairobi and if he needs to see you he'll come out to Nanyuki. You might start to go a bit bush crazy after a few months, and if that's the case then by all means go to Nairobi, but keep away from the usual watering holes and clubs, and don't fly yourself there in the company aircraft. We don't want anyone to get suspicious and start asking questions. Use a local charter. There is good business to be had there, but my contact will see to all that." That had been six months ago.

Adam flew back to Kampala once a month, on a scheduled flight. Now they were sitting on Luca's veranda, drinking beer. Although an intensely private man himself, Luca felt as though it was time to lay some ghosts to rest.

"I'm sorry about Kate and everything that happened, Adam. I was very fond of her and of Molly, but that was the price that had to be paid and you had to pay it. I know you don't want to talk about it, but I'd like to know when it all started to go wrong, before you came to me for help. I was close enough to both of you to see that there were problems coming up. So tell me?"

Adam stared out into the night. Kate. He had loved her very much. He turned to look at Luca and his eyes narrowed with memory.

"If I recall we had a deal? You didn't want to know why I needed the money?" He shrugged his shoulders. "*She* started to change, Luca."

"How so?" Luca asked, reaching for another bottle of beer. It was still cool to the touch and water droplets had condensed on the outside of the glass. Although he had been close to both of them, and had agreed to do the occasional business trip for them, he had kept well out of the actual running of the business. They had never discussed it with anyone other than each other.

"Kate was a far better business partner than I was. You know me, Luca, blow it when you have it and face the consequences when you don't. After Kate got the company out of trouble by selling her house, everything was fine. Even after her lawyer got her to ask me for half of my company, I didn't mind. I'd rather have a solvent business than otherwise. Obviously no-one knew about any of this, we kept it highly confidential. The company finally started to make serious money and Kate was brilliant with her ideas and the publicity. She saw that the company infrastructure needed attention. She brought in a top accountant, set up computers, appointed auditors and insisted that we cut back on the marketing. She wanted to make sure the company wouldn't get into trouble again. I knew she wanted her money back. She wanted to buy a house, she disliked having to rent an apartment. I hated all the restrictions. It had all been so much fun, Luca. You remember that." He flicked his cigarette out into the garden where it arched briefly before disappearing.

"I missed her, but there was also a lot of freedom in going alone on the odd business trip. Kate was far away. I was on my own, so why not? Kate resented the freedom that I took. She didn't want to be sitting in the office either, but someone had to and she knew as well as I did that it wasn't going to be me. When I returned, she always wanted to know the details of who I had seen, how much money I had spent, which hotels I had stayed in. She wanted all the receipts to check things out."

Luca smiled to himself. Yes, he remembered having to account for everything when he returned from his trips around the lodges every year, and for the occasional overseas marketing trip he had done for them. What they had paid him had been chicken feed to what he normally earned, but it had served his purposes to be out on the road.

"But why are you asking me all this, you knew pretty much what was going on in the company?"

Luca narrowed his eyes. "Yes, I remember all that, but something doesn't stack up... but carry on, let's hear the rest of the story."

Adam reached for a fresh beer and wondered just how much Luca had worked out. "I started to look around a little. I met an American woman at a camp in Botswana. She was from New York. She was..." he paused and a flicker of doubt crossed his face. Luca was watching Adam intently. It was after one of these first few trips to New York that Adam had asked for his help. He heard a note in his friend's voice that didn't ring true.

"Kate started to get clingy and needy; she started to want more from me – not just in business but in our relationship too. She'd never asked anything from me before." Adam turned to face Luca before continuing, "And then she found out about me and the woman in New York and that was it. You remember. You were there."

"I remember," Luca said quietly. "What happened after I left for Uganda?"

"I blew money left, right and centre. I spent eight months of the year out of the country and it was much harder to get the business on my own. The international operators liked Kate. Anyway, to cut a long story short, and as you well know, I had to leave the country in a hurry.

"I had met Jessica, a few months before I had to leave. She was nuts about me. She wasn't much to look at, as you know, not like Kate, but she suited my purpose. Her parents had left her that place in England, out in the country. It was the perfect cover so I made the most of the situation." He smiled ruefully. "I really screwed up, Luca." He stood up and stretched, looking out into the darkening night. "God it's good to be back in Africa!" He glanced at his watch. "Better turn in, early flight tomorrow. See you in a month's time."

Luca picked up the thick envelope off the table and tossed it at Adam. "Hey, don't forget this."

Luca watched his retreating back as he headed into the house. His old friend was not telling him the whole story about the end of his affair with Kate and on this trip back to Uganda he had seemed edgy. Something didn't stack up. By mutual agreement, after he had left Cape Town for Uganda, they had not kept in touch apart from the time they had met in Jessica's cottage.

Adam stood under a long hot shower. His body ached and he was dog-tired. The pain in his gut made him gasp. He bent over and waited for it to pass. He knew that he had made some mistakes in his life and his biggest regret had been losing Kate. He longed for her. She would never understand – or even know – what he had done to protect her. When he heard she had moved to New York, he had put some feelers out and soon found out where she was working. It hadn't been hard.

When he was there on his next trip, he had waited for her and watched her. She had always known when he was around when they were together. He could walk into a crowded room and she would turn her head and look directly at him. He had wondered whether she had known he was there when he followed her in New York. A part of him had wanted her to see him but he had been forced to be careful that she didn't. When he had last gone back to New York, he had gone inside the store to discreetly enquire if Kate Hope was in, and they had told he that she had left the month before. He didn't know where she had gone after that. And then he had seen her in the middle of the bush in Kenya.

He remembered how he had started to taxi down the dirt strip, clouds of red dust billowing up behind him and seeing the woman standing there. Suddenly she had started to run, her hair coming loose from its clip. Squinting through his sunglasses, he had realised soon enough that it was Kate.

"Jesus, out here in the middle of no-where, and there she is!"

Ah Kate, he had thought to himself as he flew away from her. You must know that I died? Did the news trickle down to you eventually? Someone must have been on the phone to you straight away. Did you ever realise that a couple of times, when I was in New York, I walked right past the store where you worked? Once I saw you walking along 5th Avenue but you didn't see me, did you? You used to be able to sense me around in any city, but I guess those senses have all closed down now?

The pain in his gut eased and he straightened up. He stepped out of the shower and wrapped a towel around his waist. He took a look in the mirror and quickly glanced away. He knew he didn't look good these days. He was too thin and his face was gaunt and grey. He took a swig from the glass of vodka he had brought into the bathroom with him and returned to the chair on the veranda. He could do without ferrying guests around the lodges for the next week but it had to be done, the bookings had been confirmed.

He lit a cigarette with a match. The small flame glinted off the silver cross around his neck. He sighed deeply. It wouldn't be long now. He shook the match quickly, extinguishing the flame. Sooner rather than later he would have to tell Luca that Kate was more than likely living in Kenya, and that he was quite sure she had recognised him. He anticipated that Luca would advise him to move on. They didn't want the police sniffing around the company: that might lead to an even greater danger. He would have to tell him, or maybe leave him a quick note, so that when he got back in a month's time they could come up with a solid plan. He felt his eyes burn and closed them seeing her standing there on the air strip, calling his name in despair.

Strapping himself into his seat, Adam checked his instruments and filed his flight plan. He had dropped his passengers off here in the Mara and now he was heading back to Nanyuki. Waiting for the tower, a small singular structure, to give him the all-clear to commence his flight, Adam thought about the week ahead. He had four passengers to bring on safari to the Mara, then he was done for the month. Luca would have read the note he had left and would no doubt have come up with a plan. Adam anticipated that it would probably be the last time he would see Luca; he would have to leave the country.

Because now they had a problem. Kate. She was the one person who would have no trouble identifying him and blowing his cover. In the past few days since he had seen her, Adam had been flooded with feelings of guilt, for the pain he had had to cause her, as well as desire to hold her, to speak with her, to make love to her. For the first time in years he felt he owed her a full explanation and the answers to why he had done what he had done. He had written a letter to her, then sent it to his attorney in Uganda with clear instructions that it should be delivered immediately to the Muthaiga Club, in Nairobi, in the event of his death. He knew that from there it would find its way to Kate.

His radio suddenly crackled to life and the tower gave Adam the all-clear for take-off. He taxied to the end of the airstrip, turned the plane around and began to accelerate. As the plane picked up speed, it felt sluggish and when he began to ascend, the plane rose slowly. Puzzled, Adam checked his instruments. Everything looked in order. He pulled up quickly, trying to pick up some height and speed. A shadow swooped low in front of his windscreen. He frowned. It was some kind of bird. He tried to see past it but the sun was blinding him. Distracted, he pulled sharply to the right. He felt the aircraft lose what little height it had gained. Too late he saw a rocky outcrop rearing up in front of him. On impact the plane burst into flames.

The scream of fire engines ripped through the silence of the bush. When the wreckage had cooled down, the police pulled the burned remains of the pilot from the cockpit of the plane. The body was beyond recognition and would be nearly impossible to identify. They removed a silver chain from around his blackened neck. There was a cross on the end of it that had been slightly damaged by the flames.

Adam Hamilton would be impossible to identify now.

After her visit with the doctor, Kate caught a taxi back to the Norfolk Hotel. She wanted to have lunch and use their internet facilities before catching her flight back to Zanzibar. The search for Adam had exhausted her. She had searched long and hard for him with no results. None of the companies in Uganda had heard of Luca either. Perhaps, she thought bitterly, he had changed *his* name as well. Although she knew she would go on searching for both of them, she also needed to earn some money and wanted to confirm her acceptance of the job at the lodge.

Kate greeted the waiter and sat down wearily at the table. It was Friday and the place was full and noisy. It seemed more boisterous than usual. She sat quietly at a table and let herself eavesdrop on the conversations going on around her.

Who was the pilot? Which company owned the aircraft? Questions volleyed back and forth. Curious, Kate turned to the couple at the next table.

"Excuse me, what's all this about a plane crash?"

The young woman turned to Kate, relishing the opportunity of telling the story to someone who had not already heard it.

"Oh, it was terrible and so mysterious! It crashed just after take-off in the Mara. They say it was pilot error. The plane was loaded with fuel and struggled to gain height and then suddenly it turned sharply and crashed into some rocks. We don't know who it was yet, he was burned beyond recognition. The only thing known is that the aircraft was a blue and white Cessna and registered to a company no-one has ever heard of."

Kate felt the hair on the back of her neck stand up. Her gut twisted and her mouth went dry. "Adam," she whispered raggedly. "It's Adam."

Kate stood and ran hurriedly out of the restaurant. The young woman she had been speaking to guessed from her reaction that Kate knew something about the pilot, and she added that juicy morsel to her repertoire of news. Kate quickly checked back into the hotel again. She couldn't leave now, not until she had real proof.

Chapter Thirty-Six

TURNING OFF THE COMPUTER, Tom rubbed his eyes. Suddenly the telephone rang; he glanced at his watch, sleepily. It was a bit late for a call this time of night. Sitting up quickly, he reached over and punched the receive button.

Twenty minutes later he sat back, the phone still warm in his hand.

The call had been from his friend at the British High Commission in Nairobi, Mike McNeil. He had told him the most extraordinary story.

There had been a fatal accident out in the bush. A small Cessna airplane had crashed shortly after take-off and the pilot had been burnt beyond recognition. It was thought he had been English and the High Commission had become involved in trying to identify the body. The tower had confirmed the registration of the aircraft. It was registered in Kenya but belonged to a safari company in Uganda.

The company in Kampala had been informed of the crash and the death of the pilot. The owner of the company, Luca Brenner, had told them the name of the pilot: Paul Morgan. He had been questioned further and told the authorities that Paul had turned up looking for work one day and he had given him a job.

He mentioned that his pilots had habitually flown with their passports and pilot's licence and that Paul's had probably been destroyed in the crash. He had given them Paul's address in Nanyuki but they had found absolutely nothing, there was no paperwork of any kind to help them. He didn't say much more than that.

The High Commission in Nairobi was now deeply involved in the case.

231

As a matter of course, an autopsy had been carried out on what was left of the body and the dental records had been checked against an international database. The name of Paul Morgan did not exist.

"By pure chance I was having a beer at the club the day after the crash and overheard a conversation at the bar between four pilots who were discussing the accident. I got chatting to a Trish O'Connell and she told me she was convinced that the dead pilot was living under an assumed name. She showed me one of the posters that she had found pinned up outside one of the local shops. Apparently she had met him in Nairobi a couple of times and put two and two together. So that was the lead I was looking for," he had told Tom. "I asked Trish if she knew who had had been looking for this Adam Hamilton and who had been sticking the posters up all over town, but she said she didn't know. I'm not sure if I believed her. I think she was trying to protect the identity of whoever it was. We tried to call the number on the poster but it was dead."

Dental records were obtained in Cape Town and there had been a positive match to the dead pilot. There was no doubt that the deceased had had two different names, but was the same person. Adam Hamilton.

Adam Hamilton had left South Africa abruptly and taken up residence with a South African woman in England. Further investigation had revealed that he had left England two years ago, his destination unknown. He appeared to have disappeared.

More confusing facts were emerging. Mr Adam Hamilton had apparently died sometime after he left England. His former business partner was a Kate Hope. Ms Hope had apparently arrived in Kenya just two weeks before the accident, which the Embassy saw as a strange coincidence. From what they understood, she had been posting photographs of Mr Hamilton all over Nairobi, apparently looking for him. Stranger too was the fact that there had been no death recorded of a Mr Hamilton anywhere.

"Sounds like this Hamilton character faked his own death and took on a new identity," Mike had told him. "That's the line of enquiry we are pursuing. We're also trying to trace Kate Hope but she seems to have disappeared as well."

Tom's mind was racing with possibilities. Definitely this was Kate and geographically, given her history, she was on her own territory there in East Africa. Was she somehow still involved with this mystery pilot? At one point they had been business partners. Had the relationship endured for longer than the years they had been together in South Africa then? Was Kate involved in something illegal here? Why would this man, Adam, fake his own death and pitch up in Kenya. It looked as though she had gone back to this Adam. Maybe she had been part of the faked death and perhaps had arranged to meet up with Adam once the dust had settled. Perhaps there was money involved, maybe a life insurance policy? Why had Kate been sticking up posters all over town? Surely if she was involved she would know exactly where he was?

Mike McNeil had told Tom it wouldn't have been that difficult for Adam Hamilton to change his name and passport. If you had the right contacts in Europe, it could be done. Mike had also given him the last known address of Adam Hamilton and the woman he had lived with there in the UK.

Tom was relieved. He now had solid news of Kate, despite the circumstances being rather dubious. He curbed his excitement and cautioned himself. Kate could have a past he might not want to know about, or be a part of, now.

He told himself he was letting his imagination run riot with incriminating possibilities. He checked himself and re-evaluated the facts: Kate was, either willingly or unwillingly, involved in something suspicious. So far, there wasn't anything criminal, not yet anyway, but there had been a death, false identification and two people who had perhaps been partners for many years, and who both happened to be in the same part of the world at the same time when the accident happened.

He glanced at his notes next to the telephone. He would go to the address in Dorchester and see if he could learn anything of any interest. Maybe the South African woman was still living there.

Early the following evening, Tom drove up to the front of the house on the outskirts of Dorchester. The garden was tangled and overgrown and the house looked uninhabited. He pressed the buzzer and heard the chimes of a bell. He rang again before hearing slow footsteps heading towards the front door.

It opened slowly, revealing a middle-aged woman who squinted at him quizzically, a frown on her face. Taking a deep breath he took a chance and asked if this was the home of Adam Hamilton? The woman shook her head and started to close the door.

"No, please hear me out ma'am. I'm trying to find Adam Hamilton. It's really important. Are you Jessica Theron?"

The woman hesitated then rubbed her face with her hand. "You had better come in," she said wearily. "Yes, my name is Jessica Theron." She led him through to the lounge and invited him to sit down. She sat down opposite him saying nothing. The room felt cold and there was very little light. Newspapers and old magazines were piled up on the floor, along with a plate with a half-eaten sandwich on it.

"I'm sorry to call on you like this," Tom said, smiling apologetically. "I'm trying to find Adam Hamilton on behalf of a friend of mine who lives in London. I understand he used to live here?"

Jessica looked at him suspiciously and then with a deep sigh, as if the very name of the man was too much of a burden for her, she nodded reluctantly. After two years on her own, she felt a strong desire to talk to someone. Adam had disappeared and had not been in contact with her. She felt that she had nothing to lose by talking to this American.

"I met him at a cocktail party in Cape Town. He was looking for a receptionist and I got the job. I fell for him in a big way. I'd never met anyone quite like him and I was grateful that he showed any interest in me at all. He was a good looking man and we got on well enough. There were no great fireworks from his side though, but I loved him. Things started to go wrong for him and he was unhappy. He wanted to leave the country. So when he decided to leave, I went with him. I had inherited this house here and some money.

"At first we rubbed along together but he never wanted to go out anywhere, or meet anyone, in fact he rarely went out at all. He only had one visitor who lived in Uganda; I can't remember his name but Adam asked me to go out for the day as they had things to discuss.

"I think after a while I probably got on his nerves. He could be very dark company and was given to terrible rages. That was usually when he would drink."

Tom watched her as she talked. Her hair was short and lank. Her eyes had been dulled by alcohol and her skin was puffy and red. Was she a casualty of Adam, he wondered, or life in general?

"Where is he now, Jessica?"

"He's gone. He didn't want to be here anymore. He left me, as he left all the rest of them. Always running, always hiding from himself and the reality that was his life. He was always looking for something. There was this woman, you see. There always is, isn't there? Her name was Kate." Tom's heart skipped a beat; he was on the right track at last.

"He didn't talk about her but I knew about her. The travel and safari industry is small and we all knew one another. I bumped into her once. It was in the ladies' room at a travel show in London. Adam had asked me to go with him to London so I could learn more about the travel business." She sighed and rubbed her face again. "They were known as the lion and lioness amongst the industry, did you know that? They were fearless and adventurous. Everyone knew them. I suppose I had always known that we would have no future. I could never live up to Kate or what they had together. I don't really know why he chose me. I suppose I was her opposite. I knew he was going to discard me when he was ready. He was ruthless but I stayed with him."

She stood up and offered Tom a drink. He refused and she poured herself a generous glass of vodka. "I still don't understand why he threw her away when he suffered like that afterwards. It never made sense to me. If he wanted to be with her so much, he should have just fixed it," she said bitterly. "He was selfish and arrogant, but he loved her. No-one else stood a chance."

Jessica was quite drunk by now. Tom realised she must have been drinking before he arrived. Her hands shook as she lit a cigarette.

"Where is Adam now, Jessica?" Tom asked her again, gently.

She looked at him stonily. "I think he went back to her. Somewhere in Africa. It was the place where they were happiest. I came home one day and he was gone. He must have been in a big hurry because he left his pills behind; he used to take them every day. I don't know what they were for but after he left I found them. They were prescribed by a doctor in New York. I thought that was strange."

"Do you know what happened to Kate?"

"No. But he always knew where she was."

She stood up unsteadily and walked to the window. She held onto the window to keep herself balanced. Tom felt a pang of sympathy for her. "I don't have contact with anyone in the industry anymore. I don't even have a computer, so I can't help you. I don't know where he is. I've had no contact with him at all. One day he was here and the next he was gone. It's almost as if he ceased to exist. Yes, I think he went back to Africa. Kate was his talisman, she was his touchstone. I think that she was the only thing he ever regretted in his life. He loved that woman.

"Maybe he's dead. As for Kate, I have no idea. If he's not dead, maybe they're back together. If they're both in the same country, they'll find each other. They always did."

Tom thanked her for talking to him and left. With no computer and no contact with anyone in Africa, Jessica would have no knowledge of what had happened to Adam. Tom didn't feel that it was his place to tell her. He turned his car in the driveway and as he passed by the sitting room window he saw that she was still standing there staring after him. She didn't move when he waved and drove away.

On the drive back he wondered about the only visitor Adam had had when he lived here – the man from Uganda. It could only have been Luca Brenner. He had to have been involved with this somewhere along the line.

Chapter Thirty-Seven

KATE PULLED THE STRIP off the back of the envelope and sealed it. Opening the Zanzibar box, she placed it carefully where her daughter would find it. She put the keys in an envelope, which she would drop at the hotel. She had made arrangements for it to be couriered to David in Johannesburg. The taxi waited outside and she could hear the engine running. Taking a last tearful look around, Kate turned towards the big carved door and left the house in Zanzibar.

It's not what I wanted, she said to herself, but it seems to be the only answer now. She knew a place, an isolated place, where no-one would be able to find her. The future she had tried to make for herself in Zanzibar had not worked out.

Adam's terrible accident had almost unhinged her mind. Her desperation had turned to hopelessness. It will be better this way, she thought. Before leaving Nairobi, on her way back to Zanzibar, Trish had called her from the Muthaiga Club, telling her there was a letter waiting for her there.

"The whole town is abuzz with talk of the crash and the pilot. Some of the stories are quite amazing. We'll be able to dine out on the story for years. I can't believe that Paul Morgan and your old friend is one and the same person..." The line went dead in her hand.

Kate had picked the letter up on the way to the airport. Embossed on the top left-hand corner was the name and address of a legal company based in Uganda. Kate had glanced at it briefly and put it in her handbag.

Tom sat and looked out over the park hardly seeing the pale sun filtering through the leaves of the trees. Kate was in Kenya, embroiled in something he could not comprehend. Whatever was going on in her life at the moment he felt he had to be with her, no matter how bad things might be.

That evening Tom boarded the Kenya Airways flight to Nairobi. He was finally doing what he had always dreamt of doing: he was going to find the woman he loved. The aircraft sliced through the night bringing them closer.

The morning lights of Nairobi poked their way through the inky sky as the aircraft began its descent. Tom fastened his seatbelt and took a deep breath. The aircraft touched down and then nudged its way to the main terminal building. It stopped with a hissing sigh.

He checked into the Norfolk Hotel. Once he had settled in, he headed for the hotel manager's office. With the help of Mike McNeil he had been able to persuade the manager to let him look at the hotel register. Carefully checking back through the pages he finally found her name, but there was no address. He felt a twist of excitement as he looked down at her signature: Kate Hope.

Like Kate a few weeks before, he searched Nairobi for someone who would know where she might be. He checked the clubs and hotels and spoke to people in the popular restaurants. His disadvantage, however, was that he had no photograph of her and no idea what she looked like now.

At the Muthaiga Club, later that week, he found himself part of a small crowd at the bar. The Kenyan expatriate community was larger than he had imagined and this seemed to be a favourite watering hole. The people were friendly and he found himself engaged in conversation with two couples who had lived in the country for over thirty years. They invited him to join them for dinner in the dining room.

During the meal he told his dinner companions that he was looking for a woman whom he had met many years ago in London. They listened to the story politely but had never heard of the woman he talked about. During coffee, they were interrupted by the arrival at their table of one of their old friends, and introductions were made.

Deeply tanned from years in the bush, and with his dark hair caught in a ponytail plus a single gold stud in his ear, Toby McBride was instantly recognisable around Nairobi. Deep lines spread from around his friendly brown eyes as he smiled at Tom. They shook hands and Toby pulled up a chair.

Toby had been in Kenya for over forty years and was judged to be one of the best bush pilots in the country. They chatted about helicopters and fixed wing aircraft. Tom had got his private pilot's licence fifteen years ago.

Toby seemed to know just about everyone. People came up to the table to say hello, before drifting off again.

Taking a chance, Tom asked him if he knew the story behind the pilot who had crashed his plane in the Mara.

"Yes, indeed," Toby said. "It's an odd story. The pilot was not who he appeared to be. After careful investigation, he turned out to be someone called Adam Hamilton. The crash was pilot error. Apparently, after the crash, there was some drama with a woman who had pitched up at the airport and asked a lot of questions; she spoke to different pilots and badgered everyone, demanding to see the wreckage. She was a nice looking woman but she had come across as quite demented. Someone said that she lived in Zanzibar and had quite a past."

Tom's heartbeat quickened. "You don't know her name, by any chance?" he tried to ask as casually as he could.

"Yes," said Toby. "She's been in and out of Kenya for years. She used to run a lodge here. Her name is Kate Hope. I've never met her though."

"Could you fly me to Zanzibar tomorrow?" Tom asked without hesitating.

"Sure," Toby said. "I'd be pleased to, but we'll have to stay overnight. I don't mind that if you don't?" Tom shook his head. "I've always loved Zanzibar," Toby continued. "Meet me at Wilson airport at nine tomorrow morning. Any taxi will know where it is."

They arrived in Zanzibar before midday. Tom left Toby with the aircraft and caught a taxi into the old town. He was relieved that the island was small – it shouldn't be too difficult to find her house.

The taxi dropped him at Emmerson's Hotel in the town centre. He checked in and reserved a room for Toby, who would join him later. He looked through the telephone directory. There was no Kate Hope listed. He wondered whether most of the residents used mobile phones; he knew, from his various trips to Africa that they would be more reliable than landlines.

As he passed back through the lobby, Tom noticed a tall man in conversation with the receptionist. From the way the receptionist was talking with him and from what he overheard, Tom rightly assumed that the man was the owner of the hotel. Tom waited for him to finish his conversation and, when he did, he introduced himself and asked him if he knew a woman called Kate Hope.

"Yes, Kate! I know her well. She often comes here for dinner. She likes to sit up on the roof and look out over the town. I haven't seen her for a few weeks though. I think she went to Kenya. I can give you her address and perhaps her houseboy, Abraham, can tell you when she's due back. She might even be here now. I just haven't seen her for a while."

Tom walked out into the heat and followed the directions he had been given. I just can't imagine her living in a place like this, he thought, wondering how long she had been on the island.

There were no numbers on any of the large ornate doors but he found her street. The hotel owner had told him that next door to Kate's house there was a tiny school comprising of one classroom. He wouldn't be able to miss it, he was assured, as there was a brilliant orange bougainvillea plant between the house and the school. Kate's house, he told Tom, was the one with the pale blue shutters.

He found the house immediately. He lifted the heavy knocker and let it drop on the huge door. Brass reverberated against brass. There was no response. He waited a minute and tried again. There was still no response. An old African man, sitting on a stool in the shade of a door awning, watched him curiously.

"Come back at four," the old man said. "Abraham will be back then. He runs the house for Miss Kate."

Thanking him, Tom returned to the hotel. He had found Kate's house. What would she say when she saw him again? What would he say to her? He felt a little nervous. What if her lover opened the door? Maybe she hadn't just disappeared as Mike McNeil had told him, maybe she had just come home. The hours crawled by and, just before four, Tom returned to the house with the pale blue shutters.

Abraham seemed to be expecting him. Tom explained he was an old friend from many years ago and would like to see Kate. Abraham shook his head sadly, inviting him in.

He sat in Kate's lounge whilst Abraham made him a coffee, hardly believing where he was. His eyes travelled around the room. He saw her collection of books and a bronze statue that was particularly beautiful. He stood up and walked over to the huge boards of photographs. There were hundreds of them and Kate was in many of them. Her daughter in various stages of her young and adult life; with her husband, he presumed, holding a small baby at the christening. There were Kate and Molly on safari in a place, which could only be Botswana. He remembered the unusual sunsets from his recent trip there and the special light of the Okavango at that time of the day.

He looked at the photographs of her daughter and felt something stir in his memory. Tom felt as though he was travelling back through Kate's life as he looked at the photographs. Something began to bother him slightly. He carried on looking, trying to figure out what it was. That's it. Somewhere around Kate's late-forties there were no more photographs. As if everything had stopped at around that time.

He touched Kate's face in one of the photographs. She seemed to be looking straight at him, perched on the roof of a land cruiser, somewhere out in the bush. Her large eyes stared back at him, her mouth slightly curved into a smile. Now I know why I could never get her out of my head, he thought. I'm still in love with her. I never forgot her. Not since that first evening I saw her in London. He bent closer to see her better, and that's when he noticed the earrings.

Abraham padded softly back into the room, carefully placing a coffee tray on top of a Zanzibar box. Tom poured his coffee, his mind in turmoil. Abraham folded his arms behind his back and stood near the door, like a sentry.

"Abraham, I think Kate is in trouble. I want to help her. I met her many years ago and I want to find out where she is. Will Kate be home soon?" Tom asked. Abraham shook his head. "Can you tell me where she is?"

Abraham sighed softly and began to speak quietly. "Miss Kate came here to this island just over two years ago. She brought all her things from across the sea and made her home here. She seemed to be happy. She has a daughter. Miss Molly came many times to the island to be with her mother, these were very happy times. Then a month or so ago Miss Kate went to Nairobi. When she came back she seemed sad, no energy, no smiles anymore. She spent a lot of time writing, many hours, up there on the roof. Miss Kate didn't want to eat and she stayed in her bed until late in the day. Sometimes I would see her crying up there on the roof, looking out at the sea. I would leave her alone. Alone with her troubles and sadness.

"After the weekend, I came to the house and she was not here. The next day, I waited thinking that maybe she had stayed with a friend overnight but she did not come that day either. On Wednesday, when I was cleaning her room, I noticed that some of her things were gone. I checked her cupboard and saw that her small travelling bag was not there. She must have left in a hurry because there are things that she always takes with her that she left behind this time. She was not happy when she came back from Nairobi. Something was very wrong. I think that Miss Kate is in a bad place in her heart and I do not think she will come home this time."

Alarmed by Abraham's conviction, Tom finished his coffee and asked him if he could look around. Perhaps he would find something that might throw some light on what had happened and where she went. "Kate, please come back to your house. I've looked for you for years, don't let me down now?" he muttered.

Adam. Tom shook his head. It had to be something to do with him. Tom climbed the stairs leading to her room. The soft white curtains fluttered beneath the slowly circulating ceiling fan and he shivered, despite the heat. How often I have wanted to be in her bedroom, he thought, wanted to lie with her, feel her breathing next to me and to feel her in my arms. How often have I thought of waking with her in the morning, feeling her hair on my shoulder, her face in my neck. I've wanted to feel her skin, wanted to make love to her, to feel myself inside of her and to hear her cry out. He sat on the bed and looked around. He glanced at the photographs next to the bed. He saw Kate leaning towards a blond-haired man as she smiled up at him. The scent of her seemed to permeate the room.

Tom reached for his wallet. His fingers felt the hard object tucked away in the corner. He pulled it out and rolled it between his fingers. The amber earring glinted in the late afternoon sun. It was the earring that the woman had dropped in the restaurant in Cape Town. He went back downstairs and studied the photograph of Kate sitting on top of the land cruiser and then down at the earring in his hand. It was only a hunch and a ridiculous idea but it was worth a try.

"Abraham?" he called. "Could you come with me a moment please?" Abraham appeared like a genie. "Where does Kate keep her jewellery?" Tom asked. He saw Abraham's quizzical expression and realised that he was a perfect stranger asking to see what was in all likelihood a treasure trove for a thief. To reassure him, Tom held out the earring on the palm of his hand.

"Do you recognise it?" he asked. Abraham shook his head.

They walked together back to Kate's bedroom where Abraham carefully opened the wardrobe door and returned with a brown and red box. A gold dragon was painted on the lid. It was a Chinese puzzle box and made from many pieces of flat wood. There was obviously a sequence required to open it. He had seen boxes like that in China and Hong Kong.

Tom struggled with it. Pulling and pushing each piece of wood, his hands were clumsy in his haste. Frustrated, he placed it on the bed and stood up. He ran his fingers over an old leather chest as he moved towards the wardrobe. Opening the doors, he caught a faint hint of perfume. He inhaled deeply. He touched her clothes as though the gesture might bring him closer to her and give him some clue as to where she might have gone in such a desperate hurry.

Abraham picked up the box and studied it. With sure movements, he pulled and pushed the wooden fragments. Suddenly, there was a chime and the box split in half, revealing a deep drawer containing her jewellery.

Tom turned quickly from the wardrobe and tipped the contents of the box out onto the bed, his heart beating and pounding in his ears. There it was. One small amber earring. He sat heavily on the bed with an earring on the palm of each hand.

The woman in the restaurant who had been wearing the baseball cap had been Kate. Abraham looked at him even more puzzled, not understanding the significance of the earrings. It was an extraordinary, impossible, coincidence, but the evidence now lay in Tom's hands. They were identical.

Abraham carefully placed everything back in the box. He smoothed the white covers on the bed and padded quietly from the room.

Tom, feeling shaky and exhausted with emotion, climbed the stairs to the roof. He felt the warm stone underneath his hands.

Abraham followed him up to the roof with a cold glass of wine. He liked and trusted this tall American because he seemed to want to find Miss Kate. He didn't think that he would, but he would help him if he could.

"I need to ask you some more questions," Tom said. "You may not want to tell me the answers but I have to find Kate." Abraham nodded.

"Did Kate live with a man here?"

Abraham shook his head.

"Do you know who the man in the photograph next to her bed is?"

Abraham explained that he had only seen the photograph recently, before Kate went to Nairobi. It appeared one morning next to her bed. He did not know the man and had not seen him on the island.

"Perhaps it was someone from a long time ago?" he ventured.

Tom sipped the wine. Memories tumbled back to him and elements began to fall into place. The girl in the store in New York. He ran down the stairs again and stared at the photograph of the girl. She was the one who had chatted to him in the store on Madison Avenue. This was Kate's daughter, Molly; or someone incredibly like her. No wonder she had looked vaguely familiar! And, she had come from Africa, he remembered. He had met Kate's daughter and not even realised it. He had come that close to Kate twice and never known it.

He went back up to the roof garden slowly. He was aware of Abraham hovering beside him.

"Mr Tom," Abraham said quietly. "What shall I say to Miss Molly when she calls the house?"

Tom thought quickly. "Tell her that her mother has been out of contact for a few days. For all we know, Kate might have spoken to Molly." He smacked his forehead with his hand. He pulled his mobile phone from his pocket. "I'm not thinking clearly, Abraham, what is Miss Kate's mobile phone number? She must have one?"

He punched the number into his phone and held his breath. Her mobile was dead. He hung up, frustrated.

"If and when Molly calls, please tell her that I came to the house to try and find her mother. Tell her my name and that I am an old friend of Kate's. If she hasn't heard from her mother then I think she deserves to know that Kate has been missing for over two weeks. Give her my number if she wants to talk to me. Tell her that I will get in touch with the British High Commission and ask for their assistance – I have a good contact there."

He scribbled his number on his card and handed it to Abraham. "If you hear anything, please call me immediately." Abraham walked Tom to the front door. Tom shook his hand, thanked him and wished him goodnight.

The muezzin began the call to prayer for the night-time *Isha* prayers. His voice echoed all around the town, welcoming the faithful to prayer. Tom picked his way through the dark alleyways, and returned to the hotel.

He found Toby sitting in the bar, waiting for him. "Did you find Kate, Tom?" he asked, curious.

They talked over dinner and Tom felt comfortable enough to tell Toby the story that had started so many years ago in London and seemed to have ended with both the crashed aircraft some two weeks ago and Kate's disappearance.

"Well, it all sounds very romantic," Toby said, "but how the hell are you going to find out where she is now? I fly all over Kenya and Tanzania and I could certainly ask around for you. Someone must know something."

Tom glanced at Toby. "I get the feeling that she has gone somewhere where no-one will find her. I have a bad feeling about all of this, just as

Abraham does. I don't think she wants anyone to find her," he said miserably.

Toby sat back in his chair and thought about the story he had been told. It seemed incredible to him that these two people, Kate and Tom, could have crossed paths twice with neither of them realising it.

"Kenya is a fairly small place," he said at last. "Especially if you have a plane. I'll ask at the game lodges this week and I'm taking some clients to Mombasa next week, so I can ask around there for you too. How long are you planning to stay in Kenya, Tom?"

"I'm not leaving until I find her," Tom said determinedly. "So, I'll stay for as long as that takes."

Chapter Thirty-Eight

T OM MADE ONE TRIP north to Uganda. The owner of the crashed aircraft had his base there and Mike McNeil had given him all the details he needed. Tom now knew, without any doubt, that this Luca Brenner was the person who had visited Adam in Engand.

He arranged a meeting with Luca, telling him that he wanted to go on a flying safari. Luca was happy to meet with him and they discussed the various safari options.

Unable to keep up the charade, and unwilling to waste any more time, Tom interrupted Luca. "I'm trying to find Kate Hope, perhaps you can help me? Is there anything you can tell me about Adam Hamilton that would shed some light on where Kate could be?" he asked. "If Adam wasn't dead, I would probably kill the bastard myself."

Luca shifted uncomfortably in his chair, slightly alarmed at the turn of the conversation and the vehemence in the American's voice.

"Hey, listen," Luca said lightly, "I really liked the guy. He was the closest friend I had. I knew them both, years ago, in Cape Town. It amused me that he had faked his own death and it amused him. He didn't think of the pain it would cause; you couldn't help but like him, whatever he did. I wasn't surprised when he pitched up here in Uganda, I almost expected him."

"You say that you knew Adam very well but you didn't tell the whole truth to the Embassy when they were investigating his death – you didn't tell them that you knew he was using an assumed name. Why would that be? And I know for a fact that you met him in England shortly before he disappeared."

Adam's true identity was all over Kenya and Uganda, even though Luca had tried to contain the truth. Kate's name had not come up in any of the gossip so far.

This American seemed to know more than most people: he must have access to information through the British High Commission, Luca speculated. Even more disturbing was the fact that somehow this guy knew about his visit to Adam in England.

Luca looked at Tom and wondered when and where his interest in Kate had begun. In all the years he had known Kate she had never mentioned an American called Tom. Did she even know him?

"I'm sorry, I don't really know anything about you and why you're interested in Kate. Would you mind telling me why you're so keen to find her and why you're interested in all of this?"

"I think she's in trouble, Luca. I met Kate years ago in London, when she was married to her husband, Jack. I've been working in security consultancy for the last thirty years and I've been lucky enough to make the right contacts that have helped me get this far. I'm not here to get you in any trouble, Luca. I don't care what you have to do with all this. But, I do care for Kate and I want to stop her doing anything foolish. Quite frankly this business with Adam and Kate being in Kenya at the same time that he died has got me concerned that she's mixed up in all of this somehow. I was hoping you might tell me differently. Any information you give me will solely be used to help me find her."

They looked at each other, sizing each other up. They were both trying to ascertain just how well the other person knew Kate. Coming to some kind of decision, Luca said at last, "I heard she was in Zanzibar. I always meant to get in touch but when Adam pitched up here, it wasn't an option anymore. What could I have said to her? Tell her that he was alive and on my payroll? They were inevitably going to meet again – those two were destined to circumnavigate each other – and they did. Adam told me that he saw Kate, purely by chance, on an airstrip in Kenya. He left me a note before he set off on what turned out to be his final flight from Uganda. She was sitting underneath a derelict airplane, waiting to be collected by a lodge vehicle. He was pretty convinced she had recognised him." Luca lit a cigarette.

The office they were sitting in, the ones he rented in the centre of town, were small but they had a garden with a fountain in it outside and large patio doors that let the cool air in. He could see that Tom looked hot and he suggested they go and sit outside. On the way, he picked up a bottle of water for each of them. He knew he still hadn't answered Tom's question about why he hadn't told the whole truth to the British High Commission. The thing was, something about Adam's death bothered him and he wasn't sure how much he wanted to tie himself into the unfolding story. He wasn't sure how much longer he was going to hang around to find out.

"There wasn't much left of him after the crash, was there?" Luca asked matter-of-factly. "That was quite convenient. Obviously, the aircraft was insured, so I was all right. It would have bothered him that the cat was out the bag. That someone recognised him and could blow his cover. He probably felt that the game was up and the thing is, the game *was* up. Kate blew his cover without even realising it – before she'd even seen him! I heard from another pilot, in Nairobi, that a woman had been sticking up posters of Adam all over town, asking anyone for information about him. I called the number and then hung up when I heard her answer. It was Kate."

Luca stood and walked back to his desk. Opening one of the drawers, he pulled something out and returned outside. He handed a thin silver chain with a small cross to Tom.

"The police didn't have anyone to give it to so they asked me to keep it. You can have it, I'm not sentimental. Adam never took it off. Not in all the years I knew him." He passed the cross and chain over to Tom. He stared at the trickling fountain; he would miss his old friend.

"Something about that accident bothers me though, and some things don't add up at all. Under ordinary circumstances it should never have happened. The control tower think that something distracted him at the last minute, and that was it. Boom.

"The worst part of it is that I don't think it was an accident. They're saying it was pilot error and I reckon that it was but not in the way that they think. I think he had had enough you see, I think he was ill.

"So his game was up anyway, long before he saw Kate again. Either way, he had the cause and the means. It's only a shame he took one of my planes with him."

After Tom left, Luca decided to close up the office, indefinitely. He would advertise the business was for sale and wait for a buyer. Meanwhile he wanted to leave town until the dust had settled. Tanzania might be a good place to lie low for a while.

He was packing a couple of things into his bag, when his front door was kicked in. He could hear the heavy running footsteps of police officers as they made their way along the hall into his office. They must have found the drugs in one of his planes, Luca thought instantly. He knew that this day would come eventually, either here in Uganda or some other place. He'd done enough deals in drugs and arms trafficking in his lifetime to know that at some time along the road, the past was going to catch up with him. He wondered if Adam had been thinking that when his plane crashed or whether he'd been making sure that the future wouldn't get him in the end. He would have preferred to go his way, Luca thought. As would I. That's another thing we always had in common.

Four police officers swept into his office with their guns raised. Luca reached behind his back and pulled the small pistol free from its holster. He put the gun in his mouth and pulled the trigger.

Tom had rented a small cottage in Langata, on a monthly basis, and before he went to Uganda he had bought a jeep to get around in. Tom felt pretty sure that if Luca had known Kate's whereabouts, he would have told him.

He was sitting outside on the patio when he heard the tyres of a car crunching on the gravel in the driveway. He walked through the cool house and opened the front door. A car pulled up flying the Union Jack. Mike McNeil got out, patting his red face with an equally red handkerchief and looking grim-faced.

"Come in, Mike. What brings you here?"

Tom could see from the expression on Mike's face and from his demeanour that something was wrong.

"May I get you a drink?" Tom asked.

Mike shook his head. They walked into the kitchen and sat down at the kitchen table. Clearing his throat, Mike explained that news had come through to the High Commission about a white woman who had been found dead up on the Northern Frontier, close to the border with Somalia. Apparently, she had been looking after a small lodge there. The Northern Frontier, he explained, was dangerous country. Bandits crossed from Somalia on a regular basis looking for food and guns. It would appear that this woman had been alone at the lodge; there were no guests and only two members of staff. The lodge was really remote and had been up for sale. The owners had struggled to fill it with guests, what with the bandits and unforgiving terrain, and had been trying to sell it through an estate agent. The estate agents were not aware that there was anyone up there other than the staff.

"This woman was murdered, Tom."

Tom stared at him blankly, wondering why Mike thought the news of a murdered woman would be of interest to him. He raised his eyebrow in question.

"I'm telling you this because we think it might be Kate. In fact, we are pretty sure it is. She told her doctor, Charles Burton, that she was going to go up to the Northern Frontier to look after a lodge up there and Tom, I'm so sorry, but this all fits."

Tom spoke carefully. "You can't be sure of that though, can you?"

"Tom, I wouldn't be here talking to you if I wasn't sure. It's the only lodge in that neck of the woods. Her body was thrown into the bush. The staff found her the day after it had happened. We arranged for the body to be brought in, but there's not much left of her, I'm afraid. Lots of hyena and it's as hot as hell up there too."

He mopped his face again. "Actually, Tom, I will have a drink. This hasn't been an easy day for me. I have a big favour that I shouldn't ask of you – but I have to."

Tom stood and went to pour Mike a gin and tonic. Mike chose his next words carefully.

"Our problem is this. Someone has to identify the body, which will be a gruesome task for anyone. You knew her and I have to ask if you will do this," he said bluntly.

Tom looked up quickly and then turned his back to Mike. He clenched his jaw and took a deep breath. He poured himself a drink as well and took them both back to the table.

"I can't identify Kate, if it is her. I haven't seen her for over twenty years, for God's sake! I wouldn't know what she looked like now. I saw photographs of her at her house in Zanzibar, but she's older now. I don't know if I could identify her with any certainty. She could have changed beyond my limited recognition of her. I can't do it. I'm sorry."

Mike stood up, feeling awkward. He walked out onto the veranda, working through how he should ask his next question. He swirled the ice in his glass. Reluctantly, he turned back to Tom.

"Then there is another thing that I have to ask you. Would you go to see her daughter, Molly? Explain to her that she will have to identify her mother? We've told her what has happened. She's currently on the British Airways flight from London to Dar. She wants to go to her mother's house in Zanzibar before coming to Nairobi. You know where the house is, I think?"

"Yes, I know it." Tom paused, the full reality of the situation dawning on him.

"You've told her that Kate is dead?"

Mike nodded.

Tom felt something crush inside of him. He felt stunned with disbelief.

"I'll go. It's the least I can do."

After seeing Mike off and shaking his hand, Tom walked back to the patio. Sitting down, he put his head in his hands. Please God, not Kate, not now.

Chapter Thirty-Nine

MOLLY SAT ON THE SOFA in her mother's house. The two keys from the chain around her neck dangled from the lock of the open chest. She heard the brassy clang of the front door knocker and the soft footfall of Abraham as he went to answer it.

Abraham came into the lounge soon afterwards. He told her quietly that Mr Tom was here.

Molly stood up, holding the unopened letter in her hand. She was glad for the interruption. She had been sitting holding the envelope in her hands for longer than she knew.

A man in his late fifties stood in front of her. He was tall and tanned. She could tell he was American almost immediately. He was dressed in a long-sleeved white shirt, khaki trousers and safari boots. His dark hair was only slightly streaked with grey and it curled over his shirt collar. He introduced himself, recognising her immediately.

"Hello Molly, my name is Tom Fletcher. The British High Commission in Nairobi asked me to come to see you. I knew your mother many years ago, before you were born. I'm so sorry to meet you in such terrible circumstances." He didn't think it was the time to tell her that he had met her before in New York.

They shook hands.

He saw that she had been crying and he looked at her tired, pale and grief-pinched face. He followed her into the lounge and sat beside her on the sofa. Molly looked at him, tilting her head to one side.

"Yes, I remember Kate talked about you once when we were on safari. It sounds ridiculous, but I think I've met you before, Tom."

He smiled softly. She remembered him. "We have. I met you when I was in New York. You were working in a store on Madison Avenue.

We talked about Africa and I bought a book. It was just before Christmas."

"How extraordinary," Molly said. She did vaguely remember him. Abraham had told her about his visit. He had come looking for Kate.

Tom sat watching her quietly. He could hardly believe he was sitting next to Kate's daughter. He felt an ache in his chest. She should be here, he thought. Kate should be here. Molly had her mother's eyes and had some of her mannerisms.

"The silver bracelet!" Molly exclaimed loudly. "You were the one who gave her the silver bracelet. Is that right?"

"Guilty as charged," he said, nodding and smiling sadly. A flash of anxiety stabbed him in the stomach. How would he tell Molly that she would have to identify her mother's body?

"Why were you here last week?" Molly asked.

Tom told her his story. He told her how he had met Kate in London, and again in Cape Town some four years later and he had thought about her during his life and how, after his wife had died, he had decided to try and find her. He told her about how he had arrived at this point, opposite her. He left out the High Commission's request.

In the quiet that followed, Abraham came into the room to tell them he had served lunch in the roof garden. Tom and Molly went up there together. They looked out over the sea and settled down against the big cushions.

"Abraham said that you went through Kate's jewellery box whilst you were here," Molly said. "What was that about? Were you looking for her bracelet? She never took it off, you know. Not once. If it's anywhere, it's still on her," her words faltered and her eyes filled with tears.

Tom leaned across the table and squeezed her hand. He told her about the woman who had bumped into a chair near his table in the restaurant in Cape Town, and how he had found her earring on the floor. He told her that he had asked Abraham whether he could look in Kate's jewellery box after seeing a picture of Kate on the photo boards downstairs. He pulled the pair of earrings from his pocket. Molly gasped.

"Oh my God, yes, those are Kate's. So let me get this straight: you found this one on the restaurant floor and that one in her jewellery box?" she asked incredulous. Tom nodded. "I remember her telling me she had lost it. So, you missed each other in Cape Town by inches?"

"Yes, it's quite something, isn't it?"

Molly felt her skin prickle. Kate would have loved this, she thought, loved the drama and romance of it. Over lunch, Molly told him about Kate, about her own life and her partner James.

Tom asked her some of the questions that had been unanswered for years. He listened, fascinated. It was like the final stages of a jigsaw puzzle. As she talked, Molly filled in some of the missing pieces. She told him about her father Jack, and Adam, and about Kate's business and relationship bust-up, and her time in Cape Town, Kenya, New York and then Zanzibar.

Tom asked her carefully what had happened to Jack and Adam after their relationship with Kate.

"Jack and Adam are dead." Molly said, surprising herself as she said it.

"So," Tom asked, wanting to be doubly sure. "This guy, Adam – what was his surname? He died about four or five years ago?"

"It was Hamilton. His name was Adam Hamilton. The end of their relationship destroyed Kate, but Adam dying switched something off in her altogether. For years afterward, whether it was New York or Kenya, or anywhere, she would be happily talking about something and then suddenly she would look in the distance, almost as though she was looking for something, or even that she could see something, I don't really know. But I knew she was out there with him somehow, far beyond anything that I could hope to understand.

"It's funny you even mention Adam. I found some of his pictures around the house. I never thought Kate would put them out again. I'll get one, shall I? Give me a minute," she said as she went downstairs to her mother's room.

Tom waited for her to come back. So that was it then. He was beginning to understand. She must have returned to the house on the island, after the crash, which she must have heard about, and then some days later, packed her bag and rushed off again. She must have loved him very much, he thought enviously. If I had got it right when I met her again, she might have come to love me, and would never have met Adam

Adam had come back from the dead and Kate had had to go through it all again. He shook his head, really feeling for her. He looked up as Molly returned with the photograph he had seen next to the bed. He looked at it again. Now he had a face to go with the name. He put it down and then picked it up again. He swallowed the lump in his throat – she was wearing the bracelet he had given her.

He thought carefully about telling Molly about Adam's plane crash and his false identity but decided that she had enough to deal with at present. He leaned over and took both her hands in his.

"Molly," he said. "I have something to tell you. They have brought your mother back to Nairobi, as you know, and someone has to formally identify her." He saw the stricken look on her face. "It has to be you. You're the next of kin. I would offer to do it but I don't know what Kate looks like now. I'm so sorry, Molly. I've arranged for us to fly to Nairobi together tomorrow, and I'll come with you to see your mother, if you like."

The colour drained from Molly's face. "No, please don't ask me to do that, Tom. I don't want to see her dead. I want to remember her alive." She stood up hurriedly from the table, knocking her glass over, and hastily left the rooftop. Tom waited half an hour before he followed her down.

He found her in the lounge, still crying. He sat down next to her and wrapped his arms around her. She sobbed into his chest. "My mother is dead, Tom," she said hopelessly. "A senseless murder, in some remote part of Kenya. I have to make the funeral arrangements, and sort everything out. I don't think I have ever felt so terribly alone in my life."

"Molly, you have to be brave. This is hideous. I know that. I'll come with you to the mortuary. You don't have to do this by yourself. It will take a matter of seconds and then it will all be over. If you want to, we can fly up to the lodge where they found her. I think you should do this, to see where she spent her last few days. We can fly over it or we can land. It's up to you but it will help you deal with things before going to see her."

As she cried, he rocked her gently, just as he had Kate, the night before Molly was born.

Finally, exhausted by her tears, she lay down on the couch. Tom covered her with a blanket and sat in the chair opposite. He would not leave her; he would stay here all night and watch over her. He didn't want her to wake up alone, not when he knew what she would have to go through. Kate would have expected that of him.

The next morning, they flew to Nairobi. Molly was quiet and tense for most of the flight and Tom left her to her own thoughts, as he tried to deal with his own.

They took a taxi to Wilson Airport where Tom introduced her to Toby, who led them out to the small aircraft. "I won't be able to land there," Toby said, checking his instruments. "It's too bloody dangerous, but we can fly low over the lodge. As many times as you like," he said gently, looking at the grief stricken young girl.

Toby fired up the engines. He did his pre-flight check and prepared for take-off. Forty minutes later, they began to approach the lodge, flying low over the land surrounding it. The lodge was built on a low hill, a *kopje*, and a small river, peppered with boulders, flowed along and down the edge of the ridge. In the village nearby, where the staff lived, they watched the scattering of startled goats and cattle around the central *kraal*. Toby flew back and forth, trying to give them as much of a view as he could. There was plenty of game. Large herds of impala, giraffe and kudu. A herd of elephant looked up as the shadow of the aircraft passed over them.

Tom's eyes scanned the horizon. There was nothing but bush as far as the eye could see in every direction. God, Tom thought, this *is* remote. What on earth was she doing out here? He reached for Molly's hand. She was staring desolately out of the window. She hadn't said anything since they had left Nairobi.

This is where my mother died, she said to herself. She was all alone in the middle of nowhere instead of in the soft rolling savannah she had always loved. Molly saw the scrubby, rocky landscape as ugly, dangerous and hostile.

With a slow sad nod from Molly, Toby turned the aircraft around and headed back to Nairobi. Bloody shame, he thought. This story should have had a much happier ending. Poor Tom, he had come so close to meeting Kate again but he had been too late. He didn't envy what either of them had to go through next.

Tom put the phone down and walked outside to where Molly was sitting on his veranda. He had not wanted to leave her alone with her grief and he had brought her to his cottage after the flight. He told her about the arrangements that had been organised for viewing Kate's body and he asked her whether she wanted him to go with her.

She nodded woodenly.

Tom had had the Embassy move Kate's body from the morgue to the local undertakers. Mike had also told him he had spoken with Kate's doctor.

"I'll give you his number, Tom, in case you or Molly need assistance. By the way, Kate went to see him before she took the job up at the lodge. He encouraged her to take the position. He feels terrible."

Tom called Dr Burton and asked him to come to his cottage at five p.m. after the viewing. He wasn't sure what state Molly would be in and thought it might be best to have some medical help to hand, just in case.

Bruce, the very polite and slightly vacuous undertaker, was waiting for them. Taking a deep breath, Molly got out of the car and walked slowly towards the door of the funeral parlour. Tom put his arm around her shoulders, holding her up.

Bruce had done the best he could with what was left of Kate. Half the woman's body had gone, but her face, slightly reconstructed, was still recognisable. Tom and Molly stood together in front of the closed coffin. Tom indicated to Bruce that he should proceed.

Bruce gently lifted the top half of the wooden structure so that the woman's face was exposed. Molly was shaking and her eyes were squeezed shut as if she could make it all go away.

Tom glanced at her when he noticed she hadn't moved. He saw her face scrunch up as she refused to look.

"You have to look, Molly. We need you to look," he said unsteadily as he took her hand.

Molly took a deep breath, opened her eyes, and walked to the top of the coffin so that she could look down into it.

She reared back in horror; her legs buckled and she fainted. Tom caught her quickly and carried her back to the car.

He got in beside her and put on the air conditioning. Bruce came out with a blanket, which they tucked around her. They knew she would feel cold when she came around. Tom asked the driver to take them back to his cottage.

He watched her as she lay inert beside him. He was holding her hand and stroking it absent-mindedly. When they were almost at the cottage, Molly stirred and her eyes started to focus on him. He saw an expression of panic and pure terror cross her face.

Everything had happened so quickly. He hadn't even had time to look into the coffin himself. Molly started to cry and was soon sobbing and gasping for air. Dr Burton was waiting for them as they drew up to the cottage. He opened the door of the car when he saw Molly, and quickly prepared and administered an injection of sedative. After a few moments, Molly calmed down then closed her eyes again, but she didn't let go of Tom's hand. The doctor followed them in. Together, they settled Molly into bed. Whilst he did a quick check-up on her, Tom waited for him in the lounge.

"What a frightful thing for a young person to go through," Dr Burton said. "It will stay with her for years. No-one should have to do that."

"There was no alternative," Tom said. "You were Kate's doctor, weren't you?" he asked.

"Yes, I was. I didn't see her very often but if she needed me and if she was in Nairobi, I would see her."

"When was the last time you saw her?" he asked.

"A few weeks ago. She was in pretty bad shape. She was badly shaken by some news she had received. She appeared highly stressed and her blood pressure was up. I thought it best that she wasn't alone, which is why I encouraged her to take the job at the lodge. I didn't realise that it would be empty. I suspected that she might be suicidal. A mind can only take so much and from what she was saying, I think she had reached saturation point. In all the years I knew her, she had always seemed to be a fairly level-headed person to me. She was a very amusing woman, but not the last time I saw her; she was fragile, broken in fact." He shook his head sadly.

Tom saw him to the door and then went to check on Molly. He sat down next to the bed and took Molly's hand in his. I wish I could have saved her, he said to himself. If only I'd been faster or started looking for her sooner, she might still be alive.

Molly moaned quietly and turned restlessly. Tom felt emotionally drained. It was all over. All the searching had been in vain. Kate was dead and he would never be able to see her again. He had waited too long. All those years when he had the opportunity to find her and he hadn't. He'd just waited. He wondered what he had been waiting for. Why had he not gone after her? Fought for her when he had the chance? He should have tried harder. He had wasted his life with a woman he cared very little about, during which time happiness was a rarity. He had always secretly hoped that Kate would step back into his life, one way or another, and put it right. That he could start living again with her at his side. He put his head down on the side of the bed and wept for the loss of her.

Exhausted, Tom fell asleep, his head on his arms.

He heard Molly calling him and he woke up, disorientated for a moment. It was dark outside.

"Tom!" Molly called out again. He sat up, picking up her hand and shaking the sleep from his head. She opened her eyes and looked at him wide-eyed. She was trying to say something, but no words came out of her mouth.

"Shhhh," Tom said, "Wait a little. Give yourself some time. I'm here, you'll be all right. Just take your time. The worst part is over."

"No! Tom! It wasn't my mother. It wasn't Kate."

Chapter Forty

MOLLY AND TOM flew back to Zanzibar the following week, when Molly was well enough to travel. It had been a horrific time for both of them. Tom had got a phone call from Toby a day after the funeral home visit.

"I dropped the owners back at the lodge yesterday morning; they cut short their trip in Europe when they heard the news. Apparently, Kate had been offered the job and was going to get back to them. When they didn't hear from her, they found someone else to run the place. It's a terrible thing to have happened and really bad publicity for the lodge too. Kate – wherever she is – had a lucky escape; it would have been her had she taken the job."

It took a few more phone calls and meetings to unravel the mess that had been created. It was Mike who figured out where the mistake had been made.

"When things like that happen here in Kenya," Mike told Tom over lunch at the High Commission, "the authorities usually contact all the local doctors who know just about all the expatriates living here. They called and spoke with Dr Burton; he mistakenly told them that he knew the woman who had told him she intended to take the job up at the lodge on the Northern Frontier. He told them that it was Kate."

On their first evening back, Tom and Molly sat in the roof garden, planning their next course of action. Molly leaned back in the hammock and looked at him. She had become very attached to Tom over the past few weeks. She had invited him to stay on at the house in Zanzibar. Neither of them had said it, but they both harboured the hope that Kate might turn up at the house. The house had begun to feel like a beacon of hope. But, they had to figure out what to do if she didn't.

As if she had read his mind, Molly stood up and stretched.

"Tom, I need to think about getting back to London. I've got a shoot in New York in six weeks' time and there is a ton of stuff to be done before that. Also, I need to be with James. I feel so wrung out with everything that's happened. You're welcome to stay here in the house. Kate might turn up, you never know and at least you'll be surrounded by her things. Maybe you might pick up some clues? There was a project she was involved in on the coast somewhere. But, for the life of me, I can't remember what the place was called. I'd never heard of it. Kate wanted me to help her with the interiors. Next thing I heard, the whole thing had been cancelled. Maybe she went back there?"

He reached for her hand, stopping her. "Molly, there is something else that I have to tell you. No, don't look so frightened. After all you've been through, I'm quite sure you'll be able to handle what I have to say. I *was* going to tell you the first time I met you but I felt it wouldn't help matters much. Adam didn't die five years ago in England."

Molly sat down abruptly next to him. "What do you mean? If he didn't die then, when did he die?"

"About three and a half weeks ago, in Kenya."

Molly's hand flew to cover her mouth in shock. "That's not possible, Tom! That's just not possible."

"There was a plane crash at the airstrip in the Mara. The pilot who was flying was Adam. There is no doubt about it. It has transpired that he fabricated his own death and then turned up in Kenya, before heading to Uganda. He had a friend there called Luca Brenner. Luca had a flying safari business."

Molly stood up and looked out at the sea. It shimmered silver in the moonlight.

"I remember Luca! He used to help me with my French when I was at school and we used to go riding together at the weekends. Adam, Kate and Luca were always together."

Excitedly, she turned to face Tom. "I bet he'll be able to help us find her. Maybe Kate kept in touch with him? Maybe she told him where she was going? Maybe she saw Adam again? Dear God, that would have torn her up in pieces to discover he was still alive. And, it would have shattered her to find out that Adam had died again. I don't think she would have been able to handle it. Do you think she saw him, Tom? Would that explain what happened? Why she left?"

In her mind, it all began to fall in place and she spoke hurriedly as her thoughts occurred to her. "That explains why she bolted so quickly, doesn't it? She would have been desperate to get away from it all. That's why she disappeared. As soon as I came here, back to the house, I was convinced that Adam had something to do with all of this but I thought it was impossible because he was dead. But, of course, he *did* have something to do with it. Tom, we have to get hold of Luca, he'll be able to help, I'm sure of it!"

Tom stood up, putting his hands on her shoulders. He told her about his visit to Uganda, and he told her that Luca was dead.

Defeated, she looked up at him helplessly. "Tom, if anyone is going to find her, it is going to be you. I can't sit here any longer trying to figure out where she is. I want to go back to London and get away from here. She always loved the sea, Tom. She liked Malindi and Watamu, maybe she went there?"

Tom nodded, assured her that he would continue with the search and keep in touch by email if there was any news.

He walked with her to the ferry. He was going to miss her. He had become quite used to having Molly around and he had grown fond of her. Impulsively, she turned and hugged him. "I know you love her, Tom. She's out there somewhere. Please find her."

Her words echoed those of Sarah. He watched until the ferry disappeared and, with a final wave, he walked back to the house. It seemed very empty without her.

He hadn't had the heart to tell Molly the circumstances of Luca's death. Mike McNeil had phoned him and given him the details.

"Luca Brennar had a colourful past, Tom. He ran a drug dealing business in Cape Town, a very successful one I'm told. Apparently he used Adam Hamilton's company as a front sometimes. Working for him had helped spread the distribution of his stock. He travelled around the countryside on a regular basis, purportedly inspecting game lodges but in reality he was enhancing his own business network. The international business trips he did for them were also lucrative. We now know that Adam Hamilton was involved in all of this and that's why he had to leave South Africa so suddenly. The drug squad were closing in on him. He took over Luca's business when Luca left for Uganda. Luca went on ahead to set up the Uganda operation under cover of his flying safari business. Adam went to ground in England and, thanks to your information, we now know that Luca met up with him once in Dorchester. This is when they must have planned Adam's so-called death. Luca had many contacts in the shadowy world of drugs and it was simple for him to get new identity documents for Adam Hamilton."

Molly had explained everything to Abraham before she left. Since then, Abraham regarded Tom as some kind of hero and was happy to give him free rein over the house. Every evening Tom sat up in the roof garden and thought about Kate and Molly. He had explored the small island from top to bottom, but always returned to her house. He would stay up late into the night, reading Kate's books, touching the things that she had touched over the years. He slept in her bed and imagined impossible things. He remembered impossible things.

That one night in London.

Something they had not planned to happen, however much they might have wanted each other. After their final dinner at his apartment he had put her in a taxi, and going back into his apartment he had found the briefcase she had left behind. He didn't think twice. He had arrived at her hotel and taken the lift to her room. She had opened the door.

The chemistry between them was palpable. He hesitated before pulling her towards him and kissing her wide, happy mouth. Out of breath, Kate had pulled back. She too had hesitated, overcome by feelings she had not had for a long time. She had taken his hand and pulled him into the room. He closed the door, pulling off his jacket and tie. Tearing at each other's clothes, they had fallen onto the bed. He pulled back from her for a moment. "I love you, Kate. You're like a wild animal, one of those creatures in the bush. Difficult to pin down, probably impossible to hang onto, but I love you." She had looked at him seriously, then smiled and pulled him down on top of her.

On the flight back to London, Molly opened the letter from her mother, the one she had found in the Zanzibar box and started to read.

My darling Molly,

I have dreaded this day for you, from the moment I was able to hold you, when you were born. You have brought me much joy, love and happiness over the years. You had such a rocky start in life and no-one expected you to survive, only me. I knew you were a fighter, a survivor: and you will survive this too.

David sent you the keys, and now you have the letter I left for you, the one you are reading now. It was difficult to write and I thought long and hard about it. I have gone to another place now, a place where I hope to find the peace I so longed for over the years. The world was a lonely empty place without Adam in it. You will read, in this letter, about our child. You have only ever known him as your cousin, Edward. But he is your half-brother and Adam is the biological father.

Lucy and Jean-Philippe are wonderful parents for Edward. I had no choice really, and I knew how desperately they wanted a baby. I never told Adam and I will leave it to you to decide if you want to speak to Lucy about this. I made a promise to her that whilst I was alive I would never divulge the names of the real parents. Knowing you as I do, I think you will probably agree that it would be kinder to leave it that way. I know you have wondered why Lucy and I appeared to have drifted apart, it must have hurt you. But I could see how hard it was for her when I did visit, when Edward was very small. If I had seen her as often as I wanted to, it would have been too hard on her. I decided to pull away from her and give her the chance to have Edward all to herself. It was a very hard thing to do, but I think she understood my motives.

This part is very difficult for me to tell you about, but you must know the truth about your father. I know you think it is Jack, but that is not so. I think you will be able to deal with this because you had so little contact with him, and then he died.

I met Tom on a business trip. It was not something I planned to do, we were in London together; there was such a very strong attraction between us. We resisted each other until it was impossible not to. Both of us knew it was wrong, but it happened anyway. By some strange coincidence he was with me the night before you were born, but he never saw you, it was a long time ago. He was the one that gave me the bracelet. You see, Molly, you were a premature baby. Tom would never have known that or guessed that he was your father.

Although I saw him again, when you were four years old, things didn't work out between us, for reasons there is no point in telling you about. He blew into my life again and then disappeared, but you did meet him. It was at Christmas, in New York, he came into the store and you chatted together. When you told me about him, over dinner that evening, I didn't make any connection, it was only when I saw his credit card slip, that I realised you had both met, but neither of you knew there was a stronger connection.

Tom was probably the right man for me. Certainly my life would not have been tossed around so violently, if we had managed to work something out and stayed together. But I was married to Jack, and Tom was separated from his wife. He had a daughter, but she died, and I know what joy he would have felt if he had known you, the way I have done. He was a good man and I would have been safer with him, but it was not to be.

Perhaps too many years have passed, but I always regretted not telling him about you, he was so devastated when his only child died.

You asked me once about your birth mark? Tom has the same mark on the back of his neck – there was never any doubt that you were his daughter.

Now we need to talk about Adam.

He didn't die in England after all – he died in Kenya. It was a terrible accident and I was in Nairobi when it happened. The world as I knew it had ended, and I was too weary to go on. Looking back now I wish, in many ways, that I had not met him. Although we had those incredibly happy years together, the pain that came afterwards was not worth it, and I will never understand why he did what he did to me. I feel that if he had truly loved me he would have told me why it all ended the way it did. It would have been a kinder thing to do, a more loving thing to do... but instead I have spent the rest of my life trying to answer just one question. "Why? Why did he leave me like that?"

This affected any other relationships that I may have had, he spoiled it all and I think that is unforgivable – he didn't give me a chance to love again and everyone deserves a second chance. I wanted to love again, to be with someone who would look after me and love me. But because of what happened it was denied me and this is something I don't think I can forgive him for. Now that he is, without any doubt, dead, his reasons for the way he treated me have gone with him.

I hope that you and James will have a happy and full life together – sometimes the high flying world that I inhabited, could demand an impossible price; perhaps yours will be more tranquil. But be happy together and never judge him before you have found out the facts. Learn from my past.

I hope I have left you with some wonderful memories of our life together, and that these memories will comfort you. When you need me, hold still, sense me, and you will feel me there next to you – just as I always have been.

Molly finished reading the letter and stared out of the aircraft window. The letter wasn't supposed to have been read until after Kate's death. But Molly had justified that by hoping the letter would give some kind of clue as to what had happened. Had she been sick? Had she thought she was dying? Or had she chosen to end her own life? What had happened when she finally met Tom again in Cape Town?

She had said quite clearly in her letter that she had wanted another chance to love again. Molly hoped with all her heart that Tom would get the second chance he so desperately wanted with her. Her mother was out there somewhere, of that she was quite convinced, but she obviously didn't want to be found by anyone.

"Oh, Kate, what a muddle you left us all with," she whispered to her reflection. "We have always kept in touch with each other, but I've heard nothing from you for weeks. Are you in such a remote place that there is no signal for your phone? The letter that I hold in my hand was never meant to be read whilst you were alive, but I still don't know if you are?

"Where are you? Where did you go?" She closed her eyes trying to assimilate everything that her mother had written. She wouldn't say anything to Tom yet.

Tom had moved to Malindi and taken a beach cottage. Exhausted by all that had happened he had needed a change. He had explored all avenues in his search and now only the coast remained.

Toby had organised, through his contacts, for Tom to be able to charter and fly himself around the coast. Abraham had told him, as Molly had, that Kate liked the beaches in and around Mombasa. She loved to swim in the warm water and to walk miles along the shore. He had checked up and down the beaches north of Mombasa. He had flown to Lamu and Manda Island. Tomorrow, he would start searching the beaches south of Mombasa, towards the Tanzanian border.

She was there somewhere, he was convinced of it.

He made himself a sandwich and then looked at his watch. Molly would be calling him soon. They talked to each other every other day, needing to be connected. He was able to keep her hopes alive and, in her own way, she had kept him going too.

Tom felt the cross and chain, that Luca had given him, in his pocket. Pulling it out, he stared at it. Adam had met a fiery end, but Tom would never forgive him for what he had put Kate through.

Every morning, he went down to the small air charter company and enquired of the passengers and pilots whether they had seen Kate. He showed them a photograph that Molly had given him. It had been taken five years ago and she looked older, of course, but the eyes were the same, and her hair and smile. Then he would fuel up and continue his search from the air.

In the evenings, he drove around the bars and hotels showing her photograph there.

No-one had seen her.

Chapter Forty-One

KATE HEARD THE WHINING ENGINE of a small aircraft. She felt irritated by the intrusion into her quiet world. She looked upwards, shading her eyes.

The small plane probably belonged to some estate agency, ferrying prospective buyers around. They liked to give them a bird's-eye view of paradise. Well, no-one would want to buy anything along this beach. It was too remote, there were too many mosquitoes, there was no internet or television and no shops or stores. No-one in their right mind would want to live here, she thought.

Tom swooped low along the beaches. He could see the odd fisherman here and there. As he turned to head out to sea he saw a woman sitting alone at the far end of the beach. The beach was extremely isolated and she seemed to be the only one on it. He saw her look up, shading her eyes with her hand. He brought the plane around for a second look, going in lower, hoping to get a closer view, but she had gone. Through the trees he thought he saw her shadow, a glimpse of a white dress, but he couldn't be sure. He checked his fuel. Enough to get him back to Malindi, but not enough for any more sweeps along the beach. He looked again, but the beach was completely deserted. He checked his map. Msembweni. Close to the Tanzanian border. He turned the aircraft and headed back to Malindi.

The sale of the villa had not gone through in the end and John, feeling guilty about Kate's plight, had been happy for her to return for as long as she wanted – or at least until a new buyer came along. But he had warned her that all the staff, except Titus, had been sent home and she would be quite alone there this time.

270

She hadn't spoken to anyone other than Titus for weeks. She moved through her days glad to be away from everything and everyone. She missed Molly but she was a young woman now. Molly didn't need her as she had done, as a little girl. She wanted her daughter to remember her as the bright vibrant person she had been, not the unhappy and insecure person she had become. Kate's money would not last much longer and she was determined she wouldn't touch the trust fund she had set in place for her daughter. There were no jobs or projects on the horizon. She didn't want Molly to know how bad things were. It was better to let go.

She glanced up again and watched the small plane disappear over the trees. She saw it arc, ready to make another sweep of the beach. She stood up quickly and ran back through the trees to the safety of the cottage.

The early evening brought clouds in from the sea and within minutes the sky went dark. The rain had started and it increased in intensity. It came down in sheets, sizzling and hissing on the ground around where Kate sat on the veranda. Anticipating yet another power cut, she went inside and brought out a candle. She scratched match after match along the side of a matchbox, and then gave up in frustration. They were too damp to light. Remembering that she had a spare lighter in her handbag, she got up to look for it. There, lying at the bottom of the bag was the letter from the attorney's office in Uganda. It was the letter she had collected from the Muthaiga Club, put in her bag and forgotten about.

She found her lighter and lit the candle. She studied the envelope carefully, holding it next to the flickering light. Running her thumb under the flap, she pulled out the sheets of paper. She breathed in sharply when she recognised the handwriting. Shakily, she sat down, his name already on her lips.

Adam.

Kate,

Where do I begin with this letter? I know you will be shocked to receive it because I don't imagine you ever thought you would hear from me again. I saw you on the airstrip. I'm pretty sure you knew it was me and that you saw me. If you did, then you'll have worked out that I didn't die in England five years ago. After seeing you I felt compelled to write to you. I gave my lawyers instructions to send this letter in the event of my death. If you are receiving it, that is what has happened and this time, it's over, Kate, I'm really gone. The big adventure is over. I could choose to leave this life without explaining anything to you, but I feel a great need for you to know the truth.

I know you have drawn your own conclusions as to what happened between us but I'm afraid you didn't know the truth, and I feel I owe you that. You still love me, don't you? Kate, I have never stopped loving you. It's been the hardest part of my existence not being with you. Seeing you again on the air strip, in the middle of nowhere, was a shock. I heard your voice, saw you running to me and calling my name, and I question how I've had the strength to keep myself away from you. You need to know that it has not been easy, and that I've never been far from you.

Those years with you were the happiest of my life, Kate, and afterwards not a day went by when I didn't think of you. I want you to know that I always knew where you were. I was immensely proud of you when you took over that game lodge and turned it into such a success. I felt I should have been with you – I imagined it, it would have been fantastic – but it was impossible in the circumstances. I know you were in New York and I saw you a few times. You were unaware of me – or were you? I like to think that you felt me with you, as you used to. I reached out to stop you once but I had to drop my hand and watch you walk away. I had to let you walk away.

I should explain. Maybe you will finally understand and perhaps one day forgive me for the pain I have caused you, if that is possible. I know what you're like, Kate. I don't expect you to but it gives me peace now to know that with this letter, you will have the opportunity to do so.

Kate, I didn't leave you for another woman. How could I ever do that? You were the only woman I ever needed or wanted. I let you believe that because it was less painful in the long run than allowing you to watch me die. I'm just hanging in there as I write this to you. I don't think I have much longer but I'll do my best. I'm familiar with my disease now. I know its habits. This disease and I have lived with, and fought against, each other for longer than I can recall.

Dr Williams diagnosed me with cancer. I made him swear that under no circumstances, none at all, was he to tell you. Can you imagine, Kate? I thought I would live indefinitely. I never took anything seriously and then suddenly I was given a death sentence. I didn't understand it myself let alone know how to tell you. There's nothing worse than knowing you are dying. It was something I could never put you through. We were so perfect together, in every aspect, and I wanted – and still want – you to remember me like that. I didn't want you to watch me dying. We've made so many other great memories; I'd rather we have those.

What you suspected about Elizabeth was true, to a degree. I met her in Botswana and it turned out she was highly specialised in the treatment of cancer. Elizabeth wanted a lot of money for the treatment and I would have to take it in the States. She worked at the John Hopkins Hospital in New York. She was ruthless and she wanted something in return – me. I knew I was dying and I was desperate to live. I wanted to live to be with you. So, I did it, I went along with what she wanted. I hoped that I could do the treatments, get back up and running and somehow carry on with you in between. It was foolish to think you wouldn't notice. You'd notice a new freckle on my face if it appeared overnight.

Elizabeth was so positive about treatments in the States and at the hospital. She told me that they had made extraordinary progress with one particular drug. We made a deal. She wanted me, and I needed her.

My trips to New York were frequent as you know and I stayed in the hospital clinic whilst I was there. There were nights at Elizabeth's house during my treatment that I'm not proud of. She was a shallow unforgiving woman. You read me correctly in many ways. I didn't like the restrictions you were placing on me. I didn't like the way we were forced to change. I behaved like a spoilt child but I also spent weeks suffering and in pain. Coming back to you was the best thing to look forward to, but you had grown suspicious and jealous. The weeks that followed were the hardest to live through. You found out about Elizabeth and jumped to a correct conclusion, factually. You would never have believed me if I had told you the truth. You didn't like the truth of life either, Kate. You would have preferred to believe that I would rather be with someone else than have known the truth that I was dying. We both preferred the fantasy that we moulded out of life, than the drab reality of it.

I put the wall up in the office not to hide from you but because I couldn't bear to see what I was doing to you. There were days when I was so sick I knew you would see and know. It was better to put that divide between us. You screwed me to the wall with David, getting me to buy you out of the business.

I put every penny that I had into the company over the years, and then when I realised the exorbitant cost for the treatment I needed, and how much it was going to cost, I had no choice but to go to Luca – I was broke, Kate.

Luca told me that working for us was a front – he was a drug dealer and unwittingly we gave him many more opportunities to flourish. He lent me the money for the treatment but there was another price to pay. He wanted me to take over his patch, as he called it. He wanted to go to Uganda and set up there. I was shocked to find that Luca did this on the side. Then, when I had to pay you out, I had to borrow more from him; I was getting in deeper and deeper. I wasn't as confident as Luca and I worried about getting busted and ending up in jail.

Elizabeth gave me the all-clear months later, but she couldn't give me any guarantees, only a supply of pills should the cancer return. We said our goodbyes and that was the end of it. But, of course by then I had lost you.

I never loved anyone like I loved you, Kate, and even as I write this, I still do.

Then one day I got the tip-off that the drug squad were closing in on me. I left the country immediately.

I went to Luca, naturally. You know what we are like – he has never asked me any questions. In time, the cancer did come back. The pains returned and I couldn't see the point of fighting any more, Kate. I'd lost you and my life had become pretty mediocre without you in it. Luca and I continued with the business in East Africa. We ferried drugs in our

planes. *I siphoned off a little here and there to manage the pain and they
helped in other ways too.*

*Forgive me, Kate. I hope that you have found love and happiness in
your life. I hope that if you haven't that this letter helps you to
understand and to move on. It's the prospect of dying for real this time
that makes me fear you might never know the truth.*

*When I close my eyes at night, I still see you. I see you standing in
the bush, your golden hair blowing in the wind, tanned, tawny and
beautiful, as always. I hear your intoxicating laugh, and hear your
voice, and a thousand images go through my mind, all of you. I
remember those ten incredible years and how very lucky we were to
have them. The places we travelled, the fun we had. It was so very good,
Kate. It has been unforgettable.*

*If I could have chosen differently, I would have opted for a long and
happy life with you. I would have married you properly if you had
wanted, and not just have given you the ring. I am comfortable that I
will die alone as this is the way that I prefer it. Hopefully the end will be
quick and of my choosing.*

*I don't know what comes after death but I hope that one day, we can
be together again and that our lives will be free. I will wait for you,
Kate. You are the love of my life.*

My eternal love to you in this my final letter.

Adam

*P.S. I remember when you told me the story about the falcon and
how it gave you strength in difficult times, how you liked to think it was
the spirit of your father. As mystical as that might seem, it's a lovely
thought. I'm sure he is never far from you. I am not much further.*

The wicker chair next to her rocked slightly. The flame of the candle
flickered suddenly. She looked out at the trees, but despite the heavy
rain, there was no wind at all. She put her hand on the arm of the chair
and shivered as she remembered his words.

"If you hold still, you will sense me, and feel me with you." And she did. His voice was as clear and familiar to her, as it had always been.

"Adam, Adam," she whispered, crying softly. "You did come back to me, just as you said you would. But you were so wrong to do this to me, so very wrong." She had moved her chair closer to him. Like an animal sensing danger, she lifted her head and breathed deeply, searching the night air for some essence of him.

She lay curled in the chair, reading and re-reading his letter.

"Yes, you should have told me Adam," she wept. "What you did was wrong, so wrong. You spoiled any chances I had of ever being happy again. Something I so desperately wanted and needed. I'm not sure I can give you the forgiveness you are asking for. I think it's too late. I'm feeling so terribly tired, Adam, so tired with the long and lonely road you made me take on my own. Every single day since you left me has been poisoned with memories of what we had together; you left me with no possibilities and no hope. How can I forgive you for taking everything away from me?"

Kate folded his letter carefully, then stood up stiffly and made her way to the bedroom.

Chapter Forty-Two

TOM PULLED UP OUTSIDE of the grocery store in Diani. Standing in a queue in the heat, he listened idly to a conversation between two local African men standing in front of him.

"She arrived from nowhere. Just one small bag, that's all. I watch her every day; she walks up and down along the beach, even when it is raining. In the evenings, she comes to sit by the sea. Just looking. She never leaves the compound. She sends Titus for food. She is the only white woman in the whole area, so she sticks out."

"Excuse me," Tom interrupted. "This woman you're talking about, where is she living?" The two men looked at him suspiciously.

"It is a place where you cannot go. It is private property south of here. There is no entry for strangers, very difficult to find," he said, turning his back on Tom.

"I'll find it and I don't need road access either," Tom muttered to himself. He suddenly remembered the flight he had taken the day before. He had been south of Mombasa and he had thought he had seen a woman on the beach. But, by the time he had turned the airplane around, the beach was empty. Had that been the woman they were talking about?

Later that evening, as he studied the map, his mobile phone rang.

"Hello, Tom, it's me, Molly. Is there any news?"

"No, nothing, yet. I'm sitting here looking at a map. I'm going to fly south near the Tanzanian border first thing tomorrow morning. I overheard a conversation in the store today. There were two men talking about a white woman living alone somewhere down there. It's worth a shot. I've exhausted every other possible lead."

Molly took a deep breath, suddenly making up her mind. "Tom, I have something I must tell you, before you find her."

Tom held his breath. He knew what she was going to say to him. That night, after they had been to the undertakers, he had stayed with her, stroking her hair and comforting her. His brain had barely registered the mark on her neck, shaped like a small crescent moon. It was days later before he thought about it again. He knew he had an identical mark on the back of his own neck. That's when he had worked out that Molly must have been premature.

"I'm your daughter, Tom." He heard her voice break with emotion. "Kate didn't have to tell me about you, but she chose to in her letter, she told me the truth."

Tom carefully folded his map and listened closely to what she was saying. He felt something move deep inside of him. Here was someone who was connected to him, by blood. Someone he could really call his own. Something he had not experienced since the death of his daughter Cassie. He tried to find the words to describe his own tumultuous feelings now. That one night in London – but it had been far more than that. He took a deep breath and spoke to her.

"Molly it just didn't enter my head that you had been a premature baby. I noticed the birth mark on the back of your neck as I tried to comfort you, after that terrible day at the undertakers.

"I knew I was your father before you did. I didn't think it was my place to tell you – you had already been through far too much."

He looked out at the African night. "I don't really know what will happen next. How she will feel when I find her – and I will find her. She would never have anticipated this; that we would meet in such extraordinary circumstances. I have to make sure she will be able to handle it all. I'm not sure what state of mind she will be in – quite rocky, I think."

"Tom, you have to find her and then you will have to cope with what she has become. The bracelet you gave her – she never took it off, so that has to mean something special, don't you think?"

He hung up the phone and sat back thinking. Kate had given him an incredible gift – a daughter, their daughter Molly. But would she be able to love him again, despite everything that had happened to her? There was only one way to find out.

At first light, Tom took off from the small airport, climbing high into the clear sky. He turned the aircraft towards the Tanzanian border. The night before he had pored over the map, trying to locate the beach where he had seen the woman. Christ, he thought, even Moses would have been daunted by that wilderness. Who in their right mind would want to cut themselves off in a place like that?

Checking his bearings, he looked up and saw a long white beach ahead of him. He checked his co-ordinates, dropped altitude, and brought the aircraft round in a tight circle, swooping low over the beach. It was deserted. Trying to decide what to do next, he glanced at the sea below. He could see two fishermen waist-deep in the water. They were waving up at him. Tom waved back. He turned the plane and circled for another look. Nothing. He looked again at the fishermen and saw that they were still waving.

He frowned. Something didn't look right. They seemed to be trying to attract his attention. He leaned forward to get a better look. They were pointing at their net and gesticulating.

I can go in a bit lower, but not much, he thought. He flew as low as he dared. The sea rippled with the stream of air from the engines. He could clearly see the faces of the two men. They were holding onto something white. He looked closer as he passed overhead, and he felt his stomach tighten. They were holding onto what looked like the woman he had seen yesterday. Her hair was billowing in the water and she was wearing a white dress.

The beach was flat and straight. The sand looked too soft to land on. He decided that he could land on the harder sand at the water's edge, if he was careful. His hands were sticky on the controls. Please don't let it be Kate, he repeated to himself as he brought the plane down to land.

The little aircraft bumped and hopped, the wheels sinking into the sand as it came to a halt.

Tom fumbled with his seatbelt, cursing at the delay it caused. Jumping out of the aircraft, he started to run. The sand impeded his speed but he kept his eyes on the two fishermen who were now pulling the woman out of the sea. Gently, they laid her on the warm dry sand, and watched him approach.

Out of breath, he reached them. Sinking to his knees, he looked at the woman.

Kate.

He gathered her in his arms and held her closely, closing his eyes in a prayer of thanks. Bending his head, he listened for her heartbeat. It was weak. He began to resuscitate her. The men watched, powerless, at the drama playing out in front of them. Tom was persistent, refusing to give up. Kate was alive, but only just. She coughed and vomited salt water and he turned her onto her side.

"Come on, Kate. Come on," he urged. "Don't leave me now that I've finally found you."

He felt her pulse. A lump came into his throat as he recognised the bracelet he had given her, all those years ago. Her heartbeat was stronger.

"What happened?" he asked the fishermen who were watching him anxiously.

In stilted English, one of them explained that they had come out fishing and the *mazungu* woman had appeared.

"Mazungu?" Tom asked.

"The white woman," the man replied, pointing at Kate.

They all knew who she was. They had all watched her, over the past weeks, walking alone on the beach or sitting looking out to sea. That morning, she had been struggling to walk and had fallen a couple of times. They had watched her putting things in her pockets, and then seen her walking into the sea, where she disappeared beneath the waves.

A falcon had appeared, as if from no-where and hovered over a spot in the water. The fishermen had headed towards the bird, drawn to its unusual behaviour.

The falcon had skimmed over the waves, always returning to the same spot. The fishermen had dived into the water, going down again and again, until they finally saw the white of her garment. Pulling her up they had heard the sound of the aircraft and had tried to attract his attention.

Tom thanked them profusely. He asked them to tell the people where she was staying that he was taking her to Malindi for medical attention.

Lifting Kate into his arms, he carried her to the plane. He settled her as best he could, making her as comfortable as possible on the seat next to him. She felt hot to the touch. He covered her with a light blanket and paused briefly to smooth her wet hair back from her face. Cupping her face with his hands, his eyes running over her face, he kissed her on the forehead. "I found you Kate, I found you!" he could hear his voice trembling with emotion. Closing the passenger door he looked up briefly, scanning the skies. Shaking his head at the story, he prepared to climb into the pilot's seat. Suddenly, out of the corner of his eye he caught a movement.

The falcon flew effortlessly from the slender palm tree. Banking gently, he dipped his wings and flew high, then disappeared into the bright light above him. Tom watched the falcon curiously, and then climbed behind the controls of the plane. With some difficulty the plane finally lifted off from the beach and into the air. Tom set his course to Malindi, holding Kate's hand in his.

He had radioed ahead for an ambulance, which was waiting for them when they landed. He travelled with her, urging her to hang on, as the paramedics stabilised her. He paced the corridors of the little hospital as he waited for the doctor.

Hours later they wheeled Kate into a private room, and left them together. Kate was heavily sedated. They told him that she had malaria. Quickly he called Molly.

"It's Tom, Molly. I found her. I found Kate." She could hear the relief, the excitement and the utter exhaustion in his voice.

"Is she all right, where was she? May I speak to her?" he heard the tears of relief across the miles.

"She was staying in a house down near the border with Tanzania. She got into some difficulty in the sea, but it's all right, don't worry, she's going to be fine. I flew her back, and she's now in hospital. I'll stay right by her side until she is well enough to go home. As soon as she is strong enough to talk, I'll let you know. Please let her sister know, won't you?"

"Yes, yes, of course I will. Is there anything wrong with her though? How does she look?"

"As beautiful as the day I first met her in an empty champagne bar in London." He laughed happily, his own eyes filling with tears. "I can't believe I finally found her, but without the fishermen and the falcon, this would never have happened. I would have been too late to save her."

"What fishermen? What falcon?"

"She was deep in the sea. Some fishermen had watched her, from quite a distance, when suddenly she disappeared under the waves. They set out to find her but there was no trace and they didn't know where to look. Suddenly this falcon appeared from no-where and started to behave in an unusual way. Flying down and skimming the water, then it hovered over one spot. Anyway they headed towards the bird and found her."

Molly felt the hair rise on the back of her neck. "A falcon? That's strange. Kate told me, when I was a little girl, that she had a falcon that always looked out for her. She thought it might be her father. I used to believe her as well. She would point him out to me if she saw him. It made her happy to think it might be him. You're giving me goose bumps, Tom."

"Well, whatever he is, falcon or some kind of reincarnation, we would have lost her without him. I'm just so happy to be with her again."

The cool morning air brought the fresh smell of the sea into her room. Opening her eyes, Kate looked around the room. Oh God, she thought, where am I now?

A young African doctor smiled at her: "Glad to have you back with us," he said. "You had a bad attack of malaria and a few other complications. We nearly lost you."

He thought she might smile, but instead, her eyes filled with tears. Turning her face away she saw a man sitting in a chair by the window. He was in shadow.

Tom sat forward when he saw Kate turn towards him.

He smiled at her. "Hello, Kate."

Seeing her confusion, he quickly walked over to the bed and took hold of her hand.

"It's all right, Kate. Everything is all right. I've been looking for you for months, years, in fact. Probably all my life."

Unable to comprehend what was happening, she closed her eyes. She felt his strong hand holding hers. I remember this, she thought. The touch of his hand. It was so long ago, and I was frightened then too.

"Tom," she whispered, opening her eyes. "How did you find me? What are you doing here?"

Quietly, he told her the story, careful not to mention Adam. That could wait for later.

Exhaustion finally pulled her back into sleep. He sat and looked at her. He watched the pulse of her heart at the base of her throat. He knew all about her now. How would she feel about that and about him? The invasive truths and her private life exposed?

Tom had come to see her every day for the past week, sitting next to her bed and holding her hand in both of his, occasionally wiping away her tears as they talked. Finally he was able to explain what had happened, and why he had left the hotel in Cape Town so unexpectedly.

Kate woke up and looked around quickly for Tom. He was standing at the window, lost in his own thoughts. She watched him quietly. Like a ship battered and broken by a violent storm, she knew she had finally drifted into calm waters. Here was a man who had stubbornly refused to give up his search for her. A man who now knew all about her life. He still loved her. He had saved her life. Kate closed her hand over the silver bracelet on her wrist. She had been given another chance.

Sensing her gaze, he turned from the window. "Kate?"

She smiled gently at him and held out her hand. "Don't let go of my hand, Tom. Don't let go of my hand."

Lightning Source UK Ltd.
Milton Keynes UK
UKOW04f2004030815

256316UK00001B/50/P